Kinky Friedman lives in a little green trailer in a little green valley deep in the heart of Texas. There are about ten million imaginary horses in the valley and quite often they gallop around Kinky's trailer, encircling the author in a terrible, ever-tightening carousel of death. Even as the hooves are pounding around him in the darkest night, one can hear, almost in counterpoint, the frail, consumptive, ascetic novelist tip-tip-tapping away on the last typewriter in Texas. In such fashion he has turned out numerous bestselling novels. Two cats, Dr Scat and Lady Argyle, a pet armadillo called Dilly, and a small black dog named Mr Magoo can sometimes be found sleeping with Kinky in his narrow, monastic, Father Damien-like bed.

KINKY FRIEDMAN

Even More Kinky Friedman

Armadillos & Old Lace
God Bless John Wayne
The Love Song of J. Edgar Hoover

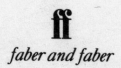

faber and faber

This omnibus edition first published in Great Britain in 2000
by Faber and Faber Limited
3 Queen Square, London WC1N 3AU

Armadillos & Old Lace first published in the USA in 1994
by Simon & Schuster, New York
First published in Great Britain in 1995
by Faber and Faber Limited

God Bless John Wayne first published in the USA in 1995
by Simon & Schuster, New York
First published in Great Britain in 1996
by Faber and Faber Limited

The Love Song of J. Edgar Hoover
first published in the USA in 1996
by Simon & Schuster, New York
First published in Great Britain in 1996
by Faber and Faber Limited

Printed in Great Britain by
Mackays of Chatham PLC, Chatham, Kent

A CIP record for this book is
available from the British Library

ISBN 0–571–20438–4

2 4 6 8 10 9 7 5 3 1

CONTENTS

Armadillos & Old Lace

God Bless John Wayne

The Love Song of J. Edgar Hoover

Armadillos & Old Lace

This book is dedicated with lots of love to Lottie Cotton

There were ten pretty girls in
the village school
There were ten pretty girls
in the village school
Some were short, some were tall
And the boy loved them all
But you can't marry ten pretty girls.

TRADITIONAL TEXAS FOLK DANCE

It was my last night in New York before saddling up the cat, grabbing my old guitar, and heading back to the family ranch in Texas for the summer. Every spring, just about the time I heard my suitcase snap, I vowed never to return to the city. Every fall, I seemed to find myself, almost inexplicably, back in the Big Apple. Sooner or later I was going to have to decide whether Texas or New York was truly my home. Then, in that quiet moment of reflection, I'd hopefully find the answer to the grand and troubling question that has haunted mankind through the ages: What is it that I really want out of life – horse-manure or pigeon shit?

Some of the boys had planned a little send-off at one of my favorite places, Big Wong's on Mott Street in Chinatown. We were sitting at a large round table close enough to the kitchen to hear the cook whistling something from the Hong Kong Hit Parade. McGovern, large Irish society columnist for the *Daily News* and master of the magical background check, had brought about fourteen cases of beer over in paper bags from the little grocery store across the street. Ratso, my flamboyant, flea-market friend, editor of *National Lampoon*, and somewhat weatherbeaten Dr Watson, had been quite disheartened when the waiter had told him: 'No more roast pork.'

'No more roast pork,' Ratso was muttering to himself. The place closed at ten o'clock and we were pushing that now.

'It's hard to keep continental dining hours at Big Wong's,' said McGovern. 'You get here after eight o'clock, you're pretty well hosed.'

Rambam, a private investigator who'd worked with me on some of my cases and was wanted in every state that began with an 'I', stared stonily at the far wall and drank his beer. The few other guests had already left us with their bottles and the bill. At the next table, the waiters and busboys, dressed entirely in white, were silently shoveling down whatever'd been left over in the kitchen. Their outfits lent a nice institutional touch to the evening. It was a quiet affair.

I could use a little quiet, I reflected. I'd become somewhat ambivalent about performing country music gigs lately and I'd come to realize that anyone who uses the word 'ambivalent' probably shouldn't have been a country singer in the first place. Going on the road as a musician was always a killer, but these days, for me, even staying home could be murder.

Over the past few years I'd tried my fine Hebrew hand as an amateur detective in the city, resulting in both the criminals and the policemen not being my friends. I was an equal opportunity offender.

Worse, the crime-solving lifestyle had brought into my life a myriad of death, destruction, heartbreak, scandal and a remorseless, lingering, spirit-sucking ennui, though several of the cases were not without charm. In my most recent adventure, which McGovern had dubbed *The Case of Elvis, Jesus and Coca-Cola*, I'd endeavored to locate a missing film about Elvis impersonators directed by my friend Tom Baker, who'd recently gone to Jesus himself. Because of that case I'd lost one or two girlfriends, depending on how you looked at it.

I glanced at my partners in crime seated around the table and wondered if they realized how much *Elvis, Jesus and Coca-Cola* had taken out of me. When I left New York this time, I figured, I might really never return. At least not until Jesus got his own postage stamp.

'You've never held a real job as long as I've known you,' Rambam was saying. 'What makes you think you need a vacation?'

'It's not a vacation,' I said, quoting my sister Marcie. 'It's a lifestyle.'

'The Kinkstah works,' said Ratso, rising above the roast pork situation to come to my defense. 'He's just finished a very grueling tour. Hey, I wonder if they have any pork gruel?'

'Believe me,' I said, 'opening for Henny Youngman at a sports bar in New Jersey on Mother's Day is hard work. I got so hammered after the show from being subjected to seven hundred video screens that I walked on my knuckles into a wall and smashed my guitar.'

'What a shame,' said Rambam. 'It's an omen. God wants you to go out and get a real job.'

'So you can be like the rest of us miserable bastards,' said McGovern. He laughed a loud, hearty, Irish laugh that seemed to echo in the little room. Several of our neighboring diners looked over briefly from their fish-head soup.

'Why is it,' said Ratso, 'that the kitchen help always gets better food than we do?'

'Racism,' said McGovern.

As Ratso began his uncanny shell game of putting money into and taking it out of a pot to pay the check, I sat back and looked around the table. McGovern, Ratso and Rambam, while very different in style and substance, were all New York down to the core of the Big Apple. There weren't many like them in the Texas Hill Country. We liked to keep it that way.

'Are you taking the cat?' McGovern asked. Ratso palmed a twenty from the middle of the table and replaced it with a five.

'Of course,' I said. 'Last year I left the cat with Winnie and by the time I came back she'd turned her into a strident feminist.' Winnie Katz ran a lesbian dance class in the loft above mine.

'It's not the first pussy Winnie's gotten her hands on,' said Rambam.

The cat would like Texas, I figured. She'd live on a beautiful ranch in a little green valley surrounded by hills. There'd be oak and cottonwood and cedar trees, streams flowing by, and lizards to chase on every rock. There'd be the spiritual elbow room available that you'd never find in the city. The freedom just to be a cat. She'd like it, all right. Of course, the cat would like an exhibit of twelfth-century Portuguese architecture if you put a can of tuna in front of it.

As we left Big Wong's and walked up Mott Street that night, I could almost feel the hot Texas sun on my shoulders and the gentle breeze rustling the sycamore against my old green trailer like the wings of a cowboy angel. In the skies over Manhattan the stars were barely bright enough to make a wish on. I'd wait until I got to Texas.

'The thing I like about the Chinese,' said Ratso, as he looked around the crowded, oblivious street, 'is that they don't hold the Jews responsible for killing Jesus.'

'Yeah,' said Rambam, 'but I think they know we contracted the lumber.'

Being in the process of lighting up and concomitantly attempting to laugh, I came precariously close to swallowing my cigar. I wondered fleetingly if there was a form of the Heimlich maneuver available for Americans who swallowed their cigars while laughing. Most likely not, I reasoned. There weren't that many people who actually smoked cigars and, for those who did, life, very probably, was not all that funny. You could always not smoke and not laugh. Then you'd probably get run over by a bookmobile.

There is, of course, a very thin line between laughing and choking to death. Both sound about the same, look about the same and, often, may feel quite similar to the occupant. The only difference is that if you're only laughing you'll eventually stop, but if you're truly choking to death, you'll go on laughing forever.

Apparently, I was only laughing. I said goodbye to my three companions as we dodged traffic on Canal Street. McGovern gave me a bear hug and Rambam clasped my shoulder with an iron grip. Ratso shook hands and copped a cigar from me. Then he borrowed my butt-cutter. Then he bummed a light.

'I'm a full-service friend,' I said.

'Well, at least you'll get some rest down there, Kinkstah,' said Ratso. 'Nothing much happens in Texas.'

'That's true,' I said. 'We've got a lot of wide open spaces.'

'Especially between people's ears,' said Ratso.

TWO

The next morning as the plane dipped like a Spanish dancer over the New York skyline, I watched the twin Trade Towers shrink to the Tinkertoys of a child, and the Statue of Liberty to the bright prize from a Cracker Jack box. Somewhere below, McGovern was probably still sleeping, dreaming of old-fashioned silk skirts rustling across make-believe ballrooms.

Ratso was down there too, someplace. Most likely tossing and turning in his cluttered warehouse of an apartment, having a nightmare about the five hundred interviews he'd soon be embarking upon in order to complete his new book on Abbie Hoffman. Abbie was down there, too, I reflected. At peace finally. Somewhere off to the left.

Rambam, no doubt, had been up all night on a stake-out. Right now he was probably sipping coffee in a parked car and watching a door or a widow or an alleyway. Those are good things to watch because, unlike many aspects of human experience, something meaningful may occasionally come out of them.

The cat had never taken kindly to the notion of leaving the loft on Vandam Street where the two of us survived more winters than the saber-toothed tiger. Like many New Yorkers, the cat believed that no life whatsoever existed outside the confines of Manhattan. I could just imagine what her mental state would be like after flying four hours in the baggage compartment in a cage next to a golden retriever and somebody's pet boa constrictor. I'd given her half a cat Valium before we'd left. The other half I'd taken myself. If mine didn't kick in soon, I figured, I might have to upgrade to heroin suppositories.

I watched New York telescope away and then disappear completely beneath the cloud cover. I thought of the troubles and tension conventions I was leaving behind. The friends. The lovers. The little black puppet head sitting all alone on top of the refrigerator. How many times, with the colorful parachute attached and the key to the building wedged in its mouth, had I thrown it out the window into the eager hands of visitors and housepests? How many times had it come back to me, still smiling one of the most genuine smiles in New York City? What the hell, I thought. Maybe I'd get a little head in Texas.

I sipped a Bloody Mary for a while, then I closed my eyes and drifted through time and space like campfire smoke. We weren't anywhere near Texas yet, but I could already see the ranch. My folks had bought the place forty years ago and in the summertime they'd operated it as a camp for boys and girls. I'd been a camper there myself, then a counselor, running the waterfront. These days, however, I felt a bit o-l-d to interact too intensely with the kids. The range of my responsibilities now rambled from dropping the laundry in town every morning in the pickup truck, to poisoning occasional mounds of fire ants, to feeding the hummingbirds, to singing a song once in a while at a campfire or hoedown. It was strenuous work.

The ranch was called Echo Hill. I had nothing but happy memories from all the years I'd been involved with the place. Now, for the first time, like echoes in a dream, I had a slight sense of foreboding about my imminent return to the Hill Country. A half-conscious uneasiness that I attributed to the fact that the guy sitting next to me in the plane looked like a mad scientist from Pakistan. If I'd known then what was awaiting me in Texas, I'd have grabbed the pilot by the beezer and told him to turn the plane around.

I woke from a fitful sleep, and having nodded out through lunch, had to make do with another Bloody Mary and a healthy piece of celery. I needed all the celery I could get. The accumulated stress of living in New York was still weighing heavily upon me. I felt vaguely troubled with a sidecar of impending doom as I looked out over what some New Yorkers call 'fly-over country'. America, I suppose. The place where celery comes from.

I drew some comfort from an old Texas axiom: Whether your destination is heaven or hell, first you have to change planes in Dallas–Forth Worth.

THREE

It was late in the afternoon when I finally arrived in San Antonio, but the weather was still hotter than a stolen tamale. It reminded me of my days with the Peace Corps working in the jungles of Borneo as an agricultural extension worker. My job had been to distribute seeds upriver to the natives. In two and a half years, however, the Peace Corps never sent me any seeds. In the end, I had to resort to distributing my own seed upriver, which had some rather unpleasant reper- cussions. But I loved the tropics and, of course, I seldom complained about the weather in Texas. Without it, no one would ever be able to start a conversation.

I breezed through the corridor to the gate and on into the terminal past straw cowboy hats, belt buckles as big as license plates, happy Hispanic families. At the Dallas–Fort Worth airport, where I'd gotten off the plane briefly to smoke a cigar, the women all had that blond, pinched look halfway between Morgan Fairchild and a praying mantis. The men at

DFW appeared to have come in on a wing and a prayer themselves. They'd looked well fed and fairly smarmy, like so many secular Jimmy Swaggarts. At the San Antonio airport the people looked like real Texans. Even the one Hare Krishna had a nice 'Y'all' going for him.

Greyhound bus stations, I reflected as I passed long rows of television chairs all individually tuned to 'Ironsides', used to tell you a lot about the character of a town. Today, it's airports. All bus stations tell you anymore is the character of the local characters, and there's damn few of them left these days in most places. I wasn't even sure if I was still one myself.

I waited at the baggage claim for a period of time roughly comparable to the length of the Holy Roman Empire.

'What comes around goes around,' I said to a man who was dressed as either a pimp or an Aryan golfer.

'True story,' he said. 'Last time I went to New Jersey the airline sent all my luggage to Las Vegas.'

'Sounds like your toilet kit had more fun than you did,' I said.

We waited.

Eventually, with suitcase, guitar and pet carrier in hand, I strolled onto the sun-blinded San Antonio sidewalk like a lost mariachi and gazed around for anybody wearing an Echo Hill T-shirt. The cat gazed around, too. She had not taken the trip very well, apparently, and at the moment, appeared to be pissed off enough to scratch out the eyes of Texas.

If someone is late to meet you in New York it is cause for major stress and consternation. But Texas is close enough to Mexico to have absorbed by some kind of cultural osmosis a healthy sense of *mañana*. In the old days at the ranch, my brother Roger always used to throw any leftover food on anybody's plate out in the backyard. 'Somethin'll git it,' he'd say.

In the same way, I knew someone would get me. The cat did not seem to share my confidence. She made loud, baleful noises and scratched unpleasantly at the bars of the cage. Several passersby stopped briefly to stare at us.

'Don't make a scene,' I said. 'We'll be at the ranch in about an hour.'

The cat continued making exaggerated mournful moaning noises and clawing at the cage. The new vice-president of the Nosey Young Women's Society came by and bent down over the pet carrier.

'Is he being mean to you?' she said to the cat. 'Did he make you fly in that little cage?'

'We're both on medication,' I said. 'We've just returned from a little fact-finding trip to Upper Baboon's Asshole.'

She left in a vintage 1937 snit.

I took a cigar out of a looped pocket in my lightweight summer hunting vest, began prenuptial arrangements and, after all preparations were complete, I fired it up with a kitchen match. Always keeping the tip of the cigar well above the flame. I sat down on a cement bench and, for the next ten minutes or so, I watched the wheels go round, as John Lennon would say. Then I got up and stretched my legs a bit until I was almost vivisected by a Dodge Dart. The bumper sticker on the Dodge, I noticed, read: 'Not A Well Woman'.

Suddenly, there was a horn honking and somebody yelling 'Kinkster!' I gazed over and saw a familiar-looking gray pickup with a familiar-looking smiling head sticking out of it. Both the truck and the head were covered with dust. It was Ben Stroud, a counselor at the ranch.

'You came a little early,' said Ben.

'That's what she told me last night,' I said, as I put the guitar and suitcase in back and the cat in front and climbed in next to Ben, who was drinking a Yoo-Hoo. Ben was not tall but he was large and loud. In Texas, you had to be large and loud. Even if you were an autistic midget. *Especially* if you were an autistic midget.

'What's new at the ranch?' I asked.

'We're still having borientation,' said Ben. 'The kids don't arrive for a few more days.'

I settled back in the cab and entertained a brief vision of the ranchers, as we called them, arriving in a cloud of dust on chartered buses. The old bell in front of the ranch office would be ringing. A small group of counselors, all wearing Echo Hill T-shirts, would be milling about, waiting for their charges in the afternoon sun. Uncle Tom, my dad, would be bringing the buses in, as always, walking in front of them motioning with his arms in the confident, stylish manner of someone leading a cavalry brigade. Uncle Tom would be wearing a light blue pith helmet that looked as if he borrowed it from someone in a Rudyard Kipling story. Tom, who was much loved and respected by the ranchers, counselors and me, had a great attachment to tradition. It seemed at times that he borrowed himself from a Rudyard Kipling story.

'Tom's assigned me as his Director of External Relations,' said Ben. 'That means I drop the laundry in town every morning and bring back his paper for him.'

'Hey,' I said, 'that was supposed to be my job! Now I'm an unemployed youth.'

'Oh, I don't know about that. You'll be helping me out. I think you may be plenty busy with other things, too. Pat Knox called Uncle Tom yesterday. She wants to talk to you. It sounds like some pretty mysterious shit.'

Pat Knox was the feisty little justice of the peace in Kerr County who'd beaten me for the job some years ago in a hotly contested campaign. One of the other unsuccessful candidates had chopped up his family collie with a hatchet two weeks before the election. He'd still received eight hundred votes.

'What the hell does Pat Knox want?' I said. 'Isn't she busy enough marrying people and going around certifying dead bodies?'

'I think that's what she wants to talk to you about.'

'Marrying people?'

'No,' said Ben. 'Dead bodies.'

The truck was zimming along headed west on I-10 through the graceful, gently rolling green hills. In the sky ahead of us, backlit by a brilliant, slowly dying sun, we could see an inordinately large number of buzzards circling. They moved methodically, timelessly, as if imbued with ghastly, fateful purpose.

'You'd be crazy to get involved,' said Ben.

'Maybe I am crazy,' I said. 'You know what Carl Jung said: "Bring me a sane man and I will cure him." '

'Maybe,' said Ben, 'Carl Jung will help us with the laundry.'

FOUR

Halfway to Kerrville along I–10 Ben took a left on a smaller road. The cat and I went through periods of dreamtime as we passed a number of small towns on the way to the ranch. Pipe Creek: so named because a local settler over a hundred years ago ran back into his burning cabin to fetch his favorite pipe after an Indian attack. Bandera: 'the Cowboy Capital of the World', where Ben and I stopped at the Old Spanish Trail Restaurant and had dinner in the John Wayne Room. The John Wayne Room's sole motif, other than an old covered wagon used as a salad bar and two defunct pinball machines, was fifty-seven photos, pictures, sketches and sculptures of John Wayne. This thematic approach led to a rather macho orientation among the regulars, and did not serve particularly well as a digestive aid to the occasional traveling butterfly collector from Teaneck, New Jersey.

I had the Mexican Plate and Ben ordered 'The Duke', a chicken fried steak approximately the size and appearance of a yellow-and-white-streaked beach umbrella. Many of our fellow diners wore straw cowboy hats and belt buckles the size of license plates. Possibly they were on their way to the San Antonio airport.

By the time we walked out of the OST, dusk was falling over the old western town. We headed up Highway 16 toward Medina. I offered the cat a few residual pieces of 'The Duke', but she demurred. We rode to Medina in silence.

Medina was a very small town that had been dying for over a hundred years and actually seemed to almost thrive on that notion. Sometime back in Old Testament days, it had voted not to serve or sell alcoholic beverages. It was open to some debate whether this policy had caused the town's long decline, or whether it had been responsible for eliciting God's favor in enabling the place to die so successfully for so long.

'Stop for a drink?' I said to Ben.

'You kiddin'? I doubt if they'd even let me recycle my Yoo-Hoo.'

I thought briefly of what our longtime friend Earl Buckelew, who'd lived in the area for over seventy years, once said about the place: 'Medina is as dry as a popcorn fart.'

'This town is so small,' I said to the cat, 'that if you blink you won't even see it.'

The cat blinked.

Medina wasn't there.

We drove a number of miles farther down 16, then took a left and rolled in a cloud of dust across a cattle guard, down a country road and into the sunset toward Echo Hill. The ranch was set back about two and a half miles from the scenic little highway, but ever since we passed Pipe Creek we'd been in a world that most New Yorkers never got to see. They believed the deer, the jackrabbits, the raccoons, the sun setting the sky on fire in the west, the cypress trees bathing their knees in the little creek, the pale moon shyly peeking over the mountain – they believed these things only really existed in a Disney movie or a children's storybook. I closed my eyes for a moment, turned a page in my mind. When I opened my eyes again everything was still there. Only New York was gone.

We splashed through a water crossing and two more cattle guards, then turned where the sign said Echo Hill Ranch. Ben drove across a small causeway, then deposited me and the cat and our belongings in front of an antique green trailer that looked like it might've once been the object of a failed timeshare arrangement between John Steinbeck and Jack Kerouac. Clearly, it wasn't going anywhere else again, geographically speaking. I felt as much at home as a jet-set gypsy has any right to feel.

I opened the door of the trailer, brushed away a few cobwebs, and turned on a lamp. A happy little raccoon family had apparently been living there over the winter.

'If they want to stay,' I said to the cat, 'they'll have to pay rent.'

The cat said nothing, but it was obvious that she was not amused. In fact, I'd long held a theory that the cat hated every living thing except me. She was ambivalent about me. And that was a nice word for it.

I opened the cage and the cat warily looked out. In a moment she emerged and appeared to gaze in some disgust around the little trailer. It was getting more decrepit every summer, and one of these days even I was going to realize that man can't live on funk alone. The cat stayed a few seconds longer, then shot out the open door like a bottle-rocket.

'What'd you expect,' I shouted after her. 'A condo?'

She'd be back, I thought. Certain cats and certain women always come back. The trouble is that no man is ever quite certain which ones they are.

I lay down on my bunk to take a quick power nap before going up to the lodge to see Tom and say hello to everybody. Ben had said that Tom was having an orientation meeting with the staff in the dining hall. I figured I might do the same for a while here in the trailer. Orient myself to the sound of crickets instead of traffic. Before I closed my eyes I noticed on the far wall that the large framed pictures of Hank Williams and Mahatma Gandhi were still hanging there side by side. They were a little dusty and off-center, but who wasn't that ever did anything great? They stared down at me and I met their cool gaze. Then I closed my eyes for a moment and, from the after-images of the two faces, little karmic hummingbirds seemed to fly to my pillow.

When I opened my eyes again Hank was smiling at me with that sad spiritually copyrighted crooked smile and Gandhi's eyes were twinkling like the helpless stars above us all. Just before I fell asleep, I recalled, for some reason, what John Lennon had repeatedly asked the Beatles during their meteoric rise to fame: 'Did we pass the audition, boys?'

FIVE

I woke up from my power nap to find that the cat had not returned. I put on my boots and headed up to the lodge. Across the night-time Texas skies someone had unrolled a shimmering blanket of stars. I walked up the little hill toward the lights of the lodge. My father was sitting on an ancient redwood chair on the front lawn, staring into the darkness. He'd made a lot of wishes in seventy years and some of them had come true.

He'd seen thousands of boys and girls grow up here over the years. Many of them had gone away into the grown-up world imbued with an intangible gift my mother, Aunt Min, had called the 'Echo Hill Way'. The world, in all this time, had not really become a different or a better place. But the world, as most people knew it, stopped at the Echo Hill cattle guard. Here, everybody was somebody. Everybody had fun. Everybody got to first base once in their lives. Many would, no doubt, be picked off later, but at least they'd had a chance.

Many of the early architects of the 'Echo Hill Way' were now among the missing and missed. My mother had died in 1985. Uncle Floyd Potter, my high school biology teacher and, for many years, our nature-study man, went to Jesus soon after that. Floyd's wife, Aunt Joan, had helped direct the camp for as long as I could remember. Her birthday, 18 August, fell on the same date as Min and Tom's anniversary. They had all been very close. Close as the cottonwoods standing by the river.

Slim, too, had passed, as some colloquially refer to dying. Slim had washed dishes, served the 'bug juice' and drank warm Jax beer as he listened to the Astros lose a million ball games on his old radio. Death is always colloquial.

Doc and Aunt Hilda Phelps had been the first to go. They'd always been older, I suppose. Doc was Tom's friend from the air force days who helped Tom and Min start the ranch. Hilda, his Australian wife, had taught handicrafts at Echo Hill, and, when I was six years old, had taught me 'Waltzing Matilda'. For several years I sang the song as 'Waltzing with Hilda'.

There were many ghosts at Echo Hill, but most of them were friendly. They mixed in quite gracefully with the dust and the campfire smoke and the river and the stars.

Tom was almost all that was left now of the old days. He looked out over the beautiful valley, now quiet except for the horses and the deer. The lights of some of the cabins twinkled merrily. Laughter drifted down from the dining hall, where my sister Marcie was still meeting with some of the counselors. It was hard to believe that within a few days over a hundred kids would be running around the place. It was hard to believe that forty years had gone by and Echo Hill was still the same. Only the names had been changed to protect the innocent.

I opened the gate and walked up the path. Sam, Tom's

myopic Jewish shepherd, barked furiously, ran at me, and came within a hair of biting my ass before he recognized me and smiled like a coal-scuttle.

'Sambo!' Tom shouted. 'Pick on someone your own size.'

'That dog keeps eating like a boar hog,' I said as I hugged my father, 'we'll have to get him a golf cart.'

'Sam's doing fine,' said Tom. 'Large mammals always put on a little weight in the winter.'

Tom would never hear a bad word about Sam. In truth, Sam was a wonderful dog. Tom had gotten him from the pound in the year following my mother's death, and Sam had been a friend indeed. He was a terrific, possibly overzealous watch-dog who scared most visitors to within an inch of their lives, but he loved children. The only people he hated were teenage boys, people in uniforms and Mexicans. 'What can I say?' Tom had once offered after Sam had chased a Mexican worker onto the roof of the pickup truck. 'The dog's a racist.'

Tom had put on a little weight himself over the year, adding to an already protuberant abdomen, but he could still whip almost all comers in tennis. Other than an extremely large gut, which he did not recognize he had, he looked very fit and virile.

We talked for a while about the ranch, the staff, the upcoming summer and, finally, the conversation worked its way around to another matter.

'You got a rather strange message on the machine today from Pat Knox. I still think she did you the greatest favor of your life by keeping you from being elected justice of the peace in Kerrville.'

'Yeah,' I said. 'That could've been ugly. It's a good thing my fellow Kerrverts returned me to the private sector.'

'If you'd won that job, what would you have done with it?'

'Pretty much what I'm doing now,' I said.

'That's what I was afraid of,' said Tom.

20

I took out a cigar, lopped the butt off and achieved ignition. I puffed a few easygoing puffs and gazed out over the flat.

'Doesn't the ranch look beautiful?' Tom said.

'Sure does,' I said, staring down the quiet, peaceful line of bunkhouses, which appeared to be bracing themselves for an onslaught of shouting, boisterous ranchers. 'So what did Pat Knox want?'

'I have no idea,' said Tom. 'It was strange. She said some things were happening that she didn't understand. She sounded very upset about it. She said she needed to talk to a man of your talents.'

'Musical?'

Tom laughed. 'Not unless she wants you to perform at somebody's funeral. From her tone, it sounds pretty serious. When she mentioned "a man of your talents", I think she must've been referring to some of your forays into crime-solving in New York.'

I took a few more thoughtful puffs on the cigar and watched the moon rising over the mountain.

'Or,' I said, 'she may just want me to drop off her laundry.'

SIX

The next morning with the sun shining brightly on Echo Hill, the nearby mountain from which the camp took its name, I called Pat Knox. It was such a beautiful day that it seemed nothing, with the exception of the cat's not having returned, could be wrong in the world. Of course, Echo Hill was not the world. With a cup of coffee and a cigar under way, I sat at the tiny desk in my trailer and spoke to the secretary at the office of the justice of the peace, precinct one, Kerrville, Texas.

'Oh,' said the secretary, 'she'll be tickled pink. You're just the person she's been wanting to talk to. She'll be so relieved.'

'Relieved?' I said. 'Is Kerrville under siege?' I thought of my campaign slogan in my ill-fated race against her boss: 'I'll keep us out of war with Fredericksburg.' Fredericksburg was a little German town about twenty miles down the road where they still tied their shoes with little Nazis.

'We're not exactly under *siege*, darlin',' she said, 'unless you want to count the Yankees, the yuppies, the developers, the retirees – '

'That's what I was hoping to be,' I said.

'I think the judge has other ideas,' she said.

I held the line and waited. I wondered what was going on. Perhaps Judge Knox had just received word that nine warships had broken through the Confederate blockade. I was pouring another cup of coffee when Her Honor came on the line.

'Can you come into town today?' she said. 'I don't want to talk on the phone. There may be spies.'

'Spies?' I said. 'In Kerrville? Do they wear satellite dishes on their cowboy hats?'

The feisty little judge was not amused. 'This is serious,' she said. 'If what I think is happenin' is really happenin', this little sleepy town is gonna have an ugly awakenin'.'

It was a fairly ugly awakening for me, too, I thought. My first day back in Texas, the cat's gone, I'm trying to drink my second cup of coffee and I'm already being sucked into some kind of foreign intrigue. Of all the happy campers who'd soon be at the ranch, I was definitely not one. With the cat gone, there wasn't even anyone around to talk to. When you have to talk to a cat that isn't there, you might as well be talking to yourself.

I poured a third cup of coffee, lit a second cigar and wandered over to see my kid sister next door. Marcie, who, along with Tom, directed the camp, lived in a big white trailer that looked as if it had belonged in its first life to Jim

Rockford. Marcie was very busy getting the camp ready to open and she was also having some trouble getting her eyes open because she'd stayed up so late meeting with the staff. She did not display a great deal of concern about the cat being missing.

'I'm sure your cat will come back,' she said.

'I don't know,' I said. 'This has never happened before.'

'It may never happen again, either,' she said. 'Especially if Sambo gets hold of the cat.'

I paced up and down Marcie's trailer as she was getting dressed, forgetting how much my cigar smoke always irritated her when she first woke up. Of course, almost everything irritated Marcie when she first woke up. She, as siblings often will, believed that it was I who was the grumpy one and that she herself had a constantly cheery, pleasant disposition. Both of us frequently confronted Tom with the well-considered opinion that he was grumpier than either of us. Tom would either laugh it off or sullenly deny it, depending on how grumpy he was feeling at the time. Whenever he laughed it off, it usually made me and Marcie pretty grumpy.

'I mourn the fact,' I said, 'that young people today don't drink coffee and that they don't have more compassion for cats.'

'I mourn the fact,' said Marcie, 'that I've got exactly one day to get this camp open and somebody's marching up and down my trailer smoking a cigar when I'm trying to get dressed.'

'I mourn the fact,' I said, 'that more effort hasn't been made on the part of the directors to more fully integrate me into the camp program.'

'I mourn the fact,' said Marcie, 'that you won't get your ass out of my trailer.'

I walked up to the lodge just as Tom was filling the hummingbird feeders. The lodge was set in an area surrounded by a white wooden fence to keep the horses out, which it rarely did. Eighty-seven trees grew inside the fence, according to Tom. One of them, very close to the lodge, was dead. That was the one the hummingbirds always established as their home base when they returned to the Hill Country from South America or wherever the hell hummingbirds come from. They arrived punctually on 15 March and stayed until about the end of August. It was a good thing they weren't housepests.

More than thirty years ago, my mother had started feeding the hummingbirds, dissolving sugar in red-dyed water and hanging the glass feeders on the eaves of the porch. The job had now devolved to Tom and myself. There were more than fifty hummingbirds around now, and during happy hour things could get pretty busy. I thought of Tom as my assistant hummingbird feeder. He thought of me as his assistant hummingbird feeder. Somehow, we managed.

Tom was hanging the last feeder on a nail and Ben Stroud was walking behind him trying to make up a list of things to get in town.

'Why are you following me?' Tom said to Ben.

Ben, aware that this was pretty much of a rhetorical question, did not give an answer. Instead, in the manner of a Talmudic scholar, he asked another question.

'Should I get the paper for you in town?' he asked. 'I'm getting the laundry and the softballs and the donuts.'

'I could get Tom's paper,' I said to Ben. 'I'm going into Kerrville for lunch.'

'No, I'll get it,' said Ben. 'I've got a whole list of shit to do.'

Tom walked over to the redwood furniture, which was older than most of the counselors, and sat down in his favorite chair. Ben wandered over to check a thing or two on his town list.

'Why are you following me?' Tom said to Ben.

Tom and Ben and I sat and talked for a while, then they both had things to do. I wandered around the ranch like a stray horse for about an hour, talked to a few of the old counselors who were getting their activities set up, and ran into Marcie down at the picnic area. We'd both gotten over our little sibling snit from earlier that morning.

'Care to join me for lunch at the Del Norte?' I asked.

'I've got to stay here,' she said. 'Camp's starting tomorrow, one of the cooks hasn't shown up yet, and Tom snapped his wig this morning when he couldn't find a typewriter ribbon. Who are you having lunch with?'

'The Honorable Pat Knox,' I said.

'Pat Knox? Isn't she the one who beat you like a drum in the election?'

'I'm not bitter,' I said.

I saddled up Dusty, my mother's old wood-paneled Chrysler convertible, waved at my cousin Bucky, who was rounding up horses on the East Flat, and headed into Kerrville. I was thinking I could use a little liquor drink to cut the phlegm. I was also thinking how being here at camp would, of necessity, cut into my cocktail hour. My normal habits and lifestyle in New York were not especially healthy for green plants or children. Not that I was a role model particularly. I just felt that if kids were going to screw up their lives, they ought to figure out how to do it themselves.

Dusty was a talking car. My mother had always said it was a good car for lonely people. I hadn't been back long enough to know whether or not I was lonely yet, but I was interested in hearing what Dusty had to say. As I drove down the gravel county road to the highway, Dusty demonstrated just how perceptive she was.

'Your washer fluid is low,' she said.

SEVEN

'I want to talk to you,' said Pat Knox in deeply conspiratorial tones, 'about four little old ladies.' We were sitting at a corner table in the Del Norte Restaurant, a place I'd often referred to as the best restaurant in the world. At least it was the best restaurant in Kerrville.

'Four little old ladies?' I said. 'Do they want me to join a quilting bee?'

'No,' said the little judge. 'They're dead.'

'Eighty-six that quilting bee.'

'If you're just gonna make fun of me, I might as well be talking to the sheriff. That's what she did, too.'

Not for the first time did I think what a strange town was Kerrville, Texas. For decades it had enjoyed a redneck macho milieu, overpopulated with pickup trucks sporting loaded gun racks in their rear windows. Now, suddenly, Kerrville had a lady sheriff and a lady justice of the peace. What was the world coming to?

The judge summoned up all the dignity and controlled anger within her four foot eleven and one-half inch frame, which was fairly considerable when she stared at you across the table. I sipped my coffee and hoped the waitress would bring me my chicken fried steak before Pat Knox reached into her leather briefcase and pulled out a pearl-handled Beretta.

'When I first met you during the campaign,' she said, 'I didn't like you.'

'Quite understandable,' I said. 'I have a certain superficial charm that holds up for about three minutes when I meet people. After that, it's usually downhill.'

'I must've stayed around for five minutes,' she said, as she reached into her leather briefcase. I readied myself.

As fate would have it, she only extracted a sheaf of papers, but in her eyes I could still see the Beretta.

'It was later in the campaign, Richard,' she said, using my Christian name, 'that I met you one day in the bank, and thought I saw that you were really a gentleman.'

'We all make mistakes,' I said.

'I don't think I made one,' she said.

I had become so accustomed to dealing with NYPD types that I almost didn't realize that this little woman was complimenting me and asking for my help. I didn't really see how I could help and I wasn't even sure what the problem was, but I felt a little ashamed about being a smart-ass. Maybe all law enforcement people brought it out in me.

The waitress came with our orders just as Pat was showing me a map of the Texas Hill Country with four little X's scattered around a fairly wide area.

'Each X indicates an isolated location in which one of these old ladies – all of them were widows – lived. And died.'

I studied the map politely as I cut into my chicken fried steak.

'The sheriff has listed the deaths as accidental, natural or suicide. She feels that four deaths in five months does not establish any kind of pattern and I can't say I really disagree with her about that. Anyway, I don't have the power to call for a formal investigation.'

I took a bite of chicken fried steak. It's an over-ordered dish in Texas and most of the time it's nothing you'd want to write home about even if you had a home. I was wondering what Pat was getting at. Did she want me to share her work load? That would've taken a lot of nerve after vanquishing me in the election.

'The first lady drowned in the bathtub near Bandera – '

'Household accident number 437,' I said.

'The second burned to death in her home near Pipe Creek.'

'Did she run back in trying to fetch her pipe?'

Pat Knox looked at me with disappointment in her eyes. The look quickly changed to a flat, hard, tail-gunner's expression.

27

'The third death occurred near Mountain Home. The victim was shot with a gun. The weapon was found near the body.'

'That was the suicide?'

'You New Yorkers sure don't miss a beat.'

'Hold the weddin',' I said. 'I come from Texas.'

'You could've fooled me.'

'And it's no disgrace to come from Texas,' I said. 'It's just a disgrace to have to come back here.'

Her Honor laughed briefly. I assured her I was kidding. She continued reading her book of the dead and I continued eating my chicken fried steak which I hoped was dead.

'The fourth death occurred just outside of town on the road to Ingram. The woman required an oxygen supply and apparently the bottle had come disconnected. That's it.'

'That's it?'

'Now three of the deaths didn't even occur in this county, so they're not really my jurisdiction –'

'Or mine.'

'That's correct. But I've talked to other JP's, to members of the families. I've conducted my own private investigation – I always do. Crime scenes, blood splatters, photos. I've kept records on all of this.'

I was only half listening now. I was thinking how a handful of deaths of elderly people wouldn't amount to a hill of beans in crazy old New York. It wouldn't even make good table conversation. I wondered again why the judge had called me. Did she want to show me how hard the job was and how overworked she was? Was she trying to rub it in that I'd lost the election?

'Okay, Pat, so what's all this mean? Put it on a bumper sticker for me.'

'I know they were murdered.'

Great, I thought. The whole thing is coming down like some gothic novel. Pat Knox is Joan of Arc. Pat Knox is Cassandra warning the warriors of Troy. Pat Knox is Martha Mitchell reporting that Secret Service agents had kidnapped her and shot her in the butt with a hypodermic needle. Who listens to these people? No one. Not until a little B&E job at Watergate brings down a presidency. Not until the Trojan Horse is taken into the gates of the city. Not until we all can hear the voices that once were only in Joan's head.

'I believe you,' I said.

The judge sighed deeply. 'But there's more,' she said. 'When I was a child I witnessed sexual molestation occurring for a period of several years within the family next door. I'm almost psychic about any aura of sexual violence in the air.'

I sipped my coffee and waited.

'I know this sounds crazy,' she said. 'But I also believe they were raped.'

'Pat,' I said, 'the sheriff is very well-liked around here and by all accounts very efficient. In fact, as you know, she just solved a triple murder case recently. Maybe she *is* invest-igating and just chooses not to tell you.' I could understand why the sheriff might not take the judge to her bosom, so to speak.

'I hope to hell you're right,' she said, ''cause I'm damn near worried sick about this.'

'Remember what Mark Twain said: "I've had many troubles in my life, but most of them never happened." '

The judge did not look convinced. She picked up her brief-case and stood up, indicating that our little luncheon was over.

'Tell that to Nigger Jim,' she said.

EIGHT

The following night, ten little girls stood outside the green trailer in the moonlight. It was pushing Cinderella time. They were all in their pajamas and many of them had brought cameras. They were hoping to get a picture of Dilly. He was there, too. Dilly was my pet armadillo.

There are those who say armadillos do not make good animal companions, but they have obviously never known the joys of tickling one behind its ears or hearing it knocking on their trailer door in the early hours of the morning for a midnight snack of milk, bacon grease and cat food. There was a note of sadness in my heart as I brought the cat food out to Dilly amidst the throng of giggling, awestruck members of the Bluebonnets. I had a lot of cat food, I reflected, for a man without a cat.

The Bluebonnets and Dilly, however, were oblivious to my own personal sorrows. Dilly was enjoying himself immensely, and quite frequently, rising to the occasion on his two hind claws. Whenever this happened, the flash of paparazzi cameras fairly lasered the darkness of the surrounding cedar trees.

There was something rather poignant, almost spiritual, about the little scene. For armadillos, as practically every Texan knows, are the very shyest of creatures, who, ironically, have been fated to co-inhabit a state populated with the very loudest, brashest of human beings. Nevertheless, they've been here since the time of the dinosaurs, and they're not about to let a silly race of people eighty-six them out this late in the game.

For those who are not intimately familiar with the armadillo, it is a small, armored creature about the size of . . . well, a cat. Its shell, as John D. MacDonald once observed, is often made into baskets and sold by the roadside. MacDonald also expressed a wish that somewhere in the universe there existed a planet inhabited by sentient armadillos who carved out humans and sold them as baskets by the roadside.

'Can armadillos hurt you?' asked Marisa.

'No,' I said. 'Only people can.'

'Is Dilly going to have a baby?' asked Michelle.

'No, Dilly is a boy. And armadillos never have just one

baby; they always have a litter of four. And the four are always either all boys or all girls.' I was quite an armadillologist.

'Can we pat Dilly?' asked Alene.

'Of course,' I said. 'But do it gently or you'll scare him. Armadillos almost never get this close to people. Dilly is a very special armadillo.'

The girls crowded around Dilly and he seemed to luxuriate in all the attention. Some of them stroked his armored shell. Some tickled him behind the ears. He even posed for pictures with the girls like a little primeval spirit come to save the world from itself. For some only slightly sick reason, I thought of Christ in the manger.

'Of course,' I said, 'armadillos have been known to carry leprosy.'

The two counselors stiffened and recoiled a bit, but the Bluebonnets remained in their attentive circle around Dilly.

'What's leprosy?' asked Jessica.

'Disease where your nose falls off,' I said.

The girls stopped petting Dilly and looked at me with that serious, half-believing expression children sometimes acquire when they suspect the adult they're listening to may be insane. I shrugged.

'Don't worry,' I said. 'They don't pass it along to people. Only to other armadillos. Besides, Dilly's already been up to the infirmary and the nurse gave him a health check.'

As if to demonstrate his general fitness, Dilly jumped about two feet in the air, then bolted inside the trailer with about six little girls almost literally on his tail. Like a young rhinoceros, he slammed into everything in sight, knocking over the forlorn bowls of cat food and water, my guitar and a small lamp. At incredible land speeds he scooted across the floor, back and forth, with the screaming Bluebonnets alternately running after him and then away from him. Eventually, he bolted out the door and into the night, and I began attempting to shoehorn personnel out of the trailer and back to their bunk.

'What's this?' asked Briana, holding up a piece of paper.

I glanced at the page. It was a sketch of Kerr, Bandera and several neighboring counties. Four black X's appeared at various loci on the paper.

'Where'd you get this, Bri?'

'I found it on the floor,' she said.

I looked at the page again. This time, with the little girls standing around me under the moonlight, an almost palpable evil seemed to emanate from it.

'Is it a treasure map?' shouted Bri.

'No,' I said. 'It's Dilly's health chart.'

At roughly 2:09 in the morning, in the middle of a rather gnarly nightmare about little girls transforming instantaneously into little old ladies, I woke up suddenly to hear a thump on the non-functioning air conditioner outside my window. Moments later, the cat jumped through the open window and, either deliberately or accidentally, landed on my testicles.

NINE

I woke up the next morning to the ringing of the old bell by the office and the sounds of radio station ECHO echoing off the hills. The disc jockey, Alex Hoffman, sometimes referred to as Phallax Hoseman, ran the station out of the media room. His first selection, unfortunately, was 'The Purple People Eater'. ECHO was staffed and run by the ranchers, but it still reflected Phallax's rather eclectic influence, ranging from 'Wipe-Out' to early Bob Dylan, to 'Happy Birthday from the Army', to 'Schwinn 24' by a little-known Texas group called King Arthur and the Carrots. ECHO, at Hoseman's behest, also played Harry Chapin's 'Cat's in the Cradle' at least two hundred times a day.

The cat was sleeping beside me on the bed and, except for a rather irritated look in her eye, showed no signs of joining me to face the day. It was quite evident, however, from the way she was twitching her left ear, that she did not like the song 'Purple People Eater'.

'I'll be sure to mention it to Phallax,' I told her, as I put on my boots, opened the creaky door of the green trailer and stared at the large porthole painting of a cross section of a watermelon. The painting had been done many years ago by a talented, somewhat eccentric counselor named Jules LeMelle who'd insisted that his only free time to do the work was at 6:00 A.M. So he'd painted the door and one inner wall of the trailer in a watermelon motif over a period of about a week while I tried to sleep with some weird guy drawing psychedelic watermelon designs inside my trailer.

LeMelle had gotten the idea from a story I'd told him about a Kappa Alpha fraternity float I'd once seen in a parade at the University of Texas. The float, as I remembered it, had been a huge construction of a watermelon with live little black children dancing around on it, ostensibly representing the seeds. It'd happened so long ago that, if I hadn't known better, I'd have thought I'd dreamed it. But it had happened, I had mentioned it to Jules LeMelle and he'd painted psychedelic watermelons all over the inner wall and door of my trailer. The natural green color of the outside of the trailer served as a perfect giant watermelon rind for the pink porthole painting when the door was closed.

As I walked up the little road to the dining hall to get some of Rosie's coffee, a dim memory of the Kappa Alpha float passed by in my mind again. Racism was easier to spot in those days. So was Jules LeMelle, for that matter. I wondered very briefly what ever had happened to him. I also wondered very briefly what ever had happened to all the rest of us.

I walked into the dining hall with the old ranch brands still on the rafters where Aunt Hilda had painted them forty years ago. The tables and chairs all looked bright and cheerful now that the kids were back. They'd been sitting alone all winter. The giant Mexican chess sets stood, with tall kings and queens, bishops, rooks, knights, pawns all in a row, each waiting for little hands. Darkened old black-and-white photos on the walls. A row of little girls standing together in front of their bunkhouse in 1953. I recognized Bunny Slipakoff, my first girlfriend, standing shyly on the right-hand side. I thought it was Bunny.

I went over to the giant lumberjack coffee urn. On the wall beside it hung the large Navajo sand painting Doc and Aunt Hilda had brought back from their stay on the reservation. The painting had hung there as long as I could remember. Now Doc and Aunt Hilda were gone and the sand painting was still there. I drew a cup of coffee and sat down alone at one of the long tables. I sipped the coffee and let my eyes gently wash across the sand painting. It was replete with suns and stars and dancers and animals and rainbows. I sipped some more coffee and noticed that the colors were still as bright as I remembered them. Forty years was a long time to a rainbow.

I looked over the counter into the kitchen and saw Elese sitting at the table sculpting orthodox rabbi heads or something out of lettuce. Rosie, the Hawaiian cook, came out of the kitchen into the dining hall and offered me one of her home-made sweet rolls.

'That's the best offer I've had today,' I said.

'I can't believe that,' said Rosie. She was a great cook, played the ukulele and gave an excellent haircut.

'What's for dinner tonight?'

'Hamburgers,' she said. 'Down at the picnic area.'

'Sambo usually eats about twelve of them,' I said.

'He does like my cookin',' said Rosie. 'I don't think it's nice that some of the counselors call him "Cujo".'

Rosie went back to the kitchen and I wandered over to the Crafts Corral, where Eric Roth, with about ten kids surrounding him, was checking out the kiln. Ceramic leaf ashtrays were always a happening thing at Echo Hill. Almost no one on the planet smoked anymore but still we turned out hundreds of ceramic leaf ashtrays. I wasn't sure what today's beleaguered parents could use them for. Maybe paperweights for their divorce papers.

At a far table, engulfed by a mob of eager ranchers, stood Aunt Anita. Today, Aunt Anita appeared to be teaching the kids how to make the ever-popular 'monkey's fist', but, in truth, there was almost nothing Aunt Anita couldn't construct out of string. Maybe, I thought, I should put her in touch with Pat Knox.

I stood at the window outside the Crafts Corral and noticed that Eric had a new assistant. She was bending over the kiln and from where I was standing, behind her, she looked like she was going to be a big boost to a lot more than just the handicrafts program. She seemed to have been delicately formed on some celestial potter's wheel.

'Pam's from Oklahoma,' Eric said, following my gaze.

'I'm Richard Kinky "Big Dick" Friedman,' I said by way of introduction. 'And I never met a Pam I didn't like.'

Pam had short blond hair and green, partly cloudy eyes that seemed to cut into me like dust blowing across the barren landscape of my soul.

'What's the "Big Dick" stand for?' she said.

The little repartee was interrupted by Eddie Wolff, a huge, gentle counselor and wrangler, shouting from the office like a giant, slightly agitated teddy bear you knew you'd better listen to. There was a long-distance phone call for me, apparently. Of course, being so far from the city, every call that came into the ranch was long-distance.

I went over to the office, picked up the blower and heard Pat Knox's secretary, Paula, tell me to hold on for the judge.

I hadn't thought about the judge for about nine hours and I was feeling pretty good about it.

'Have you gone over the material I gave you?' Pat asked.

'I've started,' I lied. 'Been kind of busy here lately unpacking my Frisbee. Doing squat thrusts in the parking lot.'

'Get crackin',' she said. 'There's gonna be a full moon out tonight. Lots of strange critters'll be stirrin'.'

I walked out of the office, past two new counselors I didn't recognize who were taking down the big WELCOME RANCHERS sign on the bulletin board. Walking along the dusty road to the green trailer I heard a New York angel whisper in my ear. 'Don't get involved,' it said.

I opened the door to the trailer and saw that the cat was in precisely the same position she was lying in when I left. As I walked across the floor to the little desk she opened her eyes.

'Pat Knox is as crazy as a betsy-bug,' I said.

The cat looked at me, yawned, then closed her eyes.

'I know what you mean,' I said.

TEN

It was almost Gary Cooper time and I was sitting out behind the trailer in the hot sun alternately watching the river flow and forking through the folder Pat Knox had given me. It wasn't clear that I was getting anywhere but at least I was working on my tan. All I was wearing were my Jesus boots, the same bathing suit I'd owned for twenty-five years and an increasingly surly expression.

'I don't understand the purpose of the exercise,' I said to the cat, who sat on the large wooden spool that served as a table.

The cat said nothing. She didn't understand the exercise either. She didn't even understand why we'd come to Texas.

'If I keep reading these morbid, stultifyingly dull coroner's reports,' I said, 'I'm going to jump in the river and drown.'

The cat stared at me, then gazed out at the river. Her placid, agreeable expression seemed to indicate that she thought it might not be such a bad idea.

'We don't really consider it a river,' I said. 'Around here folks call it a crick. Big Foot Wallace Crick, to be precise. Named after Big Foot Wallace, a famous frontier scout who lived with the Indians.'

The cat took on a very bored countenance. The only remote interest she had in Native Americans was that they occasionally wore feathers.

Reluctantly, I returned to Pat Knox's papers. They didn't exactly make for riveting summer reading. As she'd already told me, three of the four deaths had occurred outside her bailiwick, and there was no firsthand information here relating to them. What there was were sketchy, hearsay little short stories that you could've read to a bunk of kids if you wanted to bore them to sleep. Worse, from my point of view, there was not even the whiff of a nuance of foul play in any of the three. The closest to it was the first case, the lady who'd drowned in her bathtub in Bandera. A neighbor of the deceased told Pat's mother, Dot, that she could've sworn the woman never took a bath.

The death by fire in Pipe Creek was nothing but smoke and mirrors, and every time I looked into one of the mirrors I saw Pat Knox staring back at me like the Mad Lady of Chaillot.

'She is crazy as a betsy-bug,' I said to the cat. The cat lay like a waxen figure on the tabletop.

'*One* of us is crazy as a betsy-bug,' I said.

The cat did not respond.

The description of the third death, near Mountain Home, in which a gun was found near the body, at least demonstrated a colorful command of the vernacular on the part of that town's octogenarian justice of the peace, John Hill. 'The bullet,' Hill reportedly had said, 'didn't have no reverse on it. It went in the back of her head like it had eyes, but when it went out, I'll be damned if it didn't have a nose.'

The fourth death, the one that had taken place in Judge Knox's precinct, was the most recent, having occurred just two weeks earlier. The good judge had not only composed a mordant document that was as interminable as a Homeric lyrical poem; it might as well have been Greek. Her notes looked like they'd been written by a mariner crab.

The cat got up, stood on the paper and gazed down with a quite perplexed expression.

'Jesus,' I said. 'Somebody gave me the wrong Torah portion.'

The cat said nothing. She was of an extremely secular bent and could not be drawn easily into conversations of a religious nature. This was, quite possibly, to her credit. I've known a lot of cats in my life who've gotten all worked up on the subject. Of course, when you have nine lives, it doesn't matter if you're dead wrong eight times.

The lady who'd died recently, the fourth in the supposed string that stretched between Pat Knox's ears like the lonely string of colored lights they always hung across the road in Medina at Christmas time, was seventy-five years old and had required a special oxygen supply. Maybe the bottle had become disconnected accidentally, or maybe someone had deliberately . . .

'Goddamnit,' I said. 'Move your foot!'

The cat glared at me, then, rather grudgingly, moved off the paper. Cats have a uncanny ability to find precisely that particular patch of paper which you're trying to read. They find it and they proceed to stand, sit or lie down on only that portion which is germane. Indeed, if editors, lawyers and amateur private detectives were more patient, they could avoid reading reams of irrelevant material. They could just light up cigars, sit back and let cats settle on the document in question.

In this case, it wouldn't have worked. There was nothing in the judge's papers that suggested any pattern, any foul play, or, I might add, any particular grasp on reality. The part the cat had obscured merely noted that the victim, Prudence South, had, as a hobby, made little hats for cats. The fact that the cat had chosen this information to obfuscate might be cosmic, or might've had a certain significance to the cat, but it meant nothing to me. Except that I was damn sure going to let Pat Knox attack her own windmills.

I stacked the papers neatly and placed an eighty-million-year-old fossil on top of them as a paperweight.

'Wish I was that well preserved,' I said.

The cat did not reply. Tact was not her long suit, but she knew better than to poke fun at the middle-aged.

I leaned back and lit a cigar and for a while the two of us sat peacefully behind the green trailer in the sunshine of that little valley and watched the river flow. It flowed under a little red wooden bridge, past sycamore and cypress trees, past beautiful banks of natural rock, over the dam that Earl Buckelew had built over fifty years ago, and on down to Big Foot Falls, also, of course, named after Big Foot Wallace.

As I sat there, a great sense of peace and calm invaded my somewhat weatherbeaten spirit. The travails of New York City, the urgent scrawlings of Judge Knox, my own private loneliness of heart, began to float away on the currents of the little sunlit stream. It seemed almost to be murmuring to me, and I thought of the old camp song my mother had always liked: 'Peace I ask of thee, O river, / Peace, peace, peace.'

The next thing I knew the bell was ringing and the quiet of siesta was over. What appeared to be at least three bunkhouses of ranchers began boisterously descending upon the green trailer and the little stream beyond for their shallow-water swimming tests. The cat, a black and white cartoon character, shot off the table and into the bowels of the trailer like a missile seeking peace. But peace, as so many children of the world have learned, is harder to find than tits on a mule.

ELEVEN

The first few days of camp went by like a scorpion skittering across a bunkhouse floor. The troubled outside world disappeared and was replaced, for all practical purposes, by cook-outs, water fights, horseback riding, softball games and isolated spates of homesickness that soon gave way to unbridled fun. The gray, desperate adult world all but vanished in the world of sunshine and childhood at Echo Hill.

As for me, the specter of murder and mayhem had been pushed to a dark corner table of my mind and the cruelty and suffering that grown-ups routinely inflicted upon other grown-ups was simply not on the menu. The most serious altercation I'd allowed myself to become involved in was one night when I entered the Bronco Busters bunkhouse and broke up a pillow fight. My universe was demarcated by a circle of hills; the only things that mattered were the ones that occurred within that little green valley.

'It's so peaceful,' I said to Pam as I stood by the window of the Crafts Corral. 'Makes you want to just resign from the human race. Maybe I'll retire.'

'What is it you'd retire from?' she said.

'That's a good question. I see you're ignorant of my talents.'

'Totally,' said Pam, but she smiled a quick, mischievous smile to mollify what she imagined to be my wounded ego. She didn't realize that I'd left it on a curb in New York many years ago.

'Had a country band once. In the early seventies. Kinky Friedman and the Texas Jewboys. We toured the country and irritated a lot of Americans. Now I sing mostly at campfires, whorehouses, the occasional bar mitzvah.'

'The only thing I remember about the seventies,' said Pam, 'was getting my first tricycle for Christmas.' She turned her back to me for a moment and bent down to select some paint from a cabinet. I almost swallowed my cigar.

'It stands to reason you never heard of me,' I said. 'You were jumping rope in the schoolyard when I was ordering room service. Also, Oklahoma isn't the bar mitzvah capital of the world.'

'Not like Texas?'

'There's a lot of Jews in Texas, actually. I'm just the oldest living one who doesn't own any real estate. But I'm glad you never heard of me. I've had my share of groupies.'

'I don't think you'll have to worry,' she said.

I had her right where I wanted her, I thought, as I wandered away in the direction of the Nature Shack. She probably didn't realize that, after a few more weeks of isolation from the outside, Echo Hill took on almost the sexual ambience of a bar at closing time. All I had to do was play my cards right. I didn't know of anyone who'd really done that yet, but there was always a first time. In life, they don't always remember to cut the deck.

That night I stood in the shadows of the campfire and watched the children watching the fire. Their eyes reflected a bright hope you didn't see much on the streets of the city. Any city. I was about to play a song for the kids and Marcie was introducing me. The atmosphere backstage was quite relaxed, more so even than when I drank a very large amount of Jack Daniel's at the Lone Star Café in New York and had to be rolled onstage on a gurney.

Except for the few kids who always shine their flashlights in your face, it was a pretty good crowd. Some familiar faces, some new ones. Not your glitzy New York–LA-type audience. Just a large, cheerful group of young kids sitting on blankets in their bunkhouse groups, far away from home but close to the campfire. The ceiling was glittering with stars and the crickets provided a nice little rhythm section. It was a good room to work.

I sang a song that was always quite popular at camp. I'd written it when I was just eleven years old, standing backstage rehearsing for my bar mitzvahs with my little yamaha on my head. The lyrics went as follows:

> *Ol' Ben Lucas*
> *Had a lot of mucus*
> *Comin' right out of his nose.*
> *He'd pick and pick*
> *'Til it made you sick*
> *But back again it grows.*

> *When it's cotton-pickin' time in Texas*
> *Boys, it's booger-pickin' time for Ben.*
> *He'd raise that finger, mean and hostile,*
> *Stick it in that waiting nostril*
> *Here he comes with a green one once again.*

Everybody sang the 'Ol' Ben Lucas' chorus several more times, then I ankled it out of there with Marcie shouting, 'Let's give Kinky a big 1–2–3 HOW!!!' The ranchers all joined in on the 1–2–3 HOW part, which was the equivalent of applause in the city, and they shouted it as loudly and as sharply as they could, an act that generated countless echoes off the surrounding hills.

I wasn't as pumped up as James Brown after a show, but it did feel good hearing the echoes as I packed up my guitar and slipped off into the dark, beautiful, anonymous night. Every performer, no matter how great, is a ham at heart. Whether you're playing Carnegie Hall or a campfire for kids, it's still another show in your hip pocket.

Part of my job at camp, along with the overwhelming responsibility of being hummingbird man and occasionally dropping off laundry in town, was security. Not that anyone expected six Islamic fundamentalists in a blue sedan to drive up to the flagpole. I was just supposed to walk around, turn on some of the lights at night and, as Tom says, 'maintain a presence'. It wasn't very difficult. I'd been doing it most of my life.

The ranch was eerily silent with the kids all out at the campfire. The cat was sitting on top of the trailer watching the horses grazing on the latest project by the Echo Hill Garden Club. The Echo Hill Garden Club didn't usually have a lot of luck. If the horses didn't eat their latest project, the deer invariably would. Not only did we not get the opportunity to reap what we sowed, we rarely got a chance to even see it.

I'd put my guitar up and was just lighting a cigar and pouring a little shot when the phone rang.

'Start talkin',' I said.

'This is Pat.' I didn't have to ask, Pat who? I was currently a one-Pat man.

'Yes, Pat,' I said patiently.

'There's been another one.'

I took a couple of paternalistic puffs on the cigar.

'Pat, there's always going to be another one. These are little old ladies. Little old ladies are mortal. When their time comes they fall through the trapdoor just like everybody else, no matter how hard they've crammed for the final exam.'

With the hand that wasn't holding the blower, I lifted the shot of Jack Daniel's from my faithful old bullhorn and discharged it into my mouth. The little judge was really starting to get up my sleeve. I poured another small shot.

'She was murdered,' said Pat stubbornly.

'How do you know that?' I fairly shouted. 'Did she come back and appear to you in a séance and tell you that?'

'She couldn't have done that,' said the judge. 'Her lips were sewn shut.'

TWELVE

As I entered the old courthouse the next morning I thought of the only time I'd ever seen anybody's lips sewn shut. It'd been many years ago and the lips had belonged to the shrunken head in the Bandera museum. The sight hadn't been pleasant on a head the size of a tennis ball, and I could only too well imagine the nightmare vision of an actual-size human face mutilated in the same macabre fashion. It was enough to put you right off your huevos rancheros.

The old courthouse hadn't really come to life yet, if it ever did. The old lady who'd been spliced the night before wouldn't be coming to life again either, unless it was to haunt my dreams someday when I was tucked away in the Shalom Retirement Village.

The halls seemed empty as my heart. I walked past some old wooden doors that looked like they'd been closed for a hundred years, some pebbled glass and about seven spittoons. Before I knew it I was sitting in a big office in front of a big desk behind which sat a big woman. Everything was big in Texas, I thought. Even the small towns.

'The old lady who died last night,' I said. 'The one with her lips sewn shut. That one definitely goes down as murder, right?'

'Of *course* it was murder,' said Sheriff Frances Kaiser, looking fairly murderous herself. 'Can you think of anything else you could call it?'

'There's always the possibility,' I said, 'that she might've had a nearsighted tailor?'

I chuckled a brief, good-natured chuckle. A large vein throbbed in the sheriff's neck.

'What in the dickens would lead you to believe it *wasn't* murder?' she said. 'Poor old thing was strangled and her lips sewn shut. Doesn't that sound like murder to you? Maybe you've been in New York too long.'

'This kind of wanton violence never happens in New York,' I said. 'We're all good, God-fearin' little church workers up there. Mind if I smoke?'

The sheriff gave an expansive, almost papal, wave as if she were shooing away an extremely large gnat. I fished around for a cigar in the many pockets of my beaded Indian vest. This created an awkward moment and, by the time I found the cigar and started setting fire to it, I could see that the sheriff was fresh out of charm.

Sheriff Frances Kaiser was no one to putz around with. She was a big, tall, no-nonsense type who'd grown up on a ranch near Medina. As a kid, she'd done chores around the ranch and driven the tractor. Now, in her first term in office, she was one hell of a mean-looking sheriff. I could tell she was past wondering what I was doing in her office. Through the blue cigar smoke I heard her speaking to me.

'We've heard tales of your exploits in New York. Any truth to them?'

'There's a little. You know how those New Yorkers like to brag. I was just wondering whether you had any leads in this latest case.'

'Are you offerin' us your expert help?'

'Hell, no. I figure you'd probably have things just about wrapped up by now.'

'And you'd be right,' said the sheriff, her eyes straying to a gun on her desk. 'We've already apprehended a prime suspect and the DA's convening the grand jury to get the indictment.'

'Jesus. I thought the mills of justice were supposed to grind slowly but exceedingly fine.'

'Those're the mills of the Lord,' she corrected. 'The mills of justice grind just about as fast as I tell 'em to. Don't you know about the mills of the Lord? It's in the Bible. Your people wrote it.'

'Sure, we wrote it. But we didn't like it all that much. We loved the movie.'

The room was rapidly beginning to fill up with cigar smoke and unpleasant vibes. It was difficult to pry any information from Sheriff Kaiser without mentioning Pat Knox and, from what I'd already gleaned, mentioning Pat Knox to the sheriff could be lethal. It would totally dissipate what rancid crust of credibility I'd managed to attain. Apparently, my 'exploits in New York' had impressed Kaiser about as much as my cowboy hat impressed Sergeant Mort Cooperman in the city. Well, you can't please 'em all. The only one who seemed to believe in my talents was Pat Knox, and she barely came up to Sheriff Kaiser's kneecap.

'Who's the suspect?' I said.

'I can't tell you that,' she snapped.

'Is there anything you *can* tell me besides get the hell out of your office?'

Sheriff Kaiser looked at me stonily. I was glad I wasn't being hauled up here for stealing my neighbor's goat. I waited.

'We're really very busy,' said the sheriff, as she studied her fingernails. She performed this gesture, I noticed, not with her palm outward as a woman might, but palm inward with fingers curled toward her, as somebody who drove a tractor might.

'I guess I'll wait till another time,' I said, 'to ask you to quash my parking tickets.'

'Cut the bullshit,' she said. 'I'm late for my Rotary luncheon.' She stood up. She looked bigger than God, even if you happened to be an agnostic.

'Just tell me. Do you think this murder could be related to the other deaths?'

'What other deaths?' said Kaiser irritably.

'You know, Sheriff. The little old ladies.'

'Goddamnit, you been talkin' to Pat Knox,' said the sheriff, moving toward me like an angry tractor. 'Sure you have!

That's how you knew about that old lady's lips sewn shut. What else did our wonderfully imaginative justice of the peace tell you?'

'Well, she just thinks there might be some possible connection –'

'There ain't no connection,' shouted the sheriff. 'Her brain ain't even connected! Her job is to identify the victim – not to run her own investigation! This is a retirement community. There's lots of elderly people here and sooner or later they die. We got a prime suspect right over there in the jail. But we ain't accusin' him of killin' every old person that kicks the bucket. Now you stay the hell out of this! And stop listenin' to Pat Knox!'

Like a kid following behind a fast-moving plow I followed Sheriff Kaiser out of the office.

'I always suspected she was crazy as a betsy-bug,' I said.

THIRTEEN

Dark thoughts were line dancing through my mind as I hustled my butt over to the Butt-Holdsworth Memorial Library. Somebody was right and somebody was wrong, and damned if I needed to get myself square in the middle of an Old West shoot-out between the female sheriff and the female justice of the peace. I longed for the days when men were men and chickens were highly agitato.

My library card had expired back when Christ was a cowboy but I didn't intend to check out any books. All I needed was information about some people who'd checked out. If this had been New York I'd just call McGovern and have him run down the obits for me. Here I'd have to look them up myself. It was tough being your own legman.

I backed the little convertible out of the courthouse parking lot and promptly became tied up in traffic. For a small town, Kerrville was coming on strong in the gridlock department. Of course, in New York I wouldn't have been driving. I'd have been sitting peacefully behind some guy in a turban who was honking his horn, shooting the finger and screaming Sri Lankan death threats. Here, I was waiting for an ancient Studebaker that appeared to have only been driven to church and bingo games to turn left, right or back into me. At the wheel was a little old lady who barely reached the dash.

A little old lady.

Why was I going to the Butt-Holdsworth Memorial Library to read obits? I was supposed to be on sabbatical, leaving big-city crime and strife behind me in the big city where it belonged. I should listen to the sheriff, whether or not I respected authority figures as large as tractors. They had a little murder. They caught the suspect. The grand jury was going to indict him. The mills of the Lord would keep grinding just like my teeth. People lived and when they got o-l-d they died. Pat Knox had obviously been taking Slim lessons. Slim, in his last few years when he lived alone on the ranch in the wintertime, claimed he was seeing children in trees.

There were no children in trees. And, most likely, there was no succession of little old ladies upon whom some unknown fiend was performing heinous crimes. Even if by some weird proclivity of fate it was true, why should I get myself embroiled in something a hell of a lot more unpleasant than traffic?

Soon the little old lady was gone and the guy in the pickup truck behind me was honking his horn and spitting tobacco juice. I tooled past the Smokehouse, where I bought my cigars, the Main Book Store, wherein resided Alex the parrot, the post office, from whose steps I'd campaigned for justice of the peace in the manner of Huey P. Long, and Jon Wolfmueller's store, which took care of my somewhat questionable sartorial needs. Kerrville wasn't quite my home town, I reflected, but neither was New York. My home town was probably spiritually somewhere between the two, very far away, its longitude and latitude lost in a lullaby. Its citizens were smoke. Its children, beyond any shade of doubt, resided in the trees.

I was daydreaming by the time I pulled into the Butt-Holdsworth Memorial Library parking lot, which is a conducive state of mind if you're going to the library. I'd look through old newspapers for a while. Give the obits a quick scan. Get the hell out of there. If I stayed too long I might stumble on my own name.

The woman behind the counter at the Butt-Holdsworth wasn't Marian the librarian from *The Music Man*, but she maintained roughly the same rigid sense of library decorum. She insisted upon my parking my cigar outside before I had even remembered to whisper. I walked outside, wedged the cigar between two bricks in the wall and came back in with a micro-chip on my shoulder.

'I'm looking for yesterday's fish wrappers,' I said.

'I beg your pardon.'

'Back issues of the local rag.'

'Just what are you looking for, sir?'

'The croaker section.'

'I beg your pardon.' She was starting to warm up to me.

'Worm-bait page.'

'Are you referring to the obituaries, sir?' She gave a slight *moue* of distaste.

'Dead right,' I said.

In a rather brusque manner the lady pointed me toward the last row on the far wall. I started to thank her for her help, but she'd already directed her attention to a romance novel being checked out by a woman who greatly resembled a large pelican.

All I could get out of Butt-Holdsworth was a photocopy of the news story about the previous night's victim. It was too late to cover the crime scene and too early for the obit. I mumbled to myself something Uncle Tom often said: 'This is *exactly* what I didn't want to happen.'

I couldn't find the back issues I was looking for and the lady at the desk had taken on an almost autistic countenance toward me, so I took the photocopy I'd made and picked up my cigar on the way out the door. It was still smoldering. People are rarely as resilient as cigars and most of the time they're a lot less pleasant. Especially when they're lit. I puffed on the cigar like a pneumatic lung for a few moments and pretty soon it was going again and so was I.

FOURTEEN

The *Kerrville Mountain Sun*, which called itself the 'Harvester of Happenings in the Heart of the Hills', was not only somewhat given to the use of alliteration, but had been published once a week for so long it had probably run an obit for Nebuchadnezzar.

J. Tom Graham, the publisher, welcomed me warmly. I told him what I wanted and, before long, I was seated in a dim and dusty back room poring over the ancient newsprint he'd selected for me. As I looked through the obituaries, I thought of some of the things McGovern had told me over the eternal mahogany of a million nocturnal bar conversations. He'd mentioned Alden Whitman, the *Times* obituary writer who had a sixth sense for when people were going to die. When he'd call someone and say 'This is Alden Whitman with *The New York Times*,' you knew your number was up. Whitman himself had died fairly recently. It wasn't clear whether or not anybody'd called him prior to his departure.

McGovern had written many obituaries for the *Daily News*. Often they were written when the honoree was still alive. His editor had told him to 'Get one in the can' for Hirohito when the Japanese emperor was in the hospital fading fast. McGovern had delivered within twenty-four hours but, unfortunately, the emperor got well. The same thing had occurred with Bob Hope. In fact, anytime McGovern was called upon to write an advance obit for anyone, the subject invariably got better. 'Bob Hope's been in the can for ten years,' McGovern once told me.

Finding the obits I wanted took little more than an hour out of my life. I figured I could study and compare them like baseball cards later at the ranch. I might very possibly turn up life rafts of survivors and interview them all, but the point, in the final analysis, would most likely be right on top of my head. 'Pat Knox be damned,' I said, to whatever residual ghosts might be swirling about the little room.

I saddled up Dusty and rode back to the ranch. I walked into the green trailer with a troubled mind and a hand full of death. The cat was sitting in the kitchen sink watching me curiously. The red light on the answering machine was blinking like a panic-stricken whorehouse. Across the small expanse of trailer the red light filtered through the afternoon shadows and pulsed wildly against the ancient, distorted, almost sideshow-like mirror over the sink. It looked like an answering machine from Jupiter. Next to the mirror and directly over the commode a huge, mounted longhorn steer stared malevolently down at me. A hundred years earlier it had peacefully grazed on the prairie until some great white hunter had blown it away. For years it had hung in the lobby of the Bank of Kerrville. Now, since both the steer and the Bank of Kerrville had gone belly-up, it graced the space immediately above the commode, which required somewhat of an acrobatic maneuver for those who wished to take a Nixon in the trailer. Eons ago, one of its eyes had fallen into the dumper and had never been recovered. The remaining eye appeared to be imploring me to check the answering machine.

I did.

'It's J. Tom Graham,' the tape said, 'from the *Kerrville Mountain Sun*. Please call me as soon as you get this message.'

Some shard of good sense told me not to call J. Tom Graham. Just take the news account of last night's murder – which, I'd noticed, did not mention the victim's lips being sewn shut – put it together with the four obits, and take the little stack of paper up to the Crafts Corral for Eric Roth to make into one of those little Japanese ducks. Whatever weirdness was going on in the Hill Country was none of my business. If I wasn't damn careful it might keep me from having fun at camp.

Under the gun from the steer's eyeball, I punched J. Tom's number. I lit a cigar and took a few puffs as I waited for him to come on the line. The cat watched rather disapprovingly, I thought.

'Kinkster, how are you?' said J. Tom.

'Long time between dreams,' I said.

'A dream's why I called you as a matter of fact. Just after you left, an old lady came in. Said her name was Violet Crabb – '

'That's a funny name.'

'So's Kinky. Anyway, she said her sister died a few months back in a house fire near Pipe Creek. Sounded like one of the obits you were looking for, so I thought I'd call you. She thinks her sister was murdered.'

'Go on,' I said. I felt a prickly sensation on the back of my neck and it wasn't a daddy longlegs.

'Seems her dead sister appeared to her in a dream. She was wearing a white, formal dress and walking toward her. Suddenly, she could see blood dripping from her breast and her side and her neck – '

'Hold the weddin', J. Tom. It's just some old lady's dream. Maybe Violet Crabb had gas or something. Why are you trying to spook me with this?'

'I thought you'd be interested since you were checking up on the same old lady she was dreaming about. The two of you coming in like that was a little too close for coincidence. What's goin' on, Kinkster? You wouldn't be wearing your Sherlock Holmes cap under that cowboy hat, would you?'

'Hell, no, J. Tom. You know I always wear my little yamaha under my cowboy hat. Covers my horns.'

'Yeah, well, I've been hearin' some rumors out of the courthouse to the effect that some of the recent deaths around the Hill Country may not have been from natural causes. I checked over some of those obits and there's been a lot of little old ladies droppin' like Texas houseflies around here lately.'

I paced back and forth in the trailer, like a tiger tethered to the telephone. I'd been careless letting J. Tom know what I was looking for. Now, whether I got into the case or not, I had a pesky journalist on my hands and in Kerrville it was always a slow day for news.

'Don't believe everything you read in the papers,' I said.

'You still want to hear about Violet Crabb's dream?' asked J. Tom relentlessly.

'Spit it.'

'Blood's pouring out of her sister and suddenly the white dress goes up in flames. Just before she's totally engulfed in the flames, she whispers one word.'

'Plastics?'

Graham laughed a little longer than was necessary. The cat eyed me impatiently.

'What the hell was the word?' I asked.

'Cotillion,' he said.

FIFTEEN

The next morning I woke up to a nightmare of my own. A Martian was standing in the trailer at my bedside. Each of its eyes was tunneling blinding silver beams of light into my brain. The effect was paralyzing, not to say a bit unnerving. I'd always wanted to be picked up by a UFO, but not before breakfast.

'Kinky,' said the Martian. 'Wake up!'

I sat up in bed and realized that the Martian was Marilyn Leutwyler and the tunnels of light were the sun's rays reflecting off her thick glasses. On her head, I now observed, was a rather singular silver porpoise-shaped cap that read I SAW SEA WORLD.

Marilyn had, no doubt, left her bunkhouse early, possibly to avoid bunk cleanup, and somehow slipped into my trailer, where she'd stood there like a Martian and scared the hell out of me. Security was pretty lax on the ranch. I, of course, was in charge of security.

Marilyn was what we called a 'floater'. Someone who didn't necessarily go where they were supposed to go or stay where they were supposed to stay. They tended to cause havoc with bunkhouse counselors, but I felt a certain kinship with them. I'd been a floater most of my life.

We talked about cats and bugs and handicrafts for a while and eventually I aimed her in the direction of her bunkhouse group, put some coffee on and fed the cat some tuna. While I waited for the coffee to perk I tended to my morning ablutions over the small sink next to the giant steer's head. The eyeball, I noted, was still missing. It was a good thing, too. No matter how well you washed your face or brushed your hair, in the tin, carnival mirror of the green trailer everyone looked like William Henry Harrison.

The sun was doing its best to seep through dusty windows

and rusty screens into the bowels of the trailer, but the place still gave off somewhat of a rain forest ambience. I took a cup of coffee, a cigar, the obituary notices and a rather surly attitude and stepped outside the trailer into the blinding sunlight. A group of young boys, the Mavericks, I believe, came riding by on horseback and waved and shouted. I waved and shouted back.

'Good morning,' I said.

'It's afternoon,' one kid yelled back.

Still searching for some pattern in the death notices of those little old ladies, I sat down at the shady table behind the trailer and shuffled through them again like a mildly bored riverboat gambler. The victims had nice, old-fashioned names: Virginia, the Bandera bathtub woman; Myrtle, who died in the fire at Pipe Creek and then came back to haunt her sister Violet; Amaryllis, killed by a gunshot near Mountain Home; Prudence, near Kerrville, who'd had a slight reach impediment when it came to her oxygen bottle. I also glanced at the recent news story: Octavia, near Kerrville, who had had her lips sewn together. Had this detail been included, I thought, it was doubtful that the flap, no pun intended, would ever have died down.

There didn't seem to be any link between these cases other than the obvious fact that the victims were all little old ladies. Who could have hated little old ladies that much, I wondered. Maybe the killer was an extremely disgruntled little old man.

The youngest of the women was in her early sixties; the oldest, in her late seventies. They were a surprisingly active group, belonging variously to the Bluebonnet Garden Club, the Lower Turtle Creek Volunteer Fire Department Ladies Auxiliary, the First Methodist Church Vacation Bible Class, the Daughters of the Republic of Texas, the Silver Thimble Quilting Circle and the Huffers 'n' Puffers Senior Square Dance Club.

Just thinking about all their activities was starting to wear me out. But there seemed to be no pattern here, either. At least nothing you could hook your quilt on. After another cigar and another two cups of coffee, I gave up the ghost on the obits, chucked them inside the trailer and ankled it up the little hill to the lodge. Sambo, being somewhat myopic, ran toward me barking ferociously, then, at the last moment, smiled like a rat-trap and licked my hand. After studying obits for several hours, a dog licking your hand can almost make you feel good to be alive.

Few heads turned as Sambo and I entered the lodge. Cousin Bucky, who was busy handing rifles out the front door to boys from the Crow's Nest, nodded a brief greeting. Marcie and Katy were sitting on the couch in the living room locked in an intense meeting with a trio of bunkhouse counselors. Sambo and I slipped past into the back room, where Uncle Tom was at his desk talking on the speakerphone and David Hart, the head men's counselor, was wearing a funny-looking red hat and poring over a computer terminal. Neither looked up.

'Fine,' Tom was saying in a tone that indicated the situation was anything but. 'That's just *fine*.'

'I'm sorry, Dr Friedman,' said the disembodied voice on the speakerphone. 'These ice-makers'll get a little hitch in their git-along every now and then – '

'I'm running a camp. I need that machine working now!'

'Well, we may have to order parts – '

'This is *exactly* what I didn't want to happen.'

I walked over to where David Hart was working on the evening program.

'Eddie wants to know if you'll sing "Ol' Shep" for the Hoedown,' he said. 'Phallax will be the boy and Eddie will be Ol' Shep and he'll end the song by urinating on both of you from the hidden water bottle like he did last year.'

'Smells good from here,' I said. 'Look, I've got to make a run to town.'

David Hart punched in a few things on his computer. 'We can spare you,' he said.

I picked up the obits and a few cigars from the trailer, saddled up Dusty and headed over to Earl Buckelew's place. Earl was not only a timeless old-timer, he believed that 'everything comes out in the wash if you use enough Tide.' He'd known the land and the people on the land for so long that he gave directions by the bends of rivers that weren't even there anymore. Maybe he could get inside the minds of these women. If they'd known him when they were younger he might well have broken their hearts.

Earl came out into the yard on a cane, his goats gathering around him like a biblical shepherd. Two severe strokes and the gout had slowed him considerably but they hadn't stopped him. He took me into his house, where the furniture and the pictures on the wall seemed to keep the past alive and the television appeared to run 'Wheel of Fortune' on an endless loop.

Earl studied the obituary notices for a long time, slowly shaking his head.

'You don't know any of them?' I asked.

'Don't know *them*,' he said, 'but I do know widow women. And there's three things you should never try to do. Never try to climb a barbed wire fence leanin' toward you. Never try to kiss a girl leanin' away from you. And never try to get a widow woman to tell you the truth about her age.'

I sat back in the rocker, the one that had belonged to Earl's grandfather who'd been captured by the Indians – but that was another story, and one that I didn't wish for Earl to launch into at this time. I thought about the widow women. Of course, they'd all been widows. A small detail maybe, but it might be important.

'How would I get their correct ages?' I asked.

'You could try thinking about a marriage license.'

'Earl,' I said. 'This is so sudden.'

Earl laughed. I rocked and thought it over. If I got my ass out of the rocking chair there was still time to get to the courthouse before the Comanches got me. But there was something seductive about Earl's place. Before I knew it, he was telling me about his adventures in Tahiti, which he pronounced in about eleven different ways, pausing only to spit Red Man chewing tobacco into a coffee can on the floor. I rocked comfortably in the chair, smoked my cigar, and listened to the tale I'd heard many times before, almost as if it were a modern mantra. Listening to old people and young people was a hell of a lot better than just listening to middle-aged nerds, I thought. It was certainly better than listening to yourself.

Eventually, Earl wound down and he painfully walked me out to the gate. I thanked him for his help, though I had my doubts about how much light it might shed on the investigation. I was climbing into Dusty when another thought struck me.

'Earl, have you ever heard of a cotillion?'

'Hell,' he said, 'everybody knows what that is. It's a long-necked lizard from West Texas.'

A little over an hour later I was standing under a shade tree outside the Kerr County courthouse with five copies of marriage license applications in my hands. Earl Buckelew had been right. The obituaries had been wrong. Almost all of the widow women had lied about their ages.

I took out a pen and small notepad and began doing some quick calculations, subtracting the year each woman was born from the year she'd died, which was for all of them the current year. I put my pen and pad away after the first two. It wasn't necessary. The pattern was not only abundantly evident, it was crazier than any you'd be likely to find on a quilt. It made me almost shiver under the shade tree.

Each of the five, at the time of her death, had been exactly seventy-six years old.

Happy Birthday.

SIXTEEN

June shed its cocoon; July opened one eye. The summer was rolling obliviously along like a wayward beachball thrown onto the field of a nationally televised sporting event by some California sicko. Over a week had passed since I'd stood on the lawn of the Kerr County courthouse and uncovered a dark secret under the summer sun. I'd kept it to myself. One reason was the horrific nature of some of its possible interpretations. Another reason was that most of the people I talked to these days were about three feet tall. They weren't ready for it yet. I wasn't sure that I was, either.

It was Sunday and I was joining the Bronco Busters' table in the dining hall for lunch. Everyone at the table was seven or eight years old except Ben and Eric, the two counselors, who sat on either side of the little group like enormous bookends. Sunday lunch was always fried chicken and everybody wore their whites. It was Rosie and Elese's fried chicken, but before that it'd been Louise's fried chicken. Before that, long before any of the Bronco Busters had been born, it was Hattie's fried chicken. Before that the chicken had been running around pecking apple cores in the backyard of the Garden of Eden.

The fried chicken was still great and, as always, a big favorite at Echo Hill. Seldom was heard a discouraging word like 'cholesterol'. As Earl Buckelew once commented: 'Hell, when I was growin' up, we didn't even know we had *blood*.'

I'd barely laid my hot green peppers out on the table – no Bronco Buster had ever eaten a hot pepper – when the kids began singing the noonday prayer. It was a little number from *Johnny Appleseed* and it went as follows:

> *Oh the Lord is good to me*
> *And so I thank the Lord*

For giving me the things I need
The sun and the rain and the appleseed
The Lord's been good to me. Amen. Dig in.

Eating a fried chicken lunch with a tableful of seven-year-olds will certainly take your mind off weightier matters. Along with the chicken and the mashed potatoes and gravy, the adult world with its ponderous problems just seems to disappear. Conversation is limited to bunkhouse activities, hikes, horses, snakes, water fights, softball, archery and riflery. The subject of girls never even comes up.

'Is Uncle Tom really your father?'

'Yup.'

'And Marcie's your sister?'

'Yup.'

'Wow.'

'My dad says he was in your bunk when you were ranchers and that one night you both snuck up and put horse manure in the counselor's bed.'

'Very possible.'

'Don't get any ideas,' said Ben, towering over the table like a giant Buddha.

As I sat amongst the Bronco Busters, a gentle sense of arrested social development came over me. My gaze wandered across the crowded dining hall and my mind wandered back across the hot dusty summers to a time before any of these children were born. I remembered being seven years old myself and watching the oldest boys' bunk playing with their food, mixing it with ketchup and bug juice in a bowl in the middle of the table. Their counselor that summer was an Israeli named Tuvia who'd fought in a number of wars and seen men starve to death in some godforsaken biblical desert. Tuvia took the bowl and three of the culprits away from the dining hall and apparently made them eat the mess, because I vividly remember hearing various retching noises occurring through the choruses as the rest of the ranch was singing a round called 'I Like the Flowers'. From that day forth I've never had any inclination to play with food.

There were two more things Tuvia did that I would never forget. Once, when the rope snapped during flag lowering and Old Glory fell to the ground with the whole camp standing at mute attention in a circle, Tuvia had snatched it up, put the rope in his teeth and climbed the old cedar flagpole to tie the rope ends together. I remember thinking that he wasn't even an American.

The other thing Tuvia did was teach us a new bunk yell. It was almost forty years ago and I still remembered it. The bunk yell went precisely as follows:

> *Avivo! Avavo!*
> *Avivo, vavo, voo-hey!*
> *Lefty, Befty, Billillilla Lefty,*
> *Chingala, Mingala,*
> *Loof, Loof, Loof,*
> *Yea, Bunk Seven!*

That was all in the mid-fifties before the bunks had names. Now Tuvia himself was just a name, remembered only by a very few of us. A member of a lost tribe that wanders somewhere within the soul. Sooner or later all of us would be members of that tribe.

To the boisterous strains of 'When They Built the Ship Titanic' I handed my plate and silverware to the ranch KP and slipped out ahead of the throng. I smoked a cigar by the old bell that stood by the office. I looked out at the empty flat soon to be swarming with scores of ranchers. From inside the dining hall the kids were now singing 'Happy Birthday' to Eddie Wolff. At the end of the normal birthday song they tagged it with a rather unusual traditional Echo Hill verse. Sung in a minor key in the style of a funeral dirge, it went like this:

Happy birthday, happy birthday,
Misery is in the air,
People dying everywhere,
Happy birthday, happy birthday.

'Not inappropriate,' I said to the bell, 'considering recent events.'

But the bell held its tongue.

SEVENTEEN

Though it was clear to me that five women had been croaked on their seventy-sixth birthday, I was still somewhat disinclined to rush with the news to Pat Knox or Sheriff Kaiser. As far as the JP was concerned, a little bit of the little judge went a long way. I didn't want this whole megillah to turn into a Nancy Drew affair with the judge playing Nancy and me in the role of one of her little chums, both of us futilely attempting to operate outside the powers that be. As for Sheriff Kaiser, it was indubitably her attitude that a little bit of Kinky went a long way. It was a hell of an understatement to say that she would not be particularly desirous of entertaining another audience with me. The last one had been a tension convention, the repellent memory of which neither of us was soon likely to forget.

On the other hand, since the day I'd learned that terrible secret on the courthouse lawn, the onus of that dark knowledge had been weighing heavily on my conscience. I now knew beyond any shadow of a doubt that these five deaths could not be written off to coincidence. They were murders – a string, a chain, a cheap imitation necklace strung together by a madman – the end of which was nowhere in sight.

This knowledge pressed brutishly against the translucent

butterfly wings of my soul as I flitted in and out of camp activities, my mind always returning to the little old ladies who'd been hastened, if ever so slightly, through death's door. If even one more victim were to be killed while I was the sole possessor of a crucial clue to the murderer's dark agenda it would take a hell of a lot of Tide to make everything come out in the wash.

I puffed on the cigar and wandered the flat on that sunny Sunday afternoon until the singing stopped in the dining hall. After a few moments I heard Uncle Tom's voice saying 'Well . . . ?' and answered by an army of children shouting 'What are we *waiting* for!' Then the doors of the dining hall flew open and the peaceful little valley was suddenly alive with children running, shouting and laughing. The hills seemed to echo their energy and joy, and it was a little sad to think how very briefly they would stay this way before joining all the other gray, weatherbeaten souls in the quotidian adult world.

I left my cigar on the ledge and walked into the nearly deserted dining hall, where Uncle Tom was wearing his blue safari hat and working out a chess problem with an eight-year-old boy named Danny. They stood on either side of a huge wooden board I'd bought in Nuevo Laredo in another lifetime. With the chessboard at table level, the king and queen were slightly taller than Danny.

As I stood a little distance away there seemed something rather poignant about the tableau. The innocent intensity of the small boy and the equally intense sincerity of the large man. Chess, like life, is one of those rarest of endeavors that should never be taken lightly. In the case of life, it should, of course, never be taken at all.

'Treat adults like children and children like adults!' I said, quoting Tom after the little tableau had dissolved and Danny had rushed off to buy Cokes with the other kids.

'Why not?' he said to the rows of empty tables and benches. 'Almost nothing's ever been accomplished the other way.'

'True,' I said. 'As I'm finding out in this current Kerrville caper.'

'What's the latest with Pat Knox's little mystery?'

'It's not really Pat Knox's little mystery.'

'Whose is it?'

'I'm not sure. But whoever it is is going to have his or her hands rather full. I think I've stepped on something and it ain't third base. I was going through the marriage license applications down at the courthouse the other day and I discovered that all five victims were seventy-six years old.'

'The likelihood of that occurring naturally is statistically very small.'

'Tom, they were all killed on their birthdays.'

'Sure. Fine. Whatever. Sonny boy, you've got to turn this over to the sheriff. We're running a children's camp here. We can't allow the ranch to become involved with anything like this. We're not equipped to handle it. We're not geared –'

'I'll meet with the sheriff, all right? I'll go into town tomorrow.'

David Hart, wearing his funny red hat and carrying a clipboard, wandered into the dining hall just in time to hear my last sentence. He looked down briefly at his clipboard.

'We can spare you,' he said.

EIGHTEEN

Even then, on that torpid Monday afternoon in July as I was driving Miss Dusty to Kerrville, some part of my consciousness, some dim forgotten street corner of my peripheral vision, was stirring with the unpleasant notion that the baton pass to Sheriff Kaiser would not entirely extricate me from the ancient rusted meat hook that was this case. Maybe it was a deeper, darker well than a small-town sheriff's department could fathom or plumb. Maybe God, in his divine even-handed perversity, was watching over all amateur Jewish private investigators and wished them to receive credit for stumbling over vital clues. That was unlikely, I figured, as I smoked a cigar and sped with the top down beneath a canopy of cottonwoods, cypress and Spanish oak. God had created them, so they'd told me in Sunday school. God had also created a rather tedious situation with me and Sheriff Frances Kaiser. Not that I particularly blamed God. I wasn't even sure if God was a he, she or it. Possibly, he was the guy on the dim street corner of my peripheral vision who was looking for spare change for a sex change.

Maybe he was none of the above.

'A door is ajar,' said Dusty.

'Nice of you to mention it,' I said, 'but why'd you wait till I was halfway to Kerrville?' I opened the driver's door and slammed it shut again.

'Thank you,' said Dusty.

'You're welcome,' I said.

As Dusty and I climbed the steep hill between the ranch and Kerrville, I noticed that the sky was growing increasingly foreboding. If you were writing a Victorian novel you might say the clouds were becoming edged with pewter. In Texas, we'd say they were getting dark.

However you described it, the changing weather was only a physical manifestation of what I sensed were deeper, deadlier changes. Changes within the psyche of a killer capable of restraint and of remarkable rage. Changes in a weatherbeaten, war-torn world that was capable of absolutely anything. No big deal. I'd turn my evidence of murder most methodical over to the powers that be. That'd be all she wrote, so I thought. At the time, assuredly, I did not expect the hand of fate to be quite so well manicured. Nor was I aware that it might indeed be clutching quite such a prolific or such a poisoned pen.

Thunder was crashing and lightning was forking the

summer sky as I parked Dusty near the courthouse on Earl Garrett Street. The cat, I figured, was probably hiding under the bed in the trailer. She did not particularly like the sound of thunder, and Sambo liked it even less. It wasn't all that popular with me, either, in spite of Ratso's oft-noted contention that thunderstorms produce 'negative ionization' which is 'psychologically beneficial' to people. Ratso says that pounding surf can produce the same effects as thunderstorms in making you feel more energetic and creative – though, to my knowledge, Ratso's never been near an ocean in his life, having rarely left the confines of Manhattan, which, according to Ratso, is a positive-ion environment conducive to suicide. Ratso also says that rich people often secretly install negative-ion generating machines in all the rooms of their houses, which helps them constantly think up more ways of making money and thereby maintain their wealth.

I asked Ratso once, as I looked around his hideously cluttered apartment, why he hadn't bought a negative-ion generator for his own place. Aside from the obvious reason that there wasn't any room for it. His answer was: 'They don't sell 'em on Canal Street.'

I walked patiently, luxuriantly through the storm to the courthouse and shook the rain off my cowboy hat into a nearby spittoon. The halls were dark, and so was the look on the secretary's face when I told her I had to see the sheriff but I didn't have an appointment.

'Always make an appointment if you want to see the sheriff,' said the secretary. 'She's got a very busy schedule and she hardly ever sees anyone without an appointment.'

'I'll write that down in my Big Chief tablet,' I said.

Considerably later, and much to the secretary's surprise, I found myself looking across the big desk at Sheriff Kaiser. I don't know whether or not the sheriff had a negative-ion generator going for her but the room certainly had an almost palpable negative atmosphere. The secretary left and closed the door behind her.

'What do you want?' said the sheriff.

'Not a thing,' I said. 'Just have a look at these.'

In a manner roughly akin to Bret Maverick, I fanned out the five copies of the marriage license applications on the desk before the sheriff.

'What're these?' she said.

'Five of a kind.'

As Frances Kaiser adjusted her glasses and picked up the documents I walked over to the window and watched the storm. I lit a cigar and watched the trees on the courthouse lawn sway with an almost violent grace like dancers in Borneo. I imagined the emotions that must've been traversing the sheriff's face as she read. Doubt, astonishment, thinly veiled anger. I was sure she'd been working diligently to get the grand jury seated, possibly prodding the DA to get his case together in order to gain an indictment against the suspect still in custody. The man she believed had sewn an old lady's lips together. Now all that might be out the window. Into the storm.

Once the forces of the law are set into motion, once the DA goes for an indictment, the grand jury almost invariably rubber-stamps his recommendation. As Rambam once said: 'If the DA really wanted it, the grand jury would indict a couch.' But now the forces of the law in this little town might have to take a step backward and rethink things a bit. Outside the window the forces of nature continued wild and unabated. They were not influenced by the DA's recommendation. They were not subject to the sheriff's authority. They did seem to be moderately interested in exactly how far they could propel a deputy's straw cowboy hat across the courthouse lawn and down Main Street.

'I see,' said the sheriff, as she stared past the window out into the fury of the storm. Her face was an emotionless porcelain mask that in some strange way seemed more unnerving than any display of mere emotion. I puffed politely on the cigar and waited.

'You obtained these documents –'

'Down the hall,' I said. 'But it was Earl Buckelew's idea to check the marriage license applications.'

'Ol' Earl,' said the sheriff, her eyes going back in time. 'We used to sneak onto his place and go fishin' when I was a kid.'

'The same. He claims widow women always lie about their ages.'

Sheriff Kaiser smiled. It was a nice smile. Sheriffs usually don't get to smile a lot but when they do it's always appreciated. Kind of like Ronald Reagan giving a turkey to an orphanage on Thanksgiving.

The sheriff stood up, got rid of the smile and stacked the pages neatly on her desk. It was a gesture of dismissal and I edged toward the door.

'You've been a good citizen,' she said. 'We'll take it from here.'

'I just did what anybody would do.'

'If that was really true,' she said, 'I'd be out of a job.'

I opened the door and headed for the hallway.

'One more thing,' the sheriff called after me.

I turned around. She was standing like a giant in the doorway.

'Tell Earl Buckelew that one of the little Kaiser girls said hello.'

NINETEEN

It was around eleven that night when the phone rang in the green trailer. Pam Stoner, the green-eyed handicrafts counselor from Oklahoma, and I were getting acquainted on a big flat rock out back. We had a Roy Rogers blanket that had somehow survived the lifetime of childhood and a few shots of Jack Daniel's with a little Mr Pibb backing it up. The cat was watching from the roof of the trailer.

'I'd better take this call,' I said.

'You really *are* Jewish,' said Pam Stoner.

'The ugly head of anti-Semitism rears up out of a peaceful, bucolic setting,' I said, as I, too, reared up and moved toward the trailer.

'Bring the bottle with you when you come back,' she said. She was smiling and her star-colored eyes seemed to be shimmering in the moonlight. A whippoorwill was calling from a nearby juniper tree. Maybe that should've been the call I took.

I grabbed the bottle with one hand and took the persistent blower from its cradle with the other.

'Syrian Embassy,' I said.

'This is Pat Knox,' said the blower, 'returning your call. I already know what happened at the sheriff's office today, so you don't need to fill me in on that. You done good.'

'Thanks, Your Honor. Looks like the sheriff now realizes these five deaths are related.'

'Gettin' her to realize it is only half the battle. The other half is gettin' her to do somethin' about it.'

'She assured me the full force of the law will be behind the case.'

Pat Knox laughed. It was a long, hearty, bitter laugh. When she recovered, her tone was dangerous and conspiratorial in nature.

'You and I have sure put her on the right track, but if you'll pardon the choice of words, this case may just be too kinky for the sheriff.'

'It may be too kinky for me, too.' I twisted the top off the bottle of Jack and took a short pull.

'That's not quite true,' said the judge. 'And if there's one thing I know about you it's that you've got the kind of mind that loves a good mystery.'

I looked out the back window of the trailer and saw Pam

lying on her back on the big rock in a very suggestive position.

'That's right, Judge. Me and Miss Marple love a good mystery. What've you got?'

'Come see for yourself. You're not gonna quit on me, are you? Let that big ol' sheriff scare you?'

The big ol' sheriff didn't scare me. In fact, she'd turned in a rather poignant performance that afternoon. But there was something almost sirenlike in Pat Knox's appeal. And I wasn't referring to the thing that's mounted on the top of police cars.

I looked out the window and saw that nothing was going to be mounted around the ranch that night. Pam was asleep on the rock.

'Okay,' I said. 'Where do we meet?'

'Midnight. The Garden of Memories.'

'The cemetery?'

'Boo!' said Pat Knox, and she hung up.

TWENTY

If you've got to go to a bone orchard, midnight's about as good a time as any. Things are just beginning to get stirring and you avoid the crowds. It was a funny thing, but the closer I got to the cemetery the more I felt drawn to it. Sort of like a part-time ghoul returning to the crypt. Of course, all ghouls are pretty much part-time. Being a ghoul twenty-four hours a day would kill anybody. Such were my thoughts as I drove up to the gates of the Garden of Memories. One other little thought that was in my mind was that Sheriff Kaiser probably wouldn't approve of whatever Judge Knox and I were going to be doing here. But who was afraid of the big ol' sheriff?

I hooked a right off Sidney Baker Street and urged Dusty

slowly through the main entrance to the bone orchard. The place was quieter even than the Butt-Holdsworth Memorial Library. Between the two of them there'd been a lot of books and a lot of people checked out. But there was no one here to say 'Ssshhh . . .' Only the wind whispering in the shadows of the willow trees.

There didn't seem to be any human forms moving around or any vehicles parked along the entrance road. I drove a little farther until the town of Kerrville had disappeared behind me and the bone orchard had pretty well swallowed me up. It was not an entirely unpleasant sensation. There was a certain sense of peace to it. Kind of like the way it must feel to be inside a McDonald's after closing time. Of course, there was no closing time here. There was not even any time here. It didn't at the moment particularly feel like there was any here here.

So I hit the brights.

Dark forms and figures began springing up all over the graveyard. Dripping half-shadows of passengers aboard the *Titanic* descended from the willow branches. A partially drawn shade of Ichabod Crane galloped by with hooves of distant thunder. Cowboys and Indians and Jews and gypsies and homosexuals and tiny little Cambodians and soldiers and sailors and airmen from wars that are now trivia questions leapt up out of the night in the manner of game show contestants with the answers to the mysteries of life. But none of them spoke a word. Imagination can be a blessing, I thought, but it can also be pretty tedious.

I puffed my cigar nervously.

Dusty shuddered.

Then, off to the side, glowing darkly through the night with the ageless intensity of Anne Frank's eyes, came a beacon no less welcome than had it shone down from the Old North Church or skipped softly across the waters that gently lapped at Daisy Buchanan's pier.

Then the light vanished along with any residual personal

enjoyment I had at being in that particular locus at that particular time. I pulled Dusty over to the side of the little road, not that there was a lot of oncoming traffic, and waited. The light did not come on again.

I got out of the car, performed a few square-dance maneuvers around the headstones and, following the directions of an old Bob Dylan song, 'walked ten thousand miles in the miles of a graveyard'. I bumped into an ill-placed tombstone and almost burned my forehead. Recovering my balance I took stock of the desolate landscape. Where the light had been there was nothing. All around me in every direction there was nothing. It was like the sensation you sometimes get when you're standing in the middle of a busy shopping mall.

I stared up at the scythelike moon and the little freckling of stars and tapped a cigar ash onto the ground.

'Ashes to ashes,' I said.

'I wouldn't be so sure of that,' said a voice that scared the shit out of me.

I landed a few moments later, practically impaling myself upon a small wooden cross. I struggled to my feet, glanced at the cross, and then at Judge Knox.

'It's a good thing it wasn't one of those pointy-headed stars of David,' I said.

'There are *some* advantages to living in Kerrville,' she said.

'And dying in Kerrville,' I said. 'A lot of people seem to be doing it. By the way, why are we here?'

'Follow me,' she said.

As I trudged behind the little judge and her shining path through the darkened country graveyard, no elegies came to mind. The only things that popped up were more shades, more shadows, more questions, the primary one from the latter category still being: 'What the hell are we doing here?'

Finally, we reached an area in the back of the cemetery in which this season's crop appeared to have been recently planted. The ground looked fresh, there were more flowers, and the stones were new enough to gleam slightly in what moonlight there was. These were definitely not the kind of stones that gather no moss. They'd soon be gathering plenty of it, along with litter, lichens, birdshit and, conceivably, the occasional teenage swastika. Like many of the living, these stone faces seemed resigned to whatever fate lay before them.

'Three of our little ladies are buried here,' said the judge. 'The second victim, Myrtle Crabb, got burned up in the fire at Pipe Creek. They just went ahead and cremated her.'

'Might as well dance with who brung you.'

'Her son, I understand, drives around with her ashes on his motorcycle.'

'Every mother's dream.'

'The fourth victim, Prudence South, the one who needed the oxygen bottle, she's buried in a little church cemetery out the other side of town. So that leaves victims one, three and five buried here. C'mon, I'll show you.'

The judge walked like a determined little rooster to a plot about thirty feet away. I followed faithfully, puffing on my faithful cigar and beginning to realize that Judge Knox was either pulling a somewhat premature Halloween prank by bringing me here or she was really onto something.

'Here's Virginia. Supposedly drowned in the tub in Bandera.'

She had a nice shiny granite stone. On the grave itself was one yellow rose. Pat Knox turned and I followed her farther into the graveyard.

'Amaryllis,' she said. 'Supposedly shot herself.'

'In the back of the head. Wouldn't that be difficult?'

'For a seventy-six-year-old arthritic little lady, damn near impossible.'

Amaryllis had a smaller, more modest stone. There was a vase of wilting flowers on the grave. Beside the vase were three yellow roses.

'Come along,' said the judge.

I stepped around and over the macabre obstacle course and followed her to the other side of the recently planted section. The night seemed to have gotten a good bit chillier and there was a fog rolling in from somewhere. There weren't any oceans around. Where was the fog coming from, I wondered. Possibly, all bone orchards get a little misty after midnight. Who's to say that they don't?

'Octavia,' said a voice out of the fog.

I remembered Octavia. Her lips had been sewn together. Not an item you easily forget. I walked around the grave. The marker was a stone cross. There was a scroll on a little pedestal acknowledging her as an active lifetime member of the Daughters of the Republic of Texas. On the grave were six yellow roses.

'Six yellow roses,' I said. 'Either somebody's made a floral typo or we're missing one of our little ladies.'

'This person's pretty meticulous. I think if we hunt around a little we'll find there's been a victim we've overlooked.'

'When did you first notice the flowers?'

'I've been checking some vandalism in this cemetery the past few days. The flowers weren't on the graves when I came by late this afternoon. Somebody put 'em here tonight.'

'Looks like I'm drawn to this case whether I like it or not. I'm trapped like an insect in amber. You win, Judge.'

'I knew you'd see things my way,' she said, smiling a slightly cadaverous smile.

'Since you've got the contacts and the resources,' I said, 'why don't you try to locate our missing victim?'

'I'll do that,' she said. 'What are you going to be doing?'

I puffed on the cigar and blew a little smoke into the foggy night.

' "There's a yellow rose of Texas",' I said, ' "that I am going to see".'

Bright and early the next morning after I'd delivered a Gandhi-like truckload of ranch laundry to a nice lady named Arlena at the Country Clean Laundromat, I went to the Del Norte Restaurant for breakfast. Heuvos rancheros without the yolks – my one healthy-heart habit. Chain-smoke Hoyo de Monterrey Rothschilds Maduros, drink as much Jameson's as Gram Parsons drank tequila in the last few months of his life, and always eat heuvos rancheros without the yolks if your waitress speaks enough English to get your order right, and you'll live forever. Your life may not be very pleasant, but you can't have everything. You've got to decide what it is you really want – ninety-seven years of shit or Mozart?

It was still not yet eight in the morning and I was walking in the alleyway between the parking lot and the stores on Earl Garrett Street quietly cursing Ben Stroud. Ben had convinced Uncle Tom that the riflery program at camp had reached such a fever pitch that Ben himself must be present to supervise the qualifications. This left me to do the early morning laundry run and David Hart, Eddie or Wayne the Wrangler to take the mid-afternoon run. The advantage to the early morning laundry run was that it was over fast, like a number of love affairs I'd been involved in. By seven forty-five I was through for the day.

Most of the stores didn't open till nine, but I thought I heard some activity inside Wolfmueller's Town and Country Clothiers. I knocked on the back door.

'Who is it?' said a muffled voice.

'Charles Starkweather,' I said.

I pushed the door open. Over about eight rows of tuxedos on movable floor racks I could barely make out Jon Wolfmueller's head. He looked up from his invoices and calculator, waved me in and returned to his work.

'Who's Charles Starkweather?' he said.

'How soon they forget. Got any coffee?'

'Right over there on the other side of the discontinued styles rack.'

'Jesus Christ. How can you have discontinued styles in Kerrville?'

Jon was busily at work back at the invoices and did not respond. I sipped some coffee and paced between the racks of clothes.

'Just wait'll the Nehru jacket hits town,' I said. 'That'll create a buzz.'

Jon paid no attention. I sipped more coffee.

'Jon,' I said, 'I need your help with something.'

'I don't have any openings for male models, if that's what you're hinting at.'

Jon did have a sense of humor lurking back there somewhere. I often, in fact, referred to him as my faithful Indian companion. He wasn't an Indian, of course. Tied to the store as he was, he didn't even make much of a companion. But good help was hard to get these days for both of us. Jon was one of the few Kerrverts I knew who seemed to enjoy my company. At least he put up with me for extended periods of time. Maybe he *was* an Indian.

One thing was for sure. Jon knew what was going on in Kerrville, and anything Jon didn't know, his wife, Sandy, who ran Pampell's drugstore and soda fountain, most assuredly did. Between the two of them I had my finger on the sometimes rather shallow pulse of Kerrville. I knew others, of course. Jody Rhoden, the photographer. Max Swafford, my former campaign manager, who abandoned the campaign right in the middle of the race to search for a gold mine in Mexico. Dylan Ferrero, who'd moved to Kerrville recently from a little town called Comfort, Texas, and communicated almost entirely in rock 'n' roll lyrics. When you're trying to keep a low profile and not irritate the sheriff, personal contacts were the only way to go. And Jon Wolfmueller was the place to start.

'Jon,' I said, 'what do you know about this grand jury they're convening about the woman who was murdered and had her lips sewn together?'

Jon pursed his lips in an unconscious manner not dissimilar to the way the victim must've appeared and thought it over. I sipped more coffee.

'I know they're having a hard time getting the grand jury together for some reason. I know the sheriff and the justice of the peace are each about ready to kill the other and sew her lips together. I don't know the name of the subject of the grand jury.'

'That's kept secret.'

'Don't bet on it. Why don't you go on over and ask Sandy?'

I headed down Earl Garrett and hung a right on Water Street till I reached Pampell's Drug Store, a building that had once belonged to the legendary Singin' Brakeman, Jimmie Rodgers, the man most credit for popularizing the guitar in America. Rodgers was a seminal country blues singer who, next to Elton Britt, was the greatest yodeler of his time or anybody else's. Jimmie wasn't around anymore. He'd died of TB in New York City when most of us were jumping rope in the schoolyard. But every time I went into Pampell's and looked up at the old balconies that had once surrounded his music hall and recording studio, I could hear a little distant Dopplered echo of a train whistle.

Sandy was setting up the soda fountain. There was already one customer, a skinny old man wearing a straw hat and a bolo tie.

'Jon just called,' she said. 'You wanted to know who's the subject of the grand jury?'

'I thought they were supposed to keep his identity secret.'

Sandy laughed. 'There's never been a secret in Kerrville that everybody didn't know,' she said.

'It's one of them funny-soundin' Mescan names,' offered

the old man. 'Rod-*ree*-gis Gui-*tar*-is. One of them hard-to-say kind of names.'

'The guy's name is Garza,' Sandy told me.

The old man nodded his head and cackled softly to himself. '*Gar*-za,' he said. 'There's a jawbreaker.'

TWENTY-TWO

I got a cup of coffee from Sandy and she vanished to the back of the store. I decided to kill a little time and pain there at the old soda fountain until nine o'clock, when the Rose Shop just across Sidney Baker Street opened up. There were only three or four florists in Kerrville. If I was going to get a lead on who'd bought the yellow roses it wasn't going to take very long. That was one advantage to being in a small town when it came to crime solving. It was the reason Miss Jane Marple, arguably Agatha Christie's greatest detective, chose to live in St Mary Mead instead of London. Jane Marple and Agatha Christie, I reflected as I sipped my coffee, were little old ladies themselves.

Jane Marple, of course, would live forever in the timeless casino of fiction, waiting for the freckled, feckless hand of a young person in Wyoming to pluck her off some dusty shelf and fall in love with the mysteries of life. Agatha Christie, like Jimmie Rodgers, wasn't around anymore but in a sense I suppose they both still were, for they continued to ply silent rivers of words and music down into the yawning rugosities of our lives. Silver threads in an otherwise drab embroidery. Too bad Jimmie and Agatha never met. Might've made an interesting couple.

'If it don't rain again by the tenth of July,' the old man with the bolo tie was saying, 'then it ain't gonna rain for the whole summer. It's gonna be a hell of a scorcher.'

'Even if it does rain,' I said, as I laid down a buck for my coffee, 'it's not going to be too pleasant.'

Jesus Christ, I thought. Here I was casually paying a buck for a cup of coffee. What was the world coming to? We dressed casually. Waved casually on the street. Nobody got too excited. Everybody went with the flow. Now some nerd had casually taken six little old ladies off the board.

'Boll weevil's comin' back again,' said the old-timer as I headed for the door.

'Ain't we all, brother,' I said.

At approximately 9:01 A.M. I crossed Sidney Baker Street and entered the Rose Shop, where an irritating little bell rang just above the door and climbed halfway into my inner ear. There was a fairly wide selection of flowers. The flowers smiled at me and I smiled back at them. No one else was in sight. No yellow roses, either.

'Someone in Texas Loves You,' read a bright ceramic wall hanging. 'God Loves You,' read a nearby colorfully painted plate.

'Make up your mind,' I said.

'Can I help you?' said a voice from above.

This is it, I thought. On a bumper sticker, vengeance is mine saith the Lord. The family of man might be fairly dysfunctional but now God was coming down to straighten things out. And She did sound slightly irritated.

I looked up and saw a rather nice pair of legs descending a ladder. The legs were attached to a lady who was holding a hanging plant. She looked pretty earthy for a florist.

Her name, I soon learned, was Betty and she knew a lot about flowers. A little more, possibly, than I wanted to know.

But she didn't have any yellow roses.

'Sometimes we'll go months without selling any yellow roses. We haven't sold any in a long while. Now June through August we do have available our special "Texas Dozen" offer. That's fifteen flowers for $29.95.'

'But no yellow roses?'

'Red.'

'But if I wanted yellow, could you get them?'

'We'd have to order them. We'd bring them in from Austin or San Antonio. It might take a few days. Stores don't usually stock them.'

'How long will roses last once you sell them?'

'Well, that depends. Outdoors, indoors. Air conditioning, no air conditioning. Drafts will kill 'em faster than anything. Never put your roses in a draft.'

'Thanks for the tip.'

Betty seemed to be working up a bit of a second wind herself.

'Now once we sell 'em we'll only guarantee 'em for twenty-four hours. If something happens to 'em within twenty-four hours you can just bring 'em right back to us and we'll see that they're replaced. If it's after twenty-four hours, you're on your own.'

'Got to be tough.'

'Did you want the Texas Dozen?'

'I'm not sure.'

'Only $29.95.'

'I don't know,' I said. 'I'm kind of like James Taylor. I just can't remember who to send 'em to.'

'Well, you've got to the end of August.'

'That's a relief.'

I thanked Betty and cut buns out of there. I got in the old gray pickup and headed out toward Ingram, to a place called Showers of Flowers. I dimly recalled buying some roses there several lifetimes ago and sending them to a long-distance lover who worked at a Cadillac dealership in Spokane. She'd sent me a nice note back. Though it was addressed 'Dear Occupant,' I'd still thought the relationship worth pursuing. Of course, it wasn't, she wasn't, and at the time, from most accounts, I probably wasn't either. But it is precisely this futility, pain and seeming absence of true communication that keep the flower shops of the world in business and, every once in a while, when shaken slightly, may even envelop the stars. Maybe I should've sent her a Texas Dozen.

Showers of Flowers was a big down-home kind of place with several greenhouses out back and flowers of every variety under the sun, so to speak. I saw the yellow roses right away. The owner, a friendly guy named Al, saw me right away.

'I remember the first time you bought flowers here,' he said. 'A long time ago when we first opened up.'

'Spokane?'

'Before Spokane. Even before Los Angeles.'

The guy was weaving a spiderweb of heartbreak right before my eyes. 'It was to Hawaii. A dozen beautiful red roses in a very nice ornate vase, as I recall. You haven't forgotten?'

It had been a long time ago. The flowers had been for Kacey, who'd died very young and been pressed between the pages of my life more than a decade ago. I'd called the hotel in Maui to make sure the flowers had gotten there. Kacey'd already left for Vancouver but I still recalled the words of the maid who was cleaning up the room. 'The lady leave the vase,' she'd said, 'but she take the flowers.'

'I haven't forgotten,' I said.

I steered the conversation gently to yellow roses.

'How many yellow roses do you sell, Al?'

'I don't sell roses. People buy them. Yellow roses are very popular in Texas. For a friend, somebody in the hospital. Red is for deep love and things like that. We also have pink, white and sonya. We grow 'em ourselves. We've got our own greenhouses here.'

'What's sonya?'

'Between pink and orange. Very pretty. We go through fifteen to twenty dozen roses a week. You always bought red before. Why do you want yellow?'

'I got a friend in the hospital who doesn't like pink or white. Really hates sonya.'

After some little badgering, my insistence upon the urgency of the matter, and my promise to treat with some semblance of confidentiality the relationship between a man and his florist, I got Al to bud a little. He'd sold yellow roses to three people over the past week. Or rather, they'd bought them. Al was understandably hesitant to show me the invoices with the customers' names and addresses.

'I can't tell you why I need this information, Al, but it's very important to me. In its own way, it means as much as Spokane, Los Angeles and even Hawaii. And if I'm not being too melodramatic, lives may be at stake.'

Al was a trusting sort. He let me copy the invoices. Names, addresses, dates. He also directed me to the other two remaining florists in the area. I thanked him and hoped to hell the flowers someone had placed in the Garden of Memories weren't purchased out of town.

The third florist was closed. On vacation since the week before. So I drove across town to the last flower shop on my list. That was another advantage to a small town, I thought. You could drive all the way across it in less time than it took to find a cab in New York. And you could smoke a cigar without anybody giving you grief.

Hitting all the flower shops in Kerrville was the kind of investigative work Rambam would've liked. The life of the real PI, he'd always contended, was made up of ninety-eight percent boring routine bullshit. The other two percent, he'd added, was merely tedious. According to Rambam, most of the time the results of long hard hours of digging in the investigative field would be inconclusive. Most cases, especially serial murders, were solved through dumb luck. Ted Bundy forgetting to fix his tail light. Jeffrey Dahmer repeatedly calling his refrigerator repair man.

The last place turned out to be a small affair on Ace Ranch Road just across the way from the Veterans Cemetery, which is a good location if you're a flower shop. The fellow who ran it was a baby-faced, middle-aged guy who looked like he was wearing one of Jon Wolfmueller's discontinued styles. There was nothing yellow in the store except his teeth.

'You don't have any yellow roses, do you?' I said. It was pretty obvious he didn't.

'We sure don't. We've got some nice summery arrangements, if you'd like that. I could get you some yellow roses, but it may take a day or two.'

'Well, I'll tell you what I'd really like. I think someone may have ordered some yellow roses from here recently. Would you have any information on that?'

He looked at me curiously for a moment. Then he smiled. It was not a nice smile. Obviously I wasn't going to be any florist's favorite customer.

'Let me check,' he said, and he disappeared into the back of the shop.

I waited. After a while I wondered if he'd passed away. Eventually he returned with a scrap of paper and my patience was rewarded.

'I don't know why you need this, buddy, but I can't see as it does anybody any harm. They were delivered here.' He handed me the paper with a name and address on it.

'Thanks,' I said. 'You've been a great help.'

'You ain't with the CIA, are you?' He laughed a loud, high-pitched, dangerous, redneck laugh. He laughed and laughed.

I laughed, too.

Then I left.

TWENTY-THREE

I figured if the case was going to be solved by dumb luck, I might as well strike while the iron was hot. I had the names and addresses of the four local people who'd purchased yellow roses within the past week. Why not run them down right now? There was an outside chance I could wrap this unsavory little booger up in a sailor's knot before lunchtime, dump the whole thing on Sheriff Kaiser's desk, and she'd pat the top of my cowboy hat and tell me what a good citizen I was. There was also an outside chance that she would become mildly agitato and have me committed to the Bandera Home for the Bewildered.

I checked the first address from Al at Showers of Flowers and gunned the old gray pickup down the road in that direction. Soft drink cans, basketballs and old .177 rifles recently used in a tableau of Ira Hayes at Iwo Jima slid back and forth across the bed of the truck, making a hell of a racket under the attached camper. I shot a quick backward glance through the window of the cab and saw a sea monster swirling around back there, trying to reach through and grab my throat. A lit cigar fell out of my mouth as I hurtled down the highway. I wasn't sure if it'd fallen on the seat between my legs or on the floor, where it'd probably roll under the seat and most likely burn me to death.

'Mother of God,' I said nervously. 'This is what I live for.' A truck loaded with bales of hay barreled by on my right at about ninety-seven miles an hour.

Without taking my eyes off the highway I rose up slightly in the saddle and frantically felt around between my legs. Nothing was there except what was supposed to be, but I did receive a dirty look from a lavender-haired lady in a late-model Buick. Then I turned my attention to the sea monster. It was an old tennis net with fresh seaweed from the waterfront threaded all through it. King Neptune had worn it the week before on Shipwreck Night. Then I found a place to pull off to the side of the road, got out, and felt around under the seat until I burned the shit out of my hand.

All in a day's work, I thought. Sometimes it requires pawn-shop balls for a private eye to stay on the case.

At a little after eleven I pulled up in front of the first address, a picturesque little house with an actual swear-to-God white picket fence in front of it. It wouldn't have sur-prised me if some very sick bastard lived there.

A guy who looked like Methuselah's older brother was mowing the lawn on the side of the house with a manual lawn mower. I got out of the truck and walked over to the guy without a thought in my head as to who to tell him I was or what in the hell I was doing there. I decided to settle on the old salesman's icebreaker.

'Good morning, sir. I'm John Wisteria from Florists Inter-national. Just checking up on how the roses are doing.'

'They're doin' just fine,' he said. 'They're settin' inside in the air conditionin' and I'm out here mowin' the goddamn lawn.'

'You want to be careful with that air conditioning,' I said. 'A draft can kill them faster than anything.'

He looked at me as if he suspected that there was a draft between my ears. 'You don't say,' he muttered. 'What'd you say your name was?'

'Well, I'm just checking,' I said, as I wrote a little imaginary note in my notebook. 'Just to make sure the yellow roses arrived here all right.'

'Of course they arrived here all right. I went to the damn florist and bought 'em. Then I brought 'em home. Gave 'em to my wife for our fifty-seventh anniversary.' He was becoming increasingly belligerent.

'That's nice,' I said. I began heading back to the truck, but now he wouldn't let me go and began screaming for his wife.

The woman struggled out onto the porch, against my protestations, and backed up her husband on every tedious detail about the yellow roses. She was a grizzled old thing who got around slowly and painfully with one of those aluminum Jerry Jeff Walkers. Her name was Marsupial or something and she was a little deaf, so the dialogue between the two of them went on interminably. If I was the kind of private eye who carried a gun I probably would've pulled it out right there and shot myself to contain my ennui. Eventually, I departed with all three of us shaking our heads in disgust and confusion, softly invoking the names of our various gods.

The visit to my next customer was fast, and required no dissembling on my part. Two moving vans were parked in front of what looked as if it might've once been a happy home. The moving men were loading his things into one truck and hers into the other. The yellow roses were in front of the house, too. In a trash bin.

There's a million stories in the city, I thought. Who the hell's to say there's not also a few in the town?

I drove to the third address. On the way I stopped for a cup of coffee and called Pat Knox's office from a pay phone. We agreed to meet for a low-profile lunch at a funky little Mexican restaurant that had a lot of black velvet art going for it and no clientele from city hall.

When I got to the third address I was not surprised. It was the hospital. Just like Al had said, yellow roses for the friend in the hospital. But I had to be sure. So I checked with the desk, went up to the fourth floor, asked directions from a nurse, and walked by the room of a woman in a hospital bed watching *Smokey and the Bandit*. The yellow roses were there by the bed. Drooping a little, but so was Burt Reynolds' cookie-duster. I was oh-for-three in my horticultural area. The last customer could wait till after lunch. One thing about dumb luck. You can't force it.

When I sat down at the little corner table at the little Mexican restaurant across from the little judge, I could tell she was in a more upbeat mood than I was. Sylvia Plath was in a more upbeat mood than I was.

'What a team,' she whispered, almost shimmering with excitement.

'I don't know,' I said. 'There're some people – possibly cases of arrested development – who maintain an interest in high school sports well into their adult years. For them the prospect of going to State is like a lighthouse to their lives. As for me, the prospect of going to State – '

'I'm talking about *us*, you bullethead. *We're* the team.'

' – is not as important as the prospect of going to the men's room.'

I did have to urinate like a racehorse. But I had another motive for getting up and leaving the table that Judge Knox was not privy to. I wanted to check out the restaurant, the little hallway and the men's room for any large, burly sheriff's deputies that might report our little rendezvous to Frances Kaiser. I wasn't paranoid or anything. The fact that I was beginning to operate with a mindset not dissimilar to that of the Spy Who Came in from the Cold did not worry me too much.

I returned to the table, sat down and stared intently at the judge.

'Jabber,' I said.

'I've found another seventy-six-year-old woman who died on her birthday. Happened about twenty miles from here in Center Point. Death was ruled accidental.'

'This is crazy. We're working practically undercover. The sheriff's doing her thing. The newspapers haven't got anything more than rumors around the courthouse to work with, so they haven't broken the story. And meanwhile, some fiend has pulled the plug on six little old ladies and God knows when or if he's ever going to stop.'

'If the papers get hold of this – and they will – there'll be a panic no one's seen the likes of since the Boston Strangler. It's up to us, Richard.'

'That's what I was afraid you were going to say.' I poked desultorily at my *carne guisada*. 'But I love it when you call me Richard.'

'What about the yellow roses?' quizzed the judge. 'What'd you find out this morning?'

'That only four purchases of yellow roses have been made in this area in the past week or so. Three of them I've accounted for. The fourth came from that little shop near the Veterans Cemetery. I thought I'd check it out after lunch. They were sent to this address.'

I handed Pat Knox the last name and address on the list. She studied the scrap of paper.

'This address isn't far from here. There's several old-age homes in that area. Could be one of them.'

'We'll both probably be in an old-age home before we solve this case,' I said.

'I'm goin' with you to this address,' said the judge. She stood up and it seemed likely that lunch was over.

'Only if you promise me a round of croquet,' I said.

TWENTY-FOUR

There didn't seem to be a lot of activity as the judge parked her car by the side entrance of the Alpine Village Retirement Center. Of course, there was probably never a lot of activity around the Alpine Village Retirement Center. It wasn't exactly the best place to go if you wanted to raise some hell.

'Looks quiet as a grave,' I said, as we got out of the car.

'Looks can be deceiving,' said the judge. 'Otherwise, why would ninety-five percent of the marriages I've performed lately end in divorce or worse?'

'What's worse than divorce?'

'You'd have to ask the other five percent.'

'Jesus,' I said, as I carefully placed my lit cigar on a nearby windowsill. 'Almost makes me glad I'm still a closet heterosexual.'

As we opened the door and walked from the sweltering summer afternoon into the side wing of the place it felt like we'd just taken up residence in the freezer department of a meat-packing plant.

'If I'd known we were going to Ice Station Zebra,' I said, 'I'd've worn my long johns.'

'Shush,' said the judge rather violently.

The hallway was strangely quiet and empty. The only figures we passed were a young black orderly pushing what looked like a scarecrow in a wheelchair. You couldn't tell if the scarecrow was a man or a woman or living or dead. About the only thing you could say for it was it sure kept the crows off the wheelchair.

My mind drifted back to when my father and I saw Doc Phelps for the last time. It was at the state hospital near Silver Spring, New Mexico. Marcie had visited him a few years earlier, before they'd put him in. She'd told me he was very thin and fragile and looked like Rip Van Winkle lying in his bed with storm clouds swirling all around his little house. He'd said that Hilda's ghost had been nagging him about weeding the garden. Then Doc had told Marcie: 'I'm a very lucky man because I've loved many people in my life and I still do.' Marcie said she'd sat by the side of his bed and cried.

By the time Tom and I saw Doc he'd been at the hospital for a while, been seated next to screaming people eating with plastic silverware, been pushed around like a sack of potatoes by young orderlies who didn't know or care that in the thirties Doc with his pretty young wife on the back of his motorcycle had driven all the way from New York to San Francisco. I'd lifted Doc's birdlike legs one at a time and put him into the front seat of the car as we took him to a restaurant for lunch. He'd smiled at me like a little child through the window, the man who'd led so many of us up the hills and down the canyons of summertime and childhood itself. At the restaurant Doc appeared to slip in and out of lucidity, somewhat in the manner of my own normal conversational style. I was yapping about Santa Monica, California, about people sitting on park benches by the sea and old folks playing shuffleboard. I said there were a lot of crazy, highly creative people out there because you could stand on the edge of the cliff and look out over the sea at night and realize that you couldn't run any farther, that that was as far as you could go.

'Hardly,' Doc said. It was one of his more lucid moments.

Doc then proceeded to tell as a recurring theme through the remainder of the meal a story or joke about a woman and the gorilla at the London Zoo. Now that I think back on it, whether the rambling narrative was a story or a joke seems kind of important because Doc was one of the kindest, wisest men I've ever known and his words might've shed some light on whether life is a story or a joke. But life, like an orderly, was pushing me along too fast to remember what he said, and now it's too late to ask him to tell me again.

On the way back to the hospital that day, Doc seemed to become disoriented. Tom asked him if he knew where we were. Doc didn't say anything. Tom asked him if he knew who Tom was. Doc seemed confused and said nothing. At the hospital the orderly put him back in the wheelchair and Tom and I went along with him to his room. It was painted some kind of institutional fluorescent off-white and there was a small bed in there with high railings on both sides like a crib for a giant baby. The orderly sat Doc in a chair and he seemed almost catatonic. In the room there was not a picture, a letter, a scrap of clothing, an indication of any kind as to the deep, richly embroidered fabric that had constituted the vibrant, colorful mantle of Doc's life.

I had stood by the door as my father directed a soft, one-sided conversation toward the anthropological remains of his old friend. Tom finally came over to the door, said goodbye one more time, and we both watched Doc stare mutely at something neither of us was yet able to see. As we started to leave, Doc, still staring into space, spoke the last words we would ever hear him say: 'I love you, Tom.'

'C'mon,' said the judge, grabbing my arm. 'Something's goin' on in the other wing.'

Indeed there was.

Nurses, orderlies and sheriff's deputies were scurrying around like mice under a birdfeeder at midnight. The focus of the activity, we soon discovered, was a room belonging to one Gertrude McLane. The same name on the scrap of paper I'd shown to Judge Knox. The recipient of a dozen yellow roses.

They were there, all right. In a vase in a corner. Gert was there, too. All we could see, however, was a stick leg and a birdlike hand reaching out from the middle of an electronically operated bed that someone had raised both ends of until they'd met cruelly at the top.

The judge and I stared in mute horror until we heard a familiar voice and wheeled around. It was the grim and imposing form of Sheriff Frances Kaiser.

'You're late for the slumber party,' she said.

TWENTY-FIVE

'Many years ago, around a campfire much like this one,' Uncle Tom was saying, 'a tribe of Indians were gathered. It was the custom of the tribe at the end of the day for the old chief to stand up by the fire and anyone with any problems or questions could ask his advice at that time. He was a wise old man and had been chief for many, many years.'

Not unlike the apocryphal Indian tribe, the children were

gathered on their blankets under the stars listening to Uncle Tom. Not unlike the chief, he was a wise old man and Uncle Tom had been Uncle Tom for many, many years. Casting my mind back upon everything that had happened since I dropped off the laundry that morning, I had a rather ennui-driven realization that Kinky had also been Kinky for many, many years. Willie Nelson had once told me that the thing he was really best at was 'getting into trouble and getting out of it'. Maybe I was only good at the first part.

'But some of the young bucks thought the chief was getting too old,' Uncle Tom continued. 'They wanted to show him up in front of the whole tribe. So they talked it over that day and finally one of them said, "Look, I've got a plan. I'll go out and find a small bird that fits inside my closed palm. Tonight at the campfire I'll ask the chief if the bird is alive or dead. If he says it's alive, I'll squeeze my hand quickly and open it and show everyone that it's dead. If he says it's dead, I'll just open my hand and the bird will fly away. Either way, in front of the whole tribe, the old chief will look like a fool." '

I was feeling kind of like a fool myself. After running into the sheriff at the rest home and witnessing several of Gert McLane's fragile extremities poking out of that bear trap of a hospital bed, we'd spent the rest of the afternoon in the sheriff's office listening to her lecture us like schoolchildren. It was her case, her jurisdiction, and she would do whatever it takes to keep us from meddling. What*ever* it takes, she'd said. It wasn't going to take too much, I thought. I was about half ready to hop on a plane for New York, where nobody gave a damn what anybody did. What was stopping me? What, indeed.

I looked around at the rapt circle of little faces all watching Uncle Tom. Even the counselors and the older kids who'd no doubt heard this story many times were listening intently. Hell, so was I.

'That night,' Uncle Tom was saying, 'after the meal and the ceremonies and the stories and the dancing were over, the old chief stood up in front of the tribe and asked if anyone had any questions or anything to say. The young buck stood up in the back and came forward into the firelight holding out a closed fist. He said, "O great chief, I have a question to ask of you. I'm holding in my hand a small bird. The question I ask you, O great and wise chief, is simply this: Is the bird in my hand living or is it dead?"

'Well, the old chief realized at once what the young buck was trying to do. He was attempting to show him up in front of the whole tribe, because whichever way the chief answered the question he would be made to appear foolish. The chief thought for a moment. Then he looked at the young man and said, "You've come to me with a question. You say you hold in your hand a small bird and you ask is the bird living or is it dead?" '

Every child was listening and watching as Uncle Tom lifted his arm dramatically toward the sky, palm upward in a closed fist, and intoned the final words of the old chief:

' "The answer to your question is: That, my son, depends on you." '

Later that night, after the bell had rung for lights out, Tom, Sambo and I were having a snack in the kitchen of the lodge. I was drinking coffee and eating a sweet roll, Tom was drinking milk and reading his newspaper, and he and Sambo were sharing a great many sweet rolls. This was a ritual with the two of them, and watching it almost gave you the sense that all was right with the world.

'No doubt about it,' I said. 'The sheriff means business this time. She can get a court order. She can have me arrested. She can make things a real nightmare for me if I stay on the case.'

'And what does Pat Knox say about this?'

'She's part of the problem. There's the big sheriff with her hands on her hips standing in the doorway watching me leave her office and sitting there behind her is the little judge winking at me. I'm caught between two women and I'm not hosin' either one of them.'

'That's a first,' said Tom, as he gave Sam another sweet roll.

'Even worse,' I said, 'is if I hang around here, lead two-hour nature hikes up Echo Hill to the crystal beds, become active in the garden club, sing songs around the campfire and, as a result, more people die. There's certain leads, weird hunches I'm working on that the sheriff would never follow up even if I could explain them to her. It takes a not quite normal mind to solve a case like this.'

'Sounds like they need you, my boy,' said Tom jovially.

'Of course they do. They just don't know it. And I don't know whether it's worth risking my health, my happiness and my personal freedom, such as they are.'

'That, my son, depends on you,' said Tom, and he turned back to the sports page of the *Austin American-Statesman*.

'Is there an echo on this ranch? All I need now is a moral dilemma. Hell, I didn't get where I am letting others tell me what to do and what not to do. I've walked my own road. I've worked hard. I'm the laundry man! I'm the hummingbird man!'

Tom put down his newspaper.

'*I'm* the hummingbird man,' he said, and he gave another sweet roll to Sambo.

TWENTY-SIX

It is not usually considered normal for a grown man to look forward each night to sleeping with a cat. But the early hours of the laundryman job and the additional stress of invest-igating the handiwork of a particularly talented serial killer were wearing me out. I was dimly aware that Pam Stoner, in her faded, perfectly fitting, sinuously crotched cutoffs, was staying up in the Crafts Corral to watch the kiln. I had all I could handle cuddling up with the cat and counting yellow roses. I had decided long before the campfire embers were cold that I was never going to squeeze my fist and kill the small bird. I was always going to open my hand and let it fly away. In a strange way I knew that what happened with this case did depend on me.

If you ever have a choice between humble and cocky, go with cocky. There's always time to be humble later, once you've been proven horrendously, irrevocably wrong. By then, of course, it's too late to be cocky.

'It may seem arrogant,' I said to the cat, 'but if I don't get to the bottom of this – find out why somebody's croaking these old ladies – I doubt if anybody ever will. Is that terribly immodest?'

The cat, who was by nature, of course, wholly self-absorbed, did not seem to particularly care.

'As Golda Meir once remarked: "Don't act so humble – you're not that great." '

The cat affected no reaction whatsoever to this statement. The politics and culture of the Middle East had never held much interest for her. Her idea of a fascinating place was probably Sardinia.

Around eleven-thirty I poured a shot of Jameson's down my neck a little too quickly and almost needed a Heimlich maneuver. Hell of a way to go. Hank Williams, Gandhi and the cat all hanging around watching you choke to death. By about the time Cinderella met the guy with the shoe fetish I'd managed to recover enough to put on my sarong and go to bed. But I didn't sleep.

I was thinking of a recurring motif in this case. Something besides the obvious – the yellow roses, the victims being old ladies all of an age. It was a little detail, I was sure – unimportant, inconsequential, just barely pricking my consciousness. Just a feeling I'd seen or heard something several times that I should've paid more attention to.

I thought of a conversation I'd had with Tom a few weeks back about baseball. I'd asked him who, in the history of baseball, was the all-time rbi leader by the all-star break.

'Jimmy Foxx,' he'd said.

'Wrong.'

'Not Jimmy Foxx?'

'Not Jimmy Foxx. Not Jimmie Rodgers. Not Jimi Hendrix.'

'Who's Jimi Hendrix?'

'Played in the Negro leagues. You give up? Okay, I'll tell you. Hank Greenberg, in 1935 – 103 rbi's at the all-star break and they didn't even pick him for the all-star team.'

We both shook our heads in dismay.

'That's right,' said Tom, 'I remember. The manager was Mickey Cochran, a vicious anti-Semite.'

'It's still a pretty good piece of trivia.'

Tom looked at me for a moment, then seemed to stare off into the long ago.

'There *is* no trivia,' he said.

As I played the conversation back, in the wide open spaces between my ears I realized that Tom's last sentence was a great truth. There is no trivia. The principle applied to life, to love, to baseball, to murder investigations. Even to trivia.

I was thinking these trivial thoughts and jimmying with the door of dreamland when I heard a loud clanging sound echoing in the darkness somewhere near my head. The cat and I both leaped sideways. To my relief, it was only someone knocking on the door of the trailer. A trailer, particularly an older model like mine that isn't ever going anywhere again, has a submarine-like metallic skin that can turn a normal knock in the darkness into almost a psychedelic auditory experience.

I opened the door of the green trailer and saw two green eyes staring into my own. It had to be either a nuclear jackrabbit or else Pam Stoner had decided to take a break from watching ceramic leaf ashtrays glowing in the kiln.

'Come in,' I said. 'You scared the shit out of me.'

'I have that effect on some men,' she said.

I walked over to the bottle of Jameson's on the little counter beside the sink and poured out two stiff shots. Pam lifted her glass in a toast.

'Here's to the big private dick,' she said. 'I hope you find out who's killing all the little old ladies.'

'How did you hear about that?'

'Oh, you know what they say. The ranch is a rumor factory. A girl hears things.'

'And all the time I thought I was successfully disguised as the lonely laundryman of life.'

'Don't worry. All your secrets will be safe with me. And I'll bet you've got a bunch.'

We clinked glasses, killed the shots and I felt my hand move softly through Pam's boyish hair and down her woman's body. She had that rare ability some women possess of looking stunning and sensual even by bug-light. I kissed her once gently. Then longer and harder until her lips took on the familiar feel of the well-worked webbing of a kid's first baseball glove.

'I'll tell you a secret,' I said.

'You already have.'

TWENTY-SEVEN

When Chuck Berry made his one and only trip to Disneyland and saw all the inflated figures of Disney characters there to greet him at the entrance, his first words reportedly were: 'Fuck you, Mickey Mouse.' That was pretty much the way I felt about the sheriff and her minions, one of which, I noticed, was waiting the next morning in a plain-wrapped squad car as Dusty and I flew over the cattle guard and drifted down Highway 16 toward Kerrville. A guy with a big head and a big cowboy hat began following us at a respectable distance.

'We seem to have picked up a tail,' I said.

'Your washer fluid is low,' said Dusty.

'After last night,' I said, somewhat confidentially, 'your washer fluid would be low, too.'

Dusty coughed politely. The sheriff's deputy stayed there like a flyspeck in the rearview mirror. It was as good a place as any for a sheriff's deputy. The dance cards they'd been dealt in life were rarely very full. Not that I myself lead a bustling, industrious existence; I just had better things to do and places to be than a flyspeck on somebody's rearview. So I decided to proceed with the investigation until I was forcibly restrained from pursuing the truth. And pursuing the truth, I knew from experience, was almost as difficult and dangerous as pursuing happiness. I also had observed in my travels that the two pursuits were somewhat star-crossed, for just when you finally found one of them you always seemed to have mysteriously misplaced the other.

I pulled Dusty into the parking lot of the little flower shop by the Veterans Cemetery, with the flyspeck still in the rearview and a sense of foreboding clouding the horizon. The guy had just opened the place and was moving pots of flowers around hither and thither when I walked in the door. I did not receive the reception I'd been expecting. The guy, who before had seemed almost ready to give me ether on a piece of Kleenex, now, quite inexplicably, seemed thrilled to see me.

'Kinkster!' he shouted. 'Let me introduce myself. Boyd Elder's the name. Why didn't you tell me you were the Kinkster?'

'I'm not the Kinkster,' I said, stalling for time to figure out what the hell was going on. 'I'm a Kinky impersonator.'

Boyd Elder laughed. He was friendlier but he still had

that dangerous, high-pitched, redneck laugh going for him. Laughter's a signature that's hard to forge.

'I've been readin' all about you,' he said. 'Right here in the *Kerrville Mountain Sun*.' He waved the newspaper before my disbelieving eyes.

'Yep,' said Elder, 'that's a right interesting case you're workin' on. How many little old ladies been killed? Is it five or six?'

'Let me see that.'

Elder forked over the paper and I skimmed the front-page story. It was today's paper, the byline was J. Tom Graham, and just about everything, including my involvement in the case, was pretty much public knowledge now. This would change the river for sure. Kick the investigation into overdrive. And, much worse, possibly create a dangerous sea change in the killer's mind, not to mention spreading sheer terror amongst the geriatric multitudes in the Hill Country. On the other hand, the case was not exactly galloping to a conclusion. Maybe if we got everything out in the open, the killer would die of exposure.

'Anything I can do,' Boyd Elder was saying, 'I'll be happy to help. Boy, can you imagine that. Comin' all the way down here from New York to tackle this murder case here in Kerrville. Once a Texan, always a Texan. Right, Kinkster? I *can* call you Kinkster?'

Boyd Elder laughed again. Same laugh. He was probably going to die laughing. If he wasn't careful I was going to speed the plow a bit and strangle him with my own hands.

'You want to help,' I said, 'here's how you can do it. Those flowers you sent to Gert McLane last week. The lady at the old folks' home on Water Street. Could you find out who ordered them?'

'They were ordered by phone. Let me check out the credit card stub. Be right back.'

He went into his office and I could hear him riffling through files and drawers and generally being busy as a little bee helping the big private dick who'd come all the way from New York just to solve the case. That hadn't been, of course, my reason for coming down to Texas, but I had to admit, it looked good in print. I scanned the story again and wondered what the hell was going to happen now. Any one of a million things. The killer could take a sabbatical till things cooled off. He could become more brazen. Try to contact the newspaper, the sheriff or even the Kinkster. He could thrive in the media attention and increase his killing pace. Anything was possible. All bets were off now.

'Here we go,' Elder was hollering. 'Good book keeping always pays off.' I took the little slip of paper from the florist.

The name on the slip was V. Finnegan. There was also a phone number and credit card number. Elder very obligingly let me take the credit card stub and the newspaper. We swapped phone numbers and hobbies and I told him I'd be in touch if I thought of anything else.

'You've been a big help,' I said. 'This may bring us a lot closer to identifying him.'

'I'm not so sure,' said Elder.

'Why not?' I said, putting the stub in my pocket and lighting up a cigar.

'*Cherchez la femme*,' he said, in an accent hideous enough to make any self-respecting frog hop for the nearest puddle. But I wasn't a frog and I wasn't a prince. I just wanted the story to be over.

'Spit it, Boyd,' I said. 'What the hell are you talking about?'

'The caller,' he said, 'was a woman.'

Elder didn't laugh.

Neither did I.

TWENTY-EIGHT

I popped into Pampell's to have a cup of coffee, settle my nerves and see if Jimmie Rodgers' ghost was still hanging around the old opera house. After the third vaguely familiar person asked me how the case was going, I got a little nervous in the service and bugged out for the dugout. I drove Dusty past the ranch cutoff and over to Earl Buckelew's place. I needed to get away from people for a while and Earl's was perfect for that. Just Earl and his six-toed black tomcat. Neither of them asked too many hard questions. I knew the sheriff would not be happy with the *Mountain Sun* story. I doubted if my father would be overly pleased with it either, since it clearly was a giant step toward the destruction of the separation between ranch and state. Not only was I prominently mentioned in the piece, but so was Echo Hill. It wasn't precisely best foot forward to base your murder investigation out of a summer camp for children.

'So now,' said Earl Buckelew, gesturing with his cane toward his own copy of the *Mountain Sun*, '*he* knows who *you* are and *you* don't know who *he* is.'

'I don't even know for sure if he's a he,' I said. 'It was a woman who ordered the flowers sent to the last victim. Also, it'd take a pretty fair seamstress to sew somebody's lips together. You don't sew, do you?'

'I don't sew, I don't chew and I don't play with girls that do.'

I showed Earl the credit card stub with the phone number. 'Looks like a local number, doesn't it?'

'That'd be Bandera.'

'Mind if I make a call or two on your phone?'

'Long's you don't call Australia,' he said. I noticed he was wearing his 'I Climbed Ayers Rock' cap. In 1985, about six months after my mother died, Earl, Tom, McGovern and I –

the Four Horsemen of the Apocalypse – had visited Piers Akerman and his family in the land down under. Our adventures, no doubt, will be chronicled on another occasion, but it is not entirely inconsequential to note that Earl enjoyed himself immensely on the trip and developed somewhat of a clinical recall whenever Australia is mentioned. I was determined to head him off before he got out the photo albums.

'Let's see what happens when I dial the number of this V. Finnegan lady who ordered the flowers.'

'It'll be disconnected,' said Earl, leaning back in his grandfather's old green rocking chair.

'We don't know that,' I said, getting up and walking over to Earl's old phone on the wall. 'Here we go – 555–8826 . . . It's been disconnected. How could you be so sure of that?'

'No killer that's worth a shit is gonna give you his phone number that easily.'

'You'd make a good detective.'

'Beginner's luck,' said Earl, and he winked. Very few people know how to wink and fewer still know when to wink, but Earl Buckelew knew both along with a lot of other human talents and that's just one little reason why I've known him forever and it still seems like the wink of an eye.

'Okay, so it's disconnected. Let's try the credit card company. It's a 1–800 number.'

'Sure you're not callin' New Zealand?'

'More likely New Jersey.'

When McGovern and I left Australia, Earl and Tom had stayed on and traveled to the outback and to New Zealand. Earl, having once been a champion sheepshearer, loved New Zealand, where there are more sheep than people. I've long suspected there may be more sheep than people in America, too, these days. It's just harder to gather the statistics or, for that matter, the wool, because it's harder to tell them apart. Having left Tom and Earl to their own adventures, McGovern and I had traversed to Tahiti, where we encountered a highly disproportionate number of transvestites and honeymooners, and from where McGovern set sail for Rarotonga and I returned for a gig I couldn't get out of in the States, thereby becoming the first white man to ever fly from Australia to the Jewish Community Center in Houston, Texas.

I dialed the 1–800 number and listened while some automated nerd ran down the whole menu of buttons to push if you wanted to hang yourself from a shower rod and finally got around to telling you what to do if you had a rotary phone. Earl, of course, had a rotary phone. For Earl it was still a rotary world and maybe, considering the frantic, mindless, unhappy nature of modern times, it was the best of all possible worlds. The recorded voice told me to wait.

I waited.

Then a real live, bright, chirpy, young woman's voice came on the line and said: 'This is Debbie Ahasuerus. How can I help you?'

'I'm just checking a recent billing on my card. I don't recall making the purchase.' I gave her the account number on the stub.

Debbie Ahasuerus had the information right at her fingertips. I hardly had time to light my cigar.

'The card member's responsibility for this account has been terminated,' she said. 'And we have a note. Our security department's been cooperating with the Kerr County Sheriff's Office on this matter. We'll just continue to leave the account open. Is that all right?' It looked like the sheriff was indeed on the case.

I took a rather unsteady puff on the cigar. 'Yes, that's fine.'

'And the corporation extends its condolences, sir, on the passing of your wife, Virginia.'

I mumbled a few appreciative words to Debbie Ahasuerus and hung up the phone. There was a ringing in my head as I turned to Earl, who was rocking in his old chair and staring thoughtfully off into the middle distance at something that probably had happened before I was born. Then the sudden reminder occurred to me, accompanied by a slight shiver, that the solution to this mystery might very well lie in something that had happened before I was born. Back when the rotary phone was the coming thing.

'Earl, you got a phone book around here?'

'Over on the table somewhere there's an old one.'

'That'd be perfect.'

I sorted through barbecue, cookies, donuts and cakes that his kids and admirers had brought him. With gout and high blood pressure, Earl's doctors had decided that he shouldn't eat anything and Earl had decided the hell with them. The phone book was there, all right. About the size of a comic book. The year was 1989. Close enough for line dancing.

Bandera made Kerrville look like a big town, so it wasn't hard to find Virginia Finnegan. There weren't any other Finnegans or any other Virginias, so that was that. However improbable it was, it had to be.

'Earl,' I said, 'you remember that old lady in Bandera who drowned in the bathtub about six months ago?'

'I recollect I do.'

'Well, here's something else to recollect. She just called the florist and ordered a dozen roses.'

TWENTY-NINE

I didn't know what the hell was going on but I sure as hell was determined to find out. Why would a woman who drowned in her bathtub be ordering roses six months later? She shouldn't even have any business ordering a rubber duck. I knew, of course, that it hadn't been Virginia Finnegan, the first apparent victim, who'd placed the order. It was no doubt somebody who had taken her credit card and, very probably, her life.

I knew from limited personal experience, and from long

late-night talks with Rambam, that some of the biggest sou-
venir hounds in the world were serial killers. They almost
never dispatched a victim without retaining something for
the wall, the album, the hidden drawer or the dusty old hope
chest up in the attic. The keepsake might be a credit card,
driver's license, photograph, article of clothing, finger, eyeball
or forget-me-not swath of pubic hair. If you stopped to think
about it, the serial killer and the trophy hunter had a surprisingly similar mindset. There was little difference in the game
they played – only in the game they hunted.

I was a hunter, too, I reflected, as I sat at my little desk in
the green trailer and listened as the shouts and laughter of the
children lightly segued into a chorus of cicadas and a lonely
whippoorwill calling long distance to its mate. I was a hunter
who tracked the wide open spaces between the ears of a
madman, just barely within shouting distance of reality. Me
and my shadow of death strollin' down the avenue. No
season. No limit. No regulations. God was the game warden.
If there was a God. And if it was a game.

The cat and I were alone, but there was a certain intensity in the air. I'd brewed a large pot of coffee that lent
an ambience vaguely reminiscent of some long-ago Bobby
Kennedy campaign headquarters. Along the inner walls of
the trailer where the little watermelon children once frolicked,
Pentagon-like profiles of the seven victims were now pinned.
But the portraits were pitifully incomplete. Patterns were not
plentiful.

Virginia Finnegan was a square dancer. Myrtle Beach
belonged to the Daughters of the Republic of Texas. Amaryllis
Davis played bridge. Prudence South was a hyperactive
Republican. Octavia Willoughby was a member of the garden
club. Beatrice Parks, Pat Knox's recently discovered victim,
had been a Red Cross volunteer once upon a time. And Gert
McLane, who'd died in bed not quite as peacefully as she
might've desired, didn't even have a hobby as far as I could

tell. What a shame, I thought, to go through life and not even be able to tell St Peter: 'I was an adult stamp collector.'

They'd all died on their birthdays. But their lives seemed to have almost nothing in common. At least nothing I could hang my cowboy hat on. In the days ahead many trips to the Butt-Holdsworth would be in order. Many phone calls to Pat Knox, J. Tom Graham, the Boyd Elders, the Debbie Ahasu-eruses of the world. Many cups of coffee.

Hank and his old pal Gandhi looked on with a glint of encouragement or possibly only curiosity in their eyes as clusters of worshipful daddy-long-legs gently undulated upon the placid, glassy waters of their respective high rodeo drag.

Uncle Tom would not be happy with this trailer as a spiritual command center for a murder investigation. Sheriff Kaiser wouldn't be rapturous, either. That made three of us, for I was hardly a happy camper myself. I was homesick for somewhere I'd never been. For life to be complete. For death to be kind. Or at least for it to be aware that it was cutting into my cocktail hour.

I'd left room on the wall for profiles of future victims. There'd be more where these came from. Death, I suspected, wasn't going to sleep. Death didn't know it yet, but neither was I.

THIRTY

'What a damned circus,' Pat Knox said as she sipped a cup of coffee and smoked a cigarette at her small desk in her small office. The door was locked. The secretary wasn't letting through any calls. It was just the two of us and a banana tree that was twice as tall as the little judge and looked about the way I felt. It made sense that if you stayed up pursuing investigative obituary half the night, in the morning you were going to feel half dead. The other half didn't feel too good, either.

'Seven victims,' said the judge, as she poured half a cup of luke joe into the pot containing the banana tree. 'Damn,' she added. 'I'm not supposed to do that. It's not good for it.'

'Who told you coffee's bad for banana trees?'

She didn't seem to hear me. Just got up and poured herself a fresh cup, killed the cigarette, lit another and sat back down at her desk.

'Seven victims,' she said. It was getting to be a mantra. 'You'd think there'd be an overall, coordinated campaign of some kind, tests for semen, DNA – anything – after seven victims.'

'The sheriff doesn't care if it's twelve maids a-milkin',' I said. 'She's going to run the investigation at her own pace – '

'And scare the livin' bejesus out of every old lady within a hundred miles of here? There's so much we're in the dark about. I hear the sheriff's brought in some psychiatrist from Waco.'

'They *have* psychiatrists in Waco?'

'What I hear, they think the killer's someone who hated his mother.'

'Where would they get that idea?'

'It's just so damn frustrating not to know what's going on. Not to be able to help. I know it's crazy but I still have the feeling these are sex crimes as well as – '

'Hold the weddin', Judge. I can tell you right now that the last one wasn't. The McLane woman died when she was sandwiched by the mechanical bed. If the guy'd raped her he'd have to have been Houdini just to get his pee-pee out in time.'

The judge killed another cigarette and stared at the banana tree. 'You do bring a certain sophistication to the case,' she said.

I belched the words: 'Thank you, Judge.'

She continued her communion with the banana tree and didn't crack a smile. There wasn't a lot to smile about. Someone in the Hill Country was getting away with murder, and damned if it seemed there was anything the two of us could do to stop him. To make matters worse we were confined to a very limited, clandestine role in the whole rancid scenario, like two hoboes plotting together under a trembling trestle as the freight train of law enforcement rumbled by overhead on the way to nowhere.

I walked over to the coffee pot, filled my cup again and studied the large map of the Hill Country that occupied almost the whole wall of the judge's office. Little pins, dates, names of victims, all reminded me a bit of my own crime setup inside the green trailer. It was kind of poignant to see how Pat had set this up in her lonely little office, ostracized from the official investigation, no one to share ideas with but the banana tree, almost like a kid with a lemonade stand in a bad location.

'Look,' I said, 'we may not have access to the experts, we don't have much manpower, we don't have state-of-the-art police procedural mechanisms – '

'What the hell *do* we have?' said the judge.

'We have two people who smoke and drink a lot of coffee and have a lot of accumulated miles along the rusty lifelines of human nature. You were the first person to realize that these deaths weren't accidental, that they were related and methodically planned. I've had some passing experience butting heads with the NYPD, and while the races haven't always been all that pleasant my track record ain't too bad. I think the two of us can solve this thing.'

The judge stood up to her full half-banana-tree height and raised her coffee mug.

I raised my cup as well.

'L'Chaim,' I said.

'What's that mean?' said the judge.

'Objects may be closer than they appear in the mirror.'

Ten cups of coffee and three trips to the little private investigator's room later, Pat Knox and I had burrowed our way through the victims' profiles once again, coming up with no consistent element other than the obvious: old widows getting themselves croaked on their seventy-sixth birthday. The judge hadn't left her desk except to get more coffee. Now we were both standing before the giant map on the wall.

'I find it amazing,' said the judge, 'that having lived full lives during a rich, colorful era in Texas history, by the time they die all anyone can recall is that Myrtle was in the Daughters of the Republic of Texas and Octavia belonged to the local garden club.'

'I find it amazing,' I said, 'that a person of your size could have such a remarkable bladder.'

'Thank you very much,' the judge said humorlessly. We both looked at the map some more.

'This is not the pattern,' I said, 'of your garden-variety serial killer. Your Ted Bundy or your Henry Lee Lucas.'

'He ain't *my* Henry Lee Lucas,' said the judge.

'The point is, Your Honor, a serial killer selects victims from a general population when, for whatever reason, they turn him on, so to speak. He has a little problem with blood lust. The killings almost always tend to escalate in terms of savagery and in their coming closer on the heels of one another. The downtime when the killer rests or goes out to play miniature golf usually becomes less and less as his murderous pace picks up. That's when he gets a little careless. That's when he usually gets caught. But I don't see any evidence of that here.'

'You're saying he's working on a pre-selected population.'

'Correct. A special population.'

'You don't think the shrink could be right? Maybe he's a

drifter, a stranger who's been knocking off old ladies in other places before he came here because he hates his mother?'

'It's unlikely. Let's say he's a monstro-wig that just blew in from Uvula, Texas, where he's been whacking little old ladies. Assume he's got some way of knowing when birthdays of geriatric widows roll around. There's lots and lots of seventy-six-year-old women who *aren't* getting croaked around here. Everywhere you go there's a little old lady right in front of you driving four miles an hour. Which brings us back to the twisted green fuse that's driving this whole case. *How* does he pick his victims? If we can determine that we might figure out *why.*'

'He's a local boy, I just know it. I don't care what crap the shrink is tellin' the sheriff, this ain't no cry for help. He don't care if he gets press or not. I think he'd just as soon as not. And he sure as hell doesn't want to get caught.'

'I agree,' I said. 'But if he's media-shy he's going to have some problems. The wire services and *Unsolved Mysteries* can't be far away. There's people in LA and New York right now who're probably working on screenplays and book deals for him. He's going to need an agent.'

'He's gonna need more than that if I get my hands on him. If I just knew where to look.'

'There's only one place you *can* start looking for a killer you can't find and you can't understand.'

'Where's that?' said the judge.

'Inside yourself,' I said.

A fat man in a plain-wrapped squad car stopped picking his nose as I slithered out of the justice of the peace's office. His eyes followed me as I crossed Main Street against the light and almost got T-boned by a cement mixer. I'd always thought it would be kind of sad for a cosmopolitan figure like myself to get his ass run over in Kerrville, Texas, but I suppose there were worse fates. Agamemnon comes to mind.

I popped into the Smokehouse to buy a box of Hoyo de

Monterrey Rothschilds from Clint and JoLyn. Before Clint and JoLyn bought the place, Bill and Betty Hardin had sold me cigars at the Smokehouse. Before that I'd bought most of my cigars in New York. Two hundred years from now when archaeologists are searching for the tomb of Shithead the First I'll probably be comfortably ensconced in hell buying cigars from Lenny Bruce and Gertrude Stein.

'Tell us about the case,' said JoLyn as I walked in the door. 'There's a big story in today's paper that if you and the sheriff and the local authorities can't find the killer they may call in the Texas Rangers.'

'They always get their man,' I said, as my eyes roved past the titles of almost every used paperback in the world except *Steal This Book*.

'That ain't the Texas Rangers,' said Clint, puffing on his pipe. 'That's the Canadian Mounties.'

'I knew somebody always got their man,' I said. 'Of course, it'd be a little silly callin' in the Canadian Mounties.'

'So it's true,' said JoLyn, 'that he's already killed seven people and there's no clues.'

'Actually, there are some clues. At the scene of each crime the killer's left a used paperback.'

'Kinky!' said JoLyn.

'He's kiddin', honey,' said Clint.

Then she leaned over the counter confidentially. 'Tell me,' JoLyn said, 'what's it like to work on a big murder case like this with the sheriff?'

'It's a thrill a minute,' I said. 'We have a very caring, sharing relationship.'

I entered the walk-in humidor before JoLyn could ask me any hard questions. The door closed behind me and left me all alone in a peaceful, rarefied atmosphere with thousands of quiescent cigars in neat little rows like children in a Romanian orphanage waiting for their moment in the sun.

Whenever I walked into the humidor I always remembered the time many years ago in LA at a big tobacco store in some big shopping mall. Kent Perkins and Jim Ryder were with me as we found ourselves inside one of the largest, lushest humidors we'd ever seen. Just being inside the humidor felt like you were making love in a tropical jungle. I've done both in my lifetime – been in humidors and made love in jungles – and which is the more satisfying experience is a hard call to make without instant replay. But the humidor seems to shut out reality to a greater degree – allows you to cast your mind back to some Tennessee Williams childhood more vivid and colorful than the one you've no doubt already repressed. And there's the added advantage of the humidor that you are very unlikely to suddenly be rear-ended by a large hippopotamus.

At any rate, Kent and Jim and I were in this humidor when for no particular reason I emitted one of the loudest, longest, most enormous farts of my adult life, much to the dismay of my other two humidoreans. At just the same moment, the owner of the store, who of course had no way of hearing or gauging the phenomenon, came striding purposefully over to the humidor, possibly to help us with cigar selection. Kent and Jim and I were all laughing by this time. As Dylan Ferrero once observed: 'Seventy-five percent of all men find farting humorous and zero percent of all women.'

'*God damn*,' said Perkins, 'that was a world-class bell ringer.'

'It sure wasn't one of them whiny, high-pitched, little Brenda Lee farts,' said Jim supportively.

At that precise moment the owner of the place walked into the humidor. One of the high-water marks of my life was watching his eager-to-please, unctuous, American smile fade as the noxious vapor wafted across the humidor signaling him that something was terribly wrong. His entire demeanor and total countenance became that of a person with the soul of a North Korean businessman . . .

A strong hand on my shoulder quickly brought me back from this blast from the past. I spun around in the little room and saw a vaguely familiar face. The kind that takes you a life-time to place and then you wish you hadn't.

It was Boyd Elder.

'Didn't mean to startle you, Kinkster,' he said.

'Never sneak up on a veteran.'

'Oh, were you in Nam, too?'

'No,' I said, taking a box of cigars down from the top shelf. 'Gallipoli.'

'You know the other day,' said Elder, 'when you were in the store I was so excited reading about your being on the murder case that I forgot to tell you something. You said to keep in touch if I thought of anything. It might be nothing. It might be important.'

'Spit it,' I said. The humidor was becoming mildly claustrophobic.

'There's a guy I know, sort of a strange survivalist type. Lives out in the country like a hermit.'

'So far it could be me,' I said.

Elder laughed. Then he got serious.

'Not quite,' he said. 'This is one of those kind of guys that somehow manage to fall through the cracks, as they say. No family. No close contacts. No driver's license. No Social Security. No phone. Gets in touch when absolutely necessary through ham radio.'

'Wish more people were like him.'

'No, you don't. He was in Vietnam, a special forces commando. Tells stories about coming back from the jungle and taking live canaries out of their cages and eating them for lunch. Half the weaponry used in the war has somehow come into his ownership. Took a piece of shrapnel in the head and has some motor control as well as emotional problems.'

'Sounds like a nice chap to sit down to tea with.'

'He lives out Harper Road.' At this juncture, Elder took out a notepad and drew a rough map for me showing how to get to the survivalist's place. I took out a cigar, went through the pre-ignition procedures and wondered if I was going to survive this conversation.

'He's also a beekeeper.'

'No law against that,' I said. 'Sherlock Holmes was a bee-keeper in his later years.'

Boyd Elder looked at me and I could tell that just describing the guy was starting to give him the heebie-jeebies.

'He also raises roses,' said Elder.

I lit the cigar, rotating it slowly in my right hand, carefully keeping the tip just above the level of the flame.

THIRTY-TWO

The guy's name was Willis Hoover. It was entirely possible that going after him would result in a futile, somewhat dangerous wild goose chase, but at this point every lead had to be followed up. I'd never had a rendezvous with a half-crazed, gun-loving survivalist at his isolated command center before. I wasn't even sure what to wear. Possibly an ancient suit of body armor might be appropriate. Bring an attack duck with me. But there had to be a first time for everything, I thought. Just as long as the first time didn't turn out to be the last thing you ever did.

So after waking up to 'Wipe-Out' and feeding the cat and slurping three cups of hot black coffee I called Pat Knox's office.

'Hello, dollface,' she said when she got on the line.

'That's Mr Dollface to you,' I said. 'Look, Judge, I'm going out to follow up a tip from Boyd Elder, the guy at the flower shop. I'm going to see this weird survivalist type who lives way out Harper Road.'

'I'll come with you.'

'Well, I don't think that'd really be best foot forward. This will be kind of a male bonding experience. The guy is close to being a feral man. Probably hates all women, children and green plants. Except roses. Loves roses. *Raises* roses, in fact.'

'Except for the roses bit, the guy sounds a lot like you.'

'Yeah. He could practically be my gay computer date. But I'd like you to find out what you can about him. Name's Willis Hoover. Does that ring a bell?'

'Not even a cuckoo.'

'Well, check him out if you can. And if I don't call you at home by ten o'clock tonight, send out the search party.'

'You sure you want to do this alone?'

'Your Honor, the guy doesn't like groups and he doesn't like anybody even faintly on the periphery of the law. He and I should get along perfectly.'

'He may also be the break we've been waiting for. Now if you run into trouble, you call.'

'Sure thing,' I said. 'And when he sews my lips shut I'll send up smoke signals with my cigar and hum a few bars of 911.'

There was no way to call Willis Hoover and I had a distinct feeling that he was the kind of person who did not like surprises. So I got my security shotgun out of the back of the closet and loaded it up with eight shells. I made sure the safety was on. Didn't want to blow my head off before I got out of the cattle guard. The gun wasn't going to be much of a threat to a guy like Hoover. He probably had a walk-in closet full of AK Fuckhead Specials or whatever happened to be the most lethal illegal weapon of the moment.

I leaned the shotgun up against the wall, poured another cup of coffee and lit up a cigar. I sat down in the sunlit doorway of the trailer and sipped the coffee, smoked the cigar and reflected upon the subject of loners in this world. There've been some very good loners down through the ages. Henry David Thoreau, Emily Dickinson, Johnny Appleseed, the woman who worked with gorillas in Africa whatever the hell her name was, even Benny Hill in the last years of his life after they cancelled his television show. These people all knew that the majority is always wrong, and even if it isn't, who gives a damn anyway. They knew that *within* is where it's at, and if nothing's happening within it doesn't really matter if your co-dependent wife throws a black-tie surprise birthday party for you and hundreds of well-wishers show up who would just as soon wish you'd fallen down a well.

I liked loners. The downside, of course, was that every serial killer who'd ever lived had also been a loner. Well, you can't have everything. People just tend to drive you crazy after a while. That's why penthouses, nunneries, sailboats, islands and jail cells do such a booming business. And trailers.

I took a solitary puff on the cigar, looked up through the blue haze and realized that I wasn't alone. Three little girls, Pia, Briana and Tiffany, were standing under the cedar tree in front of the green trailer. I stared at them like a man waking up from a dream. They returned my gaze curiously. At last, they spoke.

'Okay,' said Pia. 'Pick a number between one and ten but it can't be one or ten.'

'Can't be one or ten,' I said. Since I was going out soon to very likely get my balls blown off, another unlucky number to choose would be two.

I picked seven and kept it to myself.

'Don't tell us the number,' said Briana.

'Wouldn't think of it.'

'Now,' said Tiffany, 'multiply your number by nine. Okay?'

'Okay,' I said. 'I've got it.' I now had sixty-three, and while I liked these three little girls I wished they had not chosen this particular time to visit my trailer and browbeat me with a mathematical puzzle I did not as yet enjoy.

'Add the two digits together,' said Pia. 'All right?'

Adding the two digits together produced nine and also produced a slight degree of tedium on my part. I stoically smoked the cigar.

'Have you added them together?' shouted Bri.

'Yes!' I shouted back.

'Okay,' said Pia. 'Now subtract five.'

'Okay, I've got it.' The number was four and, congenitally unable to keep a secret of any kind, I was having difficulty retaining this life-or-death information unto myself. At least, I felt, the exercise must be nearing its conclusion.

I was wrong.

'Now,' said Bri, jumping up and down, 'find what letter of the alphabet goes with your number.'

I stared at her in mute pain.

'You know,' said Tiffany. 'One is A. Two is B. Three is C. Four is D . . .'

'All right,' I said grimly. 'I've got it.' The corresponding letter was 'D', and if this didn't cease very quickly I was going to clear my throat with a ceiling fan.

I went back inside the trailer and poured another cup of coffee to try to stave off a headache that seemed to have come on rather suddenly. When I came back the girls were still there and all three of them appeared to be highly agitato.

'Is that it?' I said. 'Can I tell you the letter?'

'No! No!' they shouted. 'Don't tell us the letter!'

'Fine,' I said dismissively. 'That was really a fun little game.'

'Okay,' said Pia. 'Now think of a *country* that begins with your letter.'

'You're kidding.'

'No,' said Bri happily, 'we're not.'

'Okay,' I said, 'I've got a country.'

'Don't tell us what it is,' warned Tiffany.

'All I'm going to tell you is I'm about ready to hang myself from the shower rod.' It was beyond my imagination that this puzzle could continue for so long and be so incredibly complex. It frazzled my remaining brain cells. But at least I had the country.

'Okay,' said Pia. 'Now think of an *animal* that begins with the *last letter* of the country.'

I stared disbelievingly into some morbid middle distance halfway between Echo Hill and the Monkey's Paw in New York. This game, if it was a game, was truly interminable.

'*Think of an animal that begins with the last letter of the country!*' said Bri as if she were speaking to a two-year-old.

'Okay,' I said grudgingly, 'I've *got* it.'

'Now,' said Tiffany, 'think of a color that *begins* with the *last letter* of your animal.' I told myself this was the last time I'd ever have even a passing relationship with a child. Even if I lived to be a kindly old man I would never speak to a child again.

'Do you have the color?' demanded Bri.

'I've *got* it,' I said.

The girls looked at me in a state of high delight. I looked back at them in a state of total ennui, which soon transformed itself to total dismay.

'We didn't know they had orange kangaroos in Denmark,' they all shouted together.

I was stunned.

'How did you do it?' I said.

'A girl can't reveal all her secrets,' said Bri. 'What's the gun for?'

The girls all craned their necks and looked into the trailer at the shotgun leaning against the far wall. I turned and gazed at it, too. It made an ugly little still-life painting.

'I may go on a little hunting trip later this evening.'

'You're not going to kill anything?' said Pia with a look of disgust.

'Of course not,' I said. 'It's strictly for self-defense.'

'Self-defense against what?' asked Tiffany.

'Orange kangaroos in Denmark,' I said. 'Now go back to your activities.'

Dusty and I wound our way up Harper Road with the shotgun in the trunk and the late afternoon sun hanging low like a stage prop in a summer-stock sky. I thought of an incident Dylan Ferrero had mentioned to me that had once occurred on Harper Road. Dylan had been driving by several years ago and saw what he thought was some kind of petting zoo by the side of the road. A number of wild animals were in caged enclosures and a group of people with young children were walking around looking at the animals, petting and feeding them. Dylan stopped because he remembered seeing a large black water buffalo like the kind he and I plowed rice patties with in Peace Corps training in Borneo. Dylan communed with the buffalo for a while and then left just as a long black limousine was pulling up.

Dylan had a few errands to run and when he came back down Harper Road about a half hour later he noticed that the water buffalo was gone. He stopped the car and looked around, and sure enough, no water buffalo. He and several stray children walked around to the back of the enclosures and there in the dust was the cleanly severed head of the water buffalo. The kids were in tears and Dylan was stunned as he asked the guy who ran the 'menagerie' what in the hell was going on. The guy explained the buffalo had been sold to a customer in the limousine who only wanted the head for his trophy collection.

'Why would he just want his head?' one little girl tearfully asked Dylan.

Dylan didn't have anything cued up in the old answer machine for that one. Indeed, it remains an adult riddle to this day.

I rarely enjoy telling or hearing animal death stories and this one doesn't shed any light or gloom on Harper Road particularly, nor does it tell us anything much about animals. The only reason I include the story here is because it tells us something about ourselves.

'Why would he just want his head?' I asked Dusty as I followed Boyd Elder's crude little map to what I expected would be Willis Hoover's crude little place.

'Prompt service is required,' said Dusty, as we turned left and headed up a steep, rocky incline.

I checked the rearview and saw nothing but road behind me. It was ironic that the one time the sheriff's department had decided not to shadow me might be the occasion on which I needed them the most. Ah well, as my old friend Slim used to say: 'You's born alone, you dies alone, you best as well get used to it.' Parts one and two of Slim's credo, of course, were usually more easily accomplished than part three.

We flew across three cattle guards down a lonely road with nothing to break our line of vision but scrub live oak and sinister cloud-shadows that seemed to palpably waver in the heat that enclosed us like a giant microwave. The only signs of life were the dark, peripheral flutterings of the buzzards as they watched from dead trees along the roadside. This definitely didn't look like the way to grandmother's house.

'Men have been known to freeze to death on the equator,' I said to Dusty. 'Especially when their washer fluid is low.'

Dusty shuddered violently.

We pulled off the gravel road near an old ramshackle log cabin that looked like the Beverly Hillbillies might've lived there before they moved. I cut the engine and carefully stepped out of the car to suss out the situation.

'Don't forget your keys,' said Dusty.

'I didn't forget them,' I said. 'We may be departing rather quickly.'

Nothing appeared to be moving around the vicinity of the cabin, so I walked a little closer. The cabin was atop a small rise, a good vantage point for Hoover to have if waves of

Mexicans, communists, Martians or pointy-headed intellectuals ever tried to capture his somewhat dilapidated command post. There was a deathly quiet about the place, broken only by what sounded like Dizzy Gillespie playing a rather large, mean kazoo. The noise seemed to be emanating from somewhere in the back of the cabin.

I crept quietly along the little path that led up the small hill and discarded several possible cover identities as I went. Jehovah's Witness didn't really fit the bill. Sneeze-guard inspector for salad bars didn't feel right either. AmWay representative had a reasonable ring to it.

Then I saw the flowers.

They literally took your breath away. Beds and beds of roses of all colors and sizes, in that lonely, godforsaken place looking for all the world as beautiful as the butterflies etched by children into the unforgiving walls of Auschwitz. Could a hand with such a remarkable green thumb have so much blood upon it? Could the same mind that created this beauty be capable of the premeditated murders of seven human beings?

With the roses to my right and the cabin to my left I headed toward the Dizzy Gillespie area across the pathway of worn-down flagstones. It was hard to believe that I could very well be tracking a serial killer right into his lair. But that was part of the problem. A serial killer doesn't usually look like a serial killer. In fact, the serial killer rarely resembles what we think of as a criminal or a monster. He does not radiate evil. More likely, he comes off in the manner of the genial host at the weekend suburban barbecue or that friendly, outgoing, nice-looking delivery man. Why would he just want his head?

The kazoo-playing was getting louder. So was the intermittent pounding of my heart. This was either a ridiculous wild goose chase or, very possibly, I was about to get goosed by God. Suddenly, the feather in my cowboy hat was flying through the air with the cowboy hat still attached. I was, unfortunately, still attached to the cowboy hat. The roses were swirling like those in a painting by a minor French Impressionist. I was caught in some kind of old-fashioned snare trap swinging upside down like a human pendulum about six feet off the ground. The kazoo music, which I'd by this time deduced to be bees, had a nice little Doppler effect going for it each time I swung back and forth. Or it just might've been the blood rushing to my head.

This was it, I thought. I either should've been more considerate of others or less considerate of others during my lifetime. I definitely should've been something, because I was going to end up as a humorous little news story: MAN STUNG 7,000 TIMES BY BEES. Of course, the tabloid play would probably be quite a bit more sizable. That depended, naturally, on a number of other factors. How much weight Delta Burke gained this week. How much Magic Johnson lost. What particular peccadillo Elvis Presley, Marilyn Monroe, Teddy Kennedy or the Virgin Mary had gotten involved in recently. Any little thing like that could blow me right out of the tub. I could almost hear the editor of the *Globe* shouting: 'Hold the back pages!'

It might make a good B movie, no pun intended, but it was always a shame when the peculiar mode of someone's death held more interest for people than the tone and timbre of the person's life. Greater men than myself had fallen victim to this unpleasant little foible of human nature. I wasn't certain that Nelson Rockefeller was a greater man than myself, but it'd certainly happened to him. Bigger in death than in life. God gave him a wife named Happy. So what does he go and do? Checks out while he's hosing his secretary. That didn't make Happy very happy.

It didn't make me very happy, either, when I saw coming toward me a little man with a head that looked like a toadstool. His gloved hands were held strangely in front of him and seemed to be shaking like a crab. He took off some kind of pith helmet with a long bee screen attached that had previously hidden the upper part of his body. Now he just looked like a kindly, congenial, chuckling, everyday serial killer.

'Glad you came by,' he said. 'Why don't you hang around for a while?'

Then he disappeared around the corner of the little cabin.

THIRTY-FOUR

Now there was a problem. Hanging six feet off the ground upside down with one foot in a noose was just the kind of activity that could be hazardous to your health. You could learn a little more than you wished to about the birds and the bees, the birds in this case being the buzzards which were already slightly tightening their little circles overhead to get a better look at the catch of the day. Buzzards will eat anything that formerly moved and now doesn't. To them everything tastes a little bit like dead armadillo.

The prospect of a huge swarm of abandoned honeybees, moderately irritated by the sudden departure of their master and coming upon me like something out of Gullible's Travels, was a most unpleasant alternative to the buzzard scenario. An equally tedious potentiality was that the animal kingdom would leave me alone and the beekeeper would return, possibly mistaking me for a large bee. And Willis Hoover's congeniality worried me. He certainly seemed friendly enough to be a serial killer.

My cowboy hat fell off and drifted and scalloped to the ground like an awkward mutant black snowflake. I continued to hang by one foot. With enormous effort I managed to reach into the right front pocket of my jeans and extract my Chinese version of the Swiss Army knife, which had undoubtedly been made by Chinese prison labor because I'd bought it for three dollars on Canal Street. I'd bought several of them at the time, all from a large Negro with purple pantyhose on his head who was talking to an imaginary childhood friend. Guy like that you don't want to christian down too hard.

I'd given one of the knives to my dad and I remembered him telling me: 'My father once gave me a knife like this and now my son has.' Funny what you think about when you have a little time on your hands.

From my ankle to my head the pain was increasing, and if I never had before I now truly empathized with every animal in the wild that was ever trapped by the clever, cruel hand of man. I opened the knife and made a few passes at the rope, but the knife was too dull and the rope was too strong. I shouted for a while, but the only answer was the buzzing of the bees and the ringing in my ears. Hoover was probably inside the cabin tapping his foot to an eight-track of The Captain and Toenail and gaily sprinkling a little Equal on his serial.

I felt like crying. I remembered I hadn't cried at my mother's funeral and when the rabbi shook my hand he'd said: 'I see it hasn't hit you yet.' I hadn't answered him then. But the truth was it'd hit me a long time ago. Now it was hitting me again. All life ever does is hit you when you least expect it, and all you can ever do is laugh or cry whenever the hell you feel like it. As they say, 'Anything worth cryin' can be smiled.'

For some reason I also thought of Patrick O'Malley, who was a homeless person back in the early seventies in Nashville when people used to call them bums. For some reason 'bum' sounds more dignified even now than 'homeless person'. Patrick was an aristocratic freak and proud to be a bum, and he hung around our little house off Music Row with Billy Swan and Willie Fong Young and Dan Beck and myself in the days when we were getting the old Texan Jewboy band together. Patrick, who's no doubt hustling handouts in heaven about now, had any number of memorable credos. One of the best was as follows: 'If there's two things I can't stand it's a shitty baby and a cryin' man.'

That was probably why I hadn't cried at my mother's funeral.

The bees, the beekeeper and the buzzards were all beginning to cut into my cocktail hour, so I made one desperate, somewhat herculean effort to grab the rope with one hand and slash it with the other. I felt the knife tearing into the strands of the rope and I felt the combined power of millions of Chinese criminals, many of them no doubt political prisoners, pulling and sawing and ripping the twisted fabric of a spiritually outdated society.

The rope gave.
Bees buzzed.
Flowers flashed by.

Then everything went black. Black as the cemetery that night when I'd met the judge. And I knew, just before the curtain came down, that the solution to these murders lay in the Garden of Memories.

THIRTY-FIVE

I woke up some time later to what sounded and felt like a racehorse pissing on a flat rock inside my head. I opened my eyes slowly in the darkness and made out the rough form of a strange man carrying a flashlight and a water bucket. He poured the water on my head and shined the flashlight in my eyes. I was glad he wasn't the beekeper. I was glad just to be at the party at all.

'Goddamnit!' he said. 'You spooked his ass!' I had no idea what he was talking about but it was oddly comforting hearing a human voice.

'Sherlock Holmes was a beekeeper,' I said.

'Fuck a bunch of beekeepers,' he said. 'Now we gotta go after his ass, and he knows these hills like a ringtail coon.'

It dawned on me that this man was a sheriff's deputy and that Willis Hoover, possibly through my intrusion, had headed for the hills.

'Is the sheriff here?' I said, rubbing my ankle.

'Sheriff was here she'd run your ass right into the sneezer. She ain't, but I am.'

'So it's just us fellas,' I said.

'Shit,' he said, and spat disgustedly on the ground dangerously near where my cowboy hat had come to rest.

In the distance I could hear more cars driving up, voices shouting in the night, dogs barking. Here and there, searchlights began to penetrate the darkness. They looked like little lighthouses on an ocean of dust.

'This here beekeeper's our number one suspect in the killin's.'

'The killin's?'

'Them little ol' ladies. Now, what's your name, buddy? Sheriff'll probably be wantin' to talk to you.'

I got up gingerly and limped over to pick up my hat. Then I took out my wallet and fished out my card and handed it over to the deputy. He shined his flashlight on it and studied it for a long while like it was a Dead Sea scroll.

The card read: 'Kinky Friedman is allowed to walk on the grounds unattended. If found elsewhere, contact: Echo Hill Ranch, Medina, Texas, 78055.' And it gave my phone number.

'I *know* the sheriff's gonna want to talk to you,' he said. 'I didn't know who you were at first but now I do. Sheriff told us about you.'

'I'm the legendary what's-his-name,' I said.

'Well, you can get goin' and stay gone,' said the deputy.

'That's good,' I said. 'I was getting tired of holding on line two.'

I put on my hat and limped away. Then I climbed into Dusty and got the hell out of there.

'A door is ajar,' said Dusty, as we drove away.

The ranch was quiet and peaceful as we splashed across the causeway and pulled into the parking area very slowly with headlights off. At Echo Hill it's always considered best to let sleeping ranchers lie. It was about a quarter past Cinderella time when I parked Dusty in front of the green trailer, went in and poured a generous shot of Jameson's, went back outside and sat in an old wooden chair, and leaned up against the trailer. One of the most comforting things to know in life is that even if you feel everyone in the world's let you down you can always lean on a trailer.

I sipped the shot and relaxed and watched the horses grazing in the parking area. Farther over on the flat I could see deer and jackrabbits and I could hear a group of counselors talking and laughing in the dining hall. On the archery range a horse was chewing the straw out from under one of the targets, another case of exactly what Uncle Tom didn't want to happen.

The little line of bunkhouses set against the base of Echo Hill itself all were in stillness with their porch lights glowing yellow like a village of island people, which in a sense, I suppose, we were. The scene looked like it'd been painted by Gauguin on tequila. I took another swallow of Jameson's and heard the dull thudding noise of the cat jumping from the roof of the trailer and landing on top of the air conditioner. The air conditioner had been dysfunctional long before most modern mental landscapers had heard of the word. Like most modern mental landscapers it blew only hot air. From the top of the air conditioner the cat's next move was to wait until I'd gone to sleep, then jump through the open window and land on my testicles. I could hardly wait.

I was getting up to walk to the Jameson bottle when the phone rang. I collared it quickly.

'Start talkin'.'

'So you made it safe and sound.' It was the judge.

'Well, let's not go that far. I've been hangin' upside down like a large grouper for most of the afternoon but I am alive and able to answer your phone call at this time.'

'Well, I found something out about Willis Hoover.'

'So did I. Never sneak up on a veteran.'

'He's done some prison time. Do you know what for?'

'Insider trading?'

'Try rape. And the victim, I understand, was an older woman.'

THIRTY-SIX

It wasn't a particularly pleasant feeling to know that Willis Hoover was roaming the hills possibly in a half-crazed predatory state and that I had done my little bit to put him wherever the hell he was geographically and emotionally. Not that I spent a lot of time blaming myself. He was a big beekeeper. Besides, with every law enforcement nerd in the Texas Hill Country scouring the hills for his ass, how long could he hold out? He couldn't remain on the run forever. Even a survivalist has to survive.

In the days following Hoover's flying the coop I hung around the ranch, although not by one foot, and tried to work out a few little matters in my still somewhat bruised head. Had the sheriff's department tailed me out to Hoover's place without my knowing it? Had Boyd Elder or someone else given the sheriff the same tripe that I'd received in the Smokehouse? Or had the sheriff checked out Hoover's criminal record, at least twenty years old apparently, and got onto him by herself? It was very much a Sherlock Holmes-Inspector LeStrade relationship I enjoyed, so to speak, with the sheriff.

As Emily Dickinson wrote: 'Though we are each unknown to ourself / and each other, / 'tis not what well conferred it, / the dying soldier asks / it is only the water.' That was Emily's convoluted and beautiful way of saying it didn't matter who actually solved this case just as long as somebody caught the bastard.

The judge, J. Tom Graham and myself began telephonically to pursue a concentrated campaign aimed at isolating the nature of the 'special population' that apparently made up the victims of this peculiar and very particular monster. Again and again, as Inspector Maigret might have done, we delved into the pasts of the victims. Needless to say, we did not find the tie that binds one life to live to search for tomorrow. The sands of time had done their job well, it seemed, for the further back we looked the less there was to see. And there appeared to be nothing, beyond the superficial similarities that everyone already knew, that might engender any special qualities exclusive to our special population.

'Most of the women were Republicans, of course,' J. Tom had told me recently.

'Hell,' I'd said, '*all* seventy-six-year-old women in the Texas Hill Country are probably Republicans. If I was a seventy-six-year-old constipated, humorless woman living in the Texas Hill Country I'd most likely be a Republican, too.'

J. Tom had laughed. 'Maybe the killer's a Democrat,' he'd said.

'I'd opt for libertarian.'

'Anyway, I just wanted you to know I'm feeding all the data on the seven victims into the computer. We may soon have some interesting results.'

'I'm not optimistic. Computers understand the human mind about as well as the Japanese understand baseball. They play by all the rules, but when a player makes an error on a Japanese team – even if he's a star player – the manager immediately benches him. That shows that even with their zealous efforts to imitate our culture like a monkey in a zoo, the Japanese have never truly understood the spirit of baseball.'

J. Tom had apparently nodded out briefly during my Japanese-computer analogy, but when he came to, he jumped right back on where he'd left off.

'It's somewhat arbitrary,' he'd said before he hung up, 'but I'm considering four to be a significant number in an universe of seven.'

'A universe of seven,' I'd repeated to the cat.

The conversation had occurred a few days ago and I still hadn't heard back from J. Tom on any computer results. It would be galling to have the case solved by a computer, I thought, but ''tis not what well conferred it, / the dying soldier asks / it is only the water.' I was beginning to understand Emily Dickinson's mind, and that was also cause for some worry on my part. On the other hand, if you could truly understand Emily Dickinson you just might be able to figure out where a guy like Willis Hoover was coming from.

THIRTY-SEVEN

It was one of those hot, almost-mythical Texas summer nights where you drop off to sleep not knowing if you're a man or a child and you wake up in the morning half-wishing you were an angel.

I never got to the angel part.

I was deep in what seemed to be a rather pleasant routine dream about my brother Roger the psychologist walking around naked with my cat on top of his head. Both parties, though it would've been quite out of character under normal circumstances, seemed to be enjoying themselves enormously. Man and cat appeared to be smiling beatifically and this, of course, caused me and Hank Williams to smile crooked little semi-beatific smiles ourselves and even produced a mischievous little serial-killer-type smirk upon the otherwise passive countenance of Gandhi, almost as if he'd broken one of his famous fasts with a hearty bite of beansprout vindaloo.

I was just considering getting some lip chap balm for Gandhi when a loud metallic sound began reverberating through the dank night air, sending all the smiles undulating slightly like large lobsters in the death-row tanks of some trendy restaurant far from the sea. Emanating occasionally from the sumptuous dinner tables could be heard the ugly sounds of rich people laughing.

Suddenly the trailer door was opening and in walked a fifteen-year-old junior counselor named Danny Carl, who was taller than the Holy Ghost returning and appeared to be about twice as agitato.

'Kinkster!' he shouted. 'Come quick! The Mavericks are on an overnight at Big Foot and there's a huge swarm of killer bees buzzing anyone who moves!'

Danny Carl was the ranch belching champion, the perennial winner of the Counselors Night belching contest, having only been defeated once at the hands, or rather, mouth, of Katy Sternberg in a much-disputed, somewhat bitter belch-off during first session the previous summer. Danny could belch the entire alphabet in one sustained belch – a sure crowd pleaser.

All championship belchers in the history of the ranch had belching regimens they followed religiously. Katy Sternberg favored Coca-Cola to enhance her efforts and, as I recall, competed one year with a sustained belch of 'Jump! Shake your booty! Jump! Jump! Shake your booty!'

Eddie Wolff, a daunting competitor, insisted upon a diet of raisin bran and Seven-Up before all major contests. Danny Carl believed exclusively in pork rinds. I myself, in my salad days before becoming a CBE (Championship Belcher Emeritus), had always sworn by the Chocolate Soldier, a hard-to-find carbonated drink that long ago had fallen out of favor, not to mention flavor.

In last summer's contest, the one in which Danny had only gotten as far as 'U' in the alphabet, there had been a nice, engaging repartee amongst the competitors, all conveyed, of course, in sustained belches. 'I'm better than you,' belched Danny, to which Eddie belched back, 'But I'm bigger.' Katy responded with 'I want to win!' to which Eddie replied 'That was good for a girl.'

Katy went on to win the championship with a terrific, gut-wrenching rendering of the phrase: 'I Am Woman, Hear Me Roar.' Wayne the wrangler, who was also involved but was never considered to be a really serious competitor, finished the contest by vomiting on the gray truck. Wayne's regimen, at this writing, is not known to me.

But Danny Carl wasn't belching now; he was scared. His demeanor did not appear to relax measurably as he saw me walk across to the little closet and extract the large 12-gauge riot gun.

'You're not going to get many of them with *that*,' he said, looking at me as if I were walking around with the cat on top of my head.

'I'm not my brother's beekeeper,' I said in a somewhat sphinxlike manner as I walked out the door and climbed into Dusty. Danny got into the passenger seat along with Sam, who didn't like the shotgun but was a car whore as long as he could sit in the front seat. There was not a lot of room in the passenger seat even for one normal-sized American and Danny's large adolescent body combined with an excited Sambo created yet another situation in which, when Danny closed his door not quite completely, Dusty found it necessary to remark: 'A door is ajar.'

Moments later, flying on adrenaline and moonlight, we splashed across Big Foot Wallace Creek and arrived at the campsite. I killed the engine and when the dust had settled we saw that the place looked deserted. I gingerly got out of the car and listened for any sound, human or otherwise. It was the otherwise I was worried about.

As our eyes adjusted to the semidark terrain we could see a group of figures by some trees down by the creek. No sign or sound of the bees. We walked down the small rise and Floyd, the nature-study counselor, came out to meet us.

'No sign of the bees for about ten minutes now,' he said, staring pointedly at the shotgun I was cradling. 'What in the hell did you bring *that* for?'

I pulled Floyd aside for a moment, waved to the kids with a confidence I didn't feel, and scanned the dark horizon for any sign of man or bee. There was none. Probably it was just a coincidence that I hadn't seen a swarm of bees in the Hill Country for many years and now I'd had close encounters with two swarms in the same week. Most likely these bees, wherever the hell they were, had never even heard of Willis Hoover. But it was a chance I couldn't take. What if they'd followed him over here? What if they'd followed *me* over here? In my head the whole situation was taking on the proportions of a Shakespearian tragedy. To bee or not to bee.

'What *did* you bring the shotgun for?' Floyd was asking me again.

In terse tones I explained to Floyd about my recent adventures with Willis Hoover. I told him Hoover was a fugitive and possible serial killer and I asked him if there was any way the bees could've accompanied him here to the ranch.

'The only way,' said Floyd, 'would be if he took the queen with him. If he did that, the rest of the swarm would very likely follow. Of course, he'd have to be pretty crazy to do that.'

'All beekeepers are crazy,' I said. 'Not to mention serial killers.'

'Well, if that's what you're worried about, it's very doubtful that this is the same swarm. It's probably just a hive that one of the kids bumped into in the dark. Bees don't usually display much activity once it's dark. I think you can put the shotgun away. You might take out a cigar and puff on it. They're not really all that fond of smoke.'

There was something in Floyd's light, knowledgeable approach and something in his eyes that reminded me strongly of his father, a man who'd known more about the out-of-doors than anyone I'd ever met, and I found this comforting. I walked over to Dusty, put the shotgun in the trunk and went down to the bank of the river where Floyd and the kids all were.

'Why'd you bring the shotgun?' asked one of the boys.

'To blow Ernest Hemingway's head off,' I said.

I took out a cigar and lit it up to buy time and calm my nerves. Floyd winked at me just like his dad would've done. I'd taken about three puffs when a loud buzzing blur that sounded like the Mighty Eighth came roaring through the air just over my left shoulder.

'Everybody in the creek!' shouted Floyd.

As the bees began swarming in a slow, low, dangerous circle, twelve kids, two counselors, Floyd and myself all hit the creek with one mighty splash. Sambo did not like to swim but I noticed him crawling under Dusty for protection. Jewish shepherds are pretty smart.

'As long as they don't start stinging anybody we're okay,' said Floyd. 'If someone gets stung a number of times the mind of the swarm may take over. Then the bees may go into an attack mode.'

'What happens then?' I asked, with only my mouth and one ear above the surface of the water.

'We're fucked,' said Floyd.

THIRTY-EIGHT

'So what happened next?' asked Marcie some time later, as she rocked in Aunt Joan's favorite old rocking chair in the white trailer.

'Well, the bees circled for a while like a giant black lariat and then some kind of group consciousness thing happened like Floyd was telling me about. The mind of the swarm told them they'd scared the shit out of us enough and it was time to go home to the hive.'

'Then what did you do?'

'We all ran like hell out of there. Floyd and Danny took the boys back to the bunk to change out of their wet clothes, and they were all last seen heading down Armadillo Canyon with Bucky to a new campsite at Three Rivers.'

'I'm surprised you didn't even get a bee in your bonnet.'

'I am, too. The Lord protects middle-aged over-the-hill country singers.'

'He didn't do too good a job with Johnny Horton,' said Marcie. Johnny Horton had recorded such hits as 'North to Alaska' and 'Sink the Bismarck' before dying in a head-on collision near the Texas-Louisiana border back when today's country singers were still spermatozoa swimming around in little black cowboy hats.

'When do you think you'll solve this murder case?'

'Probably on a cold day in Jerusalem. I have a nagging feeling there's something we're all missing but I can't for the life of me figure out what it is. It's something to do with the victims. I just feel that those seven old ladies were kind of like the swarm mentality of the bees. I've got no evidence to prove it, but I'd swear that they knew each other.'

'If they did, it could've been a very long time ago.'

'That's what's so difficult and so spooky about this case. If something happened so long ago, what kind of person would care after all that time? Who would still hold that sort of grudge? And why wait all those years?'

'What you've got to do,' said Marcie, 'is operate like the jewfish. I've got his picture here in this old fish book from the fifties.'

I glanced at the picture of the large, scaly, bloated-looking creature.

'Attractive,' I said.

'Okay,' said Marcie, 'here's what it says: "With the cunning of its race, the jewfish – " '

'It doesn't say that!'

'It sure as hell does. "With the cunning of its race, the jewfish sucks up everything around it and then spits out what it can't digest." '

'Jesus Christ. Talk about the "warlike Apache". The fuckin' jewfish. It's kind of like Sherlock Holmes, who sucked up everything around him and spit out the impossible, thereby leaving him – improbable as it might've seemed – with the truth.'

'Then you ought to be able to solve this case with what you already know. You've been investigating the damn thing for half the summer. Now go ahead and figure it out. Let the jewfish be your guide.'

I went back to the green trailer and got out my Big Chief tablet and a fresh cigar. With the cat sitting under the desk lamp watching, I reviewed my early notes on the victims like a demon in the night. What social interaction could've occurred long ago and had such impact that the victims might've still known each other later in life, as I suspected? Garden club? Bridge club? Senior square dancers? All were fairly geriatric pastimes.

Okay, starting with Amaryllis Davis. Lifelong member of the Daughters of the Republic of Texas. What did I know about the DRT? Nothing except that they were a group of old ladies who protected and kept up the Alamo as a state shrine. I'd seen them there. Tour guides. Caretakers. Lots of plaques.

Plaques. Where'd I seen a plaque recently? Ah, yes. The Garden of Memories Cemetery.

Octavia. The one we thought was the killer's fifth victim until we saw the six yellow roses on her grave. But that wasn't the point. The point was that we'd been thinking 'garden club' when it came to Octavia. Garden club and her lips having been sewn together. We hadn't computed that little stand with the plaque on it beside her grave that proclaimed her membership in the DRT. That made two – that we knew about – in a universe of six which quickly became a universe of seven.

But what about the dream that old lady had about her sister? I was frantically flipping pages in the Big Chief tablet when there came a knock on my trailer door.

'Come in,' I said, still flipping pages.

Pam Stoner walked in with her light blue shorts and dark green eyes. 'I'm taking a short break from watching the kiln,' she said. 'There's a lot of pieces in there tonight and if it gets too hot something might explode.'

'I know what you mean,' I said. She sat down on the bed and the cat immediately jumped in her lap, which was kind of a blessing because I had to concentrate tonight and it might be distracting watching her cross her legs. She was a world-class leg-crosser.

'Pam,' I said, 'ever heard of the Daughters of the Republic of Texas?'

'No,' she said. 'They're not big in Oklahoma. What do they do?'

'I don't know. They sort of protect the Alamo.'

'They're a little late for that, aren't they?'

'Well, you know, they keep it from becoming a parking lot or a Bennigan's.'

Pam thought about it for a moment, then glanced around briefly. 'Another couple years they might consider protecting your trailer,' she said with a smile.

I smiled back at those big green eyes.

'Pam,' I said, 'do you know what a cotillion is?'

'Sure. It's a formal ball.'

'You mean it's not a long-necked lizard from West Texas?'

'Your Daughters of the Republic of Texas probably held cotillions when they weren't busy protecting the Alamo. Those blue-blooded society groups always had their debutantes and coming-out parties and cotillions and secret ceremonies and stuff like that. They usually trace their family trees back to the Bible, study their coats of arms, keep a lot of secrets among themselves that nobody else really wants to know –'

'*I* want to know!'

'They *damn* sure aren't going to tell *you*.'

'No, they're probably not.'

But they'd already told me something. At least Violet Crabb had. Her sister Myrtle, the second murder victim, had come to her in a dream wearing a white formal dress and speaking the word 'cotillion'. That, if I didn't miss my guess, was three in a universe of seven. Three of the victims had probably at some time been involved with the DRT. As the cat leaped off Pam Stoner's lovely lap, I made a leap in my mind. I'd now bet anything that at one time *all* of the victims had been in the DRT. The DRT was how they'd known each other. The DRT held the secret to why they were murdered.

'In the morning I'm going to the Alamo,' I announced.

'Congratulations,' said Pam. 'In the morning I'm teaching handicrafts. Can I ask you something?' She crossed her legs.

'Anything,' I said.

'Do you have any regrets about this summer? I mean, other than not solving this case you're investigating?'

'Of course I have regrets. Everybody has regrets. Ringo Starr, the drummer for the Beatles, said his main regret was that he never got to see the Beatles. My main regret this summer is that I've been so involved with this murder investigation and you've been so busy guarding the kiln that the two of us haven't had any real chance to be together much.'

Pam laughed, somewhat ruefully, I thought, and got up and went to the door.

'I have a regret, too,' she said, stepping out into the moonlight and heading back toward the Crafts Corral.

I walked over and stood in the doorway and watched the moonbeams bouncing lightly off her beautiful backside.

'What's your regret?' I said.

She stopped and turned around and stood there for a moment. Her tennis shoes and Echo Hill T-shirt as impeccably white and pure as the snow on a postcard mountain. Her blue shorts as challenging and defiant as a battle flag in the heat of sacred war. Her eyes as proud and deep and mischievous as Ireland.

'I haven't seen a long-necked lizard yet,' she said. 'I understand they only come out at night.'

THIRTY-NINE

In most criminal investigations things will slog along interminably like slow dancers in a rather humid dream until suddenly everything seems to be coming unwrapped at once. So it was that, instead of heading off to San Antonio the first thing that morning to pursue the DRT connection at the Alamo, I found myself picking up the blower and listening very foggily to the stentorian voice of Sheriff Frances Kaiser.

'Well, we brought him in last night,' she said.

I wasn't sure if she was talking about the Christ on the cross or the duck in the hailstorm, but it worked for me.

'Who'd you bring in?' I said, as I fumbled with the many moving parts of the percolator.

'Willis Hoover,' she said. 'The beekeeper that buzzed off when you made your little unannounced visit to him.'

'Sheriff – '

'Well, I'm callin' a meetin' this mornin'. Just you, Judge Knox and myself in my office at nine o'clock. Can you make it?'

I looked at my watch. It was 8:07. 'I'll be there,' I said.

'Good,' said the sheriff. 'Now that we've caught this bird, we want to be sure we can clean him and cook him.' She hung up while I was still holding the blower.

'I'll be there,' I repeated to the cat.

I arrived at the courthouse punctually and had almost got in the front door before some officious bureaucrat wagged her finger at me for smoking in the hallway. When a bureaucrat's officious it's rarely auspicious, I thought. But the sheriff proved me wrong. The meeting was brief, harmonious and almost what is referred to in political circles as cordial. All three of us felt that Hoover was our man. None of us felt very comfortable with what we had on him, which was very damn little other than circumstantial evidence and our gut feelings.

I mentioned that I'd like to follow up on a possible DRT connection to the case, and I received affirmative head nods from both the sheriff and the judge. The judge said she was looking further into Hoover's background, and the sheriff and I expressed our approval. The sheriff said it was time for all of us to work together and do whatever it takes to nail this monster and put the fears of the community to rest. We all heartily agreed. In fact, the only thing about the meeting that was even mildly disconcerting was how much in agreement we all were and how well we seemed to get along with each other. It felt good but it didn't quite feel right.

At the end of the little meeting the sheriff said there was something she wanted to show the two of us. She led us down the hall and down another corridor and stopped outside a small courtroom.

'There he is,' she said.

The little judge and I peered around the body of the sheriff and saw Willis Hoover standing in the dock. A small man who seemed nervous and somewhat overawed with the perpetual legal peregrinations he was experiencing. His hands were shaking in their cuffs and his eyes were on his shoes.

'Don't look like a serial killer, does he?' said the sheriff.

'They never do,' I said.

'You ain't gonna let in the Boston Strangler,' said the judge, 'if he *looks* like the Boston Strangler.'

'You can stitch that one on a pillow,' I said.

A short time later Dusty and I pulled up onto I–10, set our ears back and headed for the Alamo. It was going to be a hot day, yet I still detected a trace of residual chill from peeping in upon the human refuse that was Willis Hoover. It was even now hard to separate the little, harmless-looking man from what he had allegedly done. There must be another soul within him somewhere. Of course, he hadn't been proven guilty yet, but that might now be just a matter of time. Circumstantial evidence from all three of our investigations pointed clearly at Hoover, who had the classic profile of someone who'd fallen through the cracks of society and in that way evaded detection. He'd run from me, he'd run from the law, he'd raised yellow roses, he'd served time for raping an older woman and, according to the sheriff, he'd refused to profess guilt or innocence. Now that I thought back to him standing in that room, I could almost see the evil radiating outward in sympathetic ripples, yet I also felt a somewhat grudging pity for the pathetic little creature.

The Alamo was still there, of course. I'd often said that if the state of Texas were ever engulfed in nuclear attack, the only two institutions left standing would be the Alamo and former Dallas Cowboys coach Tom Landry's hat. Of the two, the Alamo was the one I chose to always wear with pride.

With the morning burning off and the pigeons and tourists fluttering around, the sight of the Alamo caught my heart again as it nearly always did. It was a small, poignant, pockmarked little mission, standing blindly in the sunlight as if it might not survive the coming night. It was not full of itself, nor was it distinguished by the bigness that Texans often brag about, yet it was by any consensus our state's most cherished possession. But we did not really possess the Alamo; it possessed us, as it possessed free people the world over who saw it or read its story. The Alamo was not a Texas brag, I thought. It was just the opposite. The humble heart of Texas. One of the few shrines I'd ever attended worthy of a prayer.

On the battle-scarred door is a plaque – the DRT is very big on plaques – that reads:

> *Be silent, friend*
> *Here heros died*
> *To blaze a trail*
> *For other men.*

To the right of the door is another plaque. This one reads:

> QUIET
> NO SMOKING
> GENTLEMEN REMOVE HATS
> NO PICTURES
> NO REFRESHMENTS

As my friend Dr Jim Bone says: 'A lot of rules for a small company.'

I killed my cigar and took off my hat, rubbing my hair carefully so my head wouldn't look like a Lyle Lovett starter kit. That certainly wouldn't go over well with the Daughters.

Then I went inside.

Davy Crockett's beaded vest has always been like a Shroud of Turin for me. I stare silently at it and its hundreds of beady little eyes stare silently back at me. The vest was worn by a true American hero – a man who died not for home, for land, for country. In truth, he was just passing through. He died because he was in the right place at the wrong time. He died with a hell of a lot of dead Mexicans lying all around him like a bloody funeral wreath. He died before he ever saw a car or a computer or a video. He wasn't even a Texan. But he was everybody's kind of man. In a world bereft of heroes, Davy still stands tall.

These were roughly my thoughts when I noticed another figure standing rather tall beside me. It was one of the younger DRT women who'd become somewhat agitato about the unlit cigar that I'd unconsciously placed in my mouth.

'Don't light that,' she whispered.

'Don't be silly,' I whispered back. 'Do I look to you like a person who'd smoke a cigar in the Alamo?'

The young woman directed a hostile gaze at me and didn't say a word.

'Do I look to you like a person who *fought* in the Alamo?' I whispered.

Moments later she was navigating me firmly back into the sunlight into the gravitational pull of an older Daughter.

'Maybe *you* can help this gentleman,' she said.

'I'm Lydia McNutt,' said the older lady matter-of-factly.

'I'm Phil Bender,' I said. 'I'm a graduate student in anthropological choreography and I'd –'

'Well, I'll be happy to tell you about the Daughters of the Republic of Texas,' she said, obviously operating on some kind of clinical recall. 'The organization was founded in 1903 by Clara Driscoll to honor early Texas men and women who blazed the way before statehood, to honor Texas with various holidays and to preserve and protect the shrine of the Alamo. You do remember when it was that Texas became a state, don't you, Mr. Fender?'

'Uh, Bender. And I guess I'm not really too sure about –'

'Come, come, come! Surely you remember your high school history lessons. It was ten years after the Alamo, in 1846, that Texas became a state. To join our organization one must clearly establish through birth and death certificates that at least one ancestor lived in Texas before it became a part of the United States of America.'

'My field, anthropological choreography, is a very specialized one, Mrs McButt, and we – '

'McNutt,' she said, in an oblivious, almost mindless sing-
song. 'Lydia McNutt.'

'The field is so specialized,' I continued, 'that we eschew
all things of a political or patriotic nature – '

'You poor dears.'

'Yes, well . . . and my special area of interest is "Cotillions
of the Late Thirties".'

FORTY

We'd talked for a while longer as Mrs McNutt told me just a
little more than I wished to know about the current situation
of the Daughters. But, of some passing significance, she did
reveal that in the early days the blueblood, upper-class tra-
ditions of the DRT were far more dominant and ingrained
than they were today. And almost as an afterthought, she'd
pointed across the street to the Menger Hotel, in which she
believed resided an old disused ballroom furnished with
archival materials. This, for once, was exactly what I wanted
to happen.

I entered the historic old hotel with some trepidation, for
as well as Richard King, the owner of the King Ranch, dying
there and Oscar Wilde and O. Henry living there, it had been
one of the two places on earth where I'd ever truly seen a
ghost. I didn't know it as I walked in the door, but damned
if I wasn't about to see one again.

Fortunately, my friend Ernie was manning the front desk
and, it being a rather light day, he was more than happy to
guide me himself to the old ballroom.

'It hasn't been used for many years except to store things,' said Ernie. 'The room's on the second floor in the older section – not too far from where you say you saw your ghost – '

'I *did* see that ghost,' I said, as Ernie led me down an old corridor that would've felt right at home in *The Shining*.

'Oh, you'd be surprised how many of our guests have reported seeing ghosts,' said Ernie.

'Yes,' I said, 'but how many of your ghosts have reported seeing guests?'

I remembered the night quite well, actually. It'd been about ten years ago, when Ratso was down from New York on one of his famous visits to the ranch. Ratso, Dylan and I had gone out to see Jim and Neesie Beal's band, Ear Food, and I'd gotten to bed rather early without drinking alcoholic beverages. I was definitely not flying on eleven different herbs and spices when I saw the ghost. She looked like a gypsy girl or a Mexican dancer and she came to me in a state of semiconsciousness from which I leaped sideways rather quickly.

First I was sitting up in bed, then I was standing, and the vision of the girl still wouldn't go away. She seemed to be a beautiful young person from an earlier time. She was wearing silver earrings and a belt that resembled the latent homosexual silver concho belts that the great Bill Bell of Fredericksburg had made for Willie Nelson, myself and other Americans who unconsciously wanted to separate their bodies into two parts. I doubt if Bill Bell had been alive when the ghost's jewelry had been made. The conchos looked like pieces of stars.

Dylan was snoring through the whole thing in the other bed and later suggested, rather insensitively, I thought, that the whole experience had probably been the result of gas. At any rate, I'd become convinced after the vision refused to disappear that Ratso, who was inhabiting the other room of our suite, had played a prank upon the Kinkster. It was the only explanation I could come up with for my having gazed into the dark eyes of this vision for over two minutes while standing on my feet fully awake thinking I was going to Jesus or Jupiter at any moment.

I had frantically followed this vision into Ratso's room, where she finally disappeared, and I was totally prepared to upbraid Ratso for running in a girl or prostitute or whoever the hell she was while I was asleep. But Ratso himself was out like a beached flounder and his outer door was chained and double-locked as was his custom in New York. After I'd awakened him, with some little effort, his suggestion was that I call Ghostbusters.

'Did you or the ghost say anything?' Ratso asked.

'The ghost didn't say anything, but at one point I did.'

'What'd you say?'

'I believe it was "Fuck me dead." '

'Couldn't have been a real ghost,' said Ratso. 'It never would've missed an opportunity like that.'

While I'd been reliving my earlier, otherworldly experience at the Menger, Ernie had been opening a set of massive wooden doors and now he was handing me a key.

'The light switch is on the wall,' he said. 'Don't touch or move anything. Lock these doors when you're through and bring the key back to me at the desk.'

'Fine,' I said, as I gazed into the dusty, mildly primeval darkness. 'If I'm not back in about fifty years, send Richard King after me.'

Ernie left and I hit the light switch.

It looked like the Make-Believe Ballroom might've looked once you'd grown up and forgotten how to pretend. Dust covered the floor, sheets and tarps covered most of the furniture and spiderwebs covered the rows of old framed photographs on the wall. The photos could've been right out of Violet Crabb's dream. I liked old, dusty ballrooms as much as anybody but I did not share my friend McGovern's devotion to them and all they once had represented. I especially did not want to see my ghost again or hear barely audible rustlings of old silk dresses as they moved gracefully across the dance floor. I just wanted to check out a crazy little notion I had and then get the hell out of there.

I didn't know at what age young women used to 'come out' in the old days. Today it was about nine. But I was betting that in those early days eighteen to twenty-one was about right for a self-respecting debutante, if that wasn't somewhat of a contradiction in terms. So it was the late 1930s that I wanted, and I just hoped to hell I was right or a lot of dust would've been stirred up for nothing. Not to mention some pretty unhappy spiders.

1936. 1937. 1938 . . . that was about right. I took out my Kinky Honor America Bandanna and wiped away the dust and cobwebs from the 1938 photograph on the wall. There were two rows of girls – ten in all. They wore formal white cotillion gowns and their hair had been coiffed in the latest fashions of the day. Their eyes looked into me as only the eyes of old photographs can. They were trying their damnedest to pull my soul into a better world that I wasn't quite ready to discover yet. Not quite ready, but almost.

Their names printed along the bottom were quite familiar to me now: Virginia, Myrtle, Amaryllis, Prudence, Nellie (evidently Pat Knox's newly discovered victim that we'd missed the first time), Octavia and dear Gertrude (the latest victim). There were two names that I didn't know: Hattie Blocker and Dossie Tolson. I jotted the two new names down in my notebook and then I counted all the names on the photograph again.

Something was wrong here. There were ten girls but only nine names. I looked carefully at each girl, matching her with her name. The last girl in the back row was the one whose name had been deleted. So had something else. I'd only seen the phenomenon before in early revisionist Russian photographs where certain political figures had fallen from favor. Seeing it here and now in this old attic of a ballroom sent a cold, timeless, unforgiving chill of half-remembered history through my very being.

Not only was the young girl's name missing.

So was her face.

FORTY-ONE

'Mule barn,' said Earl Buckelew, as he habitually answered the phone.

'Earl!' I shouted from the pay phone in the lobby of the Menger Hotel.

'Kinky Dick!' he shouted back.

'Earl, I've got a problem. It involves two women – '

'That's always a problem.'

'The problem is that I don't know them and I'm hoping you do.' I lit a cigar in the enclosed phone booth and it soon filled up with the very pleasant aroma of good Honduran tobacco.

'Just a minute,' said Earl. 'Let me turn down the television.' I heard the sound of Earl's cane clumping across the floor to the television, then I heard it again, quite distinctly this time, on the return trip to the phone.

'Damned A-rabs and Jews goin' at it again,' he said.

'We just can't help ourselves, Earl.'

'Cowboys and Indians,' he said.

'Anyway, you ever heard of Hattie Blocker or Dossie Tolson?'

'I never heard of that last one, but Hattie – if that's the same damn one I remember . . .'

'How many Hatties can there be?'

'Oh, you go back a ways, you'd be surprised. There'd be a Hattie poppin' outta every rumble seat.'

'This one's about seventy-six years old, Earl, and she's not likely to be poppin' out of rumble seats anymore, and I've got to find her to try to get some evidence about a man we believe has already murdered seven women.'

'Yeah, she was a fine little filly.'

'Well, the question is where is she now?'

'Back in the thirties I used to take her out in my ol' blue Model A roadster. It was the first car in the Hill Country to have a radio put in it, did you know that?'

'No, I didn't, Earl. But do you know where this woman is now?'

'Hell, it's been a while – I've lost touch with her – but it seems like I heard ... if it's the same one ... she's over at Purple Hills, that place in Bandera. Some people call 'em old folks' homes.'

'Earl, one more question. This Hattie Blocker – this young girl you used to drive around in your Model A ...'

'*Fine* young filly.'

'Yes, I know. But just tell me one thing: Was she ever a debutante?'

'Not when she was with me,' he said.

Dusty and I flew out of San Antonio like a Texas blue norther heading east with a vengeance. We took I-10 to the 46 cutoff, then blew through Pipe Creek on the road to Bandera. All along the way the girl with no name or face haunted me, her fearful featureless countenance rising up like a violated vision on the dim tie-dyed horizon of American history.

I'd called ahead to the Purple Hills Nursing Home and learned that Hattie Blocker was indeed a patient there. No, it would not be a problem for her godson, Oswald T. Wombat, to pay her a visit later this afternoon. I asked the nurse how Hattie's memory was and she said her short-term memory was almost nonexistent. I said that was a blessing and asked somewhat trepidatiously about her long-term memory. If Hattie was cookin' on another planet she wasn't going to be much good helping to nail Hoover.

'The old days are about all the poor dear has left,' the nurse had said.

'Can she remember over fifty years ago?'

'Like it was yesterday.'

'That's a blessing, too,' I'd said.

Everything was a blessing, I thought. It's just that none of us knew it yet. Most people today didn't even realize that daddy'd taken the T-bird away until they tried backing out of their driveway and got skidmarks on their ass.

As I drove through the blazing streets of Bandera, the image of the young woman's body without a face began to get to me and I became somewhat garrulous with Dusty.

'I have this really spooky feeling that she's trying to tell me something,' I said. 'I've known a name without a face and a face without a name, but this poor child appears to be redlining in both departments. Yet I can hear her voice clear as a loudspeaker across a used car lot. "Help me!" she's saying. "Help me!" If we can't delve into the past and arrange this case in its accurate historical framework, Willis Hoover, even though he may be guilty as sin, is surely going to walk.'

'There is a problem in the electrical system,' said Dusty. 'Prompt service is required.'

FORTY-TWO

Hattie Blocker looked like Barbara Fritchie on a bad hair day. I'd been to Barbara Fritchie's house in Frederick, Maryland. I'd been to Anne Frank's house in Amsterdam. Now I was at Hattie Blocker's house.

There's no place like home, I always say.

The reason there's no place like home is that home is not a place. It's a time in your life when maybe you thought you were happy, a time you think back to long after your three minutes are up. I didn't have to look back. I just had to look around Hattie's empty, antiseptic little room at Purple Hills. It could've easily been Doc Phelps's last little room at the state hospital in New Mexico. There was nothing here but Hattie and her memories. And Hattie wasn't talking.

Hell, I probably wouldn't've been talking either if I'd had one of those oxygen things plugged into my nose, everyone I knew was dead and a strange-looking cowboy was sitting at my bedside acting like he was dying to light that cigar any minute.

'Hattie,' I said softly.

Nothing.

'Hattie,' I said, turning up my vocal mike, 'I really need your help with this. I just saw a beautiful picture of you with your friends at the 1938 Cotillion Ball of the Daughters of the Republic of Texas. You looked grand.'

Hattie said nothing but her eyes were shining. I pulled my chair a little closer to the bed.

'Hattie, this is very serious. I wouldn't even tell you this, but we need you to help us convict a criminal. He's already killed seven of the debutantes at the cotillion, Hattie.'

I reeled off the list as if I were reading the Tibetan Book of the Dead and noticed that Hattie seemed to be trembling slightly. This was a hell of a way to make a living.

'Virginia . . . Myrtle . . . Amaryllis . . . Prudence . . . Octavia . . . Nellie . . . Gertrude . . .'

Hattie Blocker said nothing.

I got up from the chair and walked over to the little window. Hopeless. Hopeless and undeniably cruel. Of all the times in my life when I may have taken advantage of people and situations, this had to be the lowest. Terrifying an old lady who was already walking the garden path to heaven's door. It did not make me proud to be an American.

I looked back to where Hattie lay propped up on the bed. Still motionless. Eyes straight ahead. She looked like a little bundle of twigs. I gazed out the window again.

Then a little twig snapped in my head. I had to go ahead with this inquisition. It was too late to ask the Baby Jesus what other flavors you got? Dossie Tolson could be in worse shape than Hattie Blocker, if indeed she was even still alive. The girl with no face and no name was trying to get through but I was having trouble adjusting my set. I had to keep walking down Yesterday Street and hope I could get wherever the hell I was going before today became tomorrow and yesterday was lost forever to a country funeral, a hotel fire or a cat pissing on a telephone number.

'Look, Hattie,' I said with some excitement. 'Look what's comin' up the road. It's Earl Buckelew in his blue Model A roadster. And you're sittin' right next to him. My, you look fine. And he's got that cute little rumble seat back there. Wait. I can hear his radio playin'. What's the song? Oh, I hear it now. "Don't sit under the apple tree with anyone else but me, anyone else but me, anyone else but me . . ." '

I stood perfectly still, continued staring out the window. A moment passed, I suppose. What Hollywood screenwriters are fond of calling a beat. In truth, just another step down that garden path that all of us unconsciously tread every day of our lives. Hattie was just a little ahead of us in the line.

'She was a cute little thing,' she said, in a surprisingly clear voice. 'A saucy little redhead. The boys all liked her and some of the girls were jealous.'

I gazed out the window and held my breath.

'I told that Octavia. I said, "Octavia, you got a big mouth, honey. Don't you go spreadin' scandal. You could ruin that poor girl." '

Octavia, I thought. Octavia. Oh, my fucking god. Octavia with her lips sewn together.

I waited. There was nothing for a while.

Then she said, 'Don't remember her last name anymore. The little redhead. But her first name was Susannah. Like "O Susannah, don't you cry for me." '

'Try hard, Hattie,' I said. 'Can you remember Susannah's last name?'

She was trying but I could see that it was useless.

'I want to sleep now,' she said finally.

Her face looked like a well-loved, well-worn human road map and I suspected that Robert Frost was right. She had miles to go before she slept.

'You've been very helpful, Hattie,' I said. 'God bless you.'

I squeezed her hand and walked to the door. At the door I looked back at the old woman and the little room.

'You really looked beautiful in that Model A,' I said.

Her face was still turned to the window when I left.

FORTY-THREE

Dusty was waiting for me right where I'd left her under a large Spanish oak tree in the front circular driveway of Purple Hills. I'd just climbed in and put the key in the ignition when I saw a florist's van pull up to the side entrance. Boyd Elder got out, opened the back of the van and, moments later, entered the side entrance of the building carrying a bouquet of yellow roses.

Maybe it was something Hattie Blocker had told me or maybe it was something I'd been unconsciously worried about all along, but the noose that had seemed to be tightening nicely around Willis Hoover's neck now appeared to be whirling wildly and wickedly like a lasso out of control in the hand of a very sick cowboy. I jumped out of the car and dashed across the driveway.

'Don't forget your key,' said Dusty.

The peaceful green lawns of the nursing home belied the dark thoughts fairly zimming through my brain as I scuttled across to the side entrance like a crab on cruise control. Was it possible that we all could've missed the boat so completely? Was it possible that I'd soon be staring dumbstruck at what used to be Hattie Blocker?

The side door was locked now.

I raced around again to the front of the building and my mind was racing right along with me. Of course Willis Hoover was the wrong guy. It would have been virtually impossible to have sewn Octavia's lips together with a nervous hand disorder. And if he grew yellow roses, why order them from a store? And what about Boyd Elder? Last seen owning a little flower shop. Easy access to all kinds of flowers. Last seen helping with the investigation. Pointing us in the direction of Willis Hoover. Last seen carrying yellow roses into Purple Hills. Last seen locking the goddamn door behind him.

I bolted through the main entrance and shot down the nearly deserted corridor like a runaway bowling ball past a geezer in a wheelchair wearing a Houston Oilers cap. The Oilers were having their troubles and so was I.

'Where's the fire?' he said.

I hooked a left at the far end of the hall and slowed down halfway along the side corridor. The place was all pretty quiet and peaceful, like an old library where somebody'd checked out all the books and just never brought them back. I ankled it carefully over to the vicinity of Hattie's room. I listened with dread and was mildly relieved to hear the two voices in conversation.

'. . . *two* gentlemen callers in one day,' Hattie was saying. I thought that was pushing it a bit.

'Who was the other one?' Elder asked.

'Now don't be jealous,' she teased. Ever the ingénue.

'I'm not jealous,' said Elder patiently. 'What's he look like?'

'He was *very* young,' she said. 'Wore a big black cowboy hat. Smoked a cigar. Of course, he didn't smoke it in here, what with my oxygen and all.'

I was getting a bit jealous myself that Hattie was so voluble with her second gentleman caller.

'Of course not,' Elder said. 'What'd he want?'

'Who?' said Hattie.

That's my girl.

'The cowboy with the cigar,' said Elder helpfully.

'He wanted to know about the girls. The girls in the Cotillion Ball of 1938,' she said dreamily.

'Well, isn't that something. That's why I brought you these.'

'Oh, lord, how beautiful! Are they all for me?'

'They're all for you, Hattie.'

'Thank you so much. You're so kind.'

'Here, I'll set 'em on the table where you can see 'em.'

This guy was one sick chicken.

'So nice of you to think of me.'

'Oh, they're not from me, Hattie. They're from a friend of yours.'

There was a brief, rather sinister silence as Hattie possibly realized she had damn few friends left alive in this world.

'Can't figure it out?' he said. 'They're from Susannah. Susannah Elder. You and your high-and-mighty little friends ruined her life for her all those many years ago. Now she's payin' you back. You pathetic, fucked-up, miserable old bitch, I'm sending you to hell.'

I charged through the door just in time to see Boyd Elder snip the oxygen lines and then turn the pair of garden shears toward Hattie Blocker's throat.

FORTY-FOUR

'It was a valley very similar to this one,' Uncle Tom was telling the children, 'but it was thousands of miles away and thousands of years ago.'

The ranchers were all seated on benches on the tennis

courts, gathered like multitudes around Uncle Tom as he began his story.

'There were two brothers who lived at opposite ends of the valley and they farmed their fields together, growing large crops of grain. One brother had a wife and five children and the other brother was not married and lived alone. Each year at harvest time the two brothers gathered in the grain together from the fields and divided the harvest equally between them.'

Marcie and I were sitting on a bench in back and I was fighting to ignore the dull throbbing pain in my left arm. It had been stitched up earlier that evening at Sid Peterson Hospital in Kerrville and it was wrapped in a fashion not dissimilar to that of the mummy of the Pharaoh Esophagus. But that was another of Uncle Tom's stories.

'That night after the first day of harvest,' Uncle Tom was saying, 'the bachelor brother could not sleep. He lay awake tossing and turning and he thought, "If God was so good to give me all this grain I should share a little more with my brother, who has a wife and five children to feed." So in the middle of the night the bachelor brother got up, went to his barn, filled his wheelbarrow full of grain and wheeled it across the valley where he put the grain in his brother's barn. He did this five more times that night, and then went back to bed and slept peacefully.'

'That's more than I'll be doing,' I said.

'So tell me what happened,' said Marcie.

'You mean you've heard Tom's story?'

'About eighty times.'

'Good. Let's hear it again.'

'Just about the time the bachelor brother was going to sleep,' Uncle Tom continued, 'the married brother was tossing and turning and finally he said to his wife, "You know, God has given us so much we ought to share a bit with my brother. We've got the kids to help us in our old age. He has no one." And the married brother went to his barn, loaded up his wheelbarrow in the dark, and made a number of trips himself across the valley, depositing each wheelbarrow-load in his brother's barn. Then he went back home and fell into a deep, peaceful sleep.

'In the morning both brothers went out to their barns and each saw that the grain he'd given to his brother had been fully replenished. Each believed that a miracle had occurred, but as they worked together in the fields that day neither felt quite right about mentioning it.

'That night the bachelor brother couldn't sleep. He felt if the Lord had been that good to him he could give his brother half the grain that was in his barn. So he got up, and like the previous night, delivered the grain to his married brother's barn, and then went home to sleep. About that time the married brother was thinking the same thing. He went to his barn, loaded up in the dark and proceeded to make three or four trips across the valley to his brother's barn. Then he, too, went to sleep.'

'You'd think with all this video shit today,' I said, 'this story'd put these kids to sleep, too.'

'No way,' said Marcie. 'They're riveted.'

'In the morning both brothers went to their barns and, lo and behold, another miracle had occurred. The barns were just as full as they'd been before each brother had loaded his wheelbarrow. They worked in the fields that day side by side a little uneasy about things, but they didn't say a word to each other about it.

'The third night there was a full moon. The bachelor brother again couldn't sleep. He went to his barn and thought if the Lord could give him this second miracle he could give yet half again of his harvest to his married brother with all of those mouths to feed. He filled up his wheelbarrow and began to trundle it across the valley to his brother's barn.

'At the same time, his brother began tossing and turning and finally decided that if the Lord had given him this second miracle he'd give half again of what he had to his bachelor brother who had no one to look after him. So the married brother went to his barn, loaded up his wheelbarrow and headed out across the valley.

'It was then, in the middle of the valley, in the moonlight, that the two brothers met. Each was pushing his wheelbarrow of grain to the other one's barn. And as they stood there in the bright moonlight they both realized what had occurred. It was, indeed, a miracle. It was the miracle of brotherly love.'

I thought of my own brother, Roger, in Maryland. Married with three kids. We loved each other but we'd become somewhat distant in any number of little ways over the years. We wanted to be in closer touch and we'd both vowed to do something about it, but life often gets in the way. It would be nice if we could just load up our wheelbarrows and head out across the valley.

'There was a mountain overlooking this little valley where the brothers lived,' Tom was concluding. 'It was not the biggest mountain around, nor was it especially the most beautiful. But there are those who say that the brothers did not go unnoticed. It is said that what happened in the little valley below was the reason God chose Mount Sinai upon which to give Moses the Ten Commandments.'

I confess to having had a tear in my eye upon the conclusion of Tom's story. I don't know if it was the story itself or the way Tom had told it. It might've been for my brother, or possibly, for all my brothers. Or maybe it was just the pain in my goddamn arm.

FORTY-FIVE

Later that night, after the kids were in their bunks getting ready to go to sleep, Tom, Marcie, Sambo and I sat out on the white benches on the tennis courts under the stars. I was giving them a brief rundown, so to speak, of my afternoon at Purple Hills.

'. . . so I'm tearing down this hallway shrieking like a wounded faggot – there's blood splattering from my arm all over the wall, giving the whole thing a nice Manson-family ambience – and this totally crazed maniac with a ponytail and a pair of garden shears is ten steps behind me screaming that he's going to send me to hell.'

'Sounds unpleasant,' said Marcie.

'Sounds like the perfect time to have asked him, "Why are you following me?",' said Tom.

Sambo, who was quite well attuned to Tom's humor, was smiling like a horse-collar.

'Well, I knew that already,' I said, laughing in spite of the rather hideous memory. 'Susannah Elder was the girl with no face in the old photograph. Boyd was her son, who the sheriff has since learned was her *illegitimate* son. We also now know that Susannah, as a result of the ensuing scandal, was thrown out of the DRT.'

'Just like you were thrown out of the Peace Corps,' said Marcie.

' "De-selected" is the word we like to use. And I got back in and became their fair-haired boy and spent two years in the jungles of Borneo before finally having to be returned to my own culture.'

'Let's redirect the conversation back to Susannah,' said Marcie.

'Yes, well, she never made it to Borneo. Once you get eighty-sixed from one of these high society-type outfits you *never* get back in. You're lucky if they ever speak to you again. And that's what Boyd Elder claims happened to his mother. She became depressed, alcoholic, suicidal. He remembers strange men visiting his house at all hours when he was a child. When this happened she used to lock him in the closet for hours at a time but he could hear what was going on. He told all this to the sheriff.'

'Mama sang bass, Daddy sang tenor,' said Marcie. 'We had a very dysfunctional family.'

'The sheriff wasn't all that sympathetic, either,' I said. 'After all, the guy's whacked seven little old ladies without blinking an eye.'

'But why,' said Tom, 'did Elder wait over fifty years to exact his revenge?'

'Well, that one's kind of funny,' I said. 'The sheriff did some checking this afternoon right after Elder was booked. His mother finally hit the bottom of the lifelong downward spiral that began with her being tossed out of the DRT in disgrace. She finally drank herself to death a little over nine months ago. Just a short time after that, Boyd Elder set out on his campaign of almost biblical vindication.'

'So why did he have to wait until his mother died?' said Marcie. 'If he'd always felt this way, why didn't he act sooner?'

'I'll tell you what he told the sheriff: "I don't want Mother to think I'm a bad boy." '

'That shows a certain degree of thoughtfulness,' said Marcie, getting up from the bench. 'I've got to check on how the Sunflowers are doing with their marshmallow roast. But congratulations, big brother. I'm glad you caught the bad guy.'

After Marcie left I turned to Tom and started to finish the story about my experiences at Purple Hills.

'. . . so the guy is gaining on me in the hallway and I can hear his screaming and now I can hear the garden shears clicking and as we thunder past I see two little old ladies standing there and I hear one of them say to the other, "Oh, look! It's the Senior Olympics!" '

Tom laughed, grabbed both my cheeks with his hands, and gently shook my head in a gesture of love I'd only seen him perform occasionally upon Earl, Roger, Marcie, Sambo (in his case, ears) or anyone else who was lucky enough to be the recipient of his blessing.

'You done good, sonny boy,' he said. 'Now I've got to go to a meeting with the counselors-in-training down at the dining hall.'

'But wait,' I said. 'Let me tell you what happened when Elder finally caught up with me.'

'I can't keep the CIT's waiting,' said Tom, as he walked off the tennis court. 'Tell me the rest of it tomorrow.'

'. . . so anyway,' I said to Sam, 'I'm on my back at the end of the hallway and Elder's got his knee in my stomach and he's making swooping motions with his hands trying to snip my nose off and I'm just barely holding him back. All of a sudden I see an old man standing in a corner and I shout to him, "Call the police! Call a nurse! Get help! This guy's trying to kill me!"

'So blood is gushing out of my arm and Elder's eyes are rolling back in his head and the garden shears are snipping, snipping, snipping about an inch away from my nose and the old man – he had a nice, lilting Irish tenor, as I recall – starts singing:

> *I'm a Yankee Doodle Dandy*
> *A Yankee Doodle do or die*
> *A real live nephew of my Uncle Sam*
> *Born on the Fourth of July!*

'Then I hear a tough woman's voice shout, "Freeze, Elder, or I'll blow your damned head off!"

'Elder froze. So did I.

'Moments later, after Elder was cuffed and taken away, I spoke to the sheriff.

' "Thanks," I said gratefully. "But how the hell did you ever find me here?"

' "It wasn't too hard," she said. "I've had you tailed since you left my office this morning."

'The old man was still belting it out:

> *Yankee Doodle went to London*
> *Just to ride the pony*
> *I am that Yankee Doodle Boy!!*
> *I am that Yankee Doodle Bo-y-y-y!!!*

' "Can't you shut him up?" the sheriff said to a nurse.

'The nurse shook her head.

' "No one's ever been able to," she said.'

I paused, my story over. At that precise moment an armadillo walked by the tennis court and Sam took out after him like an express train. I paced up and down the empty court for a while smoking a cigar. There was no one there, but perhaps because of Tom's story, the valley almost seemed to have a presence in it. It was to that presence that I finally spoke.

'Why do I get the feeling,' I said, 'that after all these years we're all still playing in the Negro leagues?'

New York City

'Four men in an Indian restaurant,' I said, two weeks later as I looked around the table. 'What are the chances that all of us will lead happy, fulfilling lives?'

'Fucking remote,' said Ratso, 'if the past is any indicator.'

'Or the present,' said McGovern.

'Oh, there's always a chance,' said Jim Bessman. Jim was a talented freelance writer and possibly the only optimistic vegetarian I'd ever met in my life.

'There's always a chance,' I said, 'that Ratso will pick up the check.'

'I'll drink to that,' said McGovern. 'In fact I think I'll have a Vodka McGovern.' He signaled the tall, turbaned bartender, who bowed and came over to the table. It was a fairly coochi-poochi-boomalini Indian restaurant.

'I'll take a Vodka McGovern,' said McGovern.

'A Vodka McGovern,' said the bartender smoothly, as if somebody ordered one every night. 'And how would you like this Vodka McGovern?'

'Equal portions,' said McGovern, 'of your best vodka, just-squeezed orange juice – from Israeli or California oranges, if possible. Israeli oranges are the best in the world – '

'Of course,' Ratso and I said in unison. The bartender mumbled something to the waiter in his native dialect.

' – and freshly charged club soda with a squeeze of lime. Just squeeze it, don't bruise it.'

The bartender was bowing his way away from the table, but McGovern wasn't quite finished yet.

'In a tall glass,' he called after him. 'And stirred but not shaken.'

The bartender nodded his head gravely. When you're wearing a turban it's hard to nod any other way.

'Stirred but not shaken,' said Ratso. 'That's the way James Bond orders his drinks.'

'Mr Bond is not known to me,' said McGovern.

'Speaking of James Bond,' said Jim Bessman, 'it's too bad that Rambam couldn't join us tonight.'

'Yeah,' said Ratso, looking up briefly from his tandoori chicken. 'I was kind of hoping Heinrich Himmler could have dropped by as well.'

'Saw a guy last night,' said McGovern as his Vodka McGovern arrived. 'An old man. Looked just like Heinrich Himmler. So I said, "I don't mean to offend you, but you look just like Heinrich Himmler." He says, "I *am* Heinrich Himmler. I've been living in Westchester for forty years and now I'm back and I'm gonna kill six million more Jews and three NFL players." "Who're the three NFL players?" I asked him. He says, "You see! Der Führer was right! Nobody cares about the Jews!" '

'Nobody cares about the Irish, either,' said Ratso.

'Now that we've got *that* settled,' said Bessman, 'where *is* Rambam?'

'He's in Lopbouri, Thailand,' I said. 'Jumping.'

'Jumping?' said McGovern. 'Why can't he jump right here in New York?'

'I can think of a few places he could jump *off*,' said Ratso, 'and at least one he could jump *up*.'

'Not with the Royal Thai Paratroopers,' I said.

There is a tasty pistachio ice cream dessert that many Indian restaurants feature. It is called *kulfi*. Unfortunately, 'kulfi' is also the way most Indians pronounce the word 'coffee'. This can sometimes make for a long, not to mention tedious, evening.

'I'll have some *kulfi*,' said Ratso to the waiter.

'One *kulfi*,' he said.

'I'll just have some coffee,' I said.

'One kulfi,' he said.

'You want coffee?' I asked Bessman.

'I don't drink coffee,' said Bessman, 'but I'll try some *kulfi*.'

'Two *kulfis*, one kulfi,' said the waiter.

'I'll try the *kulfi*,' said McGovern, with a hearty Irish laugh that somewhat overwhelmed the subliminal sitar music.

'You want kulfi?'

'Yes. To go with the *kulfi*.'

'Okay,' said the waiter, 'that's three *kulfis* and two kulfis.'

'Maybe I won't have that *kulfi*,' said Ratso. 'I'm watching my diet. But I will have some coffee.'

'Okay,' said the waiter, 'that's two *kulfis* and three kulfis.'

'You know,' said Ratso after the waiter had gone away, 'maybe I should've ordered decaf.'

Later that night, in the light rain, Ratso bummed a cigar, and we walked through the Village together. Waiting to cross Sixth Avenue, I took out of my coat pocket a letter I'd received from the beekeeper and, shielding it from the rain with my cowboy hat, showed it to Ratso. He read it carefully, puffing on the cigar and shaking his head several times in some untitled emotion.

'Poignant, Kinkstah,' he said. 'Poignant. The guy lives such a fragile and isolated life to begin with and then he loses his bees and he's all alone. It's hard to believe people like this really can and do exist in the world.'

He handed me the letter. I folded it and put it back in my pocket. We crossed the street against the traffic and the rain.

'Try four men in an Indian restaurant,' I said.

'Start talkin',' I said, as I picked up the blower on the left. It was later that night sometime after Cinderella's curfew and I'd been looking through a copy of *Cowpokes*, a collection of work by the World's Greatest Cowboy Cartoonist, Ace Reid.

'Hill Country update,' said a familiar voice. It was Marcie calling from Texas.

'Spit it,' I said, as I let my mind wander vaguely back to

the ranch. I was smoking a cigar and some of the smoke drifted lazily over the cat as she slept under the desk lamp. She didn't seem to mind.

'According to the Kerrville papers,' said Marcie, 'Boyd Elder's looking at life.'

'So am I,' I said.

'It's really sick,' Marcie continued. 'He's starting to get marriage proposals and movie offers.'

'That's more than I can say for myself.'

'Then there's the news about Pam and Sam.'

'Don't tell me they ran off together?'

'No. Pam is engaged to Wayne the wrangler.'

'Hell, if I sat around every night watching ceramic leaf ashtrays glaze in a kiln I'd probably be engaged to Wayne the wrangler.' I thought very fleetingly of Pam Stoner standing outside the green trailer in the moonlight. Where did summer romances go for the winter?

'What's the matter with Sam?' I said.

'Well, there's nothing really the *matter* with Sam,' said Marcie. 'It's just that he seems to have developed a rather unpleasant new habit. He's started to spend an inordinate amount of his time rolling around in horse manure.'

'When did you first notice this behavior?' I said.

'About a week ago when Sam walked into the house and the whole place has smelled like horseshit ever since.'

'I see.'

'You see,' said Marcie, 'but you don't smell.'

'Well, it's just a suggestion,' I said, 'but how about this possibility. Sam stays in the lodge and assumes responsibility for conducting ranch business from there. You know, closes up the place for the winter, mails out statements to parents. In the meantime Tom moves down to your white trailer and you move over to my green trailer. I don't know. It's just an idea.'

'We'll take it under review,' said Marcie. 'In the meantime, *why* do you think Sam is doing this? Is his inner child reaching out through such primitive behavior to express its rage and anger at his traumatic, dysfunctional early background? Do you think *that* could be it?'

'Hardly,' I said, just as Doc Phelps had replied when I suggested that the coast of California was as far away as you could run. 'Hardly.

'You ask me why Sam is rolling in the horse manure?' I continued.

'Yes, O great Chief Fuckbrain.'

'The answer is very simple. To paraphrase old Slim: "He wants to see the world." '

'You would've made a great philosopher, brother dear,' said Marcie. 'Or at least an assistant professor at one of the larger Southern party schools. By the way, Pat Knox called for your address. She says she's sending you a homemade fruitcake.'

'What does she mean by that?' I said.

Several hours later I'd just sailed into a peaceful dream riding upon the back of Dr Doolittle's giant pink sea snail. Into the dream came the unwelcome sound of a Japanese gardener with one of those leaf-blowing devices and I realized the blower by the bed was ringing. I collared the blower and heard a high-pitched, ridiculous, agitated voice.

'Help me!! Help me!!' screamed the faintly familiar macaw-like tones. 'Help me!! There's a giant swarm of bees right outside my window!!'

'Ratso, you nerd – ' I said, but the line had been disconnected.

The cat yawned mightily and went back to sleep. I got up and walked over to the kitchen window and looked down at Vandam Street. I thought of what George Christy, the columnist for the *Hollywood Reporter*, had once told me. Years ago Christy had been in a cab with Truman Capote on their way to a Peggy Lee concert. Capote was wearily watching the streets flash by and then he turned to Christy and said, 'You know, George, the more I see of life the more I know there are only 150 of us in this world.'

I looked up at the sky and there were about a million stars. A million stars for 150 people. Good odds, I thought, but a slow track.

Suddenly, it's Hoedown Night at Echo Hill and the same stars are looking down on music and dancing and bales of hay and saddles scattered across the old tennis court; and there are pigtails and ponytails and counselors with packs of non-filter cigarettes rolled up in the sleeves of their T-shirts; and Uncle Tom and Aunt Min are all dressed up in their western clothes and smiling, Uncle Floyd is smoking his cigar and Slim Dodson is serving up glazed donuts and apple juice; Doc and Hilda Phelps are standing by, stately in their Navajo finery; Dot is clapping her hands to the music and shouting encouragement from the shadows; Earl Buckelew comes riding over on horseback and our neighbor Cabbie is watching from his jeep with his old dog Rip; and Aunt Joan is teaching the smallest girls a dance.

They stand in a line facing Aunt Joan with their arms around one another's waists, tragically fragile, impossibly young. And the stars shine down and they dance beneath the constellation of my childhood.

> *There were ten pretty girls*
> *in the village school*
> *There were ten pretty girls*
> *in the village school*
> *Some were short, some were tall*
> *and the boy loved them all*
> *But you can't marry ten pretty girls.*
>
> *Five were blondes and four brunettes*
> *and one was a saucy little redhead*
> *The girls grew up, the boy left school*
> *And in '39 he married –*
> *the saucy little redhead.*

As dawn hustled the stars out of the Manhattan sky I was still sitting at my desk holding the letter from the beekeeper.

Dear Kinky,

As you've probably guessed I'm not one for writing letters. I just wanted you to know that I'm sorry I hung you out to dry that day. I also wanted to thank you. I've heard that the sheriff saved your life but I believe it was you who saved mine. There's not a lot of people who'd give a damn about saving my life. I'm the kind of person most people call a character or maybe a loner or maybe worse. But I'm really a man who's seen the world and knows that he never wants to be a part of it.

I'm sad to say my bees have never returned. They cannot really be replaced. It may sound funny to most people but I've lived by myself all my life and the bees were like friends and family to me. Now I am truly alone in this place. I'm thinking of going to Africa as a mercenary or going to Hawaii and raise orchids. If you ever go to one of those places, I hope you'll try to look me up. If you can find me.

> *Your friend,*
> *Willis Hoover*

P.S.: Small world department – Hattie Blocker died in her sleep last night. My mama's now the last surviving debutante.

ACKNOWLEDGMENTS

The author would like to thank the following Americans: Mike McGovern, my favorite Irish poet, who, over dim sum in Chinatown one morning, came up with the title *Armadillos and Old Lace*; Don Imus, long-time imaginary childhood friend and toboggan companion, for his continuing encouragement and support, up to and including plugging *Elvis, Jesus and Coca-Cola* from the intensive care unit of New York Hospital; Chuck Adams, my discerning and dedicated editor, and all the folks at Simon & Schuster for believing in me and working to help me achieve my personal goals of becoming fat, famous and financially-fixed by fifty; Esther 'Lobster' Newberg, my literary agent, for repeatedly telling people, many of whom already disliked me intensely, that I was a genius; Elisa Petrini, who survived being my editor once and, God love her, is my editor again for *Elvis, Jesus and Coca-Cola* in paperback (Bantam); and Jim Landis, Jane Meara and Lori Ames, who I'm no longer 'with', as they say, but to whom I'm eternally grateful for so generously helping me on my way.

Also, a tip of the ol' cowboy hat to: Steve Rambam, long-suffering technical advisor; Jay Wise; Max Swafford; the drop-dead gorgeous Stephanie DuPont for petulantly sitting this one out; Dennis Laviage, for supplying the Jesus joke on page 4; and last but not least, Rudyard Kipling, for providing the particularly apt similes for the three occasions on which Sambo the dog smiles. May Rudyard continue to inspire and Sambo continue to smile.

P.S.: I'd like to thank two fine ladies, both good Americans and good sports, for their help and indulgence in this obvious work of fiction: Frances A. Kaiser, Sheriff, Kerr County; and the Hon Patricia E. Knox, Justice of the Peace, Precinct 1, Kerrville, Texas.

God Bless John Wayne

To my kid sister Marcie

'And to tell you the truth this telephone booth gets
   lonesome in the rain,
But, son, I'm 23 in Nashville and I'm 47 in Maine.
And when your mama gets home would you tell her
   I phoned – it'd take a lifetime to explain
That I'm a country picker with a bumpersticker that
   says: God Bless John Wayne.'

From 'People Who Read People Magazine'
by Kinky Friedman

It was raining cool cats and kosher hot dogs in the city that afternoon and things weren't getting any sunnier as the cat looked over my shoulder at me looking over my bank statement. I was keeping us in cigars and tuna by tackling a murder investigation every now and then, but the big clients didn't seem to be queuing up on the street outside my building waiting for me to throw down the little black puppet head with the key to the front door wedged in its mouth.

In fact, things were so bad that the only person who'd sought my help recently in undertaking an investigation for him had been Ratso. Ratso was my flamboyant flea market friend who sometimes served as a rather weather-beaten Dr Watson to my postnasal Sherlock Holmes. In his role of Dr Watson he brought zero sophistication to the table – any table – but he was loyal to a fault, was possessed of a rather charming naïveté, and had a good heart, which any detective worth his low-sodium salt will tell you is invariably the greatest possible obstacle to understanding the criminal mind.

Ratso as Dr Watson I could deal with. Ratso as a client was a whole other animal, and I do mean animal. So, when Ratso first mentioned the matter to me, I demurred. About the fourth time he mentioned it, I inquired as to the nature of the investigation, and he'd said, 'Well, it's really a very personal matter,' and I'd suggested, perhaps a bit unkindly, 'then why don't you keep it to yourself?' The other bad thing about having Ratso as a client was that he'd never paid for a meal or picked up a check in his life and there was every reason to believe that working for him would very definitely not be a financial pleasure.

I was seriously thinking of hanging myself from the shower rod when the phones rang. I maintain two red telephones on my desk, each exactly an arm's length to the east and the west of the tip of my cigar. They are both attached to the same line and when they ring in tandem things can get pretty exciting around the loft.

In this particular instance, the cat leapt up onto the desk, knocking my large, Texas-shaped ashtray upside down onto my crotch. The concept of my crotch shaped like the state of Texas was something I could've probably lived with if it weren't for so many tourists gawking. I removed the ashtray and picked up the blower on the left.

'Start talkin',' I said.

'Sergeant Mort Cooperman referred us to you,' said a well-cultivated woman's voice. 'He's told us all about you.'

'Well,' I said, 'I hope it was all good.'

There was a silence on the line that lasted, I thought, a little longer than necessary. I relit a fairly ancient cigar and waited patiently.

'I'm calling on behalf of a gentleman of such prominence and the matter in question is one of such sensitivity that we could hardly turn it over to the police or any large investigative agency. The story would be headlines in all the tabloids. I cannot overemphasize the importance of discretion and decorum in this matter. That's why we settled on calling you.'

'Get off the goddamn desk,' I said to the cat in a stage whisper.

'I beg your pardon?'

'Nothing,' I said. 'Domestic problem.'

'There will, of course,' she continued, 'be a very handsome retainer.'

'My teeth are fine,' I said. 'God's my orthodontist.'

There was a fairly long silence on the line. The woman, obviously, was not amused. I looked up at the cat and saw that the cat, obviously, was not amused either. If you always spent your time trying to entertain women and cats, I reflected, life could be a hard room to work.

'He would like to meet you today,' the woman continued, 'at two o'clock at Le Cirque.'

'Korean place?' I said.

'Hardly,' said the woman.

She gave me the address of the restaurant and I jotted it down in my Big Chief Tablet. The cat watched the paper as I wrote and then gave a rather bored feline shrug.

'Just mention your name to the maître d',' said the woman, 'and he'll show you to the private table.'

'Hold the weddin',' I said. 'I'm not going out in the freezing cold and rain to some fancy frog restaurant and mention my name to some quivering-nostriled maître d' without knowing the party that is of such prominence that you can't even tell me his name over the phone.'

There was a pause. Then there was the sound of an Aryan sigh. I puffed on the cigar and waited for the blower to emit further information into my left earlobe. When the woman spoke again it was to say only one word, her tone and inflection like the low, painful murmuring of a whore in confessional.

'Rockefeller,' she said, and hung up.

I cradled the blower, sat back in my chair, and puffed thoughtfully on the cigar.

'Where have I heard that name?' I said to the cat.

TWO

I put my feet up on the desk, puffed pridefully on the cigar, and thought it over for a few moments. That's the way the really big cases happened these days, I figured. A beautiful woman in black doesn't walk into your office anymore. Instead, you get an invitation to do lunch at Le Cirque. It troubled me slightly that I hadn't even bothered to find out my potential client's first name. Of course, if your last name is Rockefeller, I reasoned, you don't really need a first name.

At one-thirty I put on my cowboy hat, heavy coat, and no-hunting vest with cigars in the little stitched ammunition loops, and walked out the door of the loft.

I left the cat in charge.

I stepped into the freight elevator, which boasted one exposed lightbulb and all the ambience of a movable meat locker, and drifted down to the little lobby like a lost snow-flake. If some scion of the Rockefeller family had gotten his tail in a crack, why would Sergeant Cooperman put them in touch with me? On the other hand, I might be the perfect choice if you wished to eschew all trappings of the establish-ment. And, though I was still in the beginner's-luck department, I did have a fairly impressive little string of crime-solving successes going for me. Cooperman, of all people, would be keenly aware of that.

I walked out onto Vandam Street and the cold rain cut through me like a drag queen with a bowie knife. The leftover slush on the sidewalk from yesterday's snow was the color of coffee and about four inches deep. It was a hell of a day to be having lunch with a Rockefeller. It was also a hell of a day to be looking for a cab. It was so cold I was ready to jump aboard any yellow four-wheeled penis with a sign on top, even if the only Rockefeller I'd ever really wanted to meet was Michael and the odds of that happening this side of the ozone layer were six-to-five against.

There were no cabs. Cabs, apparently, thought I was dead. So I ankled it through the slush in my brontosaurus foreskin cowboy boots and I counted maître d's to keep my brain stem at least active enough not to turn into a toxic icicle. I didn't like maître d's much, I reflected, and to be fair I must report that most maître d's I'd encountered didn't like me much either. I did not have what you might call a Judy Garland-like rapport with that distinctly Cerberean species. Nobody really liked maître d's at these coochi-poochi-boomalini frog places anyway, I figured. They were effete, power-hungry, phony, officious little boogers for the most part. Not even the most misunderstood child in Belgium wanted to grow up to be a maître d'. About the only charitable thing you could say about them was they were good diversionary subject matter to think about when you were freezing your Swedish meatballs off.

I hooked a left at the corner and trudged up Hudson thinking about the possibility of representing a Rockefeller on my next case. Not too shabby. The nature of the case almost didn't matter as long as I somehow managed to blither my way to a successful solution. The referrals that could flow out of something like that might really be top drawer. The prestige that would accrue to me would be almost unimaginable. I might even be able to make a living.

Of course, if I took the Rockefeller case, discretion and even secrecy would probably have to come with the territory. It would have to be a solo gig. I'd have to keep the Village Irregulars, who'd been invaluable in the past, away with a barge pole. Ratso, of course; McGovern, my large Irish legman; Rambam, the investigator who'd spent time in federal never-never land; all would have to be kept entirely in the dark. Likewise, I'd have to distance myself professionally from Mick Brennan, Pete Myers, Chinga Chavin, and Cleve, who was the easiest of all to distance myself from. He was currently residing in the Pilgrim State Mental Hospital for smoking country singers a few years back at the Lone Star Café. There were, fortunately, no plans to release Cleve anytime soon. If that fateful day ever did come, however, the only smart thing for the rest of the world to do would be to immediately check itself into the Pilgrim State Mental Hospital.

There were very few people on the street and those who were there looked like outpatients themselves. They were on the street because there was no other place for them to go and if there had been, the maître d' probably wouldn't have let them in. They all looked cold, desperate, lonely, with maybe a sidecar of criminally insane. I was glad I didn't have a rearview mirror attached to my forehead. I might've gotten a glimpse of myself.

After about ten blocks of tertiary tedium, I vaulted into a cab that appeared to be driven by the President of Lesotho, and we spun our way across the glittering, shivering web of side streets and avenues until we pulled up in front of the promised land, Le Cirque.

'Can I help you?' said the maître d', as he studied my cowboy hat. The phrase can mean almost anything in New York, depending on how it's said and who's talking down to whom.

I mentioned my name.

His nostrils quivered ever so slightly. I was very gratified.

'Right this way, Mr Friedman,' he said. I followed him through a strange city of mostly oblivious diners bent upon eating their escargots, which was fine with me. If you're not bent upon eating your escargots, your escargots will fall into your lap and leave greasy, iridescent, possibly radioactive dead snail trails that quite conceivably have a half-life of about twenty thousand years and could cause problems later down the line at the dry cleaners. It's just the snail's way of saying to the people: 'Piss off, mate.'

I followed the back of the man's head for a long time. I didn't care if he was leading me to the gates of hell or a table too close to the kitchen; at least it was warm. When you walk past people who are busy eating, you see them but they only half-see you. You'll draw a few odd looks, maybe an occasional moue of distaste. Somebody'll start a friendly smile but then think better of it; somebody'll stare at you like you're a cockroach. But most of the people will care less. And then you're gone. It's a lot like life.

The maître d' very deferentially waved me to my private table. The only thing private about it was that there was nobody else there.

'Your guest will be arriving shortly, sir,' said the maître d'.

'Guest?' I said to the man's buttocks as he walked away. '*I'm* the goddamned guest.'

I sat for a while and listened to the subtle, slightly obscene sounds of the clanking of silverware. It all seemed somehow connected – the people, the plates, the forks and knives and spoons – like one large piece of ridiculous machinery that feeds itself forever, occasionally giving out with a subdued belch over here and a high-pitched, polite little Brenda Lee-type fart over there, and quite frequently, gushing forth with the ugly sounds of rich people's laughter.

I stared at a chandelier for a while, then caught a waiter's eye and ordered a double shot of Jameson. To pass the time waiting for my drink I contented myself with making eye contact with a child at a nearby table. The kid seemed genuinely interested in my outfit and my cigar, which, out of courtesy to my fellow diners remained, for the moment, unlit.

'Ever seen a real cowboy before?' I said to the kid.

The kid's mother, whose head resembled that of a pet ferret with earrings, gave me an icy stare and then turned her withering visage on the child.

'Guess not,' I said.

By the time my second double Jameson had arrived I'd enjoyed about all the marvelous ambience I could stand and was considering lighting a cigar just to see if anybody was awake. They say if you light a cigarette the waiter immediately shows up with your food. But if you really want some action, try lighting a cigar in a restaurant. People begin oohing and aahhing and murmuring like a German forest, or coughing that dry practiced, controlled little California cough that makes you want to throttle them. Then they begin rushing hither and thither, calling 911, wagging their fingers, feigning nausea, and frenetically jumping through their assholes to show they care. If Elijah walked in right then he'd never get a table. Everybody in the place would be too clinically focused on a man smoking a cigar, and of course, Elijah couldn't sit with me. I was waiting for Rockefeller.

As it turned out, I didn't have long to wait.

I'd just killed most of my second round and was giving some serious thought to visiting the little private investigators' room, when the maître d' began walking briskly toward my private table. There was a half-obscured figure moving along right behind him in the fashionably dim aquarium lighting. Something about the second figure seemed to set off a rather jangly car alarm on a backstreet somewhere in my gray matter department.

Then, suddenly, as if in a dream, the maître d' was handing me a menu, stepping quickly aside, and immediately vanishing, as did any remaining hope I'd had of experiencing a pleasant, productive afternoon. The man sitting across from me now was wearing a coonskin cap with the animal's little head still attached to the front, eyes sewn shut. He was also wearing green pants and an especially repellent lox-colored sport coat. He was giggling to himself in a loud and rather unpleasant manner.

My anger mounted steadily as he sat across the table pretending to coolly peruse his menu while fighting to control his somewhat obvious prepubescent glee. Finally, it seemed, he could contain himself no longer.

'Allow me to introduce myself,' he said. 'I'm Ratso Rockefeller.'

THREE

Two mornings later, still slightly smarting from the Ratso Rockefeller scam, as well as getting hosed by Ratso into paying the check, I was loitering around the loft in my purple bathrobe, sipping an espresso and spending a little quality time with the cat.

'One of the truly irritating aspects of knowing Ratso,' I said to the cat, 'is that no matter how repellent his behavior, you can't stay angry at him long. That quality alone is enough to piss me off.'

The cat had never liked Ratso. Being of a far more unforgiving and intransigent nature than myself, the cat had consistently disliked Ratso for inexplicable reasons, going all the way back to the time when Ratso was a housepest at the loft and the cat had taken a Nixon in his red antique shoe, which had once belonged to a dead man. Technically, I suppose, the shoe could never actually have *belonged* to a dead man. It was just that Ratso, as a matter of custom, obtained his entire wardrobe from flea markets and back alleyways and seemed to derive an inordinate amount of pride from the fact that the previous owners of his apparel had gone to Jesus.

'How could you sustain a grudge against a guy like that?' I said to the cat.

The cat focused nine lifetimes of green-eyed feline malevolence directly through my left iris into whatever remained inside my cranium.

'I see,' I said.

I paced the loft for a few minutes. Then I came back again to the cat.

'Ratso told me something shockingly personal the other day at a very coochi-poochi-boomalini restaurant,' I said. 'He needs my help.'

But now the cat was asleep.

I was just lighting my first cigar of the morning, taking some little care to keep the tip of the cigar ever so slightly above the flame from the kitchen match, when I heard what sounded like a large, somewhat agitated pelican shrieking outside my window. My window was on the fourth floor of the old refurbished warehouse, and through the grime I could plainly see that no pelican or stork of any kind was resting on my windowsill. The only thing on the windowsill was a fairly sizable quantity of residual pigeon shit of a fashionably off-white color and shaped strikingly like a map of the later Hapsburg Empire.

This raised two distinct possibilities. Either my hearing had gone through some uncanny enhancement process recently or the pelican was a ventriloquist. As I turned the matter over in my mind, the invisible pelican shrieked again, this time much louder. Also, quite amazingly, it appeared to be calling my name.

Against my better judgment, I walked over to the window again and flung it open. A frigid tail wind blew into the loft, sending the cockroaches scurrying. The cat sat on the desk, watching me with a critical eye. She did not suffer fools gladly. In fact she did not suffer anyone gladly and this is something I'd spoken to her about on a number of occasions, usually after I'd had three or four shots of Jameson.

I stuck my head out the window and immediately felt my nose hairs turn to stalactites. I looked down and saw a large figure pacing back and forth rapidly on the frozen sidewalk below. It was Rambam.

'Throw down that fuckin' puppet head,' he shouted.

I removed the little black puppet head from the top of the refrigerator. It had a bright parachute attached, the key to the building in its mouth, and a big smile on its face, which is more than you could say for most people in New York. I tossed the puppet head out and watched it sail gracefully down into Rambam's iron grip. Then I slammed down the window and poured myself another cup of steaming espresso.

Moments later Rambam and I were sitting at the kitchen table, sipping espresso and looking at each other from opposite sides of my old chessboard. The set was rather dusty, little used these days, and at the moment featured a long, ambitious cobweb stretching all the way from the white queen to the black knight at king's bishop three.

'This is the chess set,' I said, 'that I once used to play the world grand master Samuel Reshevsky. He came to Houston, played fifty people simultaneously, beat us all. I was the youngest player. I was only seven years old at the time. Can you imagine that? Seven years old.'

I puffed on the cigar and contemplated the old board. Rambam sipped his espresso.

'What have you done for us lately?' he said.

'Well, I'm getting ready to try to help Ratso,' I said. 'He's got a little problem.'

'He certainly does,' said Rambam.

'Ratso told me something in confidence the other night,' I said, glossing over the Rockefeller ruse so as not to get Rambam distracted.

'Whatever it is,' said Rambam, 'I don't want to know.' There was no particular love lost amongst some of the Village Irregulars.

'The only reason I'm telling you is so *you* can help *me* help Ratso.'

'Why should I help Ratso?' said Rambam. 'He wouldn't piss on me if I was on fire.'

'That *is* asking a lot,' I said.

'Look. I'm working on a lot of shit right now. Just tell me what his problem is and I'll tell you how I would go about taking care of it if the problem belonged to anyone else in the world but Ratso. Then you just do what I would've done and everything'll be fine.'

'Then I'll be a real grown-up private investigator?' I said.

'No,' said Rambam. 'You'll be an idiot for helping Ratso.'

If the truth be known, I was already smiling a little bit when I thought of the unlikely countenance of Ratso Rockefeller. Besides, everything is funny if you wait long enough. This time it'd only taken me two days. For some humorless, constipated people it takes a lifetime for them to see that their mere existence is a joke and even then sometimes they don't get it.

'Ratso said that almost no one knows this about him – '

'Almost no one cares,' said Rambam.

' – but he was adopted. He was always told that his real mother died in childbirth but some new evidence has turned up to indicate she might still be alive. No one knows who the father was. He wants me to help him find his true birth parents.'

Rambam did not look excited. He got up, walked over to the espresso machine, and made himself another espresso. Then he stood by the kitchen counter and patted the cat. The cat was just perverse enough to tolerate Rambam. I, unfortunately, was just perverse enough to tolerate Ratso.

'I'll tell you what I'll do,' said Rambam finally. 'You find out the name of Ratso's birth mother and I'll help you find her wherever she's currently living, which, having observed Ratso's table manners on a number of occasions, is probably East Roratunga.'

'Thanks, Rambam,' I said. 'That's very Christian of you for an outspoken, militant Hebe.'

Rambam, however, wasn't listening. He was stroking the cat and staring out the window, shaking his head ever so slightly. There was a dangerous little smile on his face.

'That bastard,' he said.

'That's clever,' I said, 'but it's also a bit cold.'

'C'mon,' said Rambam. 'Would you ever want to adopt a little orphan Ratso?'

'Of course not,' I said, turning dramatically toward the cat to enlarge my audience. There seemed to be just a hint of disapproval in the cat's eyes.

'But I have always wanted,' I continued hurriedly, 'to adopt an adult Korean.'

FOUR

'I've looked after a lot of lost sheep in my life,' said Ratso, later that evening as we walked through the colorful, jangly streets of Little Italy. The weather had warmed up a bit and was now what New Yorkers are fond of calling 'brisk'. Anywhere else they'd call it cold as hell.

'Now,' said Ratso, as he gazed at a young family through a restaurant window, 'I find I am one.'

The notion of Ratso as a lost sheep, for some reason, saddened me. He was, no doubt, a lot of things, most of them unpleasant. But some vestige of a still, small voice within me did not want my friend to see himself in such a pathetic light. The voice said: 'Help him, but don't ever count on getting paid.'

'You're not a lost sheep,' I said. 'Just because you've fallen in love with a succession of girlfriends all of whom happen to have about forty-nine broken wings – '

'My dick isn't a psychiatrist,' said Ratso.

'If it was,' I said, 'I never would've slept on your couch.'

I thought, a bit ruefully, of the many times I'd availed myself of Ratso's couch, before I had a cat, or a loft, or anything faintly resembling a job. Back when I was a lost sheep myself. Now that I'd grown up to become an adult stamp collector, it was my turn to help Ratso. I vowed to myself that I wouldn't let him down.

'It's a funny thing,' he said, as we sat across from each other at one of the little tables in Luna's Restaurant, 'but finding out that my mother is a real person with a real identity who may still be alive has been very unsettling to me. My whole life I was led to believe she died when I was born.'

'Who told you that?'

'My dad,' said Ratso.

I thought of Ratso's dad – his adoptive father – Jack Sloman,

187

who'd died quite recently in Florida. I'd met him a few times. He was a kind man. Very proud of his son.

'I went to Florida several times to see my father before he died,' said Ratso. 'But with the stroke and Alzheimer's he was too far gone to talk. He recognized me and seemed almost to understand what I was saying, but all he could do was lie there and make noises like a little bird.'

All of us would probably make noises like a little bird some day, I thought. If we were lucky. The waiter brought our orders of linguini with red clam sauce and in addition, for Ratso, a huge cauldron of zuppa di pesce. He attacked the food like a frenzied priest going after an altar boy.

'At least your troubles don't seem to be affecting your appetite,' I said.

'I'm a lost sheep,' said Ratso. 'Not an anorexic sheep.'

'So what makes you think your real mother may still be alive?'

'My mother mentioned it last week. She's in a retirement community in Florida –'

'That's my dream,' I said. 'To be one of the Shalom Retirement Village People. Maybe your mother and I will put together a band.'

'You tried that once,' said Ratso. 'Anyway, she alluded to some new information about my real mother that my dad had kept in a safe deposit box. She said he wanted me to have it opened after he died.'

'Jesus,' I said. 'Where's the safe deposit box?'

'In a bank.'

'I know it's in a bank, Ratso. With my vast experience in the field of crime solving, I was able to deduce that. Where's the goddamn bank?'

'Florida.'

'So just have your mother go to the bank, open the safe deposit box, and send what's ever in there to you.'

Ratso extracted the tentacles of a squid from the zuppa di

pesce, put it in his mouth, and shook his head, apparently in answer to my suggestion.

'I don't want to do that,' he said. 'She's upset enough about everything already and it wouldn't be right for me to go on some active, personal crusade to find my birth parents right now. That's how I want you to help me. Go down to Florida. Talk to my mother. Talk to the bank. Get into the safe deposit box. I don't want to talk to my mother about my true birth mother just now. I don't know if I ever want to involve her in this. She is the only mother I've ever known and I don't want to hurt her. Also, I'm somewhat ambivalent myself at times about finding my real mother.'

'And I'm somewhat ambivalent about getting on a plane and going down to Florida and not knowing who's paying for it.'

'No problem,' said Ratso. 'Just put it on my tab.'

Later, as we trudged along the Italian ice of Mulberry Street, Ratso's mood seemed, if possible, to deepen. But, like all his outlandish outfits and dead men's accoutrements, he wore his self-pity well. I knew I had to help him find some answers. Either that or coddle a large Jewish meatball for the rest of my natural life.

'I appreciate your helping me,' Ratso said, as we rounded a corner and headed toward a small café he favored because they had about a thousand different kinds of cannolis.

'I haven't said I'll help yet.'

'You will.'

'I couldn't chance losing my Dr Watson. You bring such a charming naïveté to a case.'

'Especially this one,' he said grimly. He stopped under a street lamp and removed from his wallet a small, ancient-looking piece of paper.

'What's that?' I said. 'A leftover bar mitzvah card?'

'It's older than that, if you can believe it. It's the card for the lawyer who arranged my adoption.'

'Surely he's woken up in hell by now.'

'Probably. I think he was a pretty shady guy. I can't tell you how many times in the past I've thought about trying to find him, but something kept stopping me. It's like I wanted to know but I didn't want to know – now it's probably too late.'

'Well, make up your rabbit mind. I'm not going to work my balls off digging up this information and then call your ass and find out you don't want to know.'

'I want to know. I just don't want to find out on my own.' He handed me the lawyer's card.

'If I find out the truth,' I said, putting the old business card in my pocket, 'I'm going to tell you. I'm not going to hold anything back.'

'Even if it's her?' said Ratso, as he gazed across the brightly lit street, an infinite sadness in his eyes.

I followed his gaze to a squalid figure standing on the curbside beneath a window display of Mussolini T-shirts. Somehow she appeared more like an ephemeral shadow than a human being. A disreputable shawl or blanket covered her head and most of her body and what apparently were her worldly possessions resided in two large plastic garbage bags even now spilling over into the gutter. She looked for all the world like some half-forgotten character out of a Dickens novel, and when her eyes met mine very briefly they seemed like fireflies disappearing into the primeval night.

'Even if it's her,' I said.

We walked a little further and I lit a cigar. I was puffing on it thoughtfully as the café came into sight.

'Let's get one thing straight,' I said. 'I'm not going to investigate this because I feel sorry for you. You're *not* a lost sheep.'

I looked at Ratso carefully. In the neon incandescence of Little Italy his face reflected all the pain of a momentary mask of Greek tragedy.

'Okay, Sherlock,' he said. 'So I'm *not* a lost sheep. Then what the hell *am* I?'

I glanced briefly at the happy people sitting inside the little café. I puffed on the cigar and watched the smoke curl up past the street lamp and vanish in the lights of the city.

'You're a fucked-up shepherd,' I said.

FIVE

As the late-morning sun filtered feebly into the loft, the cat sat on my desk and studied the lawyer's business card. I leaned back in my chair, leisurely sipping an espresso and smoking a cigar. If the guy had handled Ratso's adoption proceedings, by my reckoning he was almost certainly worm bait by now. Either that, or his scattered ashes were doing their dead-level best to perpetuate the city's pollution problems.

'Have I missed something?' I said to the cat.

The cat said nothing. She continued her rather intense perusal of the small document.

'Guy's got to be in some vacant lot in Brooklyn,' I said. 'Probably pushing up poison ivy.'

The cat stared at the card. I puffed patiently on the cigar.

'You know, the life span of most lawyers is often briefer than their briefs. They're very anal retentive, they make a lot of money usually, and quite often in order to do that they wind up screwing a lot of people and God punishes them. Of course, as the poet Kenneth Patchen once said: "Nobody's a long time." That includes amateur detectives and cats. Especially cats who stare too long at business cards.'

I got up to pour another espresso from the large silver-and-bronze commercial-size espresso machine. The machine was sent to me several years back by a nice gentleman named Joe the Hyena, whom I've never met and with any luck never will. Why he sent it and where it might've come from is a laborious and, I suspect, rather unsavory story which falls into the some-things-are-better-not-to-know department.

I poured the espresso and was returning to the desk when a dull thudding sound began to emanate downward from the ceiling of the loft. Winnie Katz's lesbian dance class was at it again, and what exactly went on up there was another thing that I didn't really want to know. The cat looked up at the ceiling with an irritated expression, switched her tail back and forth a few times rather viciously, then resumed her vigil over the card.

'Maybe you've got something there,' I said to the cat. 'Pardon my boardinghouse reach.'

I picked up the card and studied it again, this time with a softer focus. After all, I reflected, this worn old business card, this artifact, was all Ratso had to hold on to. It'd been in his possession since he was a young boy, he'd said. It was all that was left of a mother and father he could only dream about. The mere taking of the card from Ratso, I now realized, was practically tantamount to a spiritual commitment on my part.

The lawyer's name was William Hamburger, a slightly humorous and unusual name, and that was good. Even in New York there couldn't be that many guys named Hamburger.

The firm was Hamburger & Hamburger. It was one of those firms, I briefly explained to the cat, where you could call up and say: 'Is Mr Hamburger in?' and they'd say, 'No, he's away from the office', and you could say 'Well, then, is Mr Hamburger in?' Unfortunately, the address and phone number did not look particularly humorous or promising. It was an address in Brooklyn on Court Street and the phone number was preceded by the letters 'UL', which might've stood for 'Ulster', but in this case, more appropriately could've stood for 'Ulcer', because trying to run down something this old very likely was going to give me one.

'Where there's a will, there's a lawyer,' I said to the cat. 'Let's call him.'

I dialed the number.

'Hel-lo,' said a man with an oriental accent thick enough to float wontons on. If this was William Hamburger, he must have been to Buddha and back a few times by now.

'Good morning, sir,' I said in an important voice. 'I'm trying to locate a Mr William Hamburger.'

'No have hamburger,' said the man.

'Hold the weddin',' I said. 'I don't want to *eat* hamburger – I want to *find* him. He's a lawyer who had this phone number years ago.'

'Awwwww,' said the man. 'You mean *royer*. He die many years ago. But son take over business. Move to rower Manhattan. Son big royer now.'

'Son big royer now,' I said to the cat after I'd hung up with the guy. The cat was curled up under the desk lamp and showed no reaction whatsoever. This did not surprise me, since she had demonstrated no sense of humor either, from the time I'd first known her. She did deign to open her eyes halfway and stare at me with a very thinly veiled moue of distaste. Or maybe it was a mew of distaste. This wasn't terribly surprising either, for cats are very politically correct creatures. Ethnic mimicry sends them up the wall.

I lit a fresh cigar, picked up the blower on the left, and dialed Manhattan information.

'What city?' said a bored male voice with a high-octane lisp.

'Manhattan.'

'How can I help you?' he said, in a voice that made it clear he wouldn't throw a rubber swan to a drowning man.

'How many Hamburgers you got in Manhattan?'

'Twelve billion served,' he said, really going to town on the word 'served.'

'Let me rephrase that,' I said. 'How many *people* named Hamburger you got?'

'Let me see,' he said.

I waited. He hummed. The cat slept. The investigation was not exactly roaring off the starting line. But I'd expected this. Rambam had told me that most searches for birth parents can be tedious, futile, and quite often, stultifyingly dull. So far, he wasn't wrong.

By the time the operator had finished counting Hamburgers, I was beginning preparations to hang myself by the heels from the bronze eagle on the top of the espresso machine. Finally, he stopped humming and spoke again.

'About ten,' he said.

'And how many live in lower Manhattan?'

The operator sighed a very audible, theatrical sigh. But he did resume his humming. I took this as an encouraging sign.

'Three,' he said, somewhat peevishly.

'Great,' I said. 'Can you give me those three numbers?'

He sighed again, but this time he didn't really seem to have his heart in it. Eventually, if somewhat coyly, he coughed up the information.

'Thanks,' I said. 'Sorry these weren't the kind of hamburgers you eat.'

'How can you be so sure?' he said.

I began calling the lower Manhattan Hamburgers and nailed the lawyer the first time out of the box. Things were picking up.

By stating that the matter was one of great urgency I was able to get an appointment with the lawyer – whose name was Moie Hamburger – that very afternoon. Of course, 'urgent' was not quite the proper word to apply to this investigation. The case was already older than God. Also, my client wasn't sure that he wanted to know the results. But these days New York has become so crazy that things have to be urgent. Important doesn't work anymore.

Before I left for my meeting with Moie Hamburger, I called Rambam to make sure I knew what I was looking for. Rambam said that having the lawyer run a file check would be the easiest but the guy might charge me my eldest son for the fee. I told Rambam I didn't have an eldest son. 'How can you be so sure?' he said. I told him that was the second time I'd been asked that question and I never wanted anyone to ask me that again. 'How can you be so sure?' he said.

According to Rambam, if I didn't want to spring for the file check, I'd have to check the files myself, with the lawyer's permission, of course. Rambam guessed they'd probably be in some old warehouse in Brooklyn, the thought of which caused me to roll my eyeballs toward the lesbian dance class. Again, according to Rambam, I was looking for legal files, case notes that pertained to applications for custody, or custody transfers. All actual court files, he said, would probably be sealed.

'Just like my fate is sealed,' I said.

'He's *your* friend,' said Rambam cheerfully, as he hung up the phone.

A short time later, I grabbed a handful of cigars along with my hat and coat, killed all the lights except for the cat's heat lamp on the desk, and headed for the door.

'I'm off to see the *royer*,' I said.

She didn't even flinch.

SIX

Unless you're planning on making a pilgrimage to the grave of Clarence Darrow, a visit to an attorney rarely manifests itself as a particularly spiritual experience. Folks who come to lawyers usually have a problem. By the time they leave the lawyer's office they usually have a complicated, expensive problem. Lawyers don't intentionally try to make things costlier or more tedious for their clients. They just can't help themselves. It is the way of their people.

Moie Hamburger, of the lower Manhattan Hamburgers, I suspected, was no exception. The outer office of the firm was all done up in about eleven shades of tasteful, decorous, extremely expensive-looking gray. Not only would a file check be fiscally out of the question here, you'd probably have to leave a retainer the size of the battleship *Potemkin* if you wanted them to check your hat.

I gave my name to the receptionist and she gave me a surprisingly ingenuous smile. Probably new in town. I sat down on a couch the color of twilight, picked up a *Wall Street Gerbil*, and watched as the busy little secretaries and paralegal types rushed hither and thither carrying thick sheaves of important-looking documents, all very likely generated by somebody's highly insured four-wheeled penis allegedly being tail-ended by a Dodge Dart or by some alert individual allegedly getting himself photographed down at the No-Tell Motel in the explicit act of coveting his neighbor's ass. Needless to say, everything was now safely in the hands of the lawyers.

Allegedly.

Moie Hamburger's office, I soon discovered, was comprised of still more shades of gray, including Hamburger himself, who was a bit more o-l-d than I'd expected. I lamped him for being in his late sixties, meaning he'd conceivably still have been in law school at the time his father first became fatefully entangled with the spiritual tar baby that the world now knew as Larry 'Ratso' Sloman.

Hamburger was a distinguished-looking, kindly-visaged man with a big white beard that, unlike the rhetoric of most lawyers, came to a point. Hundreds of years ago in Norway or someplace he would've made a good-looking king. More evidence for my theory that all of us are drawn to occupations for which we're horribly ill suited. Unfortunately, the theory also applied to me.

As I entered the narrow entranceway to the office, a large, hirsute individual who roughly resembled an abominable snowman with a chip on his shoulder, barreled by me on the left. I did a little, quickly improvised Texas two-step out of his way and walked over to Hamburger's large, well-polished, important-looking desk.

'What was that?' I said, nodding in the direction of the empty passageway.

'Just a client,' said Hamburger with a rueful smile, 'who's been with the firm a long time.'

'In that case,' I said, 'I'll just be a moment.'

'How can I help you, Mr Friedman?' he said, beginning to show a few signs of mild irritation.

'Why don't we start with this,' I said, as I placed the archaic business card on his desk.

'Wow,' said Hamburger, as he looked at the card. His face appeared to soften with a brief spasm of something like nostalgia, then, just as quickly, became a mask of some more contemporary countenance, possibly wariness or distrust, which almost caused him to squirm. 'How'd you come into possession of this?' he said.

'A friend gave it to me,' I said. 'I figured the way to the father was through the son.'

'That path may prove a little difficult,' said Hamburger. 'My father died twenty years ago.'

'Sorry to hear that,' I said.

'So I ask you again,' he said, with a few more slight stirrings of irritation, 'how can I help you, Mr Friedman?' The card was still on his desk but it had become again what it always had been, a thing of the past.

'My friend, the one who gave me your father's card, was adopted. Your father handled the adoption proceedings. My friend never knew his real parents. He was always led to believe his mother had died in childbirth. Now, with the death of his adoptive father, his mother has mentioned to him that there may be documents in a bank deposit box in Florida that say otherwise.'

'Have you checked these documents?' said Hamburger. There was a rather intense curiosity in his face.

'I shall,' I said. 'But first I'd like to get a little background here in New York. That would start with your old files.'

'What's your friend's name?' asked Hamburger.

'Larry Sloman,' I said. 'Known to his intimates as Ratso.' One blue vein was pulsating rather noticeably in Moie Hamburger's forehead.

'Running a formal file check on that period would be very expensive for you and not possible for us right now. What I can do is give you an authorization to our legal warehouse in Brooklyn. Just show it to the guard and go on up and sort through it yourself. Those old files, if they're still there, should be on the fifth floor, section fourteen. I'm not at all sure you'll find what you're looking for, but happy hunting.'

Hamburger drew a sheet of stationery with his firm's legal letterhead from his desk and proceeded to scribble a few sentences. He paused somewhat somberly and then signed his name, as if the document were of some grave import. I got up, he handed me the page, and I thanked him and headed for the door.

'There's something I think you ought to know,' he said. I stopped and turned around.

'Lay it on me,' I said.

'I'm not at liberty to give you any names or details,' said Hamburger, as looked into his suddenly rather chilly blue eyes. 'But you're not the first to approach me about this matter.'

Most people in Manhattan believe that if they travel outside of Manhattan proper the world is flat and they may very well fall off the map and end up in Brooklyn or Queens or worse. This is a highly evolved, extremely progressive idea, which has required generations of lasagna and pastrami sandwiches in order to fully develop. Certainly the trip was fraught with many dangers, not the least of which was that my cab driver bore a more than passing resemblance to Idi Amin. Eventually, we fell off the end of the map and ended up in front of a grim, forbidding-looking building somewhere in the bowels of Brooklyn.

I paid the cabbie, showed Hamburger's note to a large man wearing a small hat, and strode purposefully into the shadowy warehouse. The elevator to the fifth floor was a blood relative to the one in my building on Vandam Street, which, now that I thought about it, had once been a warehouse itself. It was too bad elevators only moved up and down and never got a chance to meet each other. The occupants of the elevators not only moved up and down, of course, but could also move horizontally across the board.

Section fourteen was not hard to find, and I quickly set about searching for S for Sloman. So far so good. File cabinets populated the warehouse floor, which was like a small city of its own and, par for the course, the S files were residing in the penthouse. I pulled a dusty Jacob's ladder out of the corner and climbed step by step closer to Ratso's past, which heretofore had been shrouded in mystery. I knew roughly what I was looking for: application for custody, custody transfer, case notes, etc. The warehouse was cold as hell but if the Angel of Death didn't push me off the ladder and I didn't break my neck, I felt I was getting warm.

I found the Sloman file, slipped it out of the cabinet, and

navigated my way down the ladder, holding the file in my teeth and using my cigar as ballast. The Flying Wallenda Brothers come to Brooklyn. I walked over to a grime-covered window and opened the file.

I speed-read through the usual legal mumbo-jumbo until I got to the line where Ratso's mother's name was supposed to be. Either her name was 'Court File – Sealed' or I was going to have to look elsewhere for the truth. Ratso's adoptive parents, Jack and Lilyan, were there, surrounded by massive bookends of legal pronouncements. Ratso was born at Bellevue Hospital. He'd already told me that. Somewhere in all this ancient horse manure there had to be one live maggot.

Sure enough, on the last page of the file, under the heading 'Amended Petition' I found the only real news flash in the pile. No man is an island they say, unless that island happens to be called Manhattan. Or, as my friend Speed Vogel once put it rather succinctly: 'Your heart attack, my hangnail.' And yet I was mildly surprised at how a cold fact that was forty-seven years old and unknown even to Ratso had affected me. The statement in question read: 'No claim exists to minor child except that of mother; male parent now known to be deceased.'

At least there was one less person to look for.

EIGHT

By the time I got out of the warehouse, evening was falling clumsily onto a cold, leaden landscape that appeared to have been painted by some Van Gogh on his way to the corner liquor store. That's where I was headed, too. There was a pay phone on the corner and I wanted to call Ratso.

As I ankled down to the corner, the wind seemed to pick up and the people appeared to scurry about like some new kind of rodent. Newspapers full of yesterday's heroes swirled past me along the sidewalk. I had all I could do to hold on to my cowboy hat, so I didn't give a lot of thought to a man in a black leather overcoat leaning against the side of the warehouse shielding his face by trying to light a cigarette in the wind. I was thinking about what I should tell Ratso.

When I got him on the phone I didn't tell him about his father. I just made sure he'd be there and told him I was coming by with an update on the investigation. I did this because, though his father was a distant figure that he'd never known, like a shadow on a wall in Hiroshima, his father was his father. I also didn't say anything because another distant figure, the guy in the black overcoat, had just gone inside the liquor store and was now browsing the aisles, looking furtively in my direction.

I collared the blower and scanned the street for a hack for hire. Nothing. When you need a hack in New York it's never there, and when you don't they surround you like urine-colored lava. Cabs are like women, or horses, or happiness, or money, or pet parakeets. If you pursue them with great ardor you'll never have them. If you honestly don't give a damn they'll very often light right on your shoulder, in which case the pet parakeet is, of course, preferable to the horse or the cab.

The guy in the liquor store picked up a bottle of something that looked like Southern Comfort, held it for a moment, then put it back on the shelf. He had a good face to play cards with.

I thought back to Moie Hamburger's words as I'd left his office. 'You're not the first to approach me about this matter.' Terrific. All I needed was a *Day of the Jackal*-type character following me in Brooklyn. But why would anyone care? What was there about Ratso's misbegotten birth that would give a busy New Yorker pause?

I crossed the street and headed back up the block, and the guy came out of the liquor store and began following me like a baby duck imprinting its mother's tracks. I felt like a baby shmuck imprinting Ratso's mother's tracks. This guy was not a particularly invisible tail, but who would want me tailed in the first place? The obvious candidate was Moie Hamburger, but why would he bother to say, like a bride on her wedding night, 'You're not the first'? My paranoia was redlining.

After several blocks of hide-and-seek I finally spotted a large woman in a coat that must've decimated some mink's family tree, getting out of a cab and I took her place as the occupant. I left the guy in the black overcoat running down the sidewalk toward a parked car, gave the driver Ratso's address, and told him to step on it.

'Posse after you?' said the driver.

'I'll let you know,' I said.

I looked around a few times before we left Brooklyn. No posse. No cavalry. No Indians. No reason for anybody to give a damn whether or not I awkwardly stumbled toward the truth about the birth parents of one Larry 'Ratso' Sloman. No reason at all.

To play it safe, I jetted the cab a few blocks from Ratso's place on Prince Street in the Village. I loitered around an Italian bakery and a Korean greengrocer's store, but I saw no sign of the guy in the black overcoat. It had turned into a cold, dark night and I stepped into a corner grocery on Sullivan Street to get a large black coffee to go. I took a few sips and lit a cigar out on the sidewalk.

I'd never handled a missing-person case where you turned the clock back quite this far – almost fifty years. No doubt there were procedural methods and approaches to such an investigation but I didn't know what the hell they were. Rambam wasn't being overly helpful and I didn't know who else to turn to for advice. It was also possible, I thought darkly, that Ratso wasn't telling me everything. Maybe I wasn't asking him the right questions. I sipped some more coffee, took a few puffs on the cigar, and walked briskly up to his building, where I pushed 6G, which, according to Ratso, stood for God.

After an irritatingly long wait in the cold, I heard Ratso's rodent-like voice powering over the intercom.

'Who is it?' he said.

'It's the Antichrist,' I said, 'looking for 6G.'

'Come in, Antichrist,' he said.

I strolled quickly through the dingy, urine-scented foyer where Ratso's pet bum usually slept, took the elevator up to six, and leaned on Ratso's doorbell.

'Who is it?' shouted Ratso.

'Jesus Christ! Let me in!'

'Is it *Jesus* Christ or the *Antichrist*?' said Ratso. 'Please be specific. It could be important.'

'Please, Ratso. I've got to talk to you.' I also had to urinate like a racehorse.

'Sounds like Jesus Christ.'

'Goddamnit, Ratso, I'm gonna kill you.'

'Nope. It's the Antichrist.'

Eventually, I heard the various chains and bars and tumblers moving through their machinations as Ratso began the rather laborious process of opening his triple-locked door. What in the hell he was striving so zealously to protect was another question. How in the hell I'd gotten myself involved in this investigation was still another.

At last the door swung open and there was Ratso dressed in a coonskin cap, longjohn pajamas that looked like they'd once gone West with Lewis and Clark, and a pair of red shoes that I knew from past encounters had once belonged to a dead man.

'Kinkstah!' shouted Ratso enthusiastically. 'Why didn't you say it was you?'

'I'm going for a low profile on this case,' I said, as I endeavored to carefully navigate the narrow strait between Ratso's body and several hundred hockey sticks he kept precariously balanced against his doorframe.

'What've you got?' Ratso asked eagerly.

'I've got a full bladder, Ratso,' I said. 'Now if you'll get out of my way, I'd like to shake hands with the devil.'

'You *are* the Antichrist,' I heard Ratso say as I closed the door to his overheated bathroom, which was about the size of my nose.

Moments later I was pacing back and forth in Ratso's cluttered living room with Ratso comfortably ensconced on his famous couch with the skid marks on it. I'd once called that couch and this ragged, jumbled living room home. As I glanced around at the statue of the Virgin Mary, the polar bear's head, the ten thousand books on Jesus, Hitler, and Bob Dylan, the photos of Ratso shaking hands with Richard Nixon and posing with Bob Dylan (nothing with him and Jesus or Hitler, unfortunately), the two huge television screens soundlessly, simultaneously emitting a hockey game and a porno movie, I felt comforted with the knowledge that you can't go home again.

'Your real father is dead, Ratso,' I said softly. 'According to the application for custody that I found in the legal files.'

Ratso's form on the couch seemed suddenly forsaken. He watched the screens sightlessly and seemed to almost huddle there withdrawing ever so slightly into himself.

'What about my mother?' he said.

'Her name is not filled in on the appropriate line. Instead, it reads: Court File – Sealed. I can check the records at Bellevue Hospital, but it's been a long time and it's a long shot. I may very well have to go to Florida before this is over.'

'You're a real friend, Kinkstah,' said Ratso. He picked up the remote control unit and killed the porno movie. 'I want you to find my mother,' he said.

A short time later, I'd put my coat on and lit up a fresh cigar, in preparation for departure. Ratso still remained where he was on the couch, silently following the silent hockey players while other thoughts, I knew, weaved back and forth across the far ice of his memory.

As I walked past an overpopulated coffee table on the way to the door I noticed a bill lying on top of a disorderly stack of books. It was from one Robert McLane, Private Investigator. The bill contended that Ratso was past due in paying him four hundred dollars for services rendered.

'What the hell is this?' I said, picking the bill up from the coffee table and holding it between the hockey game and Ratso's face.

'Oh, I forgot to tell you, I guess. That's a guy I hired to look into this a while back. Robert McLane. I'm sorry. He's off the case now. I should've told you, Kinkstah.'

'You're goddamn right you should've told me.'

'Anyway, he didn't find anything and I guess I never paid him.'

'There's a shocker.'

'You want to call the guy, go ahead. Use the phone in the bedroom. Compare notes or whatever. Tell him the check's in the mail.'

I took the PI's bill and headed for the bedroom, just a little surprised at Ratso. Just a little surprised. The auditory aspect of the hockey game came roaring to life just as I was closing the bedroom door. Ratso had been a rather repellent friend of mine for over twenty years. It stood to reason he was going to make a rather repellent client.

Ten minutes later I came out of the bedroom and I suppose my face and demeanor told the story, because it's a rare occasion when Ratso kills the sound on a hockey game twice in one afternoon.

'What'd you find out?' Ratso said.

I took a patient puff on the cigar and exhaled a thick plume of smoke in the general direction of the polar bear's head.

'Did you compare notes with the guy?' Ratso wanted to know.

'No, I did not compare notes with the guy,' I said, 'and there's a very good reason for it.'

'What's the reason?' said Ratso.

I put the invoice back on the coffee table and walked over to the window beside the Virgin Mary. The cigar smoke appeared to be making a nice little blue-gray halo around her head, but I didn't pay her too much attention.

'Because he's dead,' I said.

NINE

Three days later I stood at my kitchen window, looking over a cloud-shrouded Vandam Street and feeling a great spiritual kinship with Robert Louis Stevenson, who spent the last years of his life cut off from the rest of the world in voluntary exile on Samoa. I felt a certain sartorial kinship with Stevenson as well, since I was wearing a sarong and my faithful purple bathrobe and Stevenson perpetually wore a long dark blue velvet housecoat over his pajamas even when greeting formally dressed visitors who'd come to meet the great man.

'He had a pet mouse, you know,' I said to the cat. 'He lived in Hawaii for a while on Waikiki Beach before any hotels were there and before ninety-seven Japanese tourists were waiting to make a land assault upon every elevator. Before Stevenson went to sleep each night he'd take out his flute and play a little Scottish tune, and this little mouse would come out from wherever he was hiding and dance around the room. By all records, Stevenson was one of the world's worst flute players but it didn't seem to bother him or the mouse.'

The story didn't seem to bother the cat much either. She sat stoically on the windowsill and let it roll by with the clouds.

'Stevenson loved the Samoan people and they loved him, calling him Tusitala, which means teller of tales. Though he died almost exactly a hundred years ago, there is a Samoan song that is still sung to the captains of arriving ships. The song at one point inquires if Mr Robert Louis Stevenson is aboard the ship.'

The cat, at last, seemed to be paying attention to my narrative. Her eyes appeared to have changed slightly, I noticed, from their normal green perpetual pinwheels of malice to placid green pools of reflection in which I could see the sadness in my own face. It was not just a sadness for Stevenson; it was a wistful state of melancholia that I felt for my old friend Ratso and for myself.

For the past three days I'd tried in vain to learn more about McLane, the PI Ratso had hired who'd so recently gone to Jesus. The phone number I'd called from Ratso's apartment had now been disconnected. The small agency he'd run had also seemed suddenly to blip off the screen. The lawyer, Moie Hamburger, according to his secretary, was out of the country on an extended vacation. Perhaps Ratso had not been totally open with me about the situation, but clearly something was going on that neither of us understood. Some little prickling inner sense told me that he was in danger. I had a sick, persistent feeling that far from his finding his mother, something horrible might find him first. And there was nothing I could do but smoke a cigar and talk to a cat.

'Rambam's grudging help,' I continued, 'will also not be forthcoming in the foreseeable future. He left a message on the machine this morning from the airport that he's on his way to Hong Kong to investigate a slip-and-fall accident aboard a junk for a lawyer in Seattle. After that, he says, he's apparently jumping through his asshole with the paratroopers from the Burmese Airborne Battalion. There's a nice bunch of fellows to be jumping with.'

The cat jumped off the windowsill and landed on the kitchen table without a parachute. She did not care a fig about politics or governments and she liked Rambam only slightly better than she liked Ratso, which is to say not a hell of a lot.

'Anyway, we've reached an apparent dead end in the case here in New York. There's no one to investigate and no one to advise me what to do. The only other private investigator I could go to for advice is now living in California. Name's Kent Perkins. He's a big ol' good-natured Texas boy. I think you'd like him. He used to refer to his penis as "the Spoiler".'

The cat gave a little mew of distaste.

'Anyway, I left him a message but I haven't heard back from him.'

I walked over to the espresso machine, which was now giving forth a fairly decent racket and drew myself a hot, steaming cup that tasted almost as bitter as my current attitude toward this case. I paced back and forth in the drafty old loft, puffing the cigar and sipping the espresso and carrying on a one-sided conversation with myself or the cat or some silent witness. Ratso's mother, for all I knew. It wasn't very healthy really and it made me feel kind of paranoid.

'There's nothing wrong with a man talking at great length to a cat,' I said to the cat, who was now chasing a cockroach around the far corner of the kitchen counter. 'Besides, I talked to Bellevue Hospital yesterday and the bad news is that their records don't go back that far. The good news is that they didn't ask me to come in for observation.'

I glanced quickly at the cat, who was now sitting on the counter staring at me. I thought I detected something akin to a form of feline empathy in her eyes. It was also possible that the cockroach had now crawled up on the wall behind me.

'So Robert Louis Stevenson,' I said, 'had been a great friend of a Samoan chieftain named Mataafa, and once he personally arranged to release many of Mataafa's followers from a wrongful imprisonment. The Samoans, quite reasonably, hated manual labor. But once the prisoners were released, they set about building a road from the town of Apia to

Stevenson's house. The road, which still stands today in Samoa, was called "The Road of the Loving Hearts".'

A short while later, the cat was asleep, the street was noticeably darker, and I was still standing at the window, staring into the gloom. Ratso was one of my oldest and best friends, I thought. What the hell. If Robert Louis Stevenson, with his frail and sickly constitution, could travel from Scotland to the South Sea Islands, I figured I could certainly make a trip to Florida.

It could've been my natural curiosity that helped me make the decision. Or it could've been my own selfish pride that wouldn't allow me to admit failure once I'd taken on a job. Or possibly, the fact that I was now determined to go to Florida had nothing to do with me at all. Maybe it was much simpler than that.

'The Road of the Loving Hearts', it would seem, sometimes extends itself beyond Samoa.

TEN

Two days later, having ascertained from Ratso how to contact his adoptive mother once I got to Florida, I embarked upon the brief little mission that I hoped would finally shed some light on the identity of his biological mother. I'd pretty well come to the conclusion that the safe deposit box his father had mentioned to his mother was the only lead I had left. If the cupboard turned up bare in Florida, I figured, Ratso was going to have to hire Nero Wolfe.

'And that,' I said to the cat as I packed my suitcase, 'is going to cost money.'

The cat, understandably nervous about the presence of the suitcase, didn't care a flea about anyone else's problems. If the truth be known, she would probably feel just as well had

Ratso never been born. Of course, that would've made it even more difficult for me to find his mother.

Sadly, the more hopeless the case appeared to me and the more depressed I privately became about my involvement, the more upbeat and positive was Ratso's attitude.

'I know you'll find her, Kinkstah,' he'd said. 'I can tell when you're onto something.'

'Don't get your hopes up just because I'm going to Florida,' I'd said. 'We could be off on the wrong trail altogether.'

'I'd hate to think,' Ratso had said, 'that my mother was a red herring.'

When I'd packed the suitcase, I patted the cat reassuringly, fished around inside the porcelain head of Sherlock Holmes for the extra key to the loft, and headed up the stairs to Stephanie DuPont's apartment. Stephanie was a drop-dead-gorgeous five-eleven blonde I'd been establishing a rapport with over the past year to at least the point where she'd grudgingly assented to feed the cat for two days while I was away in Florida. In the past I'd left the cat with Winnie Katz, but our relationship had deteriorated dating almost exactly from the day when Stephanie and her two little dogs, Pyramus and Thisbe, walked into our lives. The sordid truth of the matter was that Winnie and I now considered ourselves rival suitors for Stephanie's affection. Whenever the lesbian dance class over my head became silent these days, I worried.

'God, nerd,' said Stephanie when she opened her door, 'what is that ridiculous hairball growing beneath your lower lip?'

I'd been experimenting lately with a slightly new formation of facial hair. Figured it'd at least go over well with the Cubans.

'I'm workin' on my white-man hater,' I said. 'What do you think?'

'Too bad,' she said. 'I was hoping it was lip cancer.'

Stephanie had a rather caustic wit about her, to put it mildly. If she hadn't been the most beautiful, smartest, sexiest, funniest, and tallest woman in the world, I doubt if any-body'd ever talk to her. But she was and they did. If they could.

'Now all you have to do,' I said, as I got out the key, 'is to feed the cat maybe once or twice a day – '

'Once.'

'Cat's not going to like that.'

'Neither am I.'

Stephanie, no doubt, still remembered the time the cat fairly shredded her beloved Maltese, Thisbe. It had been an unfortunate incident that had occurred some time ago during my rather checkered campaign to locate Uptown Judy and it hadn't exactly been brick and mortar to my relationship with Stephanie.

'It'd be nice also,' I continued, 'if you'd keep up a little presence around the loft in my absence. One idea might be to put on my cowboy hat and sit at my desk smoking a cigar late at night – '

'Stop,' she said.

Then she smiled incredulously. This was followed by a noise like a bubbling brook that seemed to emanate from somewhere in her throat.

'Was that a laugh?'

'I'm trying not to vomit.'

'That *was* a laugh. You know what I always say: "If you can make a woman laugh, you can take her to bed with you." '

'You know what my mother always told me?'

' "Don't go out with Jews"?'

'No,' said Stephanie DuPont, with the sultry little smile still ticcing lightly on her lips. 'She said: "Never, never, never go to bed with a man who wears a white-man hater." '

Then she kissed me lightly on the lips, just above the white-man hater, took the key from my hand, and closed the door.

'Not bad,' I said to the cat, as I walked back into the loft. 'First a Rockefeller, now a Dupont.'

ELEVEN

A short time later, with suitcase and cigar in hand, I was walking out the door of the loft when the phones rang. I walked back to the desk, set down my suitcase, and picked up the blower on the left.

'Start talkin',' I said.

'This is the voice of your conscience,' said the blower.

'Impossible,' I said. 'He's right here and I'm lookin' at him.' I gave a perfunctory little Nero Wolfe-like nod to Sherlock Holmes's head. His face remained impassive.

'Maybe your conscience just likes to visit Southern California,' drawled the friendly voice, placing a suggestive, somewhat primitive inflection on the word 'visit'.

'No self-respecting conscience would ever visit Southern California.'

'That's why I still keep my Texas driver's license,' said Kent Perkins.

I had a plane to catch and this little banter was getting me nowhere, but there was something about Kent that made you want to trust him. Maybe that's why he'd been so successful in the PI business. Also, it was hard to dislike a guy who'd already told you that in his will he'd left you a 1964 Lincoln Continental with suicide doors that opened from the middle of the car outward. It was the same model car that Kennedy had been shot in in Dallas, but I wasn't going to let one unfortunate incident total my karma.

Anyway, with Rambam out of the picture, Perkins was the only experienced consultant I had to work with. The fact that an adult referred to his penis as 'the Spoiler' was no reason to believe that the person didn't have the knowledge and maturity to help me with the problem at hand, so to speak. Still, it gave one pause.

Nonetheless, I sat down at the desk, laid my cigar down

in the large, Texas-shaped ashtray, and proceeded to fill Kent Perkins in on the details of the investigation as I knew them. I had to admit it felt mildly reassuring to be sharing the information with someone other than my hopelessly ambivalent, subjective, sometimes tedious, often rather repellent client.

'So what happened to the other PI?' Perkins wanted to know. 'The one Ratso hired to find his mother in the first place?'

'He went to Jesus.'

'We have a lot of that out here. People dropping whatever else they're doing and joining up with Christian fundamentalist cults.'

I didn't say anything. Just puffed patiently on the cigar.

'That is what you mean, isn't it?' said Perkins.

'I'm afraid not,' I said.

By the time I'd cradled the blower, I was ready to change my plane reservation to Fat Chance, Arkansas. Kent Perkins had, indeed, offered his personal help. Then he had given me about seven hundred good reasons why a private investigator, especially one who's a friend of his client, should never take a case of this nature. The odds of a successful conclusion after all this time were about as good as winning the lottery, he'd said, and the work would be a lot harder. Probably, Perkins had asserted, Ratso and I would no longer be friends by the conclusion of the case. There was also the off chance I might find Ratso's mother. Then dark forces often might come into play from siblings and other relatives who felt threatened by the new relationship coming to light. Finally, Perkins had set forth from personal experience the cruelest blow of all: that Ratso, after waiting a lifetime to find his real mother, might be rejected again by her as he had most likely been in the first place.

'Well, there's nothing like a healthy negative attitude,' I said to the cat, as I picked up the suitcase. 'I envy you.

Stephanie will be looking after you. I'll be back soon. Until then, you're in charge.'

Then I set out in the cold, brisk, hungover New York half-light to hail a hack for La Guardia and points south. I didn't stop feeling a certain soul chill until I was aboard the aircraft with New York City in the rearview mirror. Then I took off my overcoat for the first time.

I hadn't thought much about it but the shirt I was wearing for Florida was the one I'd bought in Hawaii several years ago. According to the guy who'd sold it to me it was an exact replica of the shirt Montgomery Clift had died in in *From Here to Eternity*. As things turned out, it was a damned near perfect sartorial choice.

TWELVE

I arrived in Florida in only slightly better condition than Dustin Hoffman in *Midnight Cowboy*. The pressures of living in New York, which can reduce the human spirit to rancid sandwich meat over a long weekend, combined with Kent Perkins's dire predictions about the case, had resulted in my hitting the tarmac in a fairly amphibious state. I was pleased to observe, at least, that many people at the Miami Airport were wearing white-man haters just like mine. Also, it was comforting to note that the vast majority of the people there were extremely o-l-d. It made me feel almost youthful. Kind of like a dead teenager. Whatever else you could say about the place, the demographics were good.

Tony Bruno, an old friend of mine from the days I was living in the tow-away zone known as Los Angeles, had once told me that there were over six hundred different kind of palm trees in the world and almost all of them had been imported and now grew in Florida. Unfortunately, most of them now seemed to be lined up in front of one kind of mall. I waved at them from my rent-a-car and they waved back along with a guy who looked like he was either the junta-appointed president of Haiti or your yard-man. I didn't have the time to find out which. When you're driving a rent-a-car in Miami, you want to be on your way.

I wasn't sure how many krauts had had their vacations rather abruptly terminated while driving rent-a-cars in Miami, but I knew it was a sizable number. The mills of the Lord grind slowly but they grind exceedingly fine. In fact, for the past few years now when, in my travels, I've come across a party of German tourists someplace I've always made it a matter of conscience to approach their table with a friendly, innocent, American smile and say: 'Have you checked out Miami?' None of them have found much humor in this. But it could be because they're Dutch or Swiss. The problem, of course, is somewhat complicated by the fact that if the tourist party had indeed been of the German persuasion, humor not being their particular long suit, they wouldn't have gotten the joke anyway. They never do.

I banished all dark thoughts from my mind as I zimmed along in my rent-a-car to pick up Ratso's mother at the Golden Flamingo Retirement Center, which was pretty near the airport. That was a good thing, because I'd forgotten to wrap my lunch in a road map. I hadn't driven a rent-a-car since Christ was a cowboy, but I found it to be a very exhilarating experience. After the first few miles you cease to care about the welfare of your vehicle, yourself, or anyone else in the world.

I passed by palm trees and parking meters and colorful shirts and sunshine glinting brightly off of every fast-food franchise under heaven. A carefree, pastel, old-time color postcard rent-a-view that made you wonder whether Cerberus, that three-headed dog of crime, greed, and ecological disaster was still guarding the gate. In Miami, as in life, staring too intently at the façade may be harmful to the eyes.

Staring too intently behind it, of course, is unthinkable. I found myself whistling 'England Swings' as I drove along and once again came to the conclusion that the world is divided into two groups of people: those who like Roger Miller and those who don't.

The Golden Flamingo Retirement Center looked like any other condo-apartment lobby-type setup except for the mandatory mental-hospital sign that stated: Today is THURSDAY. The next meal is LUNCH. This, of course, was necessary for many of the occupants of the center, the dates on whose cartons, unfortunately, had expired. There seemed to be an atmosphere of moderately restrained excitement around the place, and it didn't take me long to find out the reason: Perry Como was coming. There was a comforting, almost seductive, quality about the whole operation and I was kind of sorry I couldn't stick around and at least catch the show. Maybe sometime.

Lilyan Sloman was sitting out on the veranda feeding the birds and scanning a back issue of *National Lampoon*, which her son, Ratso, had once edited. I took one look at her and realized that far from being out where the buses don't run, she had her wits collected about her in a manner more meticulous than were my own, which, of course, wasn't saying all that much.

'Sit down, Kinky,' she said, as casually as an old lover. 'It's been a long time.'

'Yes, it has,' I said, pulling up a deck chair. I was racking my brains trying to remember the few times I'd met Lilyan, and the job wasn't made easier by the fact that I'd been by and large cookin' on another planet for most of the previous decade.

'How's Larry?' she said, looking at me with a mother's eyes.

'Larry's fine,' I said. 'I think he just wants to put an end to not knowing. He wants once and for all to find out the truth.

The last thing he told me before I left was: "I just want to spank this monkey and put it to bed." '

Lilyan laughed. 'That sounds like him,' she said. 'But I'm just worried that he may not realize that the monkey's already been sleeping for a long, long time. By the time it finally wakes up it may have become a big, hairy ape. He might not like that.'

'Or,' I said, as I watched an old man practicing his croquet shots, 'it might turn out to be a big, hairy steak, in which case Ratso *would* like it.'

'He *is* eating?' Ratso's mother asked me earnestly. She was probably the only person in the world who knew Ratso and could ask that question without getting laughed out of town.

'Let's put it this way, Lilyan,' I said. 'My initial plan to send him to that anorexia clinic in Canada has not required implementation at this time.'

'That's good,' she said, nodding to herself, then returning an ageless smile and a little wave to the man with the croquet mallet. It was a small gesture but it had in it all the shy, unmistakably ingenuous spirit of two young people meeting at their first garden party. I'd been at the party myself once, and so had Lilyan, but she'd gone for a sixty-year ride with a boy who had a car and now she was back on her own. I'd left to get cigarettes decades ago and was still standing in the checkout line behind a large Hispanic woman. In my mind I could hear Lesley Gore singing a slight paraphrasal of her song over the in-store Muzak system: 'It's my party, I can leave if I want to.' I'd left all right, and it didn't seem like I was going to be coming back anytime soon.

I watched Lilyan Sloman feeding the birds for a while. Then I watched the old guy playing croquet on a lawn as green as a cemetery. Then Lilyan and I looked at each other.

'Well,' she said, 'let's go to the bank.'

THIRTEEN

A short while later, after Lilyan Sloman had excused herself to change out of her summery frock into a dark, more businesslike outfit, she returned holding a little key to the bank safe deposit box.

'I could take the key down there myself, Lilyan,' I said. 'You don't really have to go with me.'

'It'll be better if I do,' she said. 'I know bankers, and when they see a young man from out of state with that cowboy hat and cigar holding the key to a little old lady's safe deposit box, it'll take more than a phone call to straighten things out.'

'They didn't like Pretty Boy Floyd either,' I said, as I helped her into the rent-a-car.

I turned out of the drive and at the same time turned the conversation from bankers to lawyers by asking Ratso's mother about Moie Hamburger's father, the man who handled the adoption proceedings so many years ago. The result was illuminating, and her composure appeared to ever so slightly unravel as she spoke.

'There was always something so strange about that whole business,' she said, letting the thought hang in the sultry air for a long while.

'The adoption?'

'The adoption, the lawyer himself, the agency that sent us the baby – '

'Ratso said he thought it was a Jewish adoption agency.'

'It *was* Jewish, but there was something about the whole affair that I always felt wasn't quite – '

'Kosher?' I offered.

'That wasn't exactly the word I was looking for,' she said.

'No,' I said. 'I guess not.'

We rode along in silence for a while. I noticed her handkerchief coming out of her purse occasionally as she blew her nose and occasionally dabbed at her eyes.

'I just want Larry to be happy,' she said.

'Then you're doing the right thing by helping us get to the bottom of this.'

'No. I just feel in my heart – I have for a long time – that there may be some awful secret lurking there in the past – '

'Don't be silly. You're Larry's mother – the only one he's ever known. He loves you. But this is just something he feels he has to know.'

'The only one who knew what is in that safe deposit box was Jack. He never told me. I never wanted to know. I still don't.'

As we pulled into the parking lot of the bank, I knew I was very close to holding in my hands a crucial piece of the puzzle, just as Lilyan Sloman was also holding my hand and very close to tears. We'd worked out a deal. She'd see that I got past the phalanx of bankers into the safe deposit vault without severe blows to anything but my ego. Then, when the vault clerk and I were safely within the holy of holies, each with our respective little keys, she would have the bank officer call a taxi and she would leave.

Like any adoptive mother who'd spent her life loving and raising a son, she probably felt she was close to losing a part of him forever to his 'real' mother. Like my own mother, who was no longer alive, she just wanted her son to be happy. Like any mother's son, I hugged Lilyan Sloman until the tears stopped flowing. Then we walked into the bank like Frank and Jesse James.

The vault teller, who held one of the two keys necessary to open any safe deposit box, was in an interesting position in life. He had the power to partially unlock your gold and silver, your most cherished possessions, the secrets of your honeymoon, and yet he could never luxuriate in that wealth, never have knowledge of those secrets. The key he held, I thought very fleetingly as he inserted it into the top of the box, might well be the key to happiness.

'Okay,' he said. 'Now you put yours in.'

'That's what she told me last night,' I said.

He made a forced, rather unpleasant twitch with his lips that looked like he might be experiencing gas. Then, with his key in the box and his power diminished, the energy seemed to flow out of his body and he quietly scuttled from the room. I was all alone with Ratso's past and quite possibly Ratso's future, and it seemed very damned eerie. The key in my hand felt like Benjamin Franklin had just tied it to the end of his kite. What the hell, I thought. I didn't come down here to shake hands with Donald Duck.

I opened the box.

FOURTEEN

As a friend of mine in Australia once put it: 'I was drier than a nun's nasty.' I was sitting at the counter of a little Cuban bar and restaurant somewhere along the way to the airport. In my coat pocket, next to what I sometimes liked to refer to as my heart, was a yellowed, rather innocuous-looking, sealed envelope that, if I didn't miss my bet, hadn't been opened in over forty-seven years. Anything that had waited that long could wait for me to have a drink.

The bar was kind of seedy and kind of empty but it looked like I felt. The music sounded like the kind Hank Williams might've played when he was hanging out with Jack Ruby in Havana in the days before he went to Jesus, and I do not mean that he joined a Christian fundamentalist cult. Aside from wearing white-man haters to a degree that would've made Frank Zappa proud, the Cubans have many other good qualities: they're passionate and fiery-tempered, they appreciate good cigars, and they always stock their bars with about ninety-seven different kinds of rum. I ordered a large neat glass of Mount Gay Rum and a Coca-Cola on the side in honor of Timothy B. Mayer, who first recognized the power and importance of separating the rum from the Coke. The drink was known as the Timster and the Timster himself drank a hell of a lot of Timsters with me before he, too, went to Jesus and I went back to Texas, which many New Yorkers consider to be almost as bad.

When the two glasses arrived I drank a little rum, a little Coke, a little rum, a little Coke, a little rum, a little Coke, until there was no rum left but still a lot of Coca-Cola. There will always be a lot of Coca-Cola in the world.

I told the bartender my glass was crying and he poured out another shot of Mount Gay. By this time I was feeling much better and had just about decided to slit open the envelope and then slit open Ratso's throat if it contained Jack Sloman's old collection of baseball cards.

I got out the envelope and set it down on the bar next to the glass of Mount Gay. It was a moment fraught with destiny, and I was the only one in the place who realized it. In fact, I was very damn near the only one in the place. The jukebox had suddenly gone autistic on me and the bartender had taken to swatting the occasional fly like the guy in *Casablanca* with the funny hat. Maybe it was the calm before the storm.

I picked up the envelope off the bar and my friend's fate was literally in my hands. A little rum, a little Coke, a little rum, a little Coke and I heard a voice sneaking up on me like a Miskito Indian and whispering in my ear. It sounded a lot like Lilyan Sloman. It said: 'I never wanted to know. I still don't.'

'You're right,' I said, as the bartender swatted a fly.

Then I heard another voice. It was kind of staticy and distant but not without certain natural elements of the ring of truth. An overseas call in a dream. It was the Timster's voice. It said: 'The envelope, please.'

'You're right, too,' I said, and I opened the envelope.

FIFTEEN

I was envisioning Stephanie DuPont bending over to feed the cat, the envelope was safely ensconced in my breast pocket, and I was dutifully watching for occasional weirdly placed signs depicting an aircraft taking off, when I picked up a Miskito Indian sneaking up in the rearview mirror of the rent-a-car. Upon closer inspection it looked like a krautmobile of some type but with all the four-wheeled penises out there today, it's hard to tell. As is often the case, it got bigger.

It stayed right behind me for three more pictures of airplanes taking off and I was starting to become mildly agitato. Two more pictures of airplanes and I was definitely not singing 'England Swings'. Driving a rent-a-car through a strange town and being closely tailed by a dangerous-looking, large, modern krautmobile with two sinister specimens lurking behind the windscreen was like a long-buried dream fragment from a troubled adolescence suddenly exploding and lodging itself in your skull-house. The krautmobile moved menacingly closer. I just caught a glimpse of the guy in the passenger seat playing with something in his lap. I doubted seriously if it was himself.

What would James Dean have done in a situation like this, I wondered? What would Jim Rockford do? What the hell was happening to me down here in the Land of My People? I instinctively patted the breast pocket of my coat. The envelope was still there. I shot another glance at the rearview. The krautmobile was still there, too. It had to be the envelope.

They wanted the envelope. Or else, and far worse, they wanted no one to know the information which it contained.

I cursed myself for letting the bright, mindless Florida sunshine lull me into being careless. The red flags had all been there and I must've thought it was a going-out-of-business sale. In a rather macabre fashion, maybe it was. I hadn't listened between the lines, apparently, to what both Rambam and Perkins had tried to tell me about this kind of investigation into the primeval. I'd forgotten about the guy in the black overcoat who'd tailed me in Brooklyn after I'd gotten the adoption papers from the warehouse. And what about Moie Hamburger, the son of the lawyer who'd arranged the deal, suddenly blipping off the screen? Maybe he was at the bottom of the East River right now with little gefilte fishes chasing one another through his eye sockets.

That's the way it happens, I thought, as I stared into the gaping mouth of an assault rifle that looked like it was ready to say *Ahhh*. You go on a short trip to help a friend and you leave your protective coat of good ol' New York paranoia behind. You look for answers and, incredibly enough, you even find them. Then the kraut car closes, then it pulls next to you, then the weapon rises into view like a daydream gone bad, and somewhere between the fun and the sun and the rum and the gun you follow that last airplane picture right up into the sky. A window seat to limbo if the Catholic Church is correct, where you fly a tight, tedious holding pattern through night and fog for at least a thousand years with a small Aryan child kicking the seat behind you, while next to you a fat man from Des Moines is locked in a hideous rictus of eternal vomiting upon the half-completed crossword puzzle that is all of our lives.

The other passengers to limbo, if the Catholic Church is correct, are non-baptized babies, all of whom cry incessantly for their mothers throughout the thousand-year vector. Whether said mothers are biological or adoptive raises an interesting legal point, for by the time the plane lands every family tree on earth has been totally defoliated and no one cares a thousand-year-old Chinese egg whether the sign on the terminal reads HEAVEN: NO SMOKING OR HELL: NOTHING TO DECLARE.

And then, lo and behold, a miracle had occurred. Traffic was suddenly slowing to a crawl and a Florida highway patrolman was stopping all cars beside a large sign that read: DRUG INTERDICTION CHECKPOINT AHEAD. I was so happy to have Big Brother watching over me I was about ready to hum a few bars of 'The Love Song of J. Edgar Hoover'. I stopped the rent-a-car and cautiously glanced over my shoulder.

There was a scurry of frenzied activity in the krautmobile now as it suddenly roared across the grass divider, performed a mud-slinging, gravel-gouging L.A. turn-around, and shot off in the opposite direction with several black-and-whites on its tail. The cavalry had arrived.

As for me, I exhibited the even-minded patience of the great Mahatma while the highway patrolman checked my driver's license and asked routine questions and a large German shepherd sniffed around the floorboards and the backseat area. I didn't mind. I had lots of time now. I also had the license plate number of the krautmobile just in case good German engineering carried the day.

While the highway patrol continued with their investigation, I realized with some little satisfaction that mine was in large part over. With the information I now had, the wrapping-it-up aspect should be child's play. Today would be an important day in the history of Larry 'Ratso' Sloman. The search for his mother, I felt, was all but over, along with the uncertainty, the insecurity, and the nagging doubt he'd carried with him most of his adult life. Quite literally, he was now a different man. And he didn't even know it yet.

I sat back in the driver's seat, lit up a cigar, and smiled through the open window at the nearby grove of citrus trees, the sun-dappled skyline, and the white gulls wheeling to and fro across the brush-stroke horizon of the kind of blue that seems to change ever so slightly in your imagination like half-remembered, half-closed eyes.

'You want to pop your trunk for us, sir?' the patrolman was saying.

'Well,' I said, 'there goes a hundred kilos of Peruvian marching powder.'

'We don't appreciate jokes about drugs, sir.'

'There's no drugs in the trunk,' I said, pushing the button that opened it. 'There's just my wife.'

'We don't appreciate jokes about that either,' he said, letting the 'sir' slide, and walking around to the back of the car.

A moment later he returned and waved me on my way, his face young, impassive, unsmiling, like a slightly bored eagle scout.

'Let me ask you one question, Officer,' I said. 'What kind of jokes do you guys appreciate?'

'Well,' he said, 'you're from New York. You wouldn't want to know about it.'

'I just live in New York. I'm actually from Texas.'

'Then you really wouldn't want to know about it,' he said.

SIXTEEN

An hour and a half later, from a pay phone at Miami International Airport, I called a familiar number in New York. I was delighted to find my party at home and to hear his rather raucous, rodent-like voice.

'Kinkstah!' Ratso shouted ebulliently. 'What'd you find, Kinkstah?'

'Hi, David,' I said.

There was an unusual, yet, under the circumstances, quite understandable silence on the other end of the blower. Then I heard a small, birdlike voice, in tone and timbre, possibly not terribly dissimilar to that of Ratso's father in the days before he died.

'David?' it said.

'David.'

'David,' said Ratso, still not sure he liked it. 'David.'

'Beats Goliath,' I said supportively.

'That's it? David?'

'No. There's more. Your full name is David Victor Goodman.'

'Jesus Christ.'

'I asked for it but they said that handle was taken.'

'And my mother – '

'Your mother's name was Mary Goodman. I don't know if she's still alive, but if she is, you could be meeting her soon. Of course, earlier this afternoon I didn't know if I'd still be alive to make this phone call.'

'Does Lilyan know?'

'No one knows but you and me and Mary Goodman.'

'I'm going to call Lilyan. I don't think I'll tell her yet. Just see how she's doing.'

'That'd be thoughtful,' I said. 'I wish I could call my mother, too. I just don't know the area code.'

'You talk to her more than you know, Kinkstah.'

'I hope to God you're right.'

'I'm always right,' said Ratso. 'Especially to have a friend like you.'

'Don't lay it on too thick,' I said, leaning away from the phone to check the departure board. When I put the blower next to my eardrum again Ratso was in the midst of some kind of frenetic Jewish Hare Krishna chant.

'Daaavid Victah Goodman! Daa-vid Vic-tah Goodman! DavidVictahGoodman!'

The thought of Ratso dancing around his cluttered apartment shouting his new name to the stuffed polar bear's head was enough to make me smile for a moment, which is something you don't see too often at Miami International Airport.

Sometimes good, solid amateur detective work can be its own reward. If Ratso's your client, of course, it's the only one you're probably ever going to get.

'Just think,' shouted Ratso. 'I might be Steve Goodman's twin brother, accidentally separated at birth!'

'Or you might be Benny Goodman's twin brother, accidentally separated at birth.'

'Or I might even be related to the Goodman of Goodman, Schwerner, and Cheney,' said Ratso.

Just in case you were jumping rope in the schoolyard at the time, or using rope for other purposes, Goodman, Schwerner, and Cheney were three young civil rights workers who were killed by the Klan in Mississippi in the early sixties. Cheney was black, but Goodman and Schwerner were two Jewish kids from Queens, where Ratso was from, who went down South in the cause of freedom and equality. Abbie Hoffman, too, was down in Mississippi at about that time, and the early civil rights movement, it should be noted, was generously infused with Jewish blood, if, indeed, there is such a thing. It should also be noted that good little white Christian church workers were few and far between at that particular place at that particular time. This is not really surprising, for the dangerous role of the troublemakers in history has often fallen to the Jewish people. Anne Frankly, it should be noted, in passing, that a great deal of good for the advancement of mankind has been accomplished between circumcision, where they cut off the tip of your dick, to crucifixion, where they throw the whole Jew away.

'It'd be an honor,' I said, 'to have been related to *that* Goodman.'

'The trouble is,' said Ratso, 'today most people probably think Goodman, Schwerner, and Cheney were a law firm.'

'Today,' I said, 'they probably would be a law firm. Besides, I'm going to miss my plane.'

'You know the Goodman I'd *really* like to be related to?'

said Ratso, totally oblivious of another American attempting to board an aircraft.

'I can't imagine,' I said, as I looked around nervously for the gate.

'The Goodman I'd *really* like to be related to – '

'Goddamn it, Ratso, spit it! I'm going to miss my plane.'

Ratso paused maddeningly. When he spoke again it was in a tone of great and careless dignity.

'It's just possible,' he said, 'that I'm an heir to the Goodman Egg Noodle fortune.'

There was nothing left to say. And, quite fortunately, there was no time left to say it.

SEVENTEEN

I goose-stepped to the gate just in time to hop a big silver bird flying North. I took an aisle seat somewhere in its lower intestine. It was time, I figured, as I went through the wheels-up experience, to stop patting myself on the back and start looking for Mary Goodman. Unfortunately, there were about 64 million Mary Goodmans on the East Coast. By the time I'd completed the laborious process of contacting all of them, Ratso would probably be in the Shalom Retirement Village himself, refusing to wear trousers and insisting others address him as Admiral Hornblower.

If baby Ratso had come through the offices of a Jewish adoption agency, as I now believed, the old files of temples and synagogues might be good places to start. Jews usually keep pretty methodical records. The Old Testament, which is, in large part, a somewhat glorified seed catalogue of who begat whom, who cast his seed upon the ground, and who merely coveted his neighbor's ass, has been around for thousands of years.

Now that we knew the name of the subject, we might be able to turn up an old address that could possibly be very helpful in running down her current whereabouts. Unless, of course, the building had become a state prison, a McDonald's, or a parking lot, or some other aspect of man's progress had taken place.

Kent Perkins, I remembered, had suggested I check the public library for old telephone directories from the forties. If that approach didn't work, he'd offered to get involved himself and try to locate her through CD-ROM, which was something I viewed almost as suspiciously as an Australian aboriginal might regard the little device you put inside your dumper that turns the water blue.

Of course, it would all be worth it if in the end we found Ratso's mother. Especially, I thought, if she turned out to be the Goodman of the Goodman Egg Noodle fortune. At least then, when it came time to send Ratso his bill, I might not find myself hosed to the barnyard door.

I drifted off into a fitful sleep and dreamed one of those ridiculous dreams that nobody pays any attention to because it often tells us a little more than we wish to know about ourselves. In the dream I was dressed in the same blue velvet housecoat that Robert Louis Stevenson had worn through a lifetime of ill health and convalescence. I was inside a huge mansion walking across miles and miles of bathroom tiles to open the front door. Behind me, in the glittering dining room, the Goodman Egg Noodle people were having a dinner party for the Rockefellers and the DuPonts. The entree, served, of course, upon a four-poster bed of Goodman's Egg Noodles, appeared to be a goose. When the servant, who looked very much like Supreme Court Justice Clarence 'Frogman' Thomas, cut the goose with a big, gleaming knife, inside the goose was a duck and inside the duck was a chicken, and inside the chicken was a pheasant, and inside the pheasant was a squab, and inside the squab was a quail.

I never found out what was inside the quail, because the knocking on the door grew louder and I had to go open it.

Outside in the snow was a man wearing a coonskin cap with the head of the animal attached to the front, its eyes sewn shut. He wore a pimp's flashy overcoat, a shirt that looked like it had once belonged to Engelbert Humperdinck, a pair of lox-colored pants, and red shoes that I intuitively knew had once been worn by someone who was no longer with us. He also wore a big, good-natured smile. As I ushered him to the table, no one appeared to take the slightest notice of his presence.

Suddenly, Mary Goodman, who strongly resembled Nancy Reagan auditioning for *Daughter of Dr Jekyll*, stood up and began emitting a strange Palestinian keening noise. The stranger looked at her with tragic, disbelieving eyes.

'Mom?' he said.

'We don't want him!' she screamed. 'Send him away!'

I ushered the pitiable creature back out into the snow. Before I closed the door, he turned and put his hand on my shoulder.

'Thanks a lot for helping me, pal,' he said. His eyes swirled like little sad Jacuzzis.

As he walked away I noticed that he was wearing the Robert Louis Stevenson coat and I was now attired in the formal outfit of a butler. I felt guilty, but I didn't know the nature of the crime. All I knew was I was the butler and I'd done it. I woke from the dream to find a small Aryan child kicking the back of my seat.

The rest of the flight, as they say, was uneventful. It was late by the time I got into the city, but the night was clear and a silver sliver of moon was playing hide-and-seek with me between the skyscrapers. The air felt even colder than when I'd left, but it could've been nerves. Coming back to New York is almost as hard as leaving it.

The cab spit me out at 199B Vandam Street. I paid the driver, got my suitcase out of the trunk, and let myself in through the big metal door of the old converted warehouse. I took the freight elevator up to the fourth floor and was just crossing the dusty little hallway to the door of my loft when it suddenly opened.

Stephanie DuPont stood framed in the doorway and I knew right away that something was amiss. Tall, strong, beautiful women seem to collapse into little girls faster than anyone else when something is seriously wrong. I could see it in her eyes, in her hands, and certainly in the way she threw her arms around me and practically pulled me into the room.

My first thought was that something had happened to the cat. But the cat was sleeping on my desk under her sunlamp.

'You got a call just a moment ago,' Stephanie said, in a voice I almost didn't recognize. 'I heard it on the machine. A police detective – Cooperman, I think. He said it was urgent, so I picked up the phone. He said he was at the apartment and you should get over there now – '

'Where? What apartment?'

'I don't want to be the one to tell you,' she whispered like a child. Her hand reached up to smooth her hair and her hand was shaking. I grabbed the hand and held it tight.

'What did he say?'

'It's your friend Ratso,' she said. 'He was murdered tonight.'

EIGHTEEN

Robert Louis Stevenson, during his extended stay in the South Seas, grew to love the Polynesian people, and came to believe they were the brightest, happiest, most beautiful race to populate the earth since the ancient Greeks. Stevenson felt that the white man had cut short their cultural progress before the Polynesians were able to come forth with their own Homer and their own Socrates. He wrote many letters to the Queen and the British High Commissioner on behalf of his friend Mataafa and his followers, never realizing that the British, the Germans, and the Americans had already divided up Samoa amongst themselves and sealed its fate forever.

Many years later, Don Ho echoed Stevenson's hopes for the people of the South Seas and described how he felt those hopes had been dashed in large part by the American missionaries. 'The missionaries told the people,' said Ho, 'to bow their heads and pray. By the time they looked up, their land was gone.'

Now, as I gazed numbly out of the window of the cab, I knew in my heart that a great many pieces of my life were gone, too. The South Seas of Robert Louis Stevenson were merely a divertive device to temporarily keep the tragic chords of truth from coming back, dull and relentless, as if I were a child all dressed up and trying to understand my first funeral.

As we turned off West Broadway onto Prince Street I saw the plain-wrapped squad cars and the meat wagon, sometimes referred to as 'Hamburger Helper', parked in front of Ratso's building. They looked like dim mechanical sharks hovering in a circle of gloom.

'If this is a movie,' I said, 'I want my money back.'

The driver gave me a shopworn smile. 'That'll be four dollars and seventy-five cents,' he said.

I paid him with my subconscious mind and got out of the hack. I stood for a moment on the curb and looked at Ratso's street in the cold and crystal-clear lamplight, and time seemed suspended, as if I were standing inside a historical tableau waiting for a man with a candle to stumble in or three wise guys or somebody who'd come to bury Caesar. Maybe that was my job, I thought.

For the next few hours I only recalled certain images, as if God had significantly reduced the wattage of my powers of observation until all of life was no more than a child's kaleidoscope on a gloomy day. If there was a God. Not only was my visual prowess somewhat impaired, but I kept hearing Robert Louis Stevenson's 'Requiem' inside my head. The poem marks Stevenson's grave on top of Mount Vaea in Samoa. How it got itself over to New York so fast and inside my head was a mystery to me. Possibly it had traveled along the Road of the Loving Hearts.

> *Under the wide and starry sky.*
> *Dig the grave and let me lie.*

He certainly wasn't writing about New York, I thought, as I mumbled my name to a uniform at the door of the building and he nodded me in. Ratso's bum was nowhere to be seen. Handouts were going to be harder now.

> *Glad did I live and gladly die*
> *And I laid me down with a will.*

Where there's a will, there's a lawyer, I thought as I walked through the hallway and waited for the little elevator. Only I didn't know where the hell the lawyer was. I just knew that he figured into all of this and all of this figured into all of whatever I was about to see upstairs.

The elevator came and I got aboard. It was a sad little elevator in a sad little world and it needed to go a lot higher than the sixth floor or a lot lower than the lobby, I reckoned, if it was ever going to catch up with Ratso.

The sixth floor was swarming with cops. Cops in uniform, plainclothes dicks, techs, good cops, bad cops, all with something slightly predatory or worse glinting deep behind their eyes as they moved to the ever-popular music of murder. Whether their job was wrapping up bundles of blood and gore into body bags and tossing them into meat wagons or lurking in some godforsaken hallway in the early hours of the dawn, drinking black coffee from Styrofoam cups, they liked their work. There's nothing wrong with a cop being a cop. It's just the way of their people. I took a hard right at the elevator and walked down the little hallway until I reached Ratso's door. It was open. No reason for him to ever triple-lock it again.

> *This be the verse you grave for me:*
> *Here he lies where he longed to be;*

Ratso was lying face down on the floor. A small wading pool of semi-coagulated blood was all around the upper half of his body. It was the color of pink horseradish.

A photographer and some other kind of technician were still futzing around with his body. Taking pictures of his garish outfit. A nice close-up of the red antique shoes he was wearing that had once belonged to a dead man. Now they had walked full circle.

> *Home is the sailor, home from the sea,*
> *And the hunter home from the hill.*

Detective Sergeant Fox and a cop I didn't know were at Ratso's little desk riffling through his phone book and bank statements and listening to his answering machine. 'Where are you?' a rather seductive female voice was asking. 'I've been waiting here at the Pink Pussycat for over two hours.' Fox chuckled to himself.

I looked up and saw Sergeant Mort Cooperman standing by the windows beside the statue of the Virgin Mary. They both looked grim. Cooperman shook his head at me sadly and shrugged a cop shrug. The Virgin Mary looked right at me and didn't say a thing. She'd seen it all before.

'Don't look at his face, Tex,' said Cooperman. 'He's not ready for his close-up yet.'

There was an uncomfortable silence. I continued staring at the Virgin Mary. One of us was bound to blink soon.

'If it's any consolation,' Cooperman said, 'he was dead before he hit the floor.'

'Some guys have all the luck,' I said.

NINETEEN

It is a rather ironic fact, but those familiar with the world of crime will swear that it's true. When no killer and no weapon are found at the scene, the murderer most often turns out to be the person closest to the victim in life – the spouse, the best friend, the family member, the person who called the police in the first place or possibly helped in some way with the investigation. While every cop knows this and it may make a good rule of thumb in crime solving, it does represent somewhat of a spiritual indictment of the human race. In other words, to know us is to love us. Maybe it is that we've just never been very good at one-on-one.

It was not surprising, therefore, that despite Cooperman's ostensibly sympathetic approach to the questioning, he nonetheless regarded me as a primary suspect. I was in a state of cultural mayonnaise at the time, and this was not improved by my witnessing Ratso being taken away in a body bag. One of the best friends I'd ever had was suddenly, surreally, worm bait, and now Cooperman and I were sitting on this rather sordid sofa conversing like two Chinese towkays haggling over the price of fish maws.

Strangely enough, I remember our conversation quite clearly, almost like clinical recall. Cooperman was smoking a Gauloise and lighting it with a Zippo and a vulture-like twist of his thick neck. I was smoking a cigar and lighting it with a kitchen match and a prayer. The smoke along with the Virgin Mary being there reminded me somehow of incense. If incense was supposed to spiritually cleanse a place, I remember thinking it had better get on the stick.

The dull grief that was beginning to manifest itself in my heart soon drove the Requiem for Ratso verses out of my head. And in some dark train yard of my brain, I suppose a coupling was already taking place between Ratso's murder and the now seemingly rather pointless search for his mother. Whether the two were connected I couldn't say for sure, but Cooperman was having none of it. He started the grilling off in his own inimitable, blunt, straight-ahead style. For matters of brevity, I've recorded only a small portion of our conversation here.

'Did Ratso own a sawed-off?'

'A sawed-off what?'

'Shotgun.'

'Not to my knowledge.'

'Do you own a sawed-off shotgun, Tex?'

'Not to my knowledge.'

'I thought all you cowboys rode horses and carried guns.'

'I don't have a gun and I only ride two-legged animals.'

'When was the last time you talked to your buddy?'

'Earlier this evening. I called him around seven from the Miami airport.'

'And you were down there looking for – '

'Ratso's birth mother. His adoptive father had died recently – '

'Did you find his mother?'

'No. But I learned her name. Mary Goodman.' Here Cooperman jotted down a little note on his pad.

'How did Ratso sound when you talked to him?'

'Excited. He thought he'd soon be meeting his real mother.'

'Maybe he already has.'

'Maybe.'

Cooperman killed his cigarette and promptly lit another one. I dropped a Clarence Darrow-sized ash in the little ashtray. I looked up at the photo of Ratso meeting Nixon. Ratso with Bob Dylan. Who was going to finish the Abbie Hoffman book now? I wondered. Ratso'd only been working on it for five years. Of course, he could interview Abbie himself now. That would be a scoop.

'Did he ever get into arguments, say, over matters of money or women?'

'Yes and yes.'

'Start with money. When'd he have an argument about money?'

'Every time he ever got out of a cab.'

'I see.'

'No you don't. The guy had fishhooks in his pockets. The whole time I've known him I don't think he's ever picked up the check. But this is not the kind of behavior that causes your piece to be taken off the board. Maybe it was just a basic form of neurotic Judaism in action. At heart, and in life, however, Ratso was always a man of very generous spirit. One of the kindest, most gentlehearted people I've ever known.'

'Then why does somebody ice him?' Cooperman glared at me. I looked around the room for help.

'I don't know. Ask Nixon why he went along with Watergate. Ask Bob Dylan why he wrote "Mr Tambourine Man". Ask Abbie Hoffman why he videotaped his vasectomy.'

'I'm asking you.'

'And I'm telling you the only thing I can think of that makes any sense. Somebody killed him because he and I were getting close to finding his real mother.'

Cooperman gave me a tired smile. I gave him a tired smile. I was so emotionally spindled and mutilated that I was ready to accept any social intercourse I could get.

'Let me give you some advice,' said Cooperman. 'Leave the involved plots and the conspiracy theories to the Hollywood screenwriters. When this murder is solved – and it will be – it'll be a lot simpler than that and a lot closer to home. Now what about broads? He did have broads in his life, didn't he?'

'How'd you think this couch got skid-marks on it?'

'I'm gonna want the names of all his women for the past five years.'

'That's easy. Go down to the Monkey's Paw and look on the wall of the men's dumper. Anyway, you're not suggesting a woman came in here and Sam Cooked him with a sawed-off shotgun?'

'No. A man did that. The door was forced, by the way. But that don't mean some skirt didn't have it in for Ratso. Could've hired somebody to come in here and terminate him.'

I was starting to feel a physical pain in my head and my gut as the time ticked ruthlessly by and Ratso didn't walk back in and turn on a hockey game.

'I'd like to hire somebody,' I said, 'to come in here and terminate this conversation.'

'You just did,' said Cooperman, standing up and stretching his back. 'That's the crummiest sofa I've ever sat on in my life.'

'Try sleeping on it.'

'Try not leaving town,' he said, and he walked over to confer with Fox.

TWENTY

The death of someone close to you is never as much fun as it's cracked up to be. I should know. I've been to that rodeo on a handful of occasions and every time you get thrown it gets a little bit harder for you to pick up your hat and dust it off. In fact, four cigars and half a bottle of Jameson later, at three-thirty in the morning, as I sat at my desk in the loft playing solitaire with Ratso's adoption papers, I still was having a hell of a time believing what I'd seen with my own eyes.

I poured another shot of Jameson into the old bullhorn and watched my watch wind its world-weary way to a quarter to four. It was a death watch and it didn't really give a damn about anything but methodically monitoring the seconds, minutes, and hours of all our lives. Of moments, it knew nothing. Wristwatches were always like that, I thought. Emotionless, expressionless little faces forever keeping themselves an arm's length away from your heart.

'Next time I'll get a sundial,' I said to the cat.

The cat said nothing but sat on the desk rather protectively close to me. Through some ancient feline sonar she had perhaps sensed another sea change in my heart. She'd weathered this sort of situation before and appeared to be battening down the hatches for whatever came next. If the cat had known that it was Ratso who'd gone to Jesus, I wouldn't like to predict what she might've done. Probably she'd have donned a long, green leprechaun's cap, picked up a fiddle, and danced a jig from one red telephone to the other until the cows came home, which, in New York City, could take a while. Cats, however, like humans, can never be sure for whom the bell tolls. Unlike humans, they are usually too polite to ask.

I lifted the old bullhorn toward the living room and the old couch where Ratso had stayed when he'd been a housepest at the loft. I recited the last verse from the poem Breaker Morant had written in his cell on April 19, 1902, the night before his execution.

> *Let's toss a bumper down our throat,*
> *Before we pass to Heaven,*
> *And toast: 'The trim-set petticoat*
> *We leave behind in Devon.'*

I included Breaker's last words that he shouted at the British firing squad: 'Shoot straight, you bastards!'

I killed the shot, listened hopefully for the lesbian dance class, which wasn't there, puffed on the cigar for a while, and killed that, too. Then I killed the light and went to bed. It was enough killing for one day.

The sandman, it seemed, was on sabbatical and that gave me no choice but to painfully toss and turn the sad situation over in my aching mind. I did not agree with Cooperman that a 'trim-set petticoat' was responsible for Ratso's death. Nor did I believe he'd been whacked in a feud or argument over money, though I'd felt like killing him myself on several occasions for just that same reason. It was possible that money or a woman figured into it, I thought, but not as simply or as neatly as Cooperman seemed to suspect. Whoever the agent of Ratso's death was, I strongly believed he'd been set in motion forty-seven years ago, and there were only two people I could possibly think of who might be able to tell me why. Moie Hamburger and Mary Goodman. Both, unfortunately, did not appear to be eager to answer my knock on their doors of perception.

I would find Mary Goodman, I thought, if for no other reason than to tell her that her son had been looking for her. It was the least I could do for Ratso. It was the least I could do for myself. I fell asleep to the stained-glass glare of a streetlight inexorably turning red, green, yellow, and red again, like so many Popsicle saints and jukebox witches burning in the Dark Ages of the heart.

Just before dawn I began to hear a noise like a giant locust inside my pillow. In a moderately brain-dead state I collared the bedside blower and yanked it over to what I believed was my head.

'This is the AT&T operator,' said a female voice. 'You have a collect call.'

'Who's calling, operator?'

'David Victor Goodman,' she said.

TWENTY-ONE

When I heard the rather distinctive voice of the caller powering over the blower, I knew I'd either gone to Jesus myself or Ratso was still malingering somewhere along this mortal coil. As it became increasingly apparent that Ratso was yet among us I found myself torn simultaneously between the equally compelling twin desires of jumping for joy and killing his ass again.

'Kinkstah!' he shouted. 'Kinkstah!'

'This better be good,' I said grimly, though I must confess a virtual tidal bore of relief was washing over me. In spite of the fact that it was 5:30 A.M. and I was attempting rather unsuccessfully to disentangle my Borneo sarong from a monstro morning erection, I let out with a well-modulated Texas whoop and attempted to scoop up the cat, which irritated her no end; she stalked out of the bedroom like a disdainful lover. Of course the cat wasn't my lover. Things weren't that bad. Yet.

'I've got a problem, Kinkstah,' Ratso was saying.

'I've got one, too,' I said.

'I'm up here in Woodstock and my old friend Jack Bramson is staying at my apartment. You've met Jack, haven't you?'

'Not formally.'

'Well, he's a good guy but he's not all that reliable, if you know what I mean. Now he's not picking up the phone and my answering machine's fucked-up. I ask him to look after the place for a few days and he can't even do that.'

'Maybe you're being too hard on him.'

'Well, somebody's been fucking with my answering machine – '

'At least it's safe sex – '

'I call my number, nobody answers, and my message isn't on the machine.'

'Why does everything have to have a message these days?'

'Anyway, if you don't mind, Kinkstah, I'd like you to go over today and check the machine.'

'No can do, Rat.'

'What do you mean? After all I've done for you? I helped you find your fucking girlfriend. I helped you find that fucking cat. I helped you find the fucking Nazi – '

'What more could a fellow ask?'

'I'm serious, Kinkstah. C'mon. I'm expecting some important calls. If Jack's there, tell him you talked to me and he'll let you in. If Jack's out, buzz the super's office and he'll give you a key.'

'Jack's out,' I said.

Once I'd laid it out for him, so to speak, it hadn't taken Ratso long to grasp the significance of the events of the previous night. His friend Jack Bramson, who resembled Ratso fairly closely in body type (what McGovern occasionally referred to as 'middle-aged Jewish meatball'), had been traveling rather light and had borrowed some of Ratso's wardrobe, which further increased the similarity. Bramson had been in the wrong place at the wrong time or, from Ratso's viewpoint, no doubt, in the right place at the right time, because if he hadn't been there Ratso at this writing would surely be shaking hands with the devil, and I do not mean urinating.

The fact that the killer had broken into the place with the express purpose of icing Ratso had not been lost upon him. He also appeared to be taking in my solemn imprecations that his life would be in grave danger once the mistake was discovered and that some careful plotting on both of our parts would be required to prevent the abrupt shortening of his life span. He still felt, however, that it was just as possible that someone wanted to unplug Jack Bramson as himself. Bramson, according to Ratso, had managed to irritate a goodly number of people in the short expanse of his star-crossed life. I didn't mention it, but Ratso, from time to time, had been rather facile at getting up a lot of people's sleeves, as well. One of those sleeves was mine.

Before I cradled the blower, I'd been able to extract a promise from Ratso that he'd stay in Woodstock until I could convince Cooperman that rumors of his death were greatly exaggerated. It worried me a bit that both Cooperman and Ratso did not share my belief that the investigation into Ratso's adoption had triggered the murder. Maybe I'd overidentified with my field of study a bit and Bramson's death was a separate matter. I certainly hoped so. Otherwise, finding Mary Goodman could become quite unpleasant.

At least Ratso was alive, I thought. Now if I could keep him that way long enough to locate his mother, I damned sure planned to turn the job over to her. For despite his outward show of bravado, I could hear in the timbre of his voice that grief and fear were lurking in the wings, and in the troubled days ahead I wasn't going to have a hell of a lot of time to hold his hand.

'You might call Lilyan in Florida,' I said. 'Before Cooperman calls her.'

'Why would he do that?'

'Because he thinks you're dead.'

'For a dead man, I took a pretty healthy dump this morning.'

'You might just keep that one to yourself,' I said.

'I have *kept* it to myself, Kinkstah,' said Ratso, with no small pride of accomplishment. 'For *four* whole days!'

TWENTY-TWO

The next thing on my agenda that morning, after feeding the cat and performing various personal ablutions, was the rather tricky task of calling Cooperman. Cops were funny creatures.

Once they'd discovered the victim and set out on the trail of the perpetrator, they very much preferred that the victim stay dead. Cops weren't the only ones who felt this way, granting, of course, that cops felt anything. Even those of us on the peripheries of the crime-solving community shared the quite natural proclivity of desiring our worm bait to remain worm bait and not go through any complicating identity problems, sex changes, or midlife crises.

This particular problem had come very close to home with me not so long ago in a case that McGovern had aptly dubbed 'Musical Chairs'. In this decidedly convoluted adventure, the victim stubbornly refused to remain the victim, and this rather niggling recalcitrance on his part created no end of tedium for the investigator, who, unfortunately, was me. As a result, I now found myself in a position the likes of which I'd never before known in my life. I empathized with Cooperman.

I made some coffee, putting a small bit of eggshell in with the grinds as was the habit of my old pal Tom Baker. This little ritual not only enriched the flavor of the coffee but it strongly brought back an aura of the Bakerman, possibly an aura of an era. It was a strange and young and hopeful time full of rainy mornings, sunny days, and nights so grainy and raw and mystical you felt you were living inside some old French movie. Heroes, it seemed, were close enough to be your friends. Today they seem very far away. In fact, if you want to meet a real hero these days you have to find him somewhere along a dusty dream trail, evanescent as childhood, fragile as the eggshells in your coffee.

By the time I got around to calling Cooperman, the garbage trucks were grumbling, the pigeons were on the wing, the commuters had crawled through all their tunnels, and the detective sergeant himself was already out someplace in the city hot on the track of Ratso's killer. I left word with the desk sergeant for Cooperman to call me when he checked in. I had some new information on the case. That was the way I left it and it was a good thing, because when Cooperman found out I'd had a conversation with his latest murder victim the morning after the murder, he was not going to be a happy little New Yorker.

As the morning wore on, the lesbian dance class cranked up directly above my slight hangover and Stephanie DuPont called at almost precisely the same time, which I took to be a good sign. She told me how sorry she was about the death of my friend and I told her that he wasn't really a friend, just a friend of a friend but the cops didn't know it yet so don't say anything to anyone, especially Pyramus and Thisbe. They'd yap it all over the neighborhood. I also told her that I couldn't say too much about the whole matter because it was getting extremely dangerous and I didn't want to drag her into it. This, of course, whetted her appetite enormously for additional information and I finally got off by promising to tell her more that evening over a couple of big, hairy steaks. Nothing like a little murder to improve your social life.

By Gary Cooper time I was beginning to experience a rather abnormal emotional state, the psychological term for which is the Swiss cheese effect. I could not remember important things like calling Sergeant Cooperman again or finding Mary Goodman before some homo erectus with a ski mask and a sawed-off shotgun found Ratso or myself. All my mind seemed to retain were trivial images floating by in a soup of the past. The cat vomiting into a carved meerschaum pipe of JFK's head, a beautiful girl in an almost empty Chinese restaurant lifting a peach-colored dress up to her waist to prove she was a true blonde (she was), Waylon Jennings pulling up in a long black limo as I was walking to the laundromat in Nashville in some other lifetime and saying: 'Get in. Walkin's bad for your image.'

Very possibly, my little trip to Florida combined with the rather hideous events of the previous night were creating a belated strain on my brain. With a conscious effort I took leave of my dawdling daydreams long enough to call Kent Perkins's answering machine in L.A. I told the machine my troubles. I related to it the latest wrinkles in the investigation. I said that I'd like for Kent to get his large, luminous buttocks out of the hot tub as soon as possible before this whole thing fell apart like a matzo ball in the rain. The machine took it all in understandingly and I felt better about myself and my life. Maybe I was just tired. I hadn't had a good night's sleep in about forty years and perhaps it was catching up with me. I crashed on the couch with the cat.

When I awoke, the sky was rather noticeably darker and the telephones were rather noticeably ringing. I navigated my way through the semi-gloom to the desk and picked up the blower on the left.

'Start talkin',' I said.

'Mit – Mit – Mit!!' said McGovern, invoking our oft-used code for the Man in Trouble hotline we'd devised when the body of a man who'd been dead for six months had been found in his Chicago apartment. Calling each other fairly regularly in this manner was merely a way to make sure that McGovern and I were both alive. So far, so good.

'Mit,' I responded rather grudgingly.

'You heard about Ratso?' he said breathlessly.

'No, but I heard that my three-year-old nephew David bit a woman on the ass in a shoe store yesterday in Silver Spring, Maryland.'

McGovern plowed doggedly on. I lit a cigar and wished I could see McGovern's face.

'Ratso's been murdered,' he said.

'Don't believe everything you read in the papers.' I laughed heartily. McGovern sounded thunderstruck.

'It's not in the papers yet. I'm just working on the story now. Wait a minute, Kinkster! What do you know that you aren't telling me?'

'I saw the body last night. Very convincing. Fooled me, in fact. But it wasn't Ratso. It was a Ratso impersonator. Friend of his who happened to be staying there for the weekend. Ratso's alive and well and just as obnoxious as ever.'

'This changes the story.'

'Yes, and if you'll help me, I might like to change it some more.'

Keeping things strictly off the record, I told McGovern about Ratso's new identity as David Victor Goodman and about my preparing to embark upon the search for Mary Goodman. I also told him that in the very near future his help might become essential in finding Ratso's mother if other methods didn't prove successful.

'It's great to feel needed,' he said.

'Now tread carefully with this story. No mention of anything to do with the adoption investigation, and remember, the cops may still not know that the victim wasn't Ratso.'

'That's what we members of the fifth estate like to refer to as a scoop.'

'Maybe next time Cooperman will return my phone calls. I may want to assemble the Village Irregulars on this one. Of course, Downtown Judy's gone, Rambam's out of the country, and Ratso's going to have to keep a rather low profile for a while.'

'That doesn't leave much. And I wish, just between us girls, that you'd think twice about continuing to look for Ratso's mother. Obviously, the guy thought he was killing Ratso. Next time he might think he's killing you. Remind me not to borrow your cowboy hat.'

'I told Ratso I'd find his mother.'

'But things have turned deadly now,' said McGovern with compassion in his voice. 'Why do you have to be involved personally? Why can't you turn it all over to the cops? Why do you always have to stir things up?'

I puffed patiently on the cigar and thought about why I always had to stir things up. It was a good question. It was also a good cigar.

'The answer is simple,' I told McGovern, 'but the way I

247

feel was described more eloquently by Gustave Flaubert over a hundred years ago. Flaubert said: "I feel very old sometimes. I carry on and would not like to die before having emptied a few more buckets of shit on the heads of my fellow men." '

'Maybe I *will* borrow your cowboy hat,' said McGovern.

TWENTY-THREE

Keeping information from a woman who wants to know, especially when that woman looks like Stephanie DuPont, is harder than Japanese arithmetic. So, by the time the waiter at the Derby had brought the first bottle of Château de Cat Piss, I was already spilling it, so to speak. Maybe I just wanted to hear myself tell the whole story again to see if there was something I'd missed. I hoped to hell there was, because – short of finding Mary Goodman – there was almost nothing I could do but wait around for the bad guys to realize they'd screwed up and to take another shot at it. 'It' being Ratso or myself.

This, I reflected, was an extremely daunting and dangerous position to be in. Almost as daunting and dangerous as looking across the candlelight at Stephanie DuPont.

'It seems crazy,' said Stephanie, 'to go after the mother after all this time when you could be going after that lawyer. That lawyer sounds suspish. I'm going to law school myself in a couple years, you know.'

'I'll bet I know why you're going to law school,' I said. 'You can't stand the sight of blood.'

'What I can't stand the sight of is that hairball on your lower lip. Get rid of it, Friedman.'

I poured us both another glass of wine and I noticed the

waiter standing silently above the table like a well-dressed hovercraft.

'What was that lawyer's name?' asked Stephanie.

'Hamburger.'

'And for the lady?' said the waiter.

'No, no,' I said. 'There's been a terrible misunderstanding. Hamburger's the lawyer who is, no doubt, at this very moment plotting to kill all of us. But before he does I'd like to order two big, hairy steaks. Medium rare okay, Stef?'

'Yes, schmuck-head,' she said, giggling like the schoolgirl that, I suppose, she very nearly was.

'That's Lord Schmuck-head, to you,' I said. Some day I would write a scholarly dissertation comparing why beautiful young girls call middle-aged men disrespectful names with why dogs lick their testicles. Both do it, of course, because they can. If you're the middle-aged man there's nothing you can do but take it in stride and not let it get your goat. Your goat, no doubt, wouldn't want to be disturbed. He's probably very busy licking his testicles.

'Okay,' said Stephanie, 'let's see where we are. Cooperman hasn't called you back and probably still thinks Ratso's dead.'

'That's correct.'

'Ratso's still hiding out in Woodstock so he won't *get* dead.'

'That's correct.'

'And you're sitting on your Hebe ass waiting for your friend Kent Perkins to come to New York and help you find Mary Goodman.'

'That's technically correct. Just like Jesus reportedly told the Mexicans, "Don't do anything until I get back", Kent told me not to poke around looking for Mary Goodman until he gets here. It could create a hot file and alert the wrong people.'

' "Hot file",' she said, laughing. 'I love the way you big private dicks talk.'

'Careful,' I said, 'you may have to eat those words.'

'Friedman,' she said warningly.

It was another facet of the beautiful young girl-middle-aged man scenario. The young girl's language could make a television evangelist blush and it was quite acceptable. The middle-aged man had to be forever on guard against a possible nuance or double entendre that might offend the beautiful young thing's ear. This made, occasionally, for some rather one-sided conversations, but it's been that way since Adam and Eve and Samson and Delilah and it's getting a little late in the game to try to make a rule change now.

'Now just why,' she said, pausing to acknowledge the arrival of the big, hairy steaks, 'do you hold this Kent Perkins in such high regard?'

'Well, for one thing he's a working, licensed private investigator, unlike myself.'

'Who would've guessed?'

'For another, he's an old friend. He's also Ruth Buzzi's husband.'

Stephanie DuPont laughed for a very long time. She laughed so hard there were tears in her eyes. The wine and the candlelight made them look like blue windows in the summer rain.

'What's wrong with being Ruth Buzzi's husband?' I said at last.

'Nothing,' she said. 'It's wonderful. He can stake out the set of Sesame Street.'

'Kent does know a lot about these kinds of investigations. He says you can find anybody if you look hard enough. Claims it's like following a jungle trail and looking for signs – marriages, divorces, illnesses, job changes, voting records, traffic tickets. The skill is in getting strangers to open those records for you. He says he often tells bureaucrats he's a Mormon student checking out his family's genealogy. That way they don't get their antennas up and shut down on him.'

'That's funny,' said Stephanie. 'You don't look like a Mormon student.'

'Kent Perkins says all we need to do is check back to the

1940s and find her date of birth, her social security number, and, if possible, her last known address. With that information he can track her down easily.'

'With that information Pyramus and Thisbe could track her down.'

For a while we both concentrated on the dissection procedures attendant to the meal. As Bob Dylan once said: 'A lot of people got a lot of knives and forks on their tables. They gotta cut something.' It might as well, I figured, be a big, hairy steak. That, very likely, wasn't what Bob had meant, but of course that was always open to interpretation.

'This big, hairy steak is really killer bee,' I said. 'Almost as good as Joe's Jefferson Street Café in Kerrville, Texas.'

'I wouldn't know,' she said.

Possibly, I gazed at Stephanie's eyes a little too long or a little too longingly, but if I did, she didn't seem to notice. Anyway, I like a girl with a good appetite. Evidently, she had one, because it wasn't long before we'd dusted off the big hairies, the waiter'd brought out the dessert menus, and Stephanie was back to badgering me about the investigation.

'So what *are* you going to do until Kent Perkins arrives?'

'I've been thinking a lot about tying a little red bandanna around the cat's neck and taking her out to Central Park to play Frisbee.'

Stephanie snorted a tired, cynical snort. It's extremely difficult for a woman to snort in an attractive fashion, but there was something so primitive in that simple display that it seemed downright sexy. Maybe I was reading too much into it, but she appeared capable of simultaneous sensuality, sophistication, and earthiness and you don't see that every day even in New York. To find those qualities you usually have to look at three different people, and even then, some of them might require a stunt man.

'Okay,' I said, 'I had an idea on the plane coming back from Florida that I might check with some temples and synagogues here in the city. Maybe we can find a Mary Goodman somewhere in their old files.'

'Yeah,' said Stephanie, 'that Mormon missionary shit's really gonna fly big time with some little old rabbi on Long Island.'

'I'll alter the approach slightly,' I said. 'I'll say I'm from the Church of the Latter-Day Businessman.'

Stephanie smiled very briefly and turned her attention to the waiter, who'd materialized again to take our dessert orders.

'How's the cream brûlée?' I asked. The waiter nodded approvingly. Stephanie continued to study her menu.

'You know,' I said, 'I'm somewhat of an expert on cream brûlée. I've ordered it in Houston, I've ordered it in Paris, I've ordered it in Melbourne, Australia. I've even had cream brûlée crossing the Atlantic Ocean on the *QEII*.'

There was a bit of a silence as both Stephanie and the waiter looked at me. Then they looked at each other. Then Stephanie shook her head slightly and gave a small, dry laugh.

'Maybe if you traveled a little further,' she said, 'you'd learn that it's pronounced *crème* brûlée.'

TWENTY-FOUR

No one has ever won a waiting game. This was the thought that was in my head when I woke up late the next morning with the cat sleeping on my face and my old Borneo sarong twisted tightly into a rather unpleasant tourniquet around my scrotum. When I'd finally become a homo erectus, fed the cat, made some coffee, lit my first cigar of the morning, and tried to decide whether or not to change the cat litter, it was half past Gary Cooper time and way past time to sit down at my desk and do some cold, deductive, Sherlockian thinking.

I had several crucial executive decisions to make which might have far-reaching repercussions that could impact significantly upon my life, that of my cat, and that of my client in, of course, a random and haphazard order. The cat and the coffee were both sitting on the desk and the smoke from the cigar was filtering upward toward the lesbian dance class, which, I noticed, sounded like it had turned on the juice and cut the damned thing loose. The board meeting was ready to come to order. It was fortunate, I reflected, that I didn't have any stockholders.

According to Anthony Robbins, the California motivational guru, making a decision – any decision – is one of the most important things you can do in your life – eating, sleeping, hosing, dumping, belching, and dying, presumably notwithstanding. Stephanie DuPont, who I once heard refer to Robbins as 'that horse-faced nerd who's sucking everybody dry', also puts great stock in decision-making. The truth is, if you don't make decisions for yourself, one of these days fate will come along and pluck you up by your pretty little neck. Unfortunately, if you *do* make decisions, fate will also come along and pluck you up by your pretty little neck. The wisest thing to do is to behave in a decisive manner while assiduously avoiding making any real decisions. That way everyone will respect you enormously until fate comes along and plucks you up by your pretty little neck and everyone claims it was your fault.

'As chief executive,' I said, 'I now bring this meeting to order.'

The cat looked at me with that fabled curiosity almost totally absent from her eyes. The coffee cup continued to send particles of steam toward the ceiling. The cigar also plumed a small bluish-white column ever upward like smoke from a little Mary Poppins chimney. On the rooftop, as fate would have it, were a large group of long-legged young women, many of whom were somewhat confused about their sexuality, and all of whom had fallen under the Sapphic spell of Winnie Katz. They had so little regard for men that they were no doubt oblivious to the fact that one floor below them an important board meeting was taking place.

'Gentlemen,' I said to the cat, who blinked several times rather indignantly, 'today we have a vital decision to make. There are three possible courses of action, only one of which do we have the time, energy, and manpower to pursue. Each of the three potential courses of action has its own compelling reason for why we should devote our full attention to it. The decision, gentlemen, is up to us.'

I paused here for dramatic effect and gazed purposefully about the boardroom. The cat had gone to sleep on her back with all four paws in the air. The coffee was no longer steaming. The cigar was out. Only the lesbian dance class seemed to maintain its thunder from above, as it probably would for all eternity. Unfazed by any distractions or disappointments, I finished my speech in unfaltering, decisive tones.

'Today, gentlemen, we must decide whether to go after the lawyer, whether to go after Mary Goodman, or whether to change the cat litter.'

At that very moment the phones rang. I picked up the blower on the left.

'Leprosarium for unwed mothers,' I said.

The voice that rasped through the blower belonged to Sergeant Mort Cooperman, and the message it passed along to me was enough to cause anybody's board meeting to adjourn.

Fate, it would seem, had plucked me up by my pretty little neck.

TWENTY-FIVE

The late-afternoon sky was gray, and I dodged a few premature snowflakes as I weaved across the Village for my appointment at the cop shop. Cooperman hadn't told me much over the phone but he'd told me enough to make me rather nervous in the service. When I'd told him that Ratso wasn't the victim, he'd launched into a long, knowing, fairly repellent laugh. From the laugh he transitioned to a wheeze, and then he laid the bomb on me. They'd apprehended the killer. Since we were 'colleagues of a sort', and 'in this thing together', he wanted me to come down and meet the perpetrator. I said 'How about sometime later in the week?' and he said 'How about four o'clock?' It was now three forty-seven and I was beginning to feel slightly agitato.

There was a world of things I didn't like and one of them was surprises. As a child, a surprise usually connotes something good. As an adult, the notion of a surprise often indicates you're about to be hosed. I had no idea what Cooperman planned to unveil when I got down to the precinct, but I felt pretty damn sure the surprise wasn't going to be a new pair of skates. Maybe it'd be a load of horseshit, I figured, without the pony.

A sense of personal dread began mounting inside me as I climbed the concrete steps of the precinct house, flicking my cigar at a nearby covey of trash cans. I tried to imagine what Cooperman wanted to show me that he couldn't have told me over the phone. If he'd correctly identified the victim and apprehended the killer, my cowboy hat was off to him, leaving me, of course, with my hair in the shape of the hat, looking like Lyle Lovett's smarter older brother. At the moment, however, I felt decidedly in the debit column in the gray-matter department. What the hell, I thought, it was Cooperman's show and I was merely the invited guest. The only price of admission, it appeared, was a little man inside my gut who kept elbowing me in the colon.

I opened the door and noticed immediately that the desk sergeant had a large red caterpillar crawling extremely slowly across his upper lip. I, for that matter, was in no hurry either. It turned out to be a good thing, because the desk sergeant checked briefly with Cooperman's office and then directed me to a nice cement bench without a park. It was like Cooperman to keep me waiting. It was like Cooperman to gloat over the successful wrap-up of a case. It was not like Cooperman to consider me a 'colleague' or to believe the two of us were 'in this thing together'. The only thing that Cooperman and I were in together was life, and everybody knew that life was just a magazine that had been out of circulation for many years now.

Well, I thought, if Cooperman had indeed caught Jack Bramson's murderer, a lot of the danger to Ratso would certainly be alleviated. As a result, the stress and pressure on myself would be greatly reduced and I might be allowed to go after the lawyer, find Mary Goodman, and empty the cat litter in peace. That's what I was thinking. But things are never what you think.

I was just about nodding out when the desk sergeant nodded me in, and the next thing I knew I was beyond the land of pebbled glass, sitting in front of the cluttered, battle-scarred desk of Sergeant Mort Cooperman. I did not especially like the little smile on his face. He shuffled some papers, shook a cigarette from some off-brand pack, and lit it with his Zippo. I took a fresh cigar out of my hunting vest and began prenuptial arrangements.

'Sorry,' said Sergeant Buddy Fox, as he slunk over from a file cabinet. 'No pipes or cigars.'

'The victim,' said Cooperman, 'as we learned almost immediately from the lab, was not your pal. It turned out to be a friend of his. Guy name of Jack Bramson. Lived in Queens. Looked out for the place sometimes when your pal left town for the weekend. This time, apparently, he didn't look out too good.'

'Tell me something I don't know, Sergeant.' Cooperman's smile became slightly broader, and if possible, slightly more unpleasant.

'If you're still clinging to your conspiracy theory connection of this guy getting whacked having something to do with your brilliant adoption investigation, you can forget it. We got the killer. We overheard his confession. And we got him confessing on tape.'

At this point Cooperman stood up abruptly and signaled like a traffic cop for me to follow him.

'Teatime's over,' said Fox.

Cooperman led the way down a narrow corridor past more offices, more pebbled glass, ringing telephones, muffled voices redolent with the trivia and the tragedy of the big city. It was a hallway like any other except that it held a strange, jangly sort of ambience not dissimilar to that of an emergency corridor in a big-city hospital. As you walked by you could almost feel the cool, sweet downdraft from the fateful flutter of the wings of life and death.

We descended a small flight of stairs with Cooperman in front, myself in the middle, and Fox bringing up the rear. It felt like being sandwiched between two relentless walking bookends. Several uniforms were moving about the hallway when we reached the next floor down. One walked close by us on the right. Cooperman acknowledged him with all the regard one might have for a passing dragonfly. Clearly, the detective sergeant was a man on a mission. He motioned to a guard and a large iron-barred door swung open ahead of us. We walked through it into a cool, dank, tomb-like place where Cooperman finally stopped and turned around.

'I think I told you,' he said, 'that once we caught the killer you'd see that the whole thing was pretty simple and close to home. You remember me saying that, Tex?'

I nodded. I remembered.

'Well, it did turn out to be pretty simple. And if you'll direct your attention over to that holding cell you'll see that it turned out to be about as close to home as you can get.'

I looked where Cooperman was pointing and I vaguely made out a solitary figure huddled in the corner of the cell. I walked a few steps closer and squinted my eyes to see more clearly through the gloom. But what I saw only managed to increase the gloom I felt in my heart.

It was Ratso.

TWENTY-SIX

Robert Louis Stevenson was once asked to contribute a short story for a religious tract that was being circulated in Samoa by a local missionary friend. The story that Stevenson wrote for the little magazine was known as 'The Bottle Imp' and before long became a world classic. It is the tale of a man who comes into ownership, at a very low price, of a magic imp in a bottle who will grant him any material wish he desires. The imp originally came into the world through a deal with the devil and, so the story goes, any man who dies with the imp in his possession will go to hell. Although the price of the imp is only a few cents, no one is foolish enough to purchase it, because the resale prospects are fairly hideous, along with, of course, the prospects of what happens to you if you fall through the trapdoor with the imp as part of your estate.

The man is in a frenzy to get rid of the imp but can find no buyers, so he tries to give it away. When he returns home, like magic, there is the imp again. The man leaves the bottle on a park bench, throws it into the sea, possibly endeavors to recycle it as well, all to no avail. The imp in the bottle always returns somehow to its doomed and desperate master.

It will grant him any wish in the world with the sole exception of health, happiness, and peace of mind.

The natives of Samoa, having been the first in the world to have read the story, became convinced, quite understandably, that it was not a work of fiction. They had observed firsthand their beloved friend's unaccountable moods of melancholia in paradise. They had observed his fragile, gentle nature, seen his health deteriorate to the point of death. They wondered openly how a man who appeared to have so much could be so achingly lonesome for his friends, his childhood, his home in Scotland, his own culture, and everything else that people who have everything have always longed for. The natives of Samoa came to believe that in a secret safe somewhere in his great plantation house Robert Louis Stevenson had locked away the bottle imp.

I had to admit, as I looked at Ratso, that try as I might, it sometimes seemed I could never get rid of him. He did have a singular propensity for popping up in my life in moments and places that always brought me aggravation and grief. Now, as Cooperman graciously opened the cell door to allow me a few minutes with the prisoner, I noticed that Ratso's eyes and the features of his face had vaguely come to resemble my mental image of the imp in the bottle.

If Ratso's appearance, not to mention his mere presence in the cell, had seemed distressing, the halting, one-way attempt at conversation with him was even more troubling. When he'd called me two days earlier from Woodstock he'd sounded like his normal, ebullient, bordering-on-tedious self. Now, he looked and acted like a man whose whole world had suddenly been kicked out from under him.

There was an absence of warmth and almost an absence of recognition in his eyes when I went over to him in the corner of the cell. When I asked him how he'd happened to have gotten here, he just despondently put his head in his hands. Obviously, he hadn't followed my instructions to stay in Woodstock, but this was hardly the time or place to mention it. When I asked more questions, Ratso behaved in an almost childlike, next door to autistic, manner, either shaking his head or turning away into the corner. About the only thing he said that seemed remotely intelligible was when I asked him, incredulously, if he'd actually killed Bramson.

'Hausenfluck,' he said. 'Talk to Hausenfluck.'

Ratso had mentioned Hausenfluck to me in passing during earlier conversations. He was Ratso's downstairs neighbor, an elderly man, a former schoolteacher, who, if I remembered correctly, had fairly recently been experiencing certain emotional problems largely associated with the bottle. I, too, I thought, had been recently experiencing certain emotional problems largely associated with the bottle. The only difference between Hausenfluck's situation and mine was that my bottle appeared to contain an imp.

It didn't look like I was going to get any more out of Ratso, and Cooperman was making not-so-subtle departure gestures in the doorway of the cell, so I gripped Ratso's arm and left him with the one-word advice Sancho Panza occasionally gave Don Quixote when the situation looked hopeless: 'Courage!'

Out in the hallway again I assured Cooperman that he was holding the wrong man. Regardless of Ratso's apparent state of clinical depression, it was against his very nature to have committed the crime. Cooperman took my objections in stride and calmly explained that Ratso had come back to the city early that morning, crossed the crime scene ribbons illegally, entered his own apartment, and, when his neighbor, a man named Hausenfluck, had called him, admitted he'd killed Jack Bramson. Since Ratso had picked up the phone after the message tape was rolling, the confession had been recorded on his own machine, the tape now residing in the hands of the police.

Ratso had been in custody only a few hours, but almost surely would not be offered bail because in his current mental state he was certainly a flight risk. A doctor was on the way to examine him. A formal interview was also soon to be conducted by Cooperman. But Ratso had already repeated to police what he'd told Hausenfluck on the tape: 'I killed Jack Bramson.'

'He didn't kill Jack Bramson,' I said, as we walked back up the stairs to the first floor.

'Better tell him that,' said Fox.

There was a dull throbbing in my head that caused me to have to concentrate on thinking clearly. I knew Ratso was innocent. He must've just been overwhelmed by a sudden remorse after I'd spoken to him about the loss of his friend. He'd blamed himself for Bramson's death, a quite natural thing for a close friend to do, and New York's finest had taken him literally at his word, a quite natural thing for them to do.

'Look,' said Cooperman. 'Don't you worry about him, Tex. He's in good hands. I'm gonna be interviewing him myself. A doctor's on his way. He's already called a lawyer. There's nothing you can do.'

'Who's the lawyer?' I said.

'Who'd he call, Fox?' said Cooperman. 'Funny-sounding name, wasn't it?'

'Yeah,' said Fox. 'He could've been confused. Could've thought he was ordering dinner.'

I turned to Fox impatiently, but he'd already stepped into the doorway of a little room to talk to a woman who looked like an aging prostitute. I was beginning to feel like an aging prostitute myself. I walked over to the doorway and stood there until Fox and the woman looked up.

'Can I help you, Tex?'

'Yes, Sergeant. What was that lawyer's name?'

'Hamburger,' he said.

TWENTY-SEVEN

When I left the cop shop, I did not return to the loft. The loft, I figured, was in good hands. With the cat in charge, and Sherlock, the cockroaches, and the answering machine to help out, there was almost no foreseeable situation they couldn't deal with. If something came up they couldn't handle, it wouldn't get handled. Right now I had work to do. Ratso was clearly out where the buses don't run, and if I didn't find some answers quick his ass was going to belong to the gypsies. For one who had so recently come back from the dead only to arrive at a fate worse than death, he seemed to be holding up about as well as could be expected. That was more than I could say for myself.

The snowflakes had increased in number now, and as I rambled down through Sheridan Square they wandered through the sky in all directions like yesterday's brain cells. I didn't know exactly what to do. I just knew that whatever it was, I'd better do it fast and right.

I was obviously heading somewhere, but I wasn't really thinking about it. All kinds of unbidden images from the past kept unreeling themselves in the old closed-for-the-winter drive-in theater of my brain. I saw myself, Ratso, and Mike Simmons down the street in the Monkey's Paw together on an evening just like this one many lunar landings ago. Simmons was a very bright, decent guy with a good heart and the only blemish on our relationship was that he'd hosed my last five former girlfriends before they'd had a chance to become former girlfriends.

Maybe it was, as Ratso had said, a form of latent homosexual flattery, or maybe Simmons just liked my taste in women and was too lazy to go and find them for himself, or maybe it had something to do with the fact that back then there was more marching powder around than snowflakes, but I never really got mad at Michael until the day I caught him eyeing the cat.

'Why're you looking at her that way?'

'She's beautiful. So graceful.'

'Don't get any ideas.'

'What the hell are you talking about?'

'I don't want you hosin' that cat.'

'I'd never hose your cat. It's the only meaningful female relationship you've ever had.'

And he kept his word.

For some reason, Simmons's persistent involvement in my love affairs never seemed to get up my sleeve. For one thing, he was always a gentleman about it. He even once suggested that I point out women to him that I was attracted to so he would then be able to hose them *before* I became involved with them. In this way, he averred, he would provide sort of a one-man protective health service for me in this modern era of AIDS and other sexually transmitted diseases. I mulled over the offer.

Unfortunately, Simmons left for California shortly after that and, ever since, my relationships with women seem to linger on just a little longer than either party desires, languishing, atrophying, rotting away until even friendship follows love out the door and leaves nothing behind but an old pair of red cowboy boots and a cup of blue coffee.

I stopped at a corner and jotted down Simmons's name in my little notebook. There'd been reports that he was back in town. If I could find him maybe he'd intercede in my relationship with Ratso. If Ratso got bail, Simmons could hold his hand, baby-sit him, and keep him out of further trouble, though I couldn't imagine how much deeper he could possibly dig himself. Or if Ratso stayed in jail, which now appeared likely, Simmons could bring him bologna sandwiches and lots of books about Hitler, Jesus, and Bob Dylan. Either way, Simmons could take Ratso off my hands psychologically and leave me free to pursue what was now becoming an investigation of a somewhat more desperate nature. If I couldn't find another good candidate for Jack Bramson's murderer, Ratso might very well be smoke.

As I crossed Seventh Avenue against the light, the way everybody does in New York and Paris and nobody does in Germany or Beverly Hills, I still strongly clung to the notion that if I could learn who actually killed Bramson, the secrets of Ratso's adoption would also be revealed. Bramson's death and the search for Ratso's mother were so intimately connected in my mind that not even Mike Simmons could put a wedge between them, provided, of course, that I could locate Mike Simmons. Of late, I seemed to be better at losing people than finding them, a trait that could, on occasion, prolong your life and could also, on occasion, make you wonder why you bothered.

The night was dark and cold and the snow was still falling as I trudged past a gay bar I'd once visited during the course of a murder investigation that McGovern had gotten himself mixed up in. I remembered walking into the place, sitting down at the bar, and ordering a drink. Then a guy had come up behind me and had given me the oldest gay pickup line in the world: 'Can I push in your stool for you?'

There was no question, I thought, that the Village derived much of its unique flavor from the gays, artists, and weirdos who lived there, along with, of course, the worker bees, serial killers, propeller-heads, bean counters, Reform rabbis, and pet shrinks who pretty much comprised the normal population. It was a bit disconcerting, when I stopped to think about it, that I seemed to fit into the milieu. Tonight, however, I sure as hell didn't want to stop and think about it. There'd be time for that when I found Mary Goodman.

As I crossed Sixth Avenue into SoHo, past all the trendy stores that sold stuff nobody needed, I shook all errant thoughts and snowflakes from my head. I ankled it up West Broadway and took a right on Prince Street, where I stopped in front of a familiar building that now appeared as spooky-looking as the artwork of a troubled child. The troubled child who usually lived here, I was well aware, had recently been incommoded and relocated to the sneezer.

I didn't know why Ratso hadn't told me about McLane, the now-deceased private dick he'd first hired to find his mother. I almost didn't want to know why the hell Ratso had tried to make a jailhouse call to Hamburger the lawyer. All I knew was that Ratso didn't live here anymore.

So I unfurled my butterfly net and pushed Hausenfluck's buzzer.

TWENTY-EIGHT

'Am I being rude, mother?' asked Cecil Hausenfluck in a highly agitato, near-hysterical falsetto voice.

'Is your mother in the bedroom?' I said.

'This is a studio apartment,' said Hausenfluck.

'I see.'

So there was no bedroom and there was no mother, unless, of course, she'd come back to haunt Hausenfluck in the form of the large tasseled floor lamp he'd appeared to direct his question to. God knows there were enough other things haunting the man. Why not his mother disguised as an antique floor lamp? At least he could turn her off occasionally.

'So, earlier this morning you made a telephone call to Ratso,' I said.

'Earlier this morning I made a telephone call to Ratso,' he stated, mimicking my intonation precisely.

'Why did you call him?'

'I wanted to tell him about the little children coming back and the Big Bad Wolf at the door.'

'I see,' I said again, but, of course, I didn't. No one ever really saw the things that the Cecil Hausenflucks of the world did. Well, maybe Anne Frank, Joan of Arc, and Van Gogh saw those things, but look what happened to them. They all died inconceivably hideous deaths and now they live with God, who, judging from the state of the planet these days, doesn't see too damn well Himself. Maybe Texas State Optical's got something for Him.

'Maybe this isn't a good time,' I said, as Hausenfluck began trying to establish eye contact with a half-eaten turkey drumstick on the table. 'Maybe I should come back another time and let you finish your meal.'

'I've eaten an appropriate amount for my figure,' he said, in a prim, take-no-prisoners falsetto.

'Fine,' I said. 'Let's get back to your conversation with Ratso.'

'He's a fine young man, isn't he?'

'He certainly is.'

'Well, you know, he helps me sometimes when the little children come and play tricks on me. They're little tricksters, they are. Hide my money sometimes. Last week they hid my reading glasses. Haven't found them yet.'

'What do they look like?' I said. 'These little children.'

With his right foot, Hausenfluck almost synaptically kicked his left ankle twice. It was a small thing but nonetheless rather disconcerting to the casual visitor. When he spoke, there was a total absence of guile in his features. Clearly, he believed every word he said.

'The little children have little faces and little heads just like little children but they're not little children. They're really very evil, demonic creatures. They have little, short bodies. No legs. No arms. Am I being rude, mother?'

His mother didn't answer.

Neither did I.

He was watching my face carefully now for any trace of doubt or skepticism. I shook my head slightly in a sympathetic manner and strived to achieve the vapid, expressionless countenance you affect when you know that a well-respected child molester's about to feed you a communion wafer.

'About a month ago,' Hausenfluck continued, 'I had to move all my furniture out into the hall there by the elevator just to keep them from hiding behind things. Ratso helped me move that heavy desk there into the hallway. He's a fine young fellow, isn't he?'

'He certainly is.'

'Don't know what I'd do without him.'

You're about to find out, I thought. I'd had about enough of the little children and I figured it might be time to steer things on to the Big Bad Wolf at the door and then follow that by walking out the door myself. This guy was cookin' on a planet that hadn't even been discovered yet.

'So tell me about the Big Bad Wolf at your door,' I said, as I blithely watched him kick himself twice in the ankle again. It was a painful thing to watch, but it seemed to get him on track. Maybe I'd try it myself, I thought, if I ever got home from the third ring of Saturn.

'Not *my* door,' he was saying.

'What?'

'The Big Bad Wolf was at Ratso's door.'

Hausenfluck was smiling a little smile and humming to himself now. He wasn't going to make a great government witness or anything, but he was all I had going for me at the time. I had to keep him focused on the Big Bad Wolf.

'When did you see the Big Bad Wolf?'

'Let me see. It was three nights ago, I think. Yes, that's right, because I needed Ratso's help to move all my clothes into the hallway because the little children were hiding in the closet. Did I tell you about the little children?'

'You mentioned them in passing. What did the Big Bad Wolf do?'

'He was knock, knock, knockin' on Ratso's door, just like that Bob Dylan song Ratso's always playing. Then he huffed and he puffed and he blew the door down and I got scared and I got back on the elevator and came back here and one of the little children had taken my keys and I had to wake up the super so he could let me back in.'

'But you saw the Big Bad Wolf?'

'Of course.'

'Describe him to me.'

'Well, he – GET OFF THE DRAPES!! YOU'LL RIP THE FUCKING DRAPES!!! STOP HANGING ON THE FUCKING DRAPES!!! I'M GONNA GET THE BROOM!! WHERE'D YOU HIDE THE FUCKING BROOM?!! – '

Hausenfluck was screaming now at the top of his lungs. He jumped up as if something had bitten him, violently knocking over the coffee table and sending the half-eaten turkey leg on a nice little trajectory over the floor lamp. I took a few steps forward to calm him down but he leapt across the room like a leprechaun on cruise control.

'THERE'S ONE ON THE COUCH!! HE WAS SITTING RIGHT NEXT TO ME!! GET THEM OUT OF HERE!! GET THEM OUT OF HERE!!!'

I didn't know whether to shake Hausenfluck like a rag doll or throw water on him or just try to help him get the little children out of there. I finally opted for going into the kitchen and looking for some brandy. I banged around for a while with Hausenfluck screaming in the background and every time I opened a cabinet, about eight hundred empty liquor bottles fell out on top of me which, I reasoned, could've been a contributing factor to Hausenfluck's dementia.

Eventually, I found a nearly full bottle of brandy and poured us both a healthy glass; neither of us needed much coaxing to pour it down our necks. Hausenfluck wanted to dance again and I didn't want him to drink alone so I gave us both a very generous second round. A short time later, with Cecil Hausenfluck snoring quietly on the couch, I let myself out. I closed the door softly and left him there with his little children.

I took the sad, small elevator down to the lobby and walked out of Ratso's building and went down to the corner to look

for a taxi. It had stopped snowing and the night air had sort
of a cold, crystalline, Zhivago-like comfort about it.

'Am I being rude, mother?' I said to the New York sky.

My mother didn't answer either.

TWENTY-NINE

Kent Perkins blew into town the next morning like a large,
blond California condor and he hit the ground flapping. He
wanted first of all for the two of us to take a working Los
Angeles power brunch during which I was to report to him
the details of the case from start to finish.

'I'll tell you everything I can remember,' I said, 'but I'm
not Archie Goodwin.'

'Who's Archie Goodwin?' he said.

'A fictional detective.'

'Every good detective is a fictional detective,' said Perkins.
'It's not an exact science. The guys with all the answers, the
hard-asses and headline grabbers, they rarely get the job
done. The best PI work is usually performed by people who
seem almost not to exist.'

It was a pretty insightful observation, I thought, for a guy
who'd never heard of Archie Goodwin. Of course, you
couldn't blame him. Nero Wolfe was a large, sedentary, cere-
bral, middle-aged, fat man who almost never got into a car,
much less a car chase. In order to portray him in a movie,
someone like Tom Hanks would have to bulk up to about
four hundred pounds and even then the opportunities to
emote would be severely restricted to the pushing out and
pulling in of one's lips just prior to the solution of the case.
For these reasons, Nero Wolfe had never made it to the
movies, and people in Hollywood, who seldom if ever read
books, would have no way of knowing that his sidekick was

Archie Goodwin. To be totally fair, it is also unlikely that
Archie Goodwin had ever heard of Tom Hanks.

For the first time in a long while I was starting to feel a
little better about the way the investigation was going. I'd
been able to reach Mike Simmons the night before and he
seemed very eager to step in for me and spend some quality
time with Ratso. Not that Ratso was going anywhere, but I
figured that between Simmons and the NYPD he'd be kept
safely on ice long enough for Perkins and myself to come up
with another candidate for Rikers Island.

Besides, there was something about Kent Perkins, other
than his being large and blond and from California, that
inspired confidence, or at least a measure of trust. He was
pleasant, modest, and engaging, which was more than I could
say for most of my New York friends, and though he was a
private investigator, he seemed to have a profound respect
for the law. This differed markedly from Rambam's approach,
which was that the law was an ass and needed to be kicked
periodically with a pointy-toed cowboy boot. That was probably one of the reasons why Rambam was wanted in every
state that started with an 'I'.

I took Kent Perkins to Big Wong's restaurant in Chinatown
for our power brunch. As we entered the place, the cooks
and waiters all lined up behind the counter and shouted
in unison: 'Oooh-lah-lah! Oooh-lah-lah! Kee-kee! Chee-chee!
Kee-kee! Chee-chee!'

I oooh-lah-lahed back a few times and took the reception
smoothly and graciously in the manner of Frank Sinatra
entering some small café in Little Italy.

Kent Perkins was duly impressed.

The manager, who stood behind the Jewish piano and
spoke very little English, nodded about seven times to me
and Kent and then looked around.

'Where Raz-zo?' he said.

'Don't ask,' I told him.

The 'kee-kee, chee-chee' greeting for Ratso and myself was

a tradition at Big Wong's that seldom had varied over the years, Ratso and I having very possibly frequented the place more than any man, woman, or child on the planet. The precise meaning of the words 'kee-kee, chee-chee' is open to some debate. Ratso and I have always considered them to be terms of endearment and have acted accordingly, considering the Big Wong waiters, despite the fact that few spoke English, to be some of our most loyal, reliable friends in the city. Sometimes they were our only friends in the city.

Ted Mann, the former editor of *National Lampoon* and a writer for *NYPD Blue*, is an old pal of mine and has a slightly different interpretation of the 'kee-kee, chee-chee' greeting. It is Ted's contention, and he claims he has researched the matter, that these two words are not really terms of endearment. He believes that 'kee-kee' and 'chee-chee' are actual Mandarin words that mean 'crazy' and 'smelly', respectively. Ted suspects, as well, that the Chinese waiters think of Ratso and myself as a pair of friendly, rather eccentric, homosexuals because we come in together so often and never with a woman.

Kent and I were shown to a special table in the back room and by the time we'd finished the first course of wonton mein soup I'd regurgitated upon him everything there was to know about the search for Mary Goodman. Kent made a few notes in a little notebook as I yapped, and I was heartened to observe that his pages flipped over the top of the pad like a cop's rather than to the side, like a poetry major or a cub reporter for the *Daily Planet*.

'Okay, Kink,' said Kent Perkins, 'let's start with the license number for the two good ol' boys with the assault rifle who followed you to the airport in Miami. Then we can move on to the roast pork. I love roast pork.'

'It speaks very highly of you,' I said, as I looked over my Big Chief tablet, found the license number, and recited it to Kent, who jotted it down in his little notebook and flipped another page.

During the next hour or so Perkins made more abrupt trips to the pay phone than a bookie with Tourette's syndrome. He was the only large, Aryan-looking person in the place which added a rather humorous component to the process, especially when the waiters came to our table, pointed to the front of the restaurant, then pointed at Kent and said, 'You!'

As Kent explained it, he had a friend who was a detective on the Miami police force and another contact with the Florida Department of Motor Vehicles, and he hoped to learn who owned or had leased the car before the fortune cookies arrived.

'We may be waiting a long time,' I said. 'Look around. No honkies. No fortune cookies.'

But Kent Perkins was already up answering the pay phone, jotting information in his little notebook, and staring lustfully at the large pieces of roast pork hanging behind the glass counter and dripping grease onto the chopping board. While Kent was otherwise disposed, I ordered him a large portion of roast pork. I also ordered spare ribs with black bean sauce, soya sauce chicken chopped with the bone and ginger sauce on the side, and a big helping of bok choy with oyster sauce, most of which was already navigating my lower intestine before Perkins had had a chance to touch the roast pork.

'Don't wait for me,' I said, as Perkins again returned to the table, 'go right ahead.'

'The car,' said Perkins with a big Texas smile, 'was leased by the Bimini Corporation. They're right here in little ol' New York. I've got the address and the suite number.'

'What do we do now?'

'First, I'm gonna finish this meal. As soon as I do that, we're gonna find the guy who rented that car and I'm gonna kick his ass.'

'You are?' I said, puffing speculatively on my cigar.

'That's right,' said Kent Perkins. 'And it don't take me long to eat roast pork.'

THIRTY

Kent Perkins was right. It didn't take him long to eat roast pork. What did take up a large portion of our adult lives was finding a cab in Chinatown. This, however, was not necessarily time poorly spent, for it gave me a chance to observe Kent, and it gave Kent a chance to observe New York, which he professed to be enjoying very much in spite of the fact that it was cold and rainy and every store we passed sold buddhas, Chinese parasols, and Chicago Bulls caps.

We stopped at one restaurant window filled with giant vermilion squids hanging next to rows of ducks with hooks in what used to be their eyeballs. There was also a whole pig hanging upside down with sightless eye sockets that seemed to say: 'I am the reincarnation of Mussolini.'

'Almost makes you want to be a vegetarian,' I said.

'Either that,' said Perkins, 'or corner the market on pork-belly futures.'

'What I'd really like to corner is the Bimini Corporation.'

'The fact that they rented the car that tried to whack you in Florida is very damning information.'

'I know,' I said, 'but it's not going to be easy for you to kick a whole corporation's ass.'

'I've come up against corporations before,' said Kent, as he bundled up against the cold. 'These old boys are probably slicker than owl shit on a pump handle, but when we find that head honcho I'm gonna hit him so hard his polo shirt's gonna roll up his spine like a venetian blind.'

'That's good,' I said. 'We never have any excitement here in New York.'

'We're fixin' to,' said Kent. 'This could get even more exciting than the time in L.A. when you generated that enormous toxic gas expulsion inside the tobacco humidor.'

'You sure that was me?'

There was not even a nuance of a cab anywhere along Mott Street. We walked in a light rain a little further up the block and I again reflected on the Kris Kristofferson 'walking contradiction' that was Kent Perkins. Under a macho, Texas, barnyard humoresque façade there stood an extremely intelligent, deeply sensitive American with a sense of loyalty and dedication that were becoming increasingly hard to find in the country of his birth. What he set out to do, he almost always accomplished. At that moment I came close to feeling a twinge of sympathy for whoever was standing in the well-polished, wing-tipped wheels of the CEO of the Bimini Corporation.

'By the way,' said Kent, 'when we get to this address and suite number, don't expect it to be the actual office suites of the Bimini Corporation.'

'Long as it's not a window with a pig in it, I'd call it progress.'

'All I'm saying is that if they're capable enough and big enough and bad enough to come within a Mickey Mouse whisker of sending you to Disney World forever, they're also smart enough not to have their actual headquarters at the address we're headed to. That is if we ever find a cab. C'mon, Kink, tell me the truth. Are there really taxicabs in New York?'

'Yes, Virginia, there are. They've just never heard of a man from Los Angeles walking and they're enjoying the novelty of it.'

We continued walking down the winding end of Mott Street, then turned around and retraced our steps back up toward Canal. Looking for a cab can sometimes be a zen, not to say tedious, experience. If you look too hard in too many places you'll never find one. It's often better to go to the place where you started and just wait.

'There's one thing we've got in our favor,' said Perkins, as the two of us stood under a metal awning outside the place where the pig was hanging.

'We're both Jewish?'

'Afraid not, Kink. The Spoiler's never seen a knife.'

'You could always borrow the one in my back,' I said, as I cut the butt off a new cigar, only vaguely aware of the Freudian implications of my actions.

'What I'm saying,' said Kent, in that way he had of being suddenly serious, 'is that we have a window of opportunity to work with and we should take advantage of it. At the very least, these guys believe that Ratso is dead, because they're under the impression they killed him themselves. If they're really clever, they already know they got the wrong guy and that Ratso's been arrested for the murder. Either way, they should be off their guard for a while now, and that may be all the window we need to get the drop on them.'

After that, things happened rather quickly. I lit a cigar, and, as I looked up, saw a guy getting out of a taxi just across the street.

'There's a cab,' I shouted, and both of us moved toward it like we'd been shot out of a circus cannon.

About half a nanosecond later the circus cannon returned a volley in our direction, right at the empty spot where the two of us had been standing under the awning. I turned around and saw a squid splinter into a million pieces, the pig suddenly spinning like a dreidel, and the window shattering into shiny icicles of glass.

Perkins had a gun out and was crouching behind a parked car scouring the street. I'd found the narrow sanctuary of a pay-phone booth with a little Chinese pagoda on top of it. For a moment time seemed to hang there like a dead pig. Then people began pouring out of the restaurant where, amazingly, no one had been hurt. Cars continued to drive slowly by in the rain. The rain continued to fall on the sidewalk. The sidewalk lay there like the old whore that it was, resplendent in the rain with bright shards of broken glass reflecting off it like costume jewelry.

'So much for our window of opportunity,' I said.

THIRTY-ONE

'Well, fuck me naked runnin' backwards on a tractor,' said Kent Perkins, as he glared angrily out the window of the taxi.

'I'm just happy,' I said, 'to get out of Chinatown without an acupuncture treatment.'

'It doesn't change anything,' said Kent. 'It just means we'd better be careful as a pair of porcupine pickers with the palsy.'

Kent had taken the cab driver through a series of sharp, unexpected turns, U-turns, and figure eights for the past twenty minutes and, as far as I was concerned, any possible pursuer who was still with us was welcome to hop in the cab and go along for the ride. That included my stomach.

I was moderately impressed with Perkins's diversionary tactics, especially considering that the only person in New York who appeared to know the city less well than Kent Perkins was our Cambodian cab driver. Of course, getting lost in a city deliberately is not always as easy as it looks. Lots of people get lost in lots of cities every day of the year, but, like belching or farting, only a chosen few can do it on command.

It was a funny old world, I thought, as I watched Kent leaning over the front seat to help the Cambodian navigate the mean streets of New York. The big, friendly Texan was, by any reckoning, at least three times the size of the tiny little Cambodian, yet the Cambodian had probably seen ten times the amount of shit in his life and I wasn't referring to horseshit or cow shit but to human misery, which often takes a lot longer to scrape off your boots.

A short while later, midtown on Lex, we spotted the building that the Bimini Corporation, whatever or whoever that was, had given as the address for its home office. Kent told the driver to go past it and drive around the block.

'What do you suppose the Bimini Corporation actually does?' I said. 'Other than shoot out windows in Chinatown.'

'We're about to find out,' said Kent, as he signaled the driver to pull over a good city block away from the building.

As Kent Perkins strode purposefully up the street toward the address in question, the cab driver, who must've come from western Cambodia, turned on a country music station. I immediately heard Garth Brooks. The anti-Hank. I puffed on my cigar and half-listened to Garth Brooks the way everybody does to country music these days and mourned the passing of the undecaffeinated era of the fifties and sixties. I missed Hank Williams and Johnny Horton, who both died young, tragic, perfectly timed country-music deaths, and who'd both, incidentally, been married to Billie Jean Horton. Captain Midnite, my friend in Nashville, always contended that Billie Jean had been some sort of a witch and that she'd killed Hank Williams and Johnny Horton and stunted Faron Young's growth.

My growth, unfortunately, was being stunted as well. My growth was being stunted by Ratso. When I'd first told him I'd help him find his real mother I hadn't envisaged the project becoming my life's work. Now the search had grown not only tedious but dangerous. Jack Bramson was dead, Ratso was in the sneezer, and whoever wanted to wax me in Florida was still trying to polish me off in New York.

Nevertheless, I had great confidence in Kent Perkins. Though he didn't know New York very well, he'd had great success with this line of work all through the West. He had a way with people. He was the quintessential good cop. And I trusted his instinct that getting to the bottom of the Bimini Corporation might be the fastest way to find out what had happened to Mary Goodman.

Moments later, Perkins came back to the cab and leaned his large head in the window. The look on his face was not encouraging.

'It's just a small mail drop,' he said. 'Just rows and rows

of boxes and a three-hundred-pound black woman in charge who's mean as a snake.'

'Doesn't look too promising.'

'Just give me a while. Remember, I'm very good with people.'

'You're not doing too well with me.'

'Look, give me a couple of hours. Just take the cab home and I'll call you at your place. Don't you have something to do around the house? Vacuum the den or something?'

'I don't have a den and the only vacuum I seem to be experiencing is the continued absence of information about the Bimini Corporation.'

'You'll soon know more than you ever wanted to.'

'Fine. If I never hear from you again, I'll assume you're either dead or you're just a California guy who doesn't always get back in touch when he says he will.'

'I'll call you in two hours.'

'I'll change the cat litter.'

Perkins was better than his word. I'd been back at the loft only a little over an hour when the telephone rang. As a creature of narrow habit, I answered the blower on the left.

'Bimini Corporation,' I said.

'Not according to my information,' said Perkins. 'Whatever in the blue-eyed buck-naked hell is goin' on around here, at least now we know where to find it.'

'Okay,' I said. 'Spit it.'

'The real office of Bimini Corporation is over on the West Side. I've got the address and I'm headed there now. I'm just going to look it over. I'm not going in. I think we should do that tonight. Late tonight.'

'How'd you get the address?'

'You wouldn't believe me if I told you. There's a cab. Got to go. I'll call you back.'

There wasn't a hell of a lot for me to do except change the cat litter.

So I did.

THIRTY-TWO

It was getting dark and I still hadn't heard again from Kent Perkins. I stood at the kitchen window of the loft, smoking a cigar, drinking a cup of black coffee, and watching the night creep its way across Vandam Street. I'd tried to make myself useful that afternoon by calling Moie Hamburger's office, Cooperman, Ratso in jail, and Michael Simmons. I'd gone 0-for-four. Hamburger was still gone, Cooperman was out, Ratso was in, of course, but couldn't take the call, and Simmons was 'no longer staying here' according to the rather testy young woman who'd answered the phone. I asked if she had a number for him and she said: 'Let your fingers do the walking.'

If Kent and I couldn't get somewhere with the trail of the Bimini Corporation, I had damn few cards left to play. I could coax McGovern into doing a piece for the paper about Ratso's search for his mother, but what they used to call human interest didn't hold people's interest these days. I could call a lawyer friend of mine in California, Phil Kaplan, and see if he had any hot ideas about finding Hamburger, but getting a lawyer to find a lawyer might get complicated. I could wear a sandwich board advertising for Mary Goodman and walk around the Village but most people would probably think it was performance art. I could call the local temples and synagogues posing as a Mormon missionary. That might bring interesting results. Or I could simply deal myself out, which, as the night and the light and the half-light grew darker still, I came very close to doing.

The same case that seemed to have been all but wrapped up in Florida a scant few days ago now appeared to be cracking and falling apart like the sidewalks of New York. In a mood of near-desperation, I sat down at the desk, picked up the blower, and called Phil Kaplan, the lawyer in California.

'Argue, Pearson, Harbison, & Myers,' said Margo, the receptionist with whom I often chatted while waiting for Phil.

'Any law firm that begins with Argue can't be all bad,' I said.

'Kinky!' she said enthusiastically. Some women liked the name Kinky and some didn't, and whether they were kinky or not didn't seem to have a lot to do with it. Margo just liked the name Kinky. We'd never met and that was probably a good thing.

When Phil came on the line I explained briefly what a Moie Hamburger was and why I wanted to find one. Phil sounded surprisingly optimistic about things. All people in California sound surprisingly optimistic about things.

'There's a book,' said Phil, 'called Martindale-Hubble. It's a directory of lawyers and it gives information that might very well help us find this guy.'

'I know he exists,' I said. 'I've met him once.'

'We'll find him,' said Phil, growing more confident. All people in California grow more confident the longer they talk to you. That's why most Americans keep their West Coast calls rather brief.

Phil said he'd check it out that night and get back to me tomorrow. I told him fine and thanked him.

'May all your juries be well hung,' I said, as I cradled the blower and took a fresh cigar out of Sherlock Holmes's head.

'You know,' I said to the cat, 'it makes sense that Kent would pursue the fresher trail of last week's license plate rather than try to find a woman who hasn't bothered to see her son in forty-seven years. Either she's dead or she doesn't give a damn.'

The cat sat on the desk and looked at me.

'Of course that could apply to a lot of people we haven't heard from.'

I struck a kitchen match and lit the cigar, rotating it slowly, holding it ever so slightly above the level of the flame, and watching two bright candles in the eyes of the cat as they burned away another moment of the obsidian night.

I'd just taken a puff when the phones rang. I exhaled and collared the blower on the left.

It was Kent Perkins, and he wanted me to meet him at a little coffee shop at midnight somewhere in Hell's Kitchen. He also wanted me to bring a long pole, like a fishing pole, and to wear a cowboy hat.

'Is this a scavenger hunt or a fishing expedition?' I said. 'I need to know how to dress.'

'Kink, we're going into a private underground parking garage. There's an infra-red light beam controlling the gate. I've got a lot to do between now and midnight. Just wear your hat and bring about a six-foot pole of some kind.'

'Have you thought of using the spoiler?'

'That's only for big hook-and-ladder jobs. And by the way, this is sort of a fishing expedition. You know what my dad in Texas used to tell me when I was a kid?'

'Don't tell mom I'm hosin' the baby-sitter?'

'Kink,' said Kent chidingly. 'My dad said: "Always fish where the big fish swim." '

'We'd better catch a big one fast,' I said. 'I don't plan on hanging around Hell's Kitchen all night in my Hebrew Huck Finn drag.'

THIRTY-THREE

The closest I could come to a pole in the loft was an old hockey stick that Ranger goalie John Davidson had given me back in some early ice age. I took that along with my cowboy hat, five cigars, and a small flashlight, and by eleven-thirty I was pouring a stiff shot of Jameson for the road into the old bullhorn.

'Don't worry about me,' I said to the cat. 'I'm totally pre-pared if anybody tries to come at me with a hockey puck.'

I killed the shot.

I left the cat in charge.

It was a cold, clear night and in the hack on my way to Hell's Kitchen, my mind seemed to be becoming rather colder and clearer as well. Was Ratso's supposed confession, his unusual behavior, and his strange request to speak to, of all the legions of lawyers in this world, Moie Hamburger, merely the result of remorse at the death of his friend Bramson? Or was there yet more that trusty old Dr Watson had not revealed to his lonely friend Sherlock?

It was true that Kent Perkins was a big boy, in more ways than one, but what was I getting him into here? If he weren't as smart as he was he could've passed for a near-perfect good ol' boy and the wingspan of good ol' boys isn't too long in the city. Was it fair for me to place him in a situation in which his life was clearly at risk and he was totally out of his depth? Was it fair for me to put myself in such a position? What would Ruth Buzzi or the cat say if they'd heard about the Chinatown incident?

By the time my hockey stick and I had gotten out of the cab I'd decided that after tonight Kent and I should not continue this deadly cat-and-mouse game with the dark oper-atives of Bimini Corporation. What was required was a more comprehensive understanding of what was going on behind the scenes. Tedious as it was, I needed to talk further with Ratso, which might prove difficult, since his lawyer had apparently now slapped an embargo on all visitors. I also needed to communicate and coordinate things, if possible, with Cooperman, and lastly, bring the whole thing out into the open through a McGovern column in the *Daily News*. These were definitely my next moves, I thought, as I walked to the little coffee shop on the corner, but first I owed it to Kent to see what, if anything, he'd been able to turn up tonight.

There were several shadowy figures loitering around and there was something that looked very much like duck vomit on the floor near the doorway, but otherwise, it appeared to be Hell's Kitchen's version of a clean, well-lighted place. There was no maître d', of course, but if the customer you were looking for was Kent Perkins, there was never any problem picking him out in a crowd. On this occasion it was even easier, since almost nobody else was in the place.

'Well,' I said, once I'd ordered some coffee and stowed the hockey stick under the table, 'I'm glad to see neither of us has joined a fundamentalist religious cult yet.'

'We came about as close as you can get this afternoon in Chinatown.'

'No shit.'

'Let me tell you what I have planned for this evening's entertainment. I think you'll find it enormously exciting.'

'As my friend John McCall always says: "Maybe you could just bring me some back on a piece of dry toast." '

Perkins laughed rather loudly. I've always believed that people who laugh loudly in restaurants are usually not very happy. Of course, that may only apply to crowded, upscale restaurants. On the other hand, Perkins could've merely been nervous. There was also the very slight possibility that he found my remarks humorous.

'Speaking of dry toast,' he said, 'don't order a hamburger here.'

I got out a cigar and began going through my preignition protocol in an effort to settle my nerves. I was still a little shaken, I suppose, about the spinning-pig experience that afternoon. I had a lingering idea in my head that if we weren't very careful, the next two spinning pigs were going to be me and Kent Perkins.

'Look,' I said, with some intensity, 'I want to know *how* and *why* we're breaking into this underground garage tonight.' If I was destined to be a spinning pig, I was at least entitled to know the reasons behind it.

'First of all,' said Perkins, as if he were talking to a small child, 'we're not breaking into the underground garage. We're breaking a light beam that will permit us to enter the garage. And here's why we're doing it.'

He slipped an envelope across the table to me and I slipped my butt-cutter out of my pocket, and, while I circumcised my cigar, observed that the envelope was addressed to the Bimini Corporation. I extracted a piece of paper from inside the envelope concomitantly with taking the phlegm-colored Bic lighter that had been in the family about forty-eight hours out of my no-hunting vest. I lit the cigar and looked at the note.

'This document came into my possession,' said Kent, 'with the help of the fork on my Swiss Army knife. There was a good bit of mail building up under the door of Bimini's suite, but this was the only piece close enough for me to reach and pull out without having to remain in the hallway so long that I'd have to start paying rent.'

The note, which, judging from the date, was already a week old, was simply a notice to Bimini to move the black Lincoln-Continental from parking space A12 or else it would be towed.

'The car's still there,' said Perkins. 'You can just see it if you stand close against the building and look in the driveway mirror.'

'Obviously, no one's been in the offices for a while.'

'Well, they may come in once a week. They may never come back. All we know is that the car was still there half an hour ago. And if there's two things I'm good at it's people and cars.'

'If there's two things I'm good at it's cats and cigars. But I'm sure we can find some common ground.'

'We already have some common ground,' said Perkins rather severely. 'Somebody tried to whack us in broad daylight this afternoon in Chinatown. We don't know who's behind the Bimini Corporation, but whoever it is sure knows us. And that kind of ruthless desperation tactic tells me we're on the right trail. It also means that somebody sure as hell doesn't want your friend Ratso to find his mother.'

'Well, I'll be damned,' I said, puffing the cigar thoughtfully. 'Maybe Ratso really *is* an heir to the Goodman Egg Noodle fortune.'

THIRTY-FOUR

It's not difficult for an underground parking garage to look fairly evil at midnight, and this one didn't have to try too hard. It was a down-curving driveway with an iron gate that led beneath the cynical sidewalks of Manhattan and, for all anybody knew, could've been the first circle of hell. So could a lot of other things in Manhattan. At Kent's instructions, I leaned close against the building and, sure enough, there was the black Lincoln, luxuriating in its own stubbornness like a particularly pious protester in front of an abortion clinic.

The streets and sidewalks were anything but empty at this hour, and I asked Perkins if he didn't think we ought to wait awhile, like until the year 2013. 'I'm not worried about being seen,' he said. 'I've already called the police.'

'You did what?' I said, almost dropping my hockey stick.

'I told them I was with Westside Security. They're the ones who handle this carpark. I said we'd be working on the system on and off tonight. That's just a precaution in case we set off the alarm instead of opening the gate.'

'You think the police believed it?'

'Why not? I told you I was good with people. I got the three-hundred-pound black lady down at the mail drop to give me the form for Bimini Corporation so I could add additional mailing instructions. Of course, I had to work at it a little. Told her how much I appreciated the long, hard hours she was working. Even went out and brought her a sweet-potato pie. Then she gave me the form and on it was the address of this place. Now all we've got to do is open this damn gate.'

'Too bad there isn't a night watchman. You could bring him a strawberry parfait.'

'One thing you've got to love about New York,' said Kent, as he hunkered down his large form in the middle of the driveway in front of the gate. 'Nobody sees or gives a damn about anything.'

'You'd better hope that applies also to whoever's behind the Bimini Corporation.'

'All signs point to them wanting to stay the hell away from here. I'm beginning to suspect I know why.'

'Would you care to share your suspicions with your little Jewish brother?'

If Perkins heard me, he gave no indication. He moved from side to side, still in the squatting position, holding the bars at about kneecap level and peering intently into the darkness, his gaze shifting from one side of the underground chamber to the other. I lit a fresh cigar and waited, puffing quietly by the side of the building, and blowing the smoke now and then in the direction of happy young couples or that very rare specimen, the joggerus midnightus idioticus. It was getting late in the year for them but I did manage to see a few.

'What do you plan to do?' I said at last. 'Squat there all night like an ape at the zoo?'

Perkins did not look up. If anything, he stared more intently through the iron bars. He held his arm out, palm up, in my general direction.

'Hockey stick,' he said.

I handed him the hockey stick.

'Cowboy hat,' he said.

I handed him the cowboy hat, which he placed on top of the large end of the hockey stick so that it could be moved along the ground, which gave the thing a rather uncanny resemblance to one of Cecil Hausenfluck's little children.

'Dr Perkins,' I said, 'are you sure that amputating the patient at the neck was the appropriate surgical procedure?'

Perkins did not respond but continued marching the ridiculous little mechanism closer to the infra-red beam. Finally, extending his arms fully inside the bars of the gate, he found himself just out of reach of the light beam.

'Six more inches and you would've been king,' I said.

'Horseshit and wild honey!' said Kent Perkins rather vehemently. 'One of us is going to have to Frisbee the cowboy hat.'

'That'd be your department,' I said. 'You're from California.'

'You understand what's at risk, don't you? If I toss the hat and miss the light beam, we not only don't get the gate open but, also, you'll probably never see that hat again.'

'I'd hate to see it flattened by a Mustang. Or stomped by a Cherokee.'

'Or rear-ended by a Probe,' said Kent. 'Maybe some executive will wear it to mow his lawn in Connecticut.'

'People don't mow lawns in Connecticut,' I said. 'They go to golf courses.'

'So he'll wear it to the golf course, then get tired of it and sell it for a few bucks at a garage sale.'

'People don't have garage sales in Connecticut,' I said. 'He'd probably give it to the Salvation Army or the Hadassah Thrift Shop, depending, of course, on the particular nature of his deep religious affiliations.'

'Then some Puerto Rican pimp picks it up cheap,' said Perkins, 'and gives it to a red-headed whore with a gold tooth in Spanish Harlem.'

'Who wears a peach-colored dress.'

'And who throws it in along with a Japanese basket-fuck to an executive from Connecticut, who loses it in this underground garage and it gets flattened by a Mustang.'

'It's a reasonable scenario,' I said.

'Let's hit it the first time,' said Perkins.

And he Frisbeed the cowboy hat.

For a second or two there was silence as the hat sailed across time and geography as fatefully as Columbus sailing a wishing well. Then we heard an almost medieval clanking sound. Either the gate was opening or Columbus was dying in chains. Neither event would've raised an eyebrow in New York.

'We'll be inside that Lincoln quicker than a minnow can swim a dipper,' said Perkins.

The next thing I knew, he was fooling around with the lock on the passenger-side door of the Lincoln, and I was hustling my ass down the drive to look for my cowboy hat. By the time I'd found it, checked it out for grease stains, put it on my head, and walked over to Kent, he had the door open.

'What took you so long?' I said.

'Sorry, Kink. It's been a while since I've committed a felony and I wanted to be sure I didn't scratch the finish.'

Perkins made a quick check inside the car; then his big, blond head disappeared under the darkness of the dashboard. I made a quick check around the garage and found no one stirring; then my kinky little head disappeared in a blue cloud of protective cigar smoke. All my life I'd wanted to have a big head like Perkins or McGovern. I had a chronic case of head envy and there was nothing I could do about it but walk around the garage with my hockey stick and look out for cops or robbers or the boys from the Bimini Corporation, who didn't give a damn what size head I had as long as they could take it off my shoulders and move it to the suburbs.

While Perkins was messing around under the dash-board either hot-wiring the car or looking for used gum, I jotted down the license number of the Lincoln and any other sticker or decal numbers I could find. It's always good to make yourself useful. I was just putting my little notebook away when the engine started.

'Hop in,' said Kent. 'Let's go egg Mary Goodman's house.'

'If we knew where it was,' I said.

Kent opened the glove compartment, removed some papers inside, glanced briefly at them, and put them inside his coat pocket.

'Might make for some good light summer reading,' he said.

'I'll wait for the movie.'

Then Kent reached back into the glove compartment and pushed a button and the trunk of the car began to open slowly upward, like the lid of a crypt. Since I hadn't smelled anything in over fifteen years, Kent was the first to realize that something was rotten in the state of Denmark.

'I don't know what's in there,' he said, 'but it'd stink a buzzard off a gut wagon.'

We both walked with somewhat measured tread to the back of the car and peered into the trunk. The bloated face of death was smiling up at us like a friendly AmWay representative. We weren't going to need to refer to a Martindale-Hubble directory anymore.

We'd found Moie Hamburger.

THIRTY-FIVE

Cooperman was not happy to see the hockey stick or the stiff in the trunk. He'd seen a lot of stiffs in a lot of trunks in his time, and he didn't appear to appreciate my thoughtfulness in getting in touch with him about seeing one more. I'd been under the mistaken impression that this one, just possibly, might lend some slight confirmation to my contention that somebody was indeed out there who wished very much for Ratso not to find his birth mother. I also took the opportunity to bend Cooperman's somewhat jaundiced ear with my account of the Chinatown attack upon Kent and myself, as well as to reiterate my close encounter with the krautmobile in Miami.

Not only had Cooperman and Fox taken the call, which was out of their precinct, rather grudgingly, they did not seem to feel that the rather ignominious adjournment of this lawyer's life made it any less plausible that Ratso had killed Jack Bramson. While Kent's engaging, Rockford-like appeal did appear to chip a little ice off Cooperman, it was mildly reassuring to see that some things never change in this funny old world. The cop-like glint in his eyes told me that my own rapport with the vaunted detective-sergeant was about the same as if he'd suddenly encountered Spinoza stumbling through the Bowery.

'*Two* fucking cowboys,' he said, after briefly surveying the garage and the Lincoln.

'And *one* hockey stick,' said Fox brightly.

'This was the lawyer,' I said, gesturing toward the open trunk, 'whose father made all the arrangements for Ratso's adoption. He's also the one Ratso tried to call from the precinct house when he was first arrested. Unless, of course, in his state of extreme remorse and depression, he was merely mumbling the name of the dead man's father, the person he may have blamed for originally setting all his problems into motion.'

'This certainly explains why the lawyer never called him back,' said Cooperman, chuckling dryly to himself as he stared down at the grotesque vision before us.

'You'd have thought,' said Fox, as he stepped out of the shadows, 'that he'd at least have had the courtesy to make a trunk call.'

Kent Perkins looked on wide-eyed, making an awkward effort at a smile. I didn't even try. Other than Fox asking a few questions about my hockey stick, he and Cooperman didn't really seem to have their hearts in it either. When the local precinct dicks showed up, Cooperman and Fox left and the new guys didn't know about Ratso and didn't want to. After a cursory interview or two, Kent and I were allowed to bug out for the dugout and we didn't waste any time getting out of those catacombs.

'Shit,' said Kent, once we'd gotten into the cab. 'I forgot to give the cops those papers from the glove compartment.'

'That's the best news I've heard all day,' I said. 'Let's go over to Sarge's Deli and do a little cramming for the final exam.'

It was after three by the time we got to Sarge's, but a second wind seemed to be blowing in from someplace and you could see the pages of the newspapers riffling on the sidewalk as if they were being turned by invisible hands. Third Avenue was pretty empty of traffic and so was Sarge's, but it was still three forty-five before my pastrami sandwich came in for a belly landing on table number 47.

'My father's theory about restaurants applies here,' I said, checking the hockey stick under the table.

'What'd he say? Stay out of Sarge's?'

'No, Sarge's is okay. The food is good and it gives you time to think. Plus, it's a good place to see and be seen at this hour of the night.' I looked up at the diminished parade of customers drifting close by our table like termagant ghosts. Kent nodded briefly and continued eating his bagel.

'What's your father's theory?' he said.

'Well, Tom's restaurant theory was first propounded in Austin, Texas, but certainly has universal applications. It's really very simple. His theory is: "The fewer the customers, the slower the service." '

'I'd hate to be the only people in the place,' said Kent, as he removed the papers from the glove compartment of the Lincoln and laid them down next to a large complimentary bowl of pickles.

'Do you think there's anything here?' I said, gesturing at

the documents with my lips like a native of Borneo. 'Any paper trail we can follow?'

'It's going to be difficult,' he said. 'The ignition lock was punched out.'

'So?'

'So it means the car was almost certainly stolen.'

'Terrific,' I said. 'So these papers and maps, Triple A crap, and gas receipts all belong to some little old lady who only went out to bingo games.'

'I'm afraid so,' said Kent, 'but this towing company receipt for fixing a flat tire appears to be more recent than the dates on the gas receipts. This might be what we're looking for. Remember Perkins's Theory of Stolen Vehicles, which I propounded in Los Angeles about the time Professor Friedman was propounding his Theory of Restaurant Service.'

'Which is?' I said, with an almost Gandhi-like effort at patience.

'When you steal a car you don't check for a spare.'

'To that theory,' I said, 'I'd like to add a possible corollary.'

'Which is?' said Perkins.

'You also don't check for a spare,' I said, 'if you know that it's covered by a rapidly decomposing Hamburger.'

THIRTY-SIX

Beaver & Son Towing Service was a twenty-four-hour operation. So were we. It was about a ten-minute cab ride, and when we got there it looked like the towing company had towed everything away but a lot of fence and a small temporary office set up in a trailer wedged between two larger buildings. There was a light burning in the trailer.

'Do you think Ruth's going to be angry that you've stayed out all night?' I said, as we got out of the cab.

'Yes,' said Kent.

'You *did* call her?'

'Of course. She's very understanding, but she also gets very angry. She's the world's only angry, understanding wife.'

'That's why I have a cat.'

As we walked up the little alleyway that led to the trailer, blocked out on both sides by big buildings under a Manhattan sky that had never held a harvest moon, with the towing receipt in the inside pocket of my coat, I thought, not for the first time, how much of life hangs by a silver thread of spit, by a fragile black chain of frog eggs across a country pond. This had to be the end of the road, I figured.

If this lead didn't pan, I could send all the documents to the cops and maybe they'd find the old lady in time to get the car back to her before the next bingo game. The cops weren't interested in the Bimini Corporation, and there was no way we were going to crack it without their help. There was no one else to go to. Eliot Ness was worm bait and George Smiley was probably sitting on some lichen-stained park bench feeding sparrows somewhere across the old herring pond. Whatever chance there'd been to pry anything out of Moie Hamburger had disappeared when Kent Perkins pushed the little button inside the glove compartment of the Lincoln. A Lincoln was a good car to die in, I thought. I remembered with a fleeting smile something the great French author and philosopher Jean Genet reportedly had once said as he was being driven around Chicago on a long-ago speaking tour. 'Only in America,' he'd commented, 'would they name an automobile "Galaxy".'

The cold and rather grimy tendrils of dawn were foisting themselves upon my bloodshot eyeballs like a cedar branch rattling against an ancient, rusty windowscreen. Maybe it's only some sense of cosmic hindsight, but I seemed to remember thinking, as we closed in on the place, that the little trailer, indeed, held something important for us. We peered in a window and saw a large, burly guy facing away from us, squatting over what appeared to be a small radiator.

'Never squat with your spurs on,' I said to Perkins.

'If he showed any more butt cleavage,' said Kent, 'he'd have to join a union.'

As we climbed the steps of a tiny porch, we could see through the trailer the tow truck parked in a scraggly backyard, gleaming like a crown jewel in the recycled light of the city. Even standing still there was something about the vehicle that gave you the notion of an oncoming train. On the side of the truck, in bright script, read the emblem: *Beaver and Son Towing Service*. We knocked on the door of the trailer, and the guy jumped up like a bottle rocket. He gave us a careful fish eye out the window and either he liked Kent's big, friendly Texas smile or my cowboy hat or else he was a hockey fan, because he opened the door.

'You guys liked to scare the shit out of me,' he said.

'Don't tell me,' said Kent Perkins, 'that at five o'clock in the morning in this godforsaken city I recognize a Texas accent?'

'Travis Beaver,' said the guy, sticking out a big hand in Kent's direction. 'Weatherford, Texas.'

'Hell,' said Kent, genuinely pleased, 'my name's Kent Perkins. I'm from Azle, Texas. Kink, Azle and Weatherford are both just spittin' distance from Fort Worth. Me and Travis might've played on opposing football teams. I played left tackle for the Azle Hornets.'

'I was right guard for the Weatherford Kangaroos,' said Beaver with growing excitement.

'Sting the Kangaroos!' shouted Kent.

'Swat the Hornets!' shouted Beaver.

Then he suddenly put a finger to his lips and gestured toward the back of the trailer where a small bundle appeared to be lying on an army cot. Kent and I tiptoed over and saw a tousle-headed, freckle-faced boy about ten years old, sound asleep.

'Beaver and Son,' whispered Beaver proudly, as he came over to join us. 'That's Travis Beaver, Jr.'

For just a moment the three of us watched the kid sleep. He looked like one of Peter Pan's Lost Boys, I thought. When you think of Peter Pan you're really thinking of Mary Martin. I thought of Mary Martin. And I remembered something in a dollop of cosmic trailer insight. Mary Martin had come from Weatherford, Texas. I leaned on my hockey stick for spiritual support. Maybe, dear God, Mary Martin had once been a cheerleader for the Weatherford Kangaroos. Maybe she'd once stood in a line with the other blond, young, small-town girls and the head cheerleader had said: 'Ready?' and the girls had all answered together: 'Ohh-*kay!*'

For no reason except possibly the hour, an old country music song popped into my head:

> *Just a small-town girl 'til she learned to twirl*
> *Then she set the world on fire*
> *Like a drive-in Cinderella*
> *in a Chevy named desire*
> *So leave your teddy bear at the county fair*
> *Honey, Hollywood's on the phone*
> *For a small-town girl from a small-town world*
> *you're a long, long way from home.*

I must've taken a brief vertical power nap, because suddenly I noticed that Perkins and Beaver were drinking coffee and talking earnestly at a table and I was still gawking at the kid with John Davidson's wooden memento high-sticking me in the sternum.

A short time later I was standing by the table with a cup of steaming coffee in front of me and Kent Perkins smiling to beat the band.

'Tell him, Travis,' said Kent.

'I remember the guy you're looking for,' said Beaver. 'Car was a black, late-model Lincoln with a flat tire and he said he didn't have a spare. Had to tow him and he also paid me for a new tire. This was about a week ago.'

'What'd he look like?' I said, drinking my coffee and holding my breath and, in so doing, coming dangerously close to a Danny Thomas coffee spit.

'Big fellow with long black hair and a dark, bushy beard. Gave me two C-notes and I told him that I wanted to see his driver's license because I've been getting so many counterfeit C-notes. He said no and I said then I'll just take the goddamn tire back off the car and he finally said okay and showed me his driver's license.'

Now I was definitely balancing on the edge of my hockey stick. Beaver was going for the hat trick and I wasn't about to try to check him.

'It's kind of foggy in my mind,' Beaver continued, 'but I know the address wasn't in the city. A New York driver's license but not from the city. Kind of an Indian-sounding place. Sounded a little bit like Chappaquiddick.'

'Maybe Ted Kennedy finally got around to calling a tow truck,' said Kent.

Beaver laughed. I realized once again how good Kent was at the game of painlessly pulling things out of people. Beaver was at a crucial point of breaking the case wide open and Kent had him relaxed and talking to us like old friends.

'What was the name on the driver's license?' said Kent.

Travis Beaver set down his coffee cup, put his hand on his head, and closed his eyes to concentrate. He held that position long enough to germinate several generations of fruit flies. I looked at Kent. Kent looked at me. We both looked at Travis Beaver. Then, still keeping his hand on his head, Beaver opened his eyes.

'Donald Goodman,' he said. 'Does that sound right?'

THIRTY-SEVEN

There are about a million places in New York State that have Indian names. The reason for this is that there once were about a zillion Indians living thereabouts until they traded the island of Manhattan for twenty-six dollars and a string of beads, which, as anyone who's visited New York recently can attest, was probably the best deal the Indians ever made. Every time I think of Indian names I'm reminded of the legend of the young warrior who came to the chief to inquire if he could change his name. If you've ever studied Indian lore you're no doubt familiar with the chief's sage reply: 'Why do you ask, Two Dogs Fucking?'

Of course, when you narrow it down to Indian names that sound kind of like Chappaquiddick, there's not all that much to work with. There's Chappaquitdick, the summer resort from which Richard Nixon resigned the presidency. There's Chappaquidproquo, the well-known watering hole for corporate attorneys. There's the popular spot where all the tourists invariably flock, Chappanudnick. And, finally, there's the little Indian village in which the natives were reported to have intermarried with an early group of irritated Italian immigrants, Chappamyass.

As I sat with my feet up on the desk the following afternoon, there was only one Indian name written down on my Big Chief tablet. This I now circled. Then I smiled like a self-satisfied serial killer and lifted Sherlock's porcelain cap to take a fresh cigar out of his porcelain head.

I put the Big Chief tablet on the desk and got up and walked over to the refrigerator, stopping long enough to extract a bag from the latest shipment of coffee beans that Kathy De Palma had sent me from Maui. With the unlit cigar in my mouth for general ballast, I went rapidly through a series of household activities, many thoughts percolating in my mind, not the least of which was the name on the Big Chief tablet and what it represented. I believed it to be, at least geographically speaking, the solution of the case.

I ground the coffee beans and fed them into the espresso machine with the facile grace of a Roman soldier throwing Christians to the lions. As I waited for the machine to move into overdrive, I smiled up at the little black puppet head on top of the refrigerator.

'Alas, poor Yorick,' I said, 'you've seen very little action of late. The visitors to our humble quarters have been few. But I suspect, my dear friend, that all of that is about to change.'

The little black puppet head smiled back down at me. It was not the big, broad, Texas smile Kent Perkins often utilized to mesmerize the populace. But it was not without its own simple charm. Unwavering. No guile. No hidden agenda. If I stayed there forever gazing upon that little ebony face it would mean a life lived looking only at the Greek mask of comedy, sheltered and safe from sorrow, never knowing the tragic countenance of this world. But somebody had to feed the cat.

I fed the cat.

Soon the smell of Hawaiian coffee filled the loft and I paced back and forth with the unlit cigar while the cat ate the tuna and the pigeons shit on the windowsills and the puppet head continued to smile warmly at the far wall upon which a picture of a ballet dancer had been hung by some former tenant, no doubt, who, for all I knew, may have hung himself as well. That would go a long way toward explaining some of the spiritual ambience I'd been noticing in the loft.

But it'd been a good, purposeful day, all in all. I'd green-lighted McGovern on the human interest piece on Ratso's personal quest for his long-lost birth mother. After no small amount of cajoling I'd convinced McGovern to eighty-six the bit about Ratso's current place of residence.

'We want a big, splashy spread on this,' I'd told him earlier that afternoon, 'and we need it to run within the next forty-eight hours.'

'That's up to the editor,' McGovern had said.

'Fuck the editor,' I'd told him.

'My sentiments precisely,' he'd said.

As well as getting McGovern cranked up and into operation, Simmons had also reported from the field. He'd been to see Ratso a number of times and, apparently, had gotten him in touch with a high-powered lawyer who Simmons felt might possibly get him out on bail.

'Ratso's showing marked improvement,' Simmons had said.

'If he vomited on your head it'd be marked improvement,' I'd commented at the time.

Finally, I'd spoken to Stephanie, who'd expressed growing interest in becoming a part of the mother hunt, especially now that, in her words, 'it seems to be going somewhere'. I'd also talked with Kent and we'd agreed that we'd have to swing into action soon.

'There's a strange thing about dusty old investigations like this one,' Kent had said. 'Remember, they're all open cases. That means there's usually someone in the shadows who doesn't want them ever to be solved.'

'This time,' I'd said, 'we know who that someone is. And I'm pretty damn sure I know *where* that someone is.'

When the coffee was ready, I drew a steaming cupful into my old Imus in the Morning mug and took Imus's mug, the coffee, and myself over to the desk. I took a sip of the coffee and for a moment through the steam I saw Robert Louis Stevenson sitting under a banyan tree with Princess Kaiulani. Princess Kaiulani, the last princess of Hawaii, did not have much time to gaze at a smiling puppet head. Her prince never came, she died tragically young, living only long enough to see her kingdom tumble down all around her. That is why good Hawaiian coffee always tastes a little bitter, as well as a little better than any other in the world.

I took another sip or two and studied again the one Indian word on the Big Chief tablet. The word was 'Chappaqua', an Indian name for a place in New York that would sound like Chappaquiddick to someone from out of state. As it happened, I knew the place well. Many moons ago, I'd lived there myself.

I struck a kitchen match on the leg of my old blue jeans and set fire to the cigar. I kept the tip of the cigar ever so slightly above the level of the flame and, as I did so, I could almost feel the noose tightening ever so slightly around Donald Goodman's neck.

THIRTY-EIGHT

Two mornings later McGovern's story hit the streets, and shortly after that Kent Perkins and I hit the road for Chappaqua. We stopped only long enough in the Village to pick up Mick Brennan, photographer extraordinaire, at a little dive near where the Bells of Hell used to be. The Bells of Hell had been known for many things and one of them was the night McGovern's eyeball popped out of his head when some guy blindsided him as he was sitting at the bar. McGovern contends that the eyeball popped right out of his skullhouse and hung there attached only to a viscous mucuslike connective tissue. He walked the eyeball, holding it in the palm of his hand, to the emergency room of St Vincent's Hospital, where (of great spiritual import to McGovern) Bessie Smith had died. He waited two hours in the emergency room while doctors worked furiously on other matters like separating people who'd gotten stuck together hosing. Eventually, a nurse spotted McGovern and the eyeball was popped back into his large head, larger even than Kent Perkins's, and he was able to return to the Bells of Hell just in time for final call.

The story, of course, had almost no relevance to the journey we were embarking upon except possibly as a mute reminder to keep our eyes out for trouble. There'd never been much trouble in Chappaqua and most people there probably wouldn't have recognized it if it'd ridden in on a large black hippopotamus, but, as we would soon find out, all that was getting ready to change.

Having picked up Brennan, who was sporting a camera and lens that would've given the spoiler a run for its money, Kent aimed the rent-a-car down the Saw Mill River Parkway and we headed out for a quiet day in suburbia. Brennan and Perkins were about as different as two people could be, having virtually nothing in common, so I reasoned that they would get along well together and they did. This was important because they were both to be key players in a drama that could very well place all our lives at stake. For finding Mary Goodman, I was now certain, meant dealing with Donald Goodman, a man I believed had already dealt with Jack Bramson and Moie Hamburger and would've already dealt with Kent and myself had destiny not shuffled the cards at the last minute. And if there's one thing I know about destiny it is that you can't count on it forever.

Over the past few days, Kent and I had hammered out a plan that we hoped would enable us to find Mary Goodman and gather evidence against Donald, who we believed was either her son or nephew and who obviously had a great deal to lose if Ratso got together with Mary. Finding the Goodman estate had actually been the easy part. I'd called my friend Sal Lorello, who, as well as having been my road manager for many years, had also run a limo service out of Chappaqua. Sal had driven everybody who was anybody in Westchester after being on the road with me had fairly well driven him over the edge. Then Cleve had taken over as road manager and, of course, wound up in residence at the Pilgrim State

Mental Hospital. Ratso, who'd accompanied me on practically all of my forays into crime solving, was now a registered guest of the NYPD. Good help, I reflected, as we pulled into sleepy Chappaqua, was hard to get these days. As Willie Nelson once told me: 'You've got to be able to move on to the next big town without slashing your wrists.'

'Hard to believe I lived here for two years,' I said, as we drove past the quaint little shops and houses.

'Hard to believe you stayed the weekend, mate,' said Brennan.

It hadn't taken Sal Lorello long to call me back with rough, hopefully accurate, directions to Mary Goodman's estate. Sal had never met Mary and didn't know anyone who had. Word around town was that she was an extremely wealthy, Howard Hughes-like, semi-invalid, who spent a lot of time in her garden but otherwise almost never left the sanctuary of the estate, which was, in fact, a modern-day castle.

We drove through Chappaqua and headed east on a smaller road, then turned to the right on a still smaller one. Kent stopped the car on a little bluff and studied the landscape with a pair of binoculars.

'Did you bring along your bird book?' I said to Brennan.

'Jesus Christ,' said Kent suddenly. 'The place looks like an Irish castle.'

'That it does, mate,' said Brennan, following along through the camera lens. 'Goodman, you know, is a well-respected Irish family name.' Brennan winked in my direction.

'Just don't drive this rent-a-car into the moat,' I said, as Perkins shooed Brennan and me into the car like baby chicks and roared off in the direction of the castle.

We found a small copse of trees to the side of the road that enabled us to see the main entrance and the front lawns of the place without being too conspicuous. The vision was one of Xanadu-like opulence.

'Mick,' I said, 'your job is to work your way around the perimeter and take unobtrusive *National Enquirer*-type shots.

I know you've never been unobtrusive in your life, but give it a try. The photos may be very helpful when we come back in a few days to implement phase two of the plan, the penetration of the castle.'

'Which is going to be a bitch,' said Kent. 'There's a heavily manned guardhouse and enough goons walking around to protect the Pope. Lot of security for a little old lady in a garden, no matter who she is. Of course, in this kind of operation, you'd never go in the main entrance.'

'What's this you've marked in yellow here, mate?' asked Brennan, as he looked over Kent's map of the general vicinity.

'That's the local hospital,' said Kent with a smile. 'This kind of operation, it's always a good idea to know just where it is.'

'Bloody terrific, mate,' said Brennan. But he was already adjusting his lenses.

'You know, the one thing I don't understand about this,' Brennan was saying, 'is why – '

'Hold the weddin',' I said.

At that moment, out the front drive past the guard-house came a long blue Rolls Royce driven by a big, burly man with long, disheveled black hair and a bushy black beard. The man and the vehicle rolled inexorably through the chill afternoon with the fluid ruthless motion of a maestro walking onto the podium. One glance and you knew that not even a brick wall would stop him. He was the same large, hairy mammal who'd almost left me for road-kill as he'd stormed out of Moie Hamburger's office.

'Get him, Mick,' I said.

Mick snapped away almost as fast as a fashion photographer. But getting Donald Goodman on film and getting him off-camera were two distinctly different matters. There's no such thing as innocent wealth, I thought. And on Goodman, wealth looked positively evil. A sudden sinking feeling came over me as I realized the Herculean nature of our task.

'The cops just aren't interested in Donald Goodman,' I said.

'With all his money and power I'm not sure by ourselves that we'll ever be able to catch him.'

'As my old dad in Texas used to tell me,' said Kent, ' "Justice rides a slow horse, but it always overtakes." '

'That's well and good,' said Brennan. 'But the old nag's never going to overtake that fuckwit in the Rolls.'

The blue Rolls Royce sped up the little road with the sinister grace and finality of a brush stroke on the canvas of the devil. We crouched behind the rent-a-car and watched Donald Goodman until he was out of sight. In that moment I thought again of Cecil Hausenfluck's words describing the man who huffed and puffed and blew Ratso's door down. In my mind I knew with a certainty that this was the same man.

'That's got to be him,' I said. 'He's the Big Bad Wolf.'

'If he is, mate,' said Brennan, setting down his camera, 'let's bloody well hope we're not the Three Little Pigs.'

THIRTY-NINE

We left Mick Brennan and his camera hiding behind a large elm tree with instructions to circle slowly around the side of the place and shoot anything that moved.

'Don't get caught,' said Kent. 'If you do, I'm afraid you'll be on your own.'

'Have done most of my life, mate,' said Brennan, and he set out through the woods.

'We'll pick you up in a few hours,' I said, but I wasn't sure he heard me.

Kent and I drove the car around to the rear of the big place, where Kent stopped and donned a dark blue tie and a cap that read: SECURITY. With his overcoat and clipboard he appeared to be someone to be reckoned with.

'How do I look?' he said, as he got out of the car.

'I'd hire you.'

'You already did.'

We waited and watched for a while in the bushes that abutted a narrow driveway. Traffic here seemed much busier than it had at the main entrance.

'The good news,' said Kent, 'is that a setup of this size requires lots of coming and going by way of the servants' entrance and almost certainly a heavy turnover of personnel. That's going to make it easier for us when we make our move.'

Kent paused for a moment as some kind of electrician's van pulled into the drive. As it did, an old landscaper's pickup and a butcher's van were pulling out.

'Jesus,' I said, 'everybody's here but Beaver and Son.'

'I'll just join the party,' said Kent, picking up his clipboard and striding confidently up the driveway. 'I'll be back in an hour or so.'

'What am I supposed to do?' I shouted after him.

'Just loiter around. See what you can see.'

'Have done, mate,' I said. 'Most of my life.'

I walked back to the car, got in, and took out a fresh cigar and fired her up. My problem with loitering around this place was that Kent Perkins looked like the chief of security and I looked like Lazarus after the fifth day. Well, I was on my own and I'd just have to deal with it. I wasn't quite sure what Perkins's idea was, but he'd told me it was a good one and I believed him. Then I looked up at the seemingly impregnable walls and turrets of the Goodman estate and began to have my doubts. Then I puffed on my cigar, watched the traffic come and go through the servants' entrance, and forgot all about it. When it came to loitering and daydreaming, I was definitely aces.

I was gazing lazily up through some palm trees somewhere in the South Seas when somebody rapped on my window with the barrel of a gun and I just about swallowed my cigar.

A moment later, I saw, to my great relief, Kent Perkins's big, smiling face filling up my window.

'Excuse me, sir,' he said. 'Could you tell me how to get to the Statue of Liberty?'

'Sure,' I said. 'The first thing you do is get the hell out of here.'

As we began the rather tedious process of ferreting Mick Brennan out of the woodwork without appearing too suspicious to Goodman's goons, Kent filled me in on his little infiltration maneuver.

'Donald Goodman's gone away for a week on business. That gives us a good window to work with.'

'That's great,' I said. 'The last one we had got blown out in Chinatown.'

'What I did was turn certain delivery and service people away until further notice. Mr Goodman's orders.'

'I hope you took rather copious notes of who they were.'

'Got all that. But we're going to need some help if you want to come back later in the week and replace them with our own people.'

'That's no problem,' I said. 'McGovern and Brennan, if we ever find him, will be happy to help out. And Stephanie DuPont's been harassing me to get involved in this case. Wait till you see her. Maybe she could pass as an outcall massage girl.'

'Good idea. Maybe I'll call her myself.'

'What would Ruthie do if she found out?'

'Probably just detach the Spoiler with a machete and donate it to Engine Company Number Nine.'

After searching high and low for Brennan, we found him low, shivering under the same elm tree where we'd left him.

'Shot five rolls,' he said, once he'd gotten into the car. 'Lots of men with guns and maids with tea trays.'

'Any sign of an old lady?' said Kent.

'None. But it wouldn't surprise me if she was holed up in

there somewhere. The servants carrying tea out to the garden almost made me homesick. Anyway, you've got a small army of servants on the inside ministering to a little old lady and on the outside you've got a small army of blokes with guns trying to protect her.'

'Or what is more likely,' I said, 'trying to keep her there.'

'She must be one hell of a little old lady.'

'If she's Ratso's mother,' I said, 'anything's possible.'

Anything was indeed possible, I thought, as Perkins aimed the car back in the direction of Chappaqua. And it's just when you think you've thought of everything that anything can happen. When it does, there's always some nerd who goes around shaking his head disapprovingly and very sagely muttering: 'Anything's possible'. I vowed to myself that on this particular occasion that nerd would not be me.

'Do you think Mary Goodman's really somewhere on that estate?' said Kent, taking off his security cap and loosening his tie.

'I'd bet my life on it,' I said.

FORTY

On the way from Chappaqua back to the city we got caught in the mother of all traffic jams, and Kent, over Brennan's mild protestations, took the opportunity to tell a rather poignant coming-of-age story about himself as a young man in Fort Worth, Texas.

'Every time I see a Rolls Royce,' said Kent, 'I think of the first Rolls I ever owned. It was also the last. I was about twenty-two years old, a young, hotshot land speculator, and I'd made myself some bucks and I wanted to spend 'em. So I bought a beautiful new black Rolls down in Houston, spent about six hours waxing and polishing her up, and drove her to Fort Worth to show her off to my friends and in-laws from my first wife. Ruthie's seen a lot of Rolls Royces in her time. She wouldn't have been impressed.

'But the folks in Fort Worth and especially in Azle, Texas, many of them had never actually seen one. I remember as I drove through Azle, every eye was on me and that car. I was stopped at a red light and a farmer in an old pickup pulled up next to me and said: "Nice car. My daddy used to have an ol' Packard just like that."

'I drove it to my in-laws' house and parked it in the driveway and they all came out and gawked and they were very impressed. I can still see that car. It just shone like a jewel in the Texas sun.

'Anyway, next door to my wife's folks lived my favorite uncle, Uncle Rosie. Now Uncle Rosie was blind but he knew what was going on. He could call out your name just by hearing your footsteps on the sidewalk. He passed the time "watching" John Wayne movies. I think he'd "seen" every movie John Wayne ever made, probably hundreds of times. Anyway, Uncle Rosie had been very excited about seeing the Rolls Royce. This caused a problem in my young mind because I could just imagine his hands moving up and down all over the car and ruining my new wax job.

'So, with some trepidation, I left the car in my in-laws' driveway and walked next door to where Uncle Rosie lived and, sure enough, he called my name as I came walking up the sidewalk. He was watching *She Wore a Yellow Ribbon*, starring, of course, John Wayne. He asked me if the car was here yet and I lied and told him no, but it was coming in in a couple of days.

' "I just want to feel the fancy leather on those seats," he said. "I just want to say howdy to that pretty little lady on the grille." And I thought again about my new wax job.

'Well, I told him I'd bring it right over just as soon as it arrived and I felt bad about it because the car, of course, was sitting right next door in the driveway the whole time. But it was just one of those things that happens when you're young and hopefully you learn from it and become a better person. If I had it to do over again I'd've taken Uncle Rosie by the hand and personally introduced him to the little lady on the grille and seen to it that he saw all of that car he wanted to.

'Anyway, that's not how it happened. I promised Uncle Rosie again that I'd bring the Rolls by as soon as I got it and then I left. I went home and felt like hell and decided that night that I'd go ahead and just bring the car over to him the next day, wax job be damned.

'So I woke up the next morning and I remember I was just making coffee when my wife got a call from my in-laws. Uncle Rosie had died.'

The traffic seemed to have cleared off a bit and Kent drove on with the kind of faraway look in his eyes that I thought I'd noticed several nights before when he'd been looking at Travis Beaver's sleeping son. I puffed silently on my cigar. Nobody spoke for a while. Then Brennan piped up from the backseat.

'There's a lesson in that,' he said.

'Yes, Mick?' I said. 'And what would that be?'

'Don't fuck around with blind people, mate.'

FORTY-ONE

'I'm not going to be an au pair girl,' said Stephanie DuPont defiantly. It was two days later and a small coordinating session was under way in the loft. We still had, according to Perkins, a four-day window to work with.

'Especially,' Stephanie continued, 'for some sick fuck in Chappaqua.'

'Sorry,' said McGovern, 'there's not much demand for au pair girls in Brooklyn.'

'Have you thought about being an outcall masseuse?' I said.

'No, turbo-dick,' said Stephanie.

'An au pair girl is what they're expecting,' said Kent Perkins, 'and an au pair is what they're going to get. So if you insist upon using that language, at least get the accent right.'

'I'd hate to have an au pair girl with *your* accent, mate,' said Brennan.

'Or yours,' said McGovern. He and Brennan had been drinking Guinness all afternoon from a large supply I'd purchased from Myers of Keswick on Hudson Street. As an accommodating host, I'd done my best to keep up with them.

'It's unfortunate,' I said, 'that Ratso and Rambam can't be with us to help plan this operation.'

'Yeah,' said McGovern. 'It's almost pleasant.'

'Rambam,' I continued, 'is jumping with the Burmese Army Paratroopers – '

'He can jump up my ass, mate.'

'And Ratso, of course, cannot be with us for reasons that all of you know.'

'And I was so looking forward,' said Stephanie, barely concealing her disgust, 'to meeting all the rest of your friends.'

'Probably,' said Kent, ignoring the previous exchanges, 'we'll make our move three days from now while Donald Goodman is still away and we have some chance of finding the old lady. Stephanie will be the au pair. Kink, McGovern, and myself will be housepainters. And Brennan will be an interior decorator.'

'Brilliant,' said Brennan. 'I'll need a beret and a little dickie.'

'You probably already have a little dickie,' said Stephanie.

'Bloody Christ,' said Mick. 'Where'd you find this brazen bird?' He gestured in Stephanie's direction by tilting slightly one of the many empty Guinness bottles standing in front of him.

'She just fluttered in the window of opportunity one

morning,' I said. 'And now she's become my favorite pet albatross.'

'Shut up, Hebe,' said Stephanie sweetly.

'God, I just thought of it,' I said. 'Without Ratso and Rambam, I'm the only Jew in this whole operation!'

'That's why it may have a chance of success, mate,' said Brennan.

'If everybody just plays their part,' I said, 'everything will be fine. Mick's photos should be developed by tonight and that ought to be a big help. McGovern's story in the newspaper has definitely got the town buzzing. It may even be part of the reason Donald Goodman hit the road. We're going to almost certainly make our move within three days' time, so get whatever outfits, vehicles, or props you think you might need. And remember, we have but one primary purpose in this adventure. Find Mary Goodman. After we ascertain that she's safe and sound, we can let the cops deal with Donald Goodman, her nephew or son or whatever he is.'

'Have you considered,' said McGovern, 'that he could be her husband?'

'There's certainly enough money involved,' said Kent. 'It's entirely possible.'

'So she may be robbing the cradle,' said Brennan, with a wicked smile. 'Like the Kinkster.'

Stephanie looked at Brennan with a gaze that would have withered a pressed flower. 'Don't mention Kinky,' she said, 'when I'm trying to relax.'

'One thing I can't emphasize enough,' said Kent Perkins, with an earnestness and a new intensity in his voice, as he stood tall above the little group. 'This is a mission of a decidedly dangerous nature. Donald Goodman will not be there on the day we infiltrate the place, but if he's who we think he is, he's already killed two people and just missed killing two more – me and Kinky. We don't want to run up against his security goons and, if all goes well, we shouldn't have to. Except for the housepainters, McGovern, Kink, and myself, we will all be working separately, but actually, of course, we'll all be working together. And a chain is only as strong as its weakest link.'

'That's McGovern,' said Brennan.

'Hush,' said Stephanie.

Kent raised his hands to quiet the crowd. He gazed briefly at each face like a commander sending his men on a mission from which he believes they may never return.

'And remember this,' Perkins continued, staring off Patton-like into some middle distance that only he could see, 'I will be armed. If you run into trouble, I will do all I can to help you. Kink will let you know when we're ready to go in. Good luck to you all.'

There was a moment of silence in the loft. Then McGovern laughed his loud, hearty, Irish laugh, which always seemed somehow inappropriate for indoor use.

'Who was that masked man?' he said.

FORTY-TWO

It was goosing Cinderella time, around eleven forty-five, and I was reading McGovern's story in the *Daily News* for about the thirteenth time, pouring bullhorn-size portions of Jameson down my neck to settle my nerves, and communing with Sherlock's porcelain head and the cat. The lesbian dance class had ratcheted up in the loft overhead and that, as usual, made the cat a little edgy. Sherlock, however, continued to aim his logical hazel eyes directly at mine. His eyes remained unperturbed, intense, and slightly amused at how little the world had really changed. Mine, particularly after many med-icinal rounds of Jameson, probably looked like two piss-holes in the snow. The only way I could know for sure would be to look in the mirror and the only mirror in the place was in the executive dumper, where I'd launched a large, rather fetid, nearly rhomboidal space station earlier that morning.

'Don't go in there without your hydrogen mask,' I said to the cat, while still perusing McGovern's column.

The cat, of course, said nothing. She had great disdain for any form of sophomoric, prepubescent, barnyard humor. She had, in fact, great disdain for any form of humor at all. It was really quite funny.

'You're a humorless, constipated prig,' I said to the cat.

The cat said nothing, but contented herself with switching her tail back and forth rather violently. It was, I thought, not so much a misunderstanding between a man and a cat. It was representative more of that intrinsic, deep-seated lack of trust that has always existed on some level between all men and all women. The cat looked at me with her logical hazel eyes. They remained unperturbed, intense, and slightly amused at how little the world had really changed.

McGovern's story about one devoted son's ceaseless search for his mother, to my mild surprise, had created a space station explosion of its own in New York. To those of us who knew Ratso, the pains and effort McGovern had gone through to portray him in a remotely attractive light seemed fairly amusing. McGovern's piece also provided great fodder for Don Imus and Howard Stern, the two New York-based radio titans who, as a rule, dumped on Ratso on a fairly regular basis. Now, both Imus and Stern, each after his own inimitable fashion, proceeded to dump on Ratso to a degree and an intensity that would've warmed the heart of Gustave Flaubert.

Neither knew, of course, that Ratso was in the sneezer. Nor did they know about the investigation or plan of attack that would soon be underway. Nor could they have any knowledge of the fact that if Mary Goodman wasn't living in a castle in Chappaqua, there weren't any cards left to play. Mary Goodman hadn't turned up in forty-seven years for a reason. No amount of press or publicity was going to bring her out of the woodwork at this late date. But it might've helped flush out Donald Goodman for the time being. However, there was no hard evidence on Goodman. None at all. Just a ridiculously skimpy circumstantial tissue of horseshit. Cecil Hausenfluck, a man who kicked his own ankles on a regular basis, had described Goodman to me. Travis Beaver, a tow-truck driver, had given me the name. His last name had matched the one I'd found in Jack Sloman's safe deposit box – the name of Ratso's birth mother. Then, of course, there was the matter of two dead bodies pointing vaguely to Goodman as the bad guy. But what, I thought, if Goodman was a bad guy but the wrong bad guy and Mary Goodman was no relation to him and she wasn't living in a castle in Chappaqua and there were no cards left to play?

'When there's no cards left to play,' I said to the cat, 'even destiny can't shuffle the deck.'

FORTY-THREE

I woke up the next morning with no scrotal-sarong difficulties but with something even more unpleasant. A poison dwarf was standing on the sidewalk four floors below my kitchen window screaming very personal slang obscenities at me in a piercing cockney accent. The last time I'd heard that kind of pathological timbre in a voice was when Cecil Hausenfluck had asked his mother if he was being rude. Mick Brennan, quite obviously, didn't care a bloody damn what anybody's mother thought.

'Put a sock in it, Mick,' I shouted, as I flung open the window and pitched the puppet head out into the feeble, freezing sunlight. Then I slammed the window back down and goose-stepped to the espresso machine, which I quickly cajoled into operation. Then I leaned against the kitchen counter, listened to it hiss and rattle, and waited for the inevitable.

'Goddamnit, mate,' said Brennan, as he roared in the door with the puppet head in one hand and a large envelope in the other, 'I've been up all bloody fucking night making these prints just so I could queue up and wait all bloody fucking morning for you to pop out of bed and toss me this bloody fucking puppet head.'

'Perhaps you would care for some tea,' I said in a conciliatory tone.

'Let's have a large helping of Jameson's, mate, and hold the bagels. Then we can look over these prints if you like.'

I poured a hefty shot of Irish whiskey into the bullhorn and handed it to Mick. I poured an equally hefty shot into my Imus in the Morning coffee mug, which I noticed had a little chip on its shoulder. So did I.

'Here's to your bloke Kent Perkins,' said Brennan, raising the bullhorn. 'I like him, and for all our sakes I hope he's not insane.'

'I'd say he's pretty damn clever stepping in in front of the security boys and telling the hired help to come back next week.'

We clinked our inappropriately stemmed receptacles and poured the Jameson down our necks.

'Always did believe in a hearty breakfast,' said Brennan.

'Okay, Mick, spit it. Did you get anything at all that would indicate that our little old lady may be in residence at the castle?'

'What'd you expect, mate? A double-parked aluminum walker? A close-up of her dentures smiling at you from the canasta table? I'm good but I'm not a bleeding spy satellite.'

With that proviso, Brennan slid the envelope over to me and slid himself in the direction of the door.

'I'm sure they'll prove invaluable,' I said, 'and we'll go over them very carefully before we move on the place. I was just hoping there'd be some sign of Mary Goodman. If she's not there, we can call in the dogs and piss on the fire.'

'Well, I hope we're not going in for nothing, mate. You told us Ratso's mother was there. You said you'd bet your life on it.'

'I'd still bet my life on it,' I said, as I placed the puppet head back on top of the fridge. 'I'm just wondering if the gods will be offering any odds.'

'They never have in the past, mate,' said Brennan, and he walked out the door.

That afternoon, with an imminent sense of D Day in the loft, I reviewed a small list of paint supplies as I waited for Stephanie DuPont to knock on my door. She was fashionably late. I used the time purposefully by returning a call to Mike Simmons at a new number he'd left on the machine.

'Good news,' he said, when he came on the line. 'Our new lawyer is not a piranha, he's a candiru. You know, the kind of thin little fish William Burroughs described in *Naked Lunch* that lives in the lower Amazon basin and darts up your ass or your prick and erects sharp spikes and can only be removed by surgery which, of course, is not feasible in the lower Amazon basin?'

'Was Burroughs writing from personal experience or was it just wishful thinking?'

'It was fishful thinking,' said Simmons. 'All I can tell you is that Ratso could be out of the can within twenty-four hours.'

'Allah be praised,' I said, more relieved than I might have sounded.

'Ratso seems very contrite. He knows he fucked up coming back to his apartment from Woodstock.'

'He's right.'

'He also says he should've told you in the beginning about the first detective he hired to find his mother.'

'He's right.'

'He also feels shitty because he's caused so much trouble for you and everybody else.'

'He's right again,' I said. 'Maybe there's something wrong with him.'

'Well,' said Simmons, 'we're all about to find out. He could be out on bail as early as tonight. I'm sure he'll call you and tell you all this stuff himself.'

'No doubt,' I said. 'I may be able to tell him something very soon, too. I may be able to tell him where Mary Goodman is. His mother.'

'That would make Ratso very happy.'

'Somehow I don't think Mary Goodman will quite derive the same enjoyment from this mother and child reunion.'

Later that afternoon I could see every head on Canal Street turning as Stephanie and I browsed the army-navy store circuit. None of the heads appeared to be looking at my cowboy hat.

'You're quite a hit on Canal Street,' I said.

'It's like this everywhere, ass brain,' said Stephanie. 'Or haven't you noticed?'

'Must be hard to manage,' I said, basking in the unbridled jealousy of every lowlife on the sidewalk.

'It's only hard to manage when I'm joined at the curvaceous hip by a Hebe detective nerd in a cowboy hat, smoking his hideous cigar.'

'Yeah,' I said understandingly. 'I know how that feels.'

We bought paint, brushes, white overalls, and white caps for Kent, McGovern, and myself. After some cajoling from Stephanie, I tried my outfit on in the store.

'You look like an orderly in a mental hospital,' Stephanie said, laughing.

'Not true,' I said. 'Only two professional groups always wear white caps. Rich men's sons and housepainters. I'm a housepainter.'

'I know,' said Stephanie wistfully.

'I appreciate your helping us with this surveillance,' I said, as we left the store with three large shopping bags. 'It could get a bit gnarly, you know.'

'Do you think it's a real castle?' she said with the sudden innocence of a near-child.

'I showed you Mick's pics of the place. Of course it's a real castle.'

'But just ask yourself: "If you were a real castle, would you live in Westchester?"'

'Probably not,' I said, as I unsuccessfully signaled a cab on Canal Street. 'But let's give the old castle a chance. You never know. Maybe you'll find your knight in shining armor.'

Stephanie raised her arm and a cab pulled immediately to the curb like a large, motorized puppet.

'You never know,' she said, tossing her head sharply and flailing her long blond hair halfway to Little Italy. 'Maybe we'll find Mary Goodman.'

FORTY-FOUR

Ratso didn't call. The cat and I had to content ourselves with the cold comfort of not knowing whether he was still in the sneezer or had been released on bail and was just pretending he didn't know us. For myself, I was too proud and too busy to bother with finding out. As far as the cat was concerned, she was too proud and too busy to bother with anything or anyone that did not directly please or intrigue her. If Ratso's life had depended upon it, she wouldn't have crossed the desk from one red telephone to the other. Cats are so clean.

As at least a grudging, time-share member of the wonderfully sensitive and complex human race, I feared I might be coming down with some spiritual malady akin to German measles and I did not wish for it to scar my conscience. Yes,

I still planned to take my skilled team of secret agents out to the castle in the morning to find Ratso's mother. Yes, I'd already rather significantly risked life and limb, including several that didn't even belong to me, during the course of this investigation. I'd done for Ratso what Sherlock would've done for Watson or what Nero Wolfe would've done, albeit rather grudgingly, for Archie Goodwin. But I wasn't sure, now that I thought about it, that I'd ever really been a true friend to Ratso, whatever that meant.

In my more reflective moments, I had to admit that I was often rather hard on people, particularly those I liked to think of as my friends. Don't get me wrong. I was capable of kindness and acts of generosity toward others; it was just that something inside me always balked at thinking of myself in that way. What the hell, I thought. We are what we are if we're anything at all.

It was at about that time that I noticed the cat staring at me intently. Reading my ambivalent, meandering thoughts just as surely as she sucked the very breath from my body as she slept on my chest at night. It was a dangerous, vulnerable, almost frightening feeling. Like standing naked in front of the whole world. Or walking on the street in New York.

'So I'm human,' I said to the cat. 'What do you want from me?'

The cat said nothing, but continued to stare cryptically, like the oracle of Vandam.

'Okay, so maybe Kent Perkins *was* right,' I said. 'I'm a giver in a taker's body.'

The cat said nothing.

Suddenly I felt like Cecil Hausenfluck talking to a mother who wasn't there. I got up from the desk, poured a little nightcap of Jameson into the bullshorn, and took it over to the window where I killed the shot and gazed with level eyes across the fatuous, fourth-story neverness of the city night. A little soul-searching can always be forgiven, I thought, when

319

you know that in the morning you're going to attack the castle.

FORTY-FIVE

Of course, we didn't really *attack* the castle. But if you've ever tried, you know that even merely insinuating yourself into a castle can be just about as dangerous. People who live in castles generally don't trust people who live outside castles. And they may have something there.

'Seems too easy, mate,' said Brennan the next morning as the five of us breakfasted on coffee and doughnuts in a nondescript rented van parked in front of a nearby Chappaqua diner.

'It *is* easy,' said Kent patiently.

'Just don't get caught,' added McGovern. He punctuated the comment with a machine-gun-like burst of highly infectious Irish laughter, which should've been illegal inside an enclosed van at eight o'clock in the morning.

'Most of the people working in and around the castle,' Kent continued, 'probably won't have been there much longer than us. When I checked earlier in the week there were a lot of new people, a number of temps, and a high turnover in general. That insures that nobody ever learns too much.'

'Yes,' said Stephanie, 'that's one way to look at it. But why permit people to crawl all over the place if you've got something or someone you've trying to hide?'

'I've pondered that one myself,' I said. 'It's a big operation to run an estate of this size and it'd look suspicious with no one ever around. Also, if Mary Goodman's there, or if she was there, the evidence may be limited to a small area inside the house. Donald Goodman's not going to be there anyway, so it's not a problem. But if he's got a crony or two watching over things, they certainly aren't threatened by what goes on outside the place. It may only become more dangerous, I suspect, if you have to go inside the house.'

'Comforting words for an interior decorator, mate,' said Brennan.

'Or the new French maid Donald Goodman hired,' said Stephanie.

'I was going to comment on that French maid outfit,' said Kent, 'but I was afraid God or Ruthie would strike me dead.'

'Now everybody just relax and look like you belong,' I said. 'Pretend you're in a strange neighborhood in the city. Just blend in. No one knows who Goodman may have hired or fired recently, so get your story down, keep it simple, and stick to it. And keep a look out for an old lady who may be closeted in a sun room or a little hidden garden somewhere.'

'Or a dungeon, mate.'

'Listen and observe,' I instructed, ignoring Brennan's remark. 'And be relaxed.'

'That's too much to remember,' said McGovern.

'By the time darkness falls on the castle,' said Kent Perkins dramatically, as he started the van's ignition, 'we'll have solved the mystery of Mary Goodman.'

As the van pulled out of the parking lot toward its date with destiny, each passenger, in his or her own way, seemed absorbed in placing the finishing touches on a new identity. I had to admit they looked the part. Now, if they could only act it.

'If you do meet your knight in shining armor somewhere in the castle,' I said to Stephanie, 'what do you plan to tell him?'

'Get in line,' she said.

Penetrating the grounds of the estate proved as easy as Kent had predicted, and was made even easier by the fact that every pair of male orbs in the place was totally zoning in on Stephanie DuPont in her French maid outfit. Quite possibly, we could've slipped the entire Polish Army into the front hall without anyone's being the wiser. And the front hall was just about big enough to accommodate the entire Polish Army.

The fortress was so large, indeed, that even Mick Brennan's surveillance photos had not done total justice to its magnitude nor its labyrinthine features. A body could get lost in here quite easily, I reflected, as I walked the lower floors unimpeded in my mental hospital drag, carrying a tape measure and a rather elaborate color chart. The fact was I'd already lost contact with everybody on our team except McGovern, the world's largest house painter, whom I could see through a set of stained-glass windows that would've made a Mormon missionary green with envy. McGovern was painting a forlorn-looking, frostbitten little wooden garden trellis and he appeared to be enjoying his work. I found a side door and made my way over to him.

'I'm not sure,' I said, 'that a phlegm-colored trellis is exactly what they wanted here. When the spring greenery comes in, you're going to have a real clash problem.'

'That's okay,' said McGovern. 'By the time the spring greenery comes in I'll be gone.'

'McGovern, I want you to stay right here for as long as you possibly can. There's probably acres of woods and gardens on the place, but this spot provides a great overview of the house and the grounds. You may be the only chance we'll have to know where the hell the rest of us are. I'll come out periodically to reconnoiter on all movements other than bowel and to supervise the drying of your paint.'

'I can't paint this trellis forever,' said McGovern. 'What if some groundskeeper or security guy comes out and tries to fat-arm me?'

'You've got to stay put. This is also the only comprehensive view we have of what's going on inside the castle.'

'There's something now,' said McGovern, gesturing toward an upstairs window in the fortress-like structure.

We both looked up and saw a flash of blond hair sticking

out from under a white painter's cap, as a large man who'd evidently been observing us stood up and turned around. Then a light-colored piece of cloth seemed to move downward out of our vision. Then, suddenly, in the window, apparently aimed directly at McGovern and myself, there appeared a pair of large, white, luminous buttocks.

FORTY-SIX

By Gary Cooper time, with our cover still holding nicely, we were able to swim around on the grounds and inside much of the castle in the blithe, practiced manner of the deadly candiru fish. The candiru, as Mike Simmons had gone on to explain, and as anybody who's ever urinated in the lower Amazon basin and lived to tell about it knows from empirical evidence, swims toward warmth. We, on the other fin, were swimming toward truth. And, as the afternoon wore on, our strokes grew bolder and stronger.

It soon became apparent that Perkins was correct about most of the servants and working people knowing less than we did. No one had seen an older lady on the premises, and the name Mary Goodman was usually responded to with a blank stare. There were, however, a few exceptions to this. One was an old man who looked like he'd been polishing silver in the scullery even longer than McGovern had been painting the trellis.

'Can you tell me where I can find Mary Goodman?' I asked him casually, as I went about comparing a nearby wall with my ever-present color chart.

'Oh, she's in her garden, sir,' he said, stopping his polishing almost imperceptibly, like a sleeping man pausing unknowingly before taking his next unconscious breath. 'She's not to be disturbed.'

'Where is her garden anyway?' I persisted.

'It's her private garden, sir. You'd have to check with Mr Goodman or Jennings.'

This posed somewhat of a problem, in that Mr Goodman, of course, was not on the premises and Jennings was obviously the head footman or Big Butler or somebody of such hierarchical stature that a mere housepainter like myself probably couldn't approach him with such a sensitive question. I wasn't sure how high up the ladder, as it were, I could climb.

As I thanked the old man I saw the reflection of my image in the silver plate he was polishing and I realized that one or both of us probably belonged in a mental hospital. I also realized that either Brennan or Stephanie would probably have to brace Jennings. If I were Jennings I would have given the guy in the silver plate the dust-off for sure.

I left to find Brennan, whom I'd seen about an hour before in all his sartorial splendor pushing the staff around like a little red apple. His personality was actually rather well suited for an interior decorator in a place like this, I thought. He could be as abrasive as he wished and everyone would still nod and bow and respectfully say: 'Yes, Mr Cunningham.' It was also refreshing to hear Brennan go through a whole morning without using the word 'mate'.

But Brennan was nowhere to be seen. Nor was Kent Perkins. Kent was a pro, however. He was the only one of us capable of casing the whole upstairs of the mansion and still find time to moon me and McGovern. The last time I'd seen Stephanie, she was chatting amiably with the old housekeeper and shooing me away with her hand when the woman wasn't watching. So, with the exception of Kent and Mick doing a disappearing act, the rest of our crew was fitting in so well it was beginning to make me nervous. As I remember, that was about the time things started to fall apart.

Suddenly, Brennan came running out of the house and grabbed my arm as I was attempting to light a cigar on a large veranda.

'Mate,' he said intensely, 'they're onto you.'

'Relax, Mick,' I said, with a confidence I did not particularly feel. 'You're behaving in a very un-interior-decorator-like fashion. Time may be running out for the housepainting crew – '

'It is. I overheard Jennings asking questions about the three of you.'

'But they're all still deferentially addressing you as "Mr Cunningham, sir" and Stephanie's got every pair of gonads on the grounds wrapped around her fingers with, of course, the possible exceptions of yours and mine and sometimes I'm not so sure about yours.'

'Mate, you'd better skate.'

'I don't think we'll have to. I doubt if Jennings knows for certain whether or not Goodman hired us. He's just got an enquiring mind. So do I and here's what I want you to do.'

I gave Mick a suggestion to pass along to Stephanie for me. It was nothing brilliant, really. Just an idea born of the times I'd lived my life around death.

Mick left to find Stephanie and I walked around the side of the house to see if McGovern was still at his command post. As I walked, I looked again to see where a private garden might be hiding itself, along with, of course, Mary Goodman. I searched for a good half an hour, but it was wintertime and it was hard to imagine what the place would be like in spring. Possibly, a private little winter garden might be tucked away somewhere on the sprawling grounds and Mary Goodman might be bundled up with her comforter on her divan sipping a hot camomile tea. There was also the possibility, I reflected, that just around the next corner, Judge Crater and Amelia Earhart might be busily pruning daffodils from the side lawn.

As I approached McGovern, Brennan's dire prediction seemed to be bearing its sour fruit. A large, armed security guard, almost as big as McGovern, was conversing with him in a manner that seemed far from congenial. I slowed my pace and was able to pick up the tail end of the conversation.

'On top of that, buddy,' said the burly security guard, 'this is the slowest fuckin' paint job I've ever seen.'

'This isn't a *paint* job,' said McGovern in a rather mincing, condescending whine. 'This is a *total surface restoration*.'

'We'll see about that,' said the guard, and he headed off toward the front of the house.

'I like that "total surface restoration",' I said, as I looked at my watch. 'I give our little housepainting crew about twenty minutes before they call in a forklift and get us out of here.'

'A lot can happen in twenty minutes,' said McGovern.

'And not all good,' I said. 'Here comes Kent.'

Kent Perkins was indeed approaching, looking slightly harassed and rubbing the knuckles on his right hand.

'Just had a minor altercation with a security guy,' he said, 'who won't be giving us any trouble for a while.'

'Unfortunately,' I said, 'there's about eighty-seven more of them crawling all over the place like so many burly praying mantises.'

'We're running out of time,' said McGovern, as he lazily slopped a few finishing touches on the phlegm-colored trellis. 'With nothing to show for it, I might add.'

'Not quite nothing,' said Kent with a quick smile. 'Stephanie got your message from Brennan and found this in the medicine cabinet in a disused boudoir upstairs.'

From his overalls pocket he extracted a plastic prescription bottle and held it in his palm for us to see. The name typed on the label was Mary Goodman. The date on the prescription was February 1984.

'Some of her effects, apparently, were still in the cabinet as well as other prescriptions, but, unfortunately, this was the most recent of the lot. She was definitely here, but it was over ten years ago.'

I puffed thoughtfully on my cigar and watched the cold sun shining on the mansion on the hill.

' "In last year's nests," ' I said, ' "there are no birds this year." '

'Who said that?' asked Kent.

'Don Quixote,' I said.

'That's about right,' said McGovern. 'I had a feeling we were tilting at windmills.'

'Not quite,' I said. 'Look over there.'

As we watched from our vantage point at the side of the castle, an evil baby blue Rolls Royce was rolling up the drive to the front door. We were able to see and not be seen, so we continued to watch the car as two men got out. The driver was Donald Goodman and he casually proceeded to walk into the house with the other man. When McGovern and I saw Goodman's companion, our faces must have reflected an astonishment roughly comparable to what we might have displayed at having just seen the Holy Ghost line-dancing on Country Music Television.

'Who was that?' asked Perkins.

Neither McGovern nor I answered until, after a moment, Kent must have figured it out for himself, because he didn't say anything either. We all just stood there like three fucked-up shepherds under a phlegm-colored trellis.

It was Ratso.

FORTY-SEVEN

Things moved at a breakneck pace after that. Perkins ran quickly toward the house, flattening himself against the outer wall and peering cautiously through a bay window into the great hall. McGovern and myself, not wishing to spook Ratso in a potentially dangerous situation, had to content ourselves with hiding behind a nearby hedge and watching Perkins watch Goodman. From our distant vantage point we could see dull images that we took to be Ratso and Goodman moving back and forth across our line of vision, occasionally coming very close to the window. Goodman appeared to be carrying some kind of shotgun or hunting rifle and showing it to Ratso.

'Do you own a sawed-off shotgun, Tex?'

'Not to my knowledge.'

The next thing I realized, McGovern was nudging me sharply in the ribs and Kent Perkins had discarded the paint-brush he'd been carrying and in his right hand he now held a gun. Then Goodman and Ratso disappeared from the window altogether and Perkins, in a scene vaguely reminiscent of Audie Murphy, ran toward us in a low crouch, still holding the gun, and jumped the small hedge, landing precariously close to my lit cigar.

'They're going hunting,' said Perkins.

'Well, fuck me gently with a chainsaw,' said McGovern.

'I overheard Ratso say: "I've never been pheasant hunting," ' said Kent. 'The problem is that for pheasant hunting you'd use something like a twenty-gauge and the shells would be six and a half birdshot.'

'So what's Goodman got?' I said. 'An elephant gun?'

'Damn close,' said Perkins. 'He's carrying a twelve-gauge shotgun and I could see the box of shells on the table. They're double-ought buckshot.'

'Which means?'

'Which means if they're hunting pheasant there's going to be nothing left to chew on.'

I chewed on the idea of Ratso going pheasant hunting with Donald Goodman and decided I didn't like it. I was just getting ready to figuratively spit it out when the back doors of the castle flung open and spit out the two great white hunters. Ratso was now carrying some kind of large burlap bag, presumably for the pheasant. Donald Goodman was still carrying the shotgun. They walked together into the woods.

'He's going to kill him,' said McGovern.

'He's sure going to *try*,' said Kent. 'I'm going after 'em.'
And he did.

'McGovern,' I said, 'do you think you can get into the
house and call the cops or the state police or somebody?'

'Sure,' said McGovern doubtfully. 'What do I tell them?'

'Tell them Mary Goodman's in the garden,' I said.

FORTY-EIGHT

I don't know if I could really *shoot* a pheasant,' came Ratso's
rodent-like voice out of the womb of the woods.

'You may not get the chance,' said a deep, gravelly voice I
took to be Goodman's. This was followed quickly by a short,
surgical laugh, cold as the ground I was crawling on.

In fairness to Ratso, he'd been in the calaboose during all
our efforts to track Goodman, so it stood to reason that he
might fall prey to an invitation from his long-lost rich cousin
to come up to the estate and be a country gentleman for a
weekend. It was also fair to say that the fine art of social
climbing was not lost on Ratso, and the opportunity to meet
his mother, now that he suspected she was loaded, would
draw him up here faster even than a hockey game.

At the moment, I couldn't see Ratso or Goodman and I
didn't know where the hell Kent was. I wasn't even sure why
I'd followed him into the woods. Without a weapon of my
own, the only role I could play was to stay out of the way of
Donald Goodman's buckshot.

I edged a little closer through the thick undergrowth until
I heard the soul-splintering sound of a shell being pumped
into the chamber of a shotgun. It was probably the last mortal
sound that Bambi's mother ever heard, and it wasn't exactly
music to my ears either. Then I heard it again. I crawled
more quickly, ever closer to oblivion by obliteration, the only

thought in my head being not to create the appearance of a large pheasant.

'You sure it's too cold for badminton?' asked Ratso. 'What does a pheasant look like anyway?'

'Pheasant?' Goodman laughed. 'Who said anything about a pheasant?' He laughed again. In the woods his laughter carried with a hollow, muffled, yet peculiarly penetrating sound, like the drums of death.

'Don,' said Ratso, a little unsure now, 'I thought you said we'd be hunting pheasant?'

I crawled closer. I could hear their voices quite clearly and what I heard was not reassuring.

'Pheasant?' said Goodman, who seemed to be playing with Ratso now. 'I didn't say we'd be hunting *pheasant*. I said it'd be *pleasant* to go hunting together. Do you know why?'

'Well, we *are* cousins,' said Ratso, now apparently clearly sensing that something was wrong. 'It's a good way to get to know each other. By the way, when is my mother getting here?'

'She's already here, cuz,' said Goodman, 'and you'll be meeting her soon. But we're not going to get to know each other, I'm afraid. We're just going to have a little hunting accident. Don't move or I'll kill you where you stand.'

Ratso, evidently, did not move. Neither did I. Their voices were almost on top of me now, it seemed, though through the undergrowth I could barely make out their images, like shadows in some poorly staged passion play. To move any closer, I thought, would be suicidal. So I listened, mesmerized by the deadly little scene, as if I were a creature of the wild, with nowhere to go and nowhere to stay, hypnotized by the very helplessness of being.

'It's like this, cuz,' Donald Goodman continued. 'Dear Aunt Mary and I lived very comfortably without a care in the world until the sweet old thing died about ten years ago. Of natural causes, I might add. I was so heart-broken I couldn't come to grips with the reality of dear Aunt Mary's death. So I just pretended she was still alive.'

'In other words,' said Ratso, 'you were keeping the goose that laid the golden egg even though you knew she was dead.'

'That's right, cuz,' said Donald Goodman, chuckling darkly in the dark forest. 'I like the way you pick up on things. Don't move. I mean it.'

There was an uncomfortable stillness in the woods. No birds. No animals. No Kent Perkins. Nothing but a silent shroud of sun-dappled darkness dancing its way downward to the forest floor.

'Oh, she was a strange bird, all right. I was her only known blood relation and I liked it that way. But dear Auntie had a will that she and her lawyers would never let me see. Of course, it doesn't matter now. She did speak of you now and again. She told me if God delivered her little David to her, everything she owned would be his. But I guess God didn't see it that way. He called her to her just reward long before you started hiring PIs and talking to lawyers and generally fucking things up. And now it's too late, cuz. Sorry we never got to know each other.'

There was a moment of silence almost like a silent prayer. Then came a desperate crashing of branches. Then a deafening blast. Then a bloodcurdling scream that seemed to die in the throat. Then another loud blast. Then nothing.

Nothing but the forest primeval.

FORTY-NINE

Three days later, a joint task force made up of the FBI and the New York State Police, using heat-sensing helicopters, infra-red cameras, and cadaver dogs, located the body of

Mary Goodman. She was in the garden. Interestingly enough, her remains were found not far from a curious-looking phlegm-colored trellis that seemed to stand a silent vigil over the entire operation. The joint task force, though disinclined to get involved with the murders of Jack Bramson and Moie Hamburger, had been keeping a close eye on Donald Goodman for what they deemed to be more important reasons – money laundering and federal tax fraud. To this end, they had infiltrated both Goodman's corporation and his estate near Chappaqua. The guard, for instance, that had tried to fat-arm McGovern had been working undercover for the New York State Police.

This did not surprise me nearly as much as the news I heard from Kent Perkins almost a week to the day after he'd blown away Donald Goodman. The head of the entire joint task force was a federal agent working undercover who'd been on Goodman's payroll for over eight months. The agent directing the operation was, according to Perkins, an older man who spent much of his time polishing silver plates.

Kent, incidentally, spent several days under the shadow of arrest for killing Donald Goodman with a weapon that was unlicensed in the state of New York. He was rather stoic about the whole ordeal, however, reciting to me what he said was the cop's routine rejoinder in situations of this nature. 'I'd rather be tried by twelve,' Kent had said, 'than carried by six.' As it evolved, of course, neither was necessary, and Kent Perkins, a job well done, was able to return to California, thereby repopulating that state with one more large, attractive, blond person.

Ratso, who suffered only a grazing wound to his left buttock, now stands, at this writing, to inherit slightly under fifty-seven million dollars. From this windfall, as might be expected, there will have to be extracted rather sizable legal fees that have been engendered by Ratso's having retained a candiru-like phalanx of lawyers that has, as also might be expected, become too sated with treading water in his prospective reservoir of riches to swim either toward warmth or truth.

To his credit, Ratso did leave a message on my answering machine that fateful day, telling me he was going out pheasant hunting with his new cousin. The cousin, according to Ratso, had read McGovern's piece in the *Daily News* and was making arrangements as well for Ratso to soon get together with his mother. Once Ratso was out on bail, of course, Goodman would know exactly how to get in touch with him at his apartment. He'd already killed him there once. Now, he realized, time was running out for him to eliminate this threat to his inheritance once and for all. And he moved very quickly. Goodman had also, apparently, been alerted to Ratso's quest on the radio. It isn't clear, however, at this writing, whether he'd heard it on Don Imus or on Howard Stern.

Unfortunately, I was already in Chappaqua when Ratso had called, having left the cat in charge of the loft. The cat, for whatever her reasons, failed to give me the message.

One final and rather disturbing note on Ratso. He has determined, for whatever his reasons, that his many new friends, as well as his relatively few older ones, should address him as David Victor Goodman. He is having very little success with this campaign and, I'm afraid, he's taking it all rather personally. I've counseled him that patience will win the day and that soon people will relate to his newfound identity as readily as they now appear to relate to his new-found wealth. Privately, however, I fear this will not be the case. It is a troubling but true phenomenon of life that people who, for whatever the reason, possibly through no fault of their own, have assumed animal names, invariably find them impossible to shed for all eternity. So if you are indeed saddled with one of these names, you may consort with the Rockefellers, but you will forever be a Ratso.

About three weeks later, back at the loft one afternoon, much in the manner of men in mental hospitals, I put on my white housepainter's cap and read to the cat a portion of a letter I'd recently received from Lilyan Sloman. Ratso by now had told her about the death of his birth mother and, apparently, a few other things as well.

' "You will never know," ' she says, ' "how much I appreciate what you've done for Larry." '

'That's nice,' I said. The cat, evidently, did not agree, for she switched her tail violently from side to side and stared stonily away in the opposite direction.

' "I know that you, too, have lost your mother fairly recently," ' I continued reading, ' "and I'm sure this did not make the search any easier for you. I only wanted to tell you the same thing I told Larry. No one can ever take the place of a person's real mother. But sometimes there are other places." '

'Sometimes there are other places,' I said to myself, and the cat, now that I wasn't addressing her directly, seemed to pick up my mood. She stopped thrashing her tail and crawled into my lap.

'Who knows,' I said. 'Maybe one of those places is right here in this loft.'

That night I dreamed I was driving a Rolls Royce across a vivid landscape in a tropical clime. In the front seat with me were Robert Louis Stevenson and Uncle Rosie. It was a beautiful day and everyone was smiling as we drove along an endless road under a swaying canopy of palm trees that seemed at once to belong to the sea and the sky.

Into this idyllic occasion was suddenly injected a strange thunking sound accompanied at irregular intervals by a not entirely unpleasant vibration in the area of my buttocks. This disruption continued for some miles until Robert Louis Stevenson turned around and peered deeply into the backseat of the Rolls.

'I say, old man, this *is* quite odd,' said the great author. 'There appears to be a small Aryan child kicking the back of your seat.'

In the morning, I lit my first cigar of the day and called Dr Charles Ansell, an old friend of my father's and a pre-eminent world expert on the analysis of dreams. I told Charlie the dream. I also told him that I rather suspected that the highway upon which we were traveling was the Road of the Loving Hearts.

'I can only analyze a dream,' said Charlie, 'in relation to a specific person and his or her experiences. But I can tell you a few quick points that seem to be indicated here. For instance the Rolls Royce. The wish explains the dream. You wish to give the appearance of a guy entitled to a Rolls Royce. And the palm trees. They grow tall, stiff, and erect. A palm tree is as near to a phallic reference as anything you can dream about.'

'So far,' I said, 'so good.'

'Uncle Rosie. Was he your uncle?'

'No.'

'Then he's the uncle everybody wishes he could've known better.'

'Charlie, you're readin' my mail.'

'A dream is more revealing than any form of conscious intercourse. Now what about Robert Louis Stevenson? You liked *Treasure Island*?'

'*Dr Jekyll and Mr Hyde*.'

'This is a dream analysis, not psychoanalysis. Now the small Aryan child is a problem. At first I thought he might be you, but now I think he's determined to always stand in the way of your complete happiness. His destiny is to keep you miserable. But did he inherit this role? Was he inoculated as a baby? How does he know you're a Jew? Is your other imaginary car a Mercedes? Anyway, if the kid comes back, let me know.'

'If the kid comes back I may be calling from the Pilgrim State Mental Hospital.'

'No, seriously,' said Charlie, 'it's a dream of great hope for the future. Especially the palm trees. I like the palm trees.'

'They speak very highly of you.'

'By the way, this place you describe – what is it? – lovely name – '

'The Road of the Loving Hearts?'

'That's it,' said Charlie. 'But the question I have for you is this: Do you actually know whether or not this road really exists?'

I took a measured puff on the cigar and then the cat and I watched the blue smoke drift dreamily upward toward the lesbian dance class.

'Charlie,' I said, 'you tell me.'

ACKNOWLEDGMENTS

Dear Occupant:

The author would like to express his deep gratitude to all the people who've helped him in his life, including those who have died and gone to Jesus, many of whom have reported that He looks a little like Andy Gibb. As far as the living are concerned, and you know who you are, thanks for the Hawaiian coffee, the Cuban cigars, the encouragement, and, in some cases, the valid criticism. The author does not take valid criticism well and it often causes him to become highly agitato, plunging him into prolonged periods of petulance and pique, not to mention alliteration. All this notwithstanding, much of the blame must be placed squarely on the shoulders of the usual suspects:

Esther 'Lobster' Newberg, literary agent par excellence, who loves me more than she loves anyone except Ted Williams and Bobby Kennedy. 'The Kinkster will soon be fartin' through silk,' says Lobster;

Chuck Adams, editor extraordinaire, who knows what to leave in, what to take out, and when to take a spiritual rain check. After months of working intensely with Jackie Collins, Charlton Heston, and myself, Chuck is now going over manuscripts at the Bandera Home for the Bewildered;

Don Imus, who got me with Esther, got me with Chuck, and got me expert medical advice many years ago when I noticed several drops of blood in my semen. Upon observing this singular phenomenon, I called Imus to say goodbye. I was, quite naturally, convinced that the date on my carton had expired. That, however, was not to be the case. The Baby Jesus, who, I understand, looks a little like Winston Churchill, wanted me to live so I could share this rather poignant personal experience with you, Gentile Reader. Imus's doctor merely prescribed that I refrain from overly zealous, Dylan

Thomas-like self-gratification for at least two weeks. I complied, and was eventually able to whip my illness. Imus, of course, continues to maintain a seminal role in my life.

I'd also like to thank some very important British people with whom I have professional intercourse on a fairly regular basis. None of them has brought me grief. Yet. They are as follows: Robert McCrum for discovering me; Joanna Mackle for launching me; Matthew Evans for nuturing me in matters beyond the coin of the spirit; Angela Smith for feeding me, and a special thanks to Anthony Wall for getting the show on the road.

Also a tip of the old Yamaha on my head to Deborah Rogers for playing such an integral part in helping to make the Kinkster an international household nerd.

And finally, before these acknowledgements begin to cut into my cocktail hour, I'd like to pass along a bare snippet from a rather illuminating conversation I had last week with the gorgeous Stephanie DuPont. She was in the process of reading out loud to me from an article in what she calls her bible and what the rest of us call *People* magazine. The newsflash concerned one of the members of the band U2 who'd recently forsaken his palatial rock-star residence and moved, with all attendant publicity, into a lighthouse.

'What do you think, banzai dick?'

'Waste of a lighthouse,' I said.

The Love Song of
J. Edgar Hoover

For Nelson Mandela and the Eskimos at the Airport

It was New Year's Day. I stood at the kitchen window sipping a hot, bitter espresso and gazing down at the half-deserted, fog-shrouded, broken-hearted countenance of Vandam Street. It looked a lot like I felt. On this day in 1953 Hank Williams had died somewhere along the way to a show in Canton, Ohio. Whether death is indeed preferable to doing a show in Canton, Ohio, has been a much disputed philosophical question ever since. About the only thing I could say for sure was that Hank Williams had been dead almost as long as I'd been alive, and the older I got the more he seemed to be catching up with me.

The cat sat smugly on the windowsill, smiling at a pigeon on the other side of the glass.

'You're probably a big fan of Hank Williams Jr,' I said, on a thinly disguised note of facetiousness.

The cat said nothing. She looked at me calmly for a moment, blinked several times, then returned her gaze to the pigeon.

I drank some more espresso and watched the fog. Facetiousness, I reflected, was one of many elements of subtlety that was most assuredly lost upon cats. It was also, of course, lost upon Hank Williams Jr. But that wasn't entirely his fault.

'How would you feel,' I said to the cat, 'if after every show somebody'd come backstage and said: "You were good – but you'll *never* be as good as your *daddy*?" '

The cat continued to watch the pigeon. I continued to sip my espresso. The fog continued to roll across Vandam Street until it almost seemed to take on the bleak, beckoning, ghostly visage of an early-fifties Tennessee highway heading inexorably toward the Canton, Ohio, of the mind.

I was contemplating the rather ludicrous notion of a man-

and-cat suicide pact when the phones rang. There are two phones in the loft, on opposite sides of my desk. Both of them are red and both of them are connected to the same line in order to enhance the importance of any incoming wounded I may receive. Neither of them had rung in my recent memory. I walked across the kitchen and over to the desk and picked up the blower on the left.

'Start talkin',' I said.

'My name is Polly Price,' said a husky voice. It was a woman I didn't know. As I reached inside the porcelain head of Sherlock Holmes for a cigar, I tried to think of a woman I could really say I did know.

'Polly want a private investigator?' I said hopefully.

'As a matter of fact,' she said, 'I do.'

To calm the wild beating of my heart, I lopped the butt off the cigar and lit it with a kitchen match, always keeping the level of the flame slightly below the tip of the cigar. In my narrow experience as a country singer turned amateur detective, I'd had very few real live, honest-to-God, walk-in-off-the-streets clients. One of the reasons for this was that it was impossible to walk in off the street through the locked front doors of the building to get to my fourth-floor loft unless you stood out on the sidewalk and hollered loud enough to get my attention, whereupon I would toss you down the little black puppet head with the key wedged tightly into its friendly, ingenuous smile.

'Hello. Are you there?'

'Yes,' I said. 'How did you hear about us?' I glanced briefly at the cat. She had moved over to the kitchen table by now and seemed to be taking a bit more interest in the situation.

'I'd rather not discuss anything about the case over the *phone*,' she said.

'Of course not,' I said, puffing understandingly on the cigar. Woman was probably a little out of touch with the mother ship.

'I'd like to see you in person as soon as possible,' she said, with a tone of urgency in her voice.

'Well, I have a very hectic schedule this week, but this sounds like a matter of some importance. Do you think you could be here within an hour?'

'Oh yes,' said Polly Price gratefully. 'And thank you, Mr Friedman.'

'Mucous garcias,' I said.

I gave her the address and cradled the blower. Then I sat back in the chair and puffed peacefully on the cigar, blowing a thin blue stream of smoke up towards the momentarily silent lesbian dance class in the loft above me. If Polly Price had the money, I thought, I had the time. The only other smudge on my docket was my friend McGovern's recent report that he was being followed by little green men or something to that effect. Why should I care if this mysterious woman was also being pursued by little green men? As long as her money was green.

'We've got a client!' I shouted, snapping out of my reverie, jumping up from the desk, and clapping my hands a few times to encourage the home team.

The cat, of course, was not over-fond of such sudden displays of adolescent enthusiasm. She jumped off the table and ran to the bedroom doorway where she stopped and turned, thrashing her tail back and forth rather violently. She levelled an ancient, powerful green gaze in my direction, comprising in almost equal parts distrust and disgust.

'Hold the weddin',' I said. 'This client may turn out to be a gorgeous broad.'

The cat did not seem remotely impressed. She turned and headed unmistakably in the direction of the litter box.

'Of course one never knows,' I said. 'Beauty's all in the eye of the beerholder.'

'If there's one thing I can't abide,' I said to the cat, 'it's a client who isn't punctual.'

It was well over an hour later and the cat and I by now were back at the kitchen window staring glazedly into the street. The pigeon was long gone and I had no earthly idea what exactly the cat was gazing at. I had even less of an idea what I was gazing at. There was absolutely nothing in the street but a few parked garbage trucks and several residual wisps of fog that slowly eddied away like dreams from childhood or hopes from the sixties.

I was pacing back and forth across the dusty wooden living-room floor, cursing a woman who was not there, when I heard what sounded like the mating shriek of a pelican emanating from somewhere just inside my right earlobe. I walked over briskly to the window and at first I thought the fog was playing tricks on me.

Then I saw her.

She was a tall, leggy blonde dressed elegantly in black, and she seemed to be rising out of the fog like a pirate ship. I took the puppet head from the top of the refrigerator, opened the window, and tossed the little black head with the colourful parachute attached, down to her. Much to my chagrin, she let it bounce several times on the sidewalk before finally picking it up rather squeamishly. She looked at the smiling head but did not smile back at it. Then she looked up at me smiling down from the window. She did not smile back at me either.

'Fourth floor,' I shouted, before closing the window. The cat looked on disapprovingly.

'Don't worry,' I said. 'When I've hooked a live one I know it.'

A mere matter of moments later, the puppet head was

residing comfortably back home on top of the refrigerator, the cat was residing comfortably on top of the desk, I was residing comfortably in my chair behind the desk, and Polly Price had parked her sleek torso in the nearby client's chair. She did not appear to be residing comfortably.

'You have been in Afghanistan, I perceive!' I said, as I lit a fresh cigar with a lox-coloured Bic.

'You *are* good,' she said. Her eyes widened eagerly and she leaned forward in her chair to reveal the ruthless outlines of a nice pair of zubers. 'Just like I'd heard.'

'I'm kind of semi-psychic sometimes,' I said. 'Also, those are the first words Sherlock Holmes said when Dr Stamford introduced him to Dr Watson. "You have been in Afghanistan, I perceive." '

I leaned back in the chair and puffed pontifically on the cigar, studying my new potential client. I was enjoying my field of study.

'Of course, you realize,' she said, 'that Dr Watson was no doubt wearing his Hard Rock Café/Kabul T-shirt.'

I chuckled warmly. She smiled for the first time, evidently savouring her own little joke. If this broad ever said anything really funny, she'd probably slay herself. On the other hand, there's always something especially nice about the first time a woman smiles at you. I contend that at that moment, if you observe her smile, her eyes, and her body language carefully, you can determine the nature and the depth of your future relationship with her.

'And now,' she said, 'I want you to help me find my husband.'

THREE

There are certain sacred moments in the often-jaded field of private investigation and this was decidedly one of them. It was the kind of thing you dreamed about when you were a kid. There is the mandatory moderately mysterious phone call. Then a mystical figure walks through the mist. A sombre-spirited, beautiful woman dressed entirely in black enters your modest office carrying a little black puppet head with a big smile on its face. You take the puppet head from her pale hand and place it on top of the refrigerator. You glance at the puppet head, then you look in her eyes, then your gaze averts to the refrigerator. You are hungry, but only for truth. There is no need to open the refrigerator. You already know that the world is cold.

Now my new client is sitting across from me, fumbling in her bag for a cigarette, placing it nervously between her sulky lips. I reach across the cat to light her cigarette. The flame ignites. Our eyes meet again briefly and something is silently unlocked as if by an old-fashioned hotel key. She is ready.

'And now, Mrs Price, before we find your husband we must find the answers to a few questions. First, how did you hear about me?'

'I was talking to a very nice young gentleman the other night. I was rather distraught, I'm afraid, and he seemed very kind and comforting. He recommended you highly.'

'His name?'

'His name was Ratso.'

I got up abruptly and walked over to the espresso machine to mask my disappointment and annoyance as well as my recognition of the name. It's always a bit of a letdown for a mender of destinies suddenly to find he's merely the butt of a puerile joke. Largely through my efforts, my semi-erstwhile friend Ratso had recently been able to locate his true birth mother and as a result now stood to inherit slightly under 57 million dollars. The matter was now in the courts, but the closer Ratso seemed to get to the family fortune the further he seemed to keep his distance from his old friend the Kinkster. That was fine with me.

'Want an espresso?' I said curtly.

'That would be nice.'

As if I were a part of the machinery itself, I robotically performed the standard pre-launch procedures for the espresso machine and kicked it into gear. It almost immediately started humming something that sounded vaguely like 'The March of the Siamese Children'.

' "Very nice young gentleman," you say?' Something had to be wrong here. Ratso was many things but one of them was not a very nice young gentleman.

'Yes. Very clean-cut-looking. Well dressed. Soft spoken.'

I thought about it for a moment. Something was definitely out of focus here. Even if Ratso had stood to inherit the World Bank, this transformation of style, grooming, and personality was impossible.

'Where did you meet this Ratso person?'

'In a bar.'

'Well, at least that sounds right.'

'He said he'd heard wonderful things about your reputation. He said you could probably find my husband much faster than the police without turning the whole thing into a carnival.'

'My carnival left town a long time ago.'

The espresso machine began hissing and steaming like a mad scientist's laboratory, so I drew a few cups and that seemed to settle it down a bit. Polly Price hadn't even told me her story and she'd already gotten her referral wrong. I took the two espressos over to the desk, set them between us and fixed her with a stern gaze.

'You sure this guy wasn't ungroomed, unshaven, unkempt, and wearing antique red shoes, phlegm-coloured trousers,

and a coonskin cap with a little racoon's head on the front
with its eyes sewn shut?'

'Of course not,' said my soon-to-be former client indignantly. 'Who would go out in a ridiculous outfit like that?'

Ratso, I thought.

We'd been sipping espresso and staring at each other in sullen
silence for several minutes before the solution to the Polly
Price referral puzzle came to me. The whole matter was
merely a case of mistaken identity.

'Where did you say this bar was where you met Ratso?'

'I didn't say,' she responded coyly.

I stood up dramatically, walked over to the window, puffed
purposefully with my back to her, sneering at the fog. After
allowing the tension to build for a moment, I spun quickly
round to face the woman in the chair.

'Why didn't you tell me,' I said, with a slow, deliberate,
deductive cadence to the words, 'that the bar where you met
this person was in Washington, D.C.?'

'My *God*,' she said, not a little impressed, 'you really *are*
good.'

'And now,' I said, returning to my chair with her total
confidence, 'suppose you tell me about your husband.'

Half an hour later, as twilight started to shadowbox with the
city, I knew a little more about Derrick Price than I wanted
to know. There'd been the standard private-investigator questions, the client's customary answers, the photograph of the
missing husband, the tears, the proffered handkerchief, the
plans to get together for an investigative lunch in the next
day or two, and a cash retainer in an envelope, which I didn't
count but which was to thick to slide under the door.

I didn't tell her, of course, that I was a two-Ratso man.
There was New York Ratso and there was the infinitely more
pleasant Washington Ratso, and as far as I knew, she was
unaware that I was acquainted with either of them. As Sher-

lock himself had once said: 'What you do in this world is a matter of no consequence; the question is what can you make people think you have done?'

As I watched the backs of her legs recede towards the door, I began to feel pretty good about the case. If I found her husband, it could really be a financial pleasure for the Kinkster. If I didn't, at least there would be a lot of opportunities to watch her legs. And there was a lot of leg to watch.

'One more question,' I said, as she reached for the door-knob. She turned and again I noticed the pale, lovely face, the long blonde hair, the blue eyes that came at you with the gentle ruthlessness of rain on the roof.

'*Have* you been in Afghanistan?' I said.

'Never.'

'I suspected as much.'

FOUR

Just as there's more than one way to find happiness in this world, or so I'm told, and there's more than one way to skin a cat, pardon the expression, there are also many different ways to conduct an investigation into the mysterious disap-pearance of the husband of a beautiful, long-legged blonde.

One of the most interesting ways is to get to know all you can about the missing husband by getting to know all you can about the client. This method is closely akin to the classic approach of Inspector Maigret, who, by the time he'd solved the case, had often practically fallen in love with the dead victim in his relentless efforts to get to know the nature of the killer.

Of course, my client was very much alive, and her husband, for all I knew, might've gone out for cigarettes a week ago and then, without notifying the war department, decided to go to upstate New York to attend a hot-tub seminar on how to find his inner child. If that, indeed, were the scenario, my client would've found me so that I could go out and find her husband who was busy himself, of course, finding his inner child.

'We live in a world of missing persons,' I said to the cat, as I poured a long, daunting shot of Jameson Irish whiskey into the old bull's horn.

The cat did not respond. She was sound asleep on the kitchen table, possibly dreaming she was in Afghanistan searching for her inner kitten. Judging from the peaceful expression on her face, however, it didn't appear as if she gave a damn about such matters. Maybe she was on to something.

I picked up the bull's horn, threw a silent toast to the puppet head, and killed the whole shot. It burned my throat all the way down like friendly fire, but it gave me a little buzz. One or two more like that, I thought, and I'd very likely be looking for myself.

As the cold fingers of darkness reached further into 199B Vandam Street, the cat made the short journey from the kitchen table to the desk, where she curled up under her private heat lamp and nodded out again. I found myself slowly pacing the floor of the draughty living room, a cigar in one hand and in the other the photograph of Derrick Price. I wasn't sure I could find him, and part of me, I must admit, almost didn't really want to. Maybe I'd seen too many movies like *The Maltese Falcon* or *Chinatown*, where the mysterious, grieving lady client winds up hosing the private investigator. Images of Polly Price came unbidden to my mind. As I paced, I realized that I was walking a fine line between the private side and the investigator side of my life.

I walked over to the counter and poured another Jameson into the bull's horn. Then I poured it down my neck. I'd meet Polly tomorrow, I figured. Learn everything there was to know about Derrick. All the secrets of their honeymoon. And soon, with any luck, he wouldn't be a missing person any more. Like almost everybody else in the world, I was operating under the delusion that I had ethics.

'I'll find this bastard if it spoils my whole weekend,' I said to the cat.

The cat moved not a hair. You know you're in trouble when you find yourself talking to a sleeping cat. There are far more tedious avenues of social intercourse, however. Like spending an evening with a deadly middle-class Jewish couple.

I was pondering the doorknob that Polly Price's pale hand had so recently twisted when the phones rang, making the cat and me both suddenly leap sideways. It was a slightly more traumatic experience for the cat, of course, who'd been sleeping on the middle of the desk in a position precisely equidistant from each red telephone.

'That's probably an important call,' I said, wasting a little more facetiousness on the cat, who now was busy cleaning herself on the kitchen table, pretending for all the world that the phones were not ringing.

As things came to pass, it *was* an important call. Unfortunately, as you go through life, the things you think are important are very rarely important at all, and the things you think are not important are eventually, inexorably, vitally, profoundly, soul-alteringly important. Then one day, like Robert Maxwell, you plunge off your yacht into the Mediterranean and drown yourself, saying only one last word: 'Roseglub!'

I picked up the blower on the left.

'House of Pain,' I said.

'Kinkster!' said the voice on the blower. 'It's Peter Myers.'

Cosmically enough, Peter Myers was a limey like Robert Maxwell, except that Pete Myers was alive and well and making quite a big success of his store, Myers of Keswick, on nearby Hudson Street. Myers specialized exclusively in gourmet British food, which, of course, is something of a contradiction in terms, thereby practically guaranteeing his continued good fortune in a place as perverse as New York. At the moment, however, Myers, who is usually cool and unflappable, sounded very highly agitato.

'Yes, Peter. Is anything the matter?'

'I'm afraid so. It's our large Irish friend McGovern.'

'Ah, the Irish again. Where are you calling from, Peter?'

'The back of the shop.'

'Where's McGovern?'

'The front of the shop.'

'Well, that seems like a reasonable placement job. Will he stay there?'

'Will a tropical storm stay precisely on its coordinates, Kinkster? I don't bloody well know. I don't know how much grog he's had and I'm not a bloody shrink, but he's becoming increasingly belligerent and very paranoid. He thinks he's seeing little green men.'

'They may not be little, Peter. They may not be green. They may not even be men. But if McGovern says he's seeing them, I can tell you that they're there.'

'Well, I can tell you for sure one thing that they're *not*, Kinkster.'

'What's that, Pete?'

'Customers.'

I told Peter Myers I'd be right over and I cradled the blower. As my father often commented, this was *exactly* what I didn't want to happen. I was just getting ready to start searching for Derrick Price and up pops McGovern like a large Irish Jack-in-the-box. There was nothing I could do about it, however. You were stuck with your old friends. Like I've always said: You can pick your friends and you can pick your nose, but you can't wipe your friends off on your saddle.

I put on my coat and my cowboy hat, grabbed four cigars for the road, and headed for the door.

I left the cat in charge.

FIVE

As I headed up Hudson towards Myers of Keswick, a light rain began to fall into the night street, softening the lights of the city and lending the neon an almost comforting appearance, like cotton candy at a county fair. Refereeing a little tension convention between Pete Myers and Michael McGovern ought to be a simple matter for the Kinkster, I thought. I'd known Myers since before I'd realized how to pronounce 'Myers of Keswick' correctly. Pete, ever the well-mannered Brit, never bothered to correct my pronunciation. But one day my friend Mick Brennan rather mockingly mentioned: 'You'd think they'd teach you in Texas that the "w" in Keswick is silent, mate.'

'Why don't you try to be,' I'd told him.

I'd first met McGovern in a large closet – it would have to be – in my suite at the Essex House one night when I was doing *Saturday Night Live*. Both of us were flying on about eleven different kinds of herbs and spices at the time, so I can never be sure, but I believe the personage who gets the credit or the blame for introducing us was Piers Akerman, the world's smartest, and loudest, Australian. Why the three of us were in the closet at the same time is a matter of conjecture, but at least we eventually came out, which is more than many New Yorkers can say. When we emerged, I had a new, rather large Irish friend and I noticed that the suite was now full of other new friends, many of whom had Bob Marley falling out of their left nostrils and most of whom I've never seen again. At least I didn't have to waste any time trying to wipe them off on my saddle.

As the wind and rain turned colder, and Hudson Street conjoined Eighth Avenue, my thoughts, as well, turned to another subject: Polly Price. I could fill the New York Public Library with what I didn't know about the woman. What I did know was hardly enough to make for a good icebreaker at a cocktail party.

She'd been married for ten years to Derrick Price and, as with most successful marriages these days, they lived in separate cities, getting together only on weekends. He lived in New York. She lived in Washington, which, of course, was where she'd met Washington Ratso. And, as might be expected, both of them were lawyers. I don't know what the stats are, but marriages between lawyers seem to last longer than other unions, for some reason. Possibly the prospect of two lawyers snipping each other's legs off, then jousting in motorized wheelchairs during ugly, superlitigious divorce proceedings is enough to keep any marriage together.

Strangely enough, Polly Price had not seemed sure whether or not she suspected foul play. She seemed confused by the question. She definitely did not think that Derrick could be cheating. After watching the sensual way she smoked a cigarette, I didn't think he could be either. I was relieved not to be merely chasing some husband who was chasing a skirt that obviously did not belong to his wife. According to the *National Enquirer*, 98 per cent of all those who suspect their spouses are cheating on them are correct. You can believe the *National Enquirer* or you can believe your spouse. Either one's a fairly long shot.

Only once during the initial interview had I asked Polly Price a really cold, surgical question. It was just after I'd lit her second cigarette and she'd crossed her legs for about the seventh time.

'Do you love your husband?' I'd said.

'Do you love your cat?' she'd replied.

It was a rather Talmudic and somewhat unsatisfactory response in many respects, but it did seem to demonstrate a slightly higher degree of perception in my client than I might've liked.

I legged it up Hudson past Jane Street and saw several limos parked in front of 634, Myers of Keswick. I peered in the window of the shop and noticed a number of customers politely milling about and Pete standing nervously behind the counter. There was no sign of McGovern's mammoth form anywhere to be seen. So far, so good.

I loitered in the doorway and admiringly observed the operation Pete Myers had built through years of hard work. The clientele was, according to Peter, about 95 per cent British and included everybody from royalty to the Rolling Stones. It was a loyal following that Myers of Keswick enjoyed, but it was also steeped stronger than Earl Grey tea in a sense of dignity and decorum. A guy like McGovern, if turned loose in a crowd like that, could send the whole business into the loo in a New York second.

'Where's Benny Hill!' came a loud roar from the back of the store. The customers looked around in embarrassed confusion. Pete Myers's face went white.

'Did you put him in the Dikstuffer?' came the roar again. The Dikstuffer was the actual trade name of a German sausage-making machine that Myers proudly had demonstrated for McGovern and myself in happier times. The machine forced sausage meat through a gleaming silver penislike projectile into the skin of the sausage. It was obvious from the perplexed expressions on the faces of the customers that they were unaware of the precise nature of the operation of this arcane device.

I walked through the hushed crowd just about the time Myers came flying round the counter, shaking his head and waving his arms, and we collided with an elderly Indian gentleman in a turban who was attempting to purchase four dozen curried chicken pies.

'You see what I mean, Kinkster!' said Myers in a voice of grim exasperation. 'I don't want him out here with the customers. I can't get him to shut up. How do I get him out of the bloody shop?'

'It's going to take the entire Polish army or a forklift,' I said, 'to get McGovern to go anywhere he doesn't want to go. Of course, we could put him in the Dikstuffer.' Myers did not find these suggestions humorous.

He peered cautiously through the doorway into the back of the store, as if it were the den of a particularly tedious dragon.

'I love McGovern,' said Myers. 'He's one of my oldest friends.'

'He's one of your biggest friends, too.'

'We've been pissed together dozens of times but I've never seen him like this. I tell you, Kinkster, he's mad. I can see it in his eyes. He's bloody off the boil.'

'What symptoms does the patient manifest? I mean, other than his recently expressed inquiry concerning Benny Hill and the Dikstuffer?'

'I'm not sure you grasp the seriousness of this,' said Myers, grasping my shoulder like a drowning man. 'This behaviour didn't start this evening. It's been almost two weeks now! He saw a little green man. He believes he's being followed everywhere. He's getting phone calls in the middle of the night from people he claims are dead. He needs bloody professional help!'

'OK. Settle down, Pete. You go back behind the counter and take care of your customers. I'll go back there and talk to McGovern.'

It was a good plan, but it never really got off the blocks. McGovern came lumbering through the little doorway, knocking over a large display of the ubiquitous H.P. Sauce that every Englishman, for reasons unknown to the rest of the world, pours lavishly upon everything he eats. Several bottles smashed to the floor.

'Jolly old H.P. Sauce,' shouted McGovern gleefully. 'The British national drink! And you never have to taste the fucking food!'

'I say,' said a nearby tweed-wrapped gentleman disapprovingly.

On his way to giving me a bear hug, McGovern managed

to dislodge an entire wall that had formerly been constructed of cans of mushy peas, a gooey green substance much loved by the British.

'You know what's really in those cans?' said McGovern in a loud voice.

'Out!' shouted Myers, pointing his arm towards the front door.

'Let's go, mate,' I said to McGovern in what I hoped was a Jiminy Cricket-like voice.

'See that old Indian guy,' said McGovern in a hoarse whisper everyone in the store could hear.

'No, I can't see him, Mike.'

'See that ol' bugger. The one with the receding turban – '

' "This is what comes of empire-building," ' I said, quoting *Breaker Morant* and aiming McGovern at the door.

'That old sod's been following me.'

'Maybe he wants to know what's really inside those cans of mushy peas.'

'It's *come* from the Jolly Green Giant,' shouted McGovern, as he turned in the doorway and glared at the tableau of appalled patrons.

'I *say*,' said the gentleman in the herringbone overcoat again.

'Didn't I meet you at the Boston Tea Party?' McGovern asked the man, as Myers flew round the counter again and the driver of one of the limos came over to help extricate this raging Irishman from the threshold of civilization.

'Who's this?' McGovern shouted. 'A fucking footman from the royal coach? Come to fetch the princess some barley water for her gin?' I saw Myers wince slightly at this remark and realized that it had struck, apparently, very close to the truth.

After a somewhat unpleasant altercation with the limo driver, Myers and I were finally able to coax and cajole the large, intransigent Irishman out of the little store, but not before McGovern had bombarded the few remaining customers with a rather extended series of 'Cheerios!' and 'Pip! Pip! Pip!s'.

As I walked with McGovern away from Myers of Keswick, I gave Pete Myers a thumbs-up sign through the window. It was a gesture he did not return. He was already busy picking up cans of mushy peas.

'Where are we going now?' asked McGovern, with all the innocence of childhood.

'Well,' I said, 'I know a nice little French restaurant down the street.'

SIX

One of the most important aspects of human nature for an amateur private investigator, or even an amateur human being, to be aware of, was once, like almost everything else, quite adroitly put on a bumper sticker by Sherlock Holmes. 'We are creatures of narrow habit,' he said. For amateur private investigators or students of human nature, paying close heed to this observation can often facilitate your labours in the field and lead to remarkable results. As far as amateur human beings are concerned, there is almost nothing anyone can do or say that can serve effectively to guide us through the rabbit warren of life. This, possibly, is why so few of us ever turn pro.

McGovern, like most people, was a creature of narrow habit. When he drank he was out where the buses don't run and walking on his knuckles and the world had damn well better get out of his way. But, the vast majority of the time, when McGovern was sober, he was that rarest of human beings, a true gentleman. Tonight's little outburst had occurred when he had not been drinking. Something had happened that had caused him to go off the boil, as Myers had

said, indeed, almost to the point of appearing to have under-
gone a personality transplant. I didn't know dick about art,
but something was definitely wrong with this picture.

'It all started about two weeks ago,' said McGovern, from
the small, dark table in the back of the Corner Bistro, where
I'd taken him for debriefing.

'What started? Whatever's going on, just tell me. I'll
believe.'

'Thank you, Peter Pan.'

I'd plied McGovern with several Vodka McGoverns to
return him to what I liked to think of as his normal state. For
myself, I'd had several shots of Old Grand-Dad, to keep
within barge-pole distance of whatever wavelength he was
on.

'Did I ever tell you about Leaning Jesus?'

'I think I would've remembered,' I said, downing a med-
icinal portion of my third Old Grand-Dad.

'He was a guy I knew in Chicago almost forty years ago.
Before I came to New York. I was just about sixteen when I
first met him. I was working as a switchman for the railroads,
and one night it was cold as hell and I went into a bar he
owned on the South Side. He kind of took me under his
wing. Let me drink in the place, taught me how to play gin,
taught me a lot of other things. I was just a big kid. In fact,
that's what he called me. The Kid.'

'Well, you've certainly matured a great deal since then.'

'He was an old man even at that time, it seemed. A very
strange and interesting old man.'

' "All right," said the farmer's daughter to the travelling
salesman, "Why did they call him Leaning Jesus?" '

'Well, these old guys had a lot of colourful names for each
other.'

'Which guys?'

'I'm getting to that. Anyway, he was called Leaning Jesus
because he was a thin, very biblical-looking guy with white
hair who'd been in a bad automobile accident and broken his

neck. He recovered eventually, but his head always leaned rather dramatically.'

'To which side?'

'Left.'

'Sorry, sir, but we've gotta cover every angle. We'll even try to cover *this*,' I said, leaning over rather drastically myself, lifting one buttock, and expelling a highly audible fart into the candlelit atmosphere of young couples dining together at nearby tables.

I ordered another round for both of us to sort of settle things down a bit and then pressed ahead with the discussion, having no particular idea where the hell this was going. All I knew for sure was that I finally had a fat retainer sitting patiently back at the loft waiting for me to start looking for Polly Price's husband, and here I was listening to McGovern yap at great length about some character he'd known in Chicago almost forty years ago. If I'd only thought to put the retainer in the bank, by now it would probably have acquired some interest.

'OK,' I said, once the drinks had arrived, 'what did this Leaning Jesus do?'

'What did he do?' said McGovern incredulously. 'He taught me everything I needed to know as a kid growing up on the South Side of Chicago. He taught me how to live, how to gamble, how to hide, how to fence things, how to be an artful dodger.'

'I understand that,' I said, 'but what did the guy do for a living besides owning a bar? I mean, did he have a day job?'

'I thought I told you that.'

'If you did, I must have repressed it.'

'He was Al Capone's chef,' said McGovern.

'Leaning Jesus was Al Capone's chef?'

'Absolootely,' said McGovern, in a pretty fair impersonation of one of the characters on *Amos 'n' Andy*.

'Jesus.'

'No. *Leaning* Jesus.'

I stared at McGovern for a moment, then stared at my drink, then raised my glass in a toast.

'To Leaning Jesus.'

'To Leaning Jesus.'

I believed McGovern implicitly. One of the things he never could be was a bullshitter. Besides, when you thought about it, Leaning Jesus was a perfect name for Al Capone's chef. He certainly wouldn't have been named Wolfgang Puck.

The other thing was that McGovern had known a lot of killers, murderers, and tough guys and dolls in his time labouring in the fields of the fifth estate. He'd done in-depth interviews with Richard Speck, Lieutenant Calley and Charles Manson, to name just a few. Why shouldn't Leaning Jesus have been a perfect father figure for him?

'For the past two weeks,' McGovern was saying, 'my telephone and television have gone haywire. Ringing and turning on and off and fading in and out and electronic beeps all the time. And men watching me and following me everywhere I go – '

'Little green men?'

'One of them was,' said McGovern defiantly.

I looked down at my drink again. This was worse than I'd thought. What was even sicker was that I found myself believing him.

'Look,' I said, 'don't worry about this now, bro'. Don't even think about it. There's got to be a logical explanation for all this, and you can rest assured I'll find it.'

'It all started with that phone call in the middle of the night about two weeks ago. That's when everything started fucking up.'

'Don't worry about it. We'll get to the bottom of this.'

McGovern now had a strange, dazed, faraway expression in his eyes that was not a particularly reassuring thing to see. I couldn't tell if he was drunk or sober, sane or crazier than Kafka.

'He was already a very old man when I left Chicago in

'sixty-seven. Yet, as God is my witness, he's the one who called me in the middle of the night two weeks ago.'

'Who called you two weeks ago, McGovern?'

'Leaning Jesus, of course.'

SEVEN

That night I couldn't sleep. McGovern had not been drinking before or during the Myers of Keswick incident, of that I was now certain. Therefore, I reflected, he clearly needed a major checkup from the neck up. Hearing from Leaning Jesus. Seeing a little green man. Of course, the mere fact that I'd found his ridiculous account almost credible might possibly indicate, I dimly realized, that I needed a checkup from the neck up as well. The more I lay in bed thinking about it, the crazier it all began to sound and the more convinced I became that these events had been occurring in one place and one place only – McGovern's large, well-oiled, life-marinated brain. Of course, there was another explanation for McGovern's bizarre experience, but, unpleasantly enough for all concerned, I didn't think of it at the time. If it had crossed my dusty, dream-laden desk, indeed, I probably would've dismissed the notion as more unbelievable than the one I was currently grappling with.

But McGovern's strange situation was only one of the Furies flying frenetically around my streetlamp-lit bedroom fending off Morpheus. Though I was probably the only Jew in America who never felt guilt, I began to half-see the distant spectre of Polly Price's husband, his arms stretched out to me, his eyes imploring my help. Missing persons was always a bitch. Especially in those not uncommon instances in which the missing persons didn't want to be found.

I had a few missing persons in my own life, I thought, as

I gently slid the cat off the pillow for the thirteenth time. She sulked a little while, walked around the bed a bit, and then came right back to the pillow. There has never been born a considerate cat. On the other hand, there are in this world very few truly considerate people. Considering that, it's a wonder anybody sleeps at all.

I missed people, both personally and professionally, I thought, as I lay wide awake listening to that great ceaseless buzzing energy that is New York at night. I would've liked to consult Steve Rambam, who was the PI I'd most often worked with on previous cases. He'd no doubt have some ideas on how to start searching for Derrick Price. But Rambam was in Tel Aviv – or was it Rio this week, or Sri Lanka? Another missing person just when you needed him.

The other missing person was Stephanie DuPont, the gorgeous blonde who lived, and possibly loved, on the floor above me in dangerously close proximity to Winnie Katz's lesbian dance class. Stephanie had gone to St Moritz with her family for their traditional holiday trip with all the other coochi-poochi-boomalini families of the world. Lots of missing persons there, no doubt. But I did miss Stephanie. She'd been invaluable in helping to find Ratso's mother, and she was the smartest, most attractive young person I'd ever met, and I had been having quite vivid, recurring dreams about her replacing the cat on my pillow.

Both Stephanie and Rambam were due back in the city within the next few weeks, but in the meantime I was going to have to show Polly Price something besides cigar smoke and two-way Ratso mirrors. For a while I thought about Polly Price, then I thought about her husband Derrick, then I thought about Polly again. Then I thought about replacing the cat with Polly on my pillow.

I still couldn't sleep.

I got up, made a cup of hot chocolate with marshmallows and sipped it as I smoked a cigar in the semi-dark living room. People who've never had hot chocolate, marshmallows and cigars together ought to give it a try. They say it helps you sleep.

When I got back to bed it was closing in on four a.m. and the cat lifted her head from the pillow and looked at me irritably. I lay back, stared at the ancient ceiling and tried to make my mind a blank slate, but McGovern's large, somehow childlike form kept spoiling my efforts. So I thought about Woody Hayes, the football coach, who was, of course, no relation to Ira Hayes, my personal hero. Ira, as you may know was the Pima Indian from Arizona who, along with five other men, raised the flag at Iwo Jima and appears in the famous picture taken after the battle. But that was another story, or was it a dream? At four o'clock in the morning whites and colours sometimes get mixed in your wash load.

Woody Hayes, I recalled, had once said in defence of his relentless ground game: 'When you pass the football, three things can happen and two of them are bad.' I applied this theorem to McGovern's current state of affairs and found that three things also could've been at work here. They were alcohol, insanity or he was telling the truth as he saw it. Unfortunately, of the three things that could've happened to create McGovern's bizarre situation, *all* of them were bad.

Lying awake at night wasn't entirely fruitless, I figured. Often you saw things you didn't see every day. There were a myriad of images, afterimages, dreams, almost-dreams, visions, and revisions that, like rare viruses in a rain forest, never would've survived the light. What was a mystery anyway, I wondered, but a shard, a tiny piece of the whole mosaic? And sometimes, through the infinite power of human imagination, this tiny piece falls into place.

'Everybody has the power of imagination,' I said to the cat. 'If we could only harness it.'

The cat opened one jaundiced eye briefly, then closed it.

'Hell,' I said, 'imagination's bigger than the information superhighway.'

The cat, evidently, had not heard of the information super-highway. So I explained it to her.

'You know the information superhighway,' I said. 'Where they spent 20 billion dollars so millions of people could wind up endlessly debating who was the better *Star Trek* captain?'

The cat said nothing. But then, she rarely if ever went in for pillow talk.

By the time dawn had begun flooding the city, cars were already crawling through the bridges and tunnels, people were already walking in the streets, and the cat and I were already sound asleep.

EIGHT

'Call me Polly.'

'OK, Polly.'

It was early afternoon and we were seated at a table by the men's room in a crowded little Chinese restaurant on Canal Street called Sun Sai Gai. Polly Price, looking earthier, more focused, but just as languorous and sultry as she had the evening before, was wanting to know if I'd had any ideas about how I planned to conduct the investigation. All I wanted to know was if they had any spare chopsticks lying around to prop open my eyes.

'I hadn't expected you to be burning the midnight oil quite so soon,' she said.

'You can't start too soon,' I said, 'on a missing person case.' I might as well let her think I'd been working on it. After all, she was letting me think she loved her husband.

'Today makes the fifth day Derrick's been missing?' I said, as the waiter brought a second pot of strong Chinese tea. Sometimes that's all that keeps you going.

'Yes,' she said quietly.

'You know that I work fairly intuitively and in a rather unorthodox fashion. Sort of a country-and-western Miss Jane Marple approach.'

Polly Price gave me a rather weak smile. I plodded on.

'That may well suit your needs, because, as I understand, you want this handled discreetly. It's always conceivable, no matter how well you thought you knew your husband, that he may indeed be a missing person by choice. He may have gotten in over his head on something. He was a partner, you say, with a very prestigious firm here in New York – '

'Schmeckel and Schmeckel,' she said, matter-of-factly.

'Just consider the possibility,' I said. 'When someone in his position disappears without an apparent trace – which I haven't really determined yet – but if that's the case, things could get tedious. I'll need your help to start out on the right track. To do that, you may have to park your pride, park your ego, and park many of your previously held notions about your husband at the door.'

I could feel her struggling with the idea. When she looked up at me there was the soft shine of sadness in her eyes.

'It's always hard to find parking in New York,' I said.

In the next few minutes, as the food began to appear and then disappear from the table, we began to hammer out a basic approach to the puzzle of her husband's vanishing act. We'd go from the restaurant to her husband's penthouse on the Upper West Side, where she was currently staying. I would have free rein to go over his papers, his effects, his lodgings, his car, the viaticum of his life. She would begin assembling for me everything that would help me follow a paper trail to her husband. I explained to her that we might very well have to follow the trail backwards before it would eventually lead us forwards. She seemed to understand this, though I doubted if she was fully ready to accept its implications. It's always hard to believe that someone you've loved isn't the person you thought he was.

Or she was, I thought, as I daydreamed a little. I saw a girl in a peach-coloured dress. She looked not a day older than when I'd first seen her as she drove up to the ranch in Texas in her white Thunderbird. She had a four-year-old son now. Lived in the Northwest. Working on her fourth or fifth husband, but who was counting? Geographically, culturally, philosophically undesirable, yet we were perfectly suited for each other in all the timeless, primitive, clandestine ways that can only be reckoned in daydreams. Maybe I'd take a trip some day.

'What were you *really* doing last night?' she was saying, as I felt my head give a slight, involuntary nod. She was smiling and waiting as I gathered whatever was left of my thoughts.

'It's an interesting, if somewhat tedious story,' I said. 'It mainly involves staying up half the night baby-sitting a crazy Irish poet who believes he's seeing little green men and getting phone calls from a dead mobster named Leaning Jesus.'

'C'mon, Kinky,' said Polly, laughing now for the first time that afternoon. 'I don't believe there is such a person.'

'As Leaning Jesus?'

'Well, him, too. But I'm thinking more of your journalist friend – just the image of you with your cowboy hat and cigar counselling someone who's obviously – '

'Cookin' on another planet?'

Polly Price was now laughing openly, whether from something I'd said or from hysteria, I couldn't tell. She had a wonderful, well-mannered, yet somehow wicked way of putting her hand to her mouth when she laughed. It was a beautiful hand and a beautiful mouth. It was the kind of mouth you wanted to kiss even if you had to bite her fingers.

'When this is over,' I said, 'if you and I are still speaking, maybe I'll introduce you to McGovern.'

'Great,' she said. 'If he's really cookin' on another planet, maybe we can share some recipes.'

Now there were tears in her eyes. This was exactly what I didn't want to happen. A hysterical broad for a client, who'd recently misplaced her husband and was falling to pieces right in front of my eyes, along with the special added attraction of McGovern providing a nuisance nightmare of his own to occupy the spare time I almost certainly wasn't going to have. It was a hell of a way to ring in the New Year.

I looked round and found a waiter and signalled to him to drop the hatchet. When I looked back at Polly Price, she was watching the people walking by the window with a dry-eyed, vacant gaze.

'Oh, Derrick,' she said.

I paid the bill and we got out of there. We found a taxi and headed uptown and over to the West Side.

Maybe she did love her husband.

NINE

Derrick Price's place was pretty swank and well ordered for a guy who wasn't home all that much. His penthouse, in a building with about nineteen doormen just off Riverside Drive, afforded a wraparound balcony upon which I was currently ensconced, sitting on some kind of modern, uncomfortable, wrought-iron chair, smoking a cigar and studying the view. New York was still there, all right. You just needed the Mount Palomar Observatory to see it. Polly was changing her clothes and I was changing my mind about how easy it was going to be to find the wealthy law partner who should've been sitting on this chair instead of me.

'Don't sit on that,' said Polly, coming through the sliding glass door in a slinky black outfit. 'That's a piece of modern sculpture that Derrick made himself.'

'Nice work,' I said, getting up gingerly and rubbing my backside.

'Are you all right?'

'Well, I've bifurcated my buttocks rather severely, but it's probably not the last time I'll make an ass out of myself. Let's get cracking.'

I told Polly what I felt I needed: her husband's date of birth and social security number, and any bank statements, phone bills, or credit-card statements or receipts that might provide a clue to his activities right before he disappeared. As she set about gathering these items, I poked round the apartment a bit on my own. There didn't seem to be anything out of place or just lying about. Polly had told me she'd touched very little and hadn't moved anything.

'Has the maid been in lately?' I asked, as I came into the room where Polly was excavating papers from a desk.

'Derrick doesn't have a maid.' She was still hanging in there with the present tense, I noticed. I wondered how long that was going to last.

'Big place like this,' I said. 'You'd think he'd need twelve maids a-milkin'.'

'Derrick's very anal.'

'All successful lawyers are very anal,' I said. 'That's part of their charm. I don't see a Christmas tree.'

'Derrick's very secular.'

'OK, so he's very anal and he's very secular. What else is he?'

'A very good husband,' she said, putting her head in her hands and beginning to stoke up the waterworks again. I let them flow. There was something she wasn't telling me, I thought. And that can often take an investigation from merely tedious to extremely unpleasant in a hurry.

I checked out the kitchen which looked like it'd never seen a cockroach. Of course, cockroaches had more brains than to go into a kitchen where there wasn't any food. I wandered into the living room and it, too, had the same unlived-in feel. Few personal effects. No photos of the happy couple anywhere on the tables or walls. It had the feel of a well-appointed boardroom or a suite in an upscale hotel. Maybe it wasn't that strange, I thought. Not everybody appreciated cats, dead cigars, a layer of dust on the floor and a lesbian dance class on the ceiling as much as I did.

I looked in Derrick's bedroom, where Polly had been sleeping for the past few nights. She was fairly anally retentive herself, and everything was neat as a pin, including photos and bric-à-brac and personal effects all in such a symmetry as to make even the great Hercule Poirot twirl his moustache in satisfaction. But which of the photos and effects were Polly's and which were Derrick's wasn't readily discernible.

I took the picture of Derrick that Polly had given me and compared it with several on the bed table. He didn't look as happy in my shot. Of course, in my photo he wasn't with Polly. I tried to think of him, in Dickens's phrase, as a 'fellow passenger to the grave'. Derrick Price had been a man just like myself, I thought. His flight, very possibly, had just gotten in a little earlier.

If Fibber McGee had been gay he would've come out of Derrick Price's closet in a hurry. Every suit, every tie, every shoe was in its place. It looked almost like a store display. What a pathologically impeccable man Price was. How could he come to such an untidy end?

I sat on the bed and looked out of the window at the missing man's flowerpots all in a row on the balcony. God would have to water them, I supposed. What in the hell was I doing getting myself involved in this? Maybe Polly could help me get the guy's papers together, but whatever else I thought I was looking for I wasn't going to find. It was a little like visiting your mother's grave and knowing that your mother isn't there.

What could Sergeant Cooperman find in this place, I wondered? And why does Polly Price want me here instead of New York's finest? And where is Derrick Price's car? And is Polly holding back on me or is she merely the traumatized wife bravely holding up as well as can be expected? Lots of little questions. But unlike the rows of ties and flowerpots, I had a feeling some of the answers were going to be messy as hell.

I walked back into the other room just as Polly was collecting some papers for me in a neat little pile on Derrick's desk. She also seemed to have collected herself pretty well.

'Polly,' I said, 'just as your husband may have gotten into something over his head, so might I have gotten into something over my head with this particular investigation. It looks like the only rational starting point is whatever you've been able to assemble on the desk there, and frankly, computer checks and paper chases aren't really my long suit. The consultant I rely on for that kind of thing is out of the country and I don't know when he's getting back. I want to find your husband. You want to find your husband. But what if your husband doesn't want to be found?'

Polly Price found a cigarette. I lit it for her. I liked to make myself useful.

Then she stacked the papers again neatly and put them in a large yellow envelope and handed it to me. I accepted the envelope reluctantly.

'Do you believe in God?' she said.

'I can't answer that until I talk to my lawyer,' I said. 'And right now he's missing.'

'Don't ask me how I know this,' she said. 'But you're the one who's going to find Derrick.'

TEN

I took the envelope and the keys to Price's car, walked over to the parking garage down the street, and located the small concrete space where the missing lawyer had probably paid enough a month to rent a nice house almost anywhere else in the country. The car was there. So was I. So I routinely checked the vehicle inside and out for recent dents, blood-stains, anything at all that might help me learn what had happened to Derrick Price. There was nothing. Finally, I took down the licence number, returned the keys to one of the nineteen doormen, hailed a passing hack, and headed for Vandam Street.

I had misgivings about staying on the case, but then, I had misgivings about a lot of things in life. One of them was, as my friend Dylan had once observed, how football coaches always used the word 'football' in every sentence when they're being interviewed after the game. The season was all but over now, of course, except for the Super Bowl. I was keenly aware that watching pro football was an extremely accurate index of the emptiness of one's life. None the less, I missed absentmindedly watching the players tump over on the field.

Why did Polly Price seem not to want the police to investigate the disappearance of her husband? If they did, would Cooperman's minions have any better chance of finding him than I would? I doubted it. The NYPD, I reflected, probably didn't believe in God either. I might as well lead the charge, I figured. Unless you're the lead dog, the scenery never really changes.

I'd go back to the loft and attempt to sift through Derrick Price's papers. I didn't hold out much hope for really finding anything. I was fairly ill equipped to be some kind of techno-logical, research-oriented, investigative bean counter. And yet it was all that was left. The situation only reinforced my theory that all of us are drawn to occupations that we're horribly ill suited for. It was certainly true of my cab-driver, who ran seven red lights, thought of the sidewalk as his passing lane, and almost collected ten points for hitting an albino Negro who'd made the mistake of trying to legally cross Seventh Avenue.

As the chill of twilight rain stabbed Manhattan, I faced the prospect of a long, lonely evening at the loft. It was a dead time after the holidays, the time when depressed dentists and other Americans often choose to croak themselves, and I was beginning to realize why. Everything I had in my life was on the table. The yellow envelope, yet to be opened. The bottle of Jameson, either half full or half empty, depending on whether you were a country-music line dancer or a depressed dentist. A Texas-shaped ashtray containing a half-smoked cigar that was as dead as my dreams. The old bull's horn, which I liked to think had fatally gored an indecisive matador or two in its day before it moved on to its next incarnation and began its job of fatally goring me. And the cat, who probably expressed my attitude best of all by attempting to dislodge, with a high degree of style and irritation, a flea she couldn't find.

I sat down at the empty table. There were no guests, so I could pick any chair I liked. Lots of elbow room for Daniel Boone. I poured a stiff shot and downed it and sat there for a while staring out of the grimy kitchen window at the grimy New York night. It almost made you feel grimy just to look at it. Grimy and rainy.

'Better to feel grimy and rainy than nothing at all,' I said to the cat.

The cat said nothing but began almost ritually licking herself in an area that was not particularly germane to my current investigation. Or maybe it was. Out of respect for the cat, however, I will reveal the precise locus of her attentions only to those on a need-to-know basis.

I fired up the dead cigar, poured another shot and sat at the little table staring at the yellow envelope and thinking about my life. My support system had atrophied almost entirely, it seemed. The people who had comforted, helped, and sustained me over the years, both professionally and personally, now all appeared to be far away, busy, or dead. Some of them, very possibly all three. What Doc Phelps, a dear, dead friend of our family, had once remarked about his lonely last years in New Mexico now came to mind. He'd said that he was a very lucky man because he'd loved many people in his life and he still did. I was a lucky man, too, I reflected. But what a strange way to be lucky. But then again, if you thought about it, lucky was always a little strange.

I poured the contents of the bull's horn on to my uvula and poured the contents of the yellow envelope on to the table.

'OK, Derrick,' I said, 'I'm settin' my ears back and comin' after you, boy!'

The cat did not find anything remarkable about my statement. She was used to witnessing a man in a loft talking to himself and, on this occasion, did not even deem it necessary to register a mew of distaste.

I sorted through the used confetti of Derrick Price's earthly existence for what seemed to me to be about the length of time it'd probably taken him to acquire it. Going through his credit-card receipts and phone bills reminded me vaguely of the kind of enjoyment I derived from doing taxes. For a post-technological Peter Pan like myself, it was a rather hideous labour.

'Hercules the bean counter,' I said to the cat.

The cat said nothing, because she wasn't there. She had moved into the living room and was curled up sound asleep in her rocking chair.

'My support system is atrophying even further,' I shouted.

But there was no one to hear me. Not the cat. Not Derrick Price. Not even the lesbian dance class, which, possibly in sympathy with my support system, had apparently taken a brief sabbatical. It was all fine with me. When you're a lucky man, very little else matters. I poured another shot into the bull's horn and moved right along to Derrick's bank statements. Christ, it was fascinating work.

I'd only been perusing the bank statements for about the lifetime of the sea tortoise when something on that little piece of paper seemed to jump up and bite me on the nose. If a guy like me could see it, I figured, it almost had to be a major discrepancy. But there was no way to mistake it. Derrick Price had done something *really* strange. And for him, I suspected, it had definitely not been very lucky.

I was wholly engrossed in double-checking my discovery when the phones rang. With no little degree of irritation I arose from my chosen chair, walked over to the desk, and picked up the blower on the left with a firm, masculine grip.

'Start talkin',' I said.

'All right,' said McGovern, in a voice reverberating with tones of both triumph and fear. 'He's out there now, looking in the window.'

'Who? Where?'

'A guy wearing a fedora and an overcoat, standing out in the rain on my fire escape.'

'Maybe it's Gene Kelly.'

'I *know* who it is. Can you get over here now?'

'OK, I'm on my way. But who is he?'

'He's the same fucker – '

An electronic beeping came on the line, quickly followed by a strange, extremely loud series of metallic-sounding clangs.

Then the blower went dead in my hand.

ELEVEN

It was pushing Cinderella time when I finally flagged a hack out on Hudson Street. McGovern was at least right about one thing. It was raining like a bitch. I didn't really mind. In fact, after the fashion of W. C. Fields, I truly loved the rain. There is a rather poignant little anecdote, hopefully not apocryphal, about the death of Fields. During the time he was dying, it is said that his much younger lover, actress Carlotta Monte, knowing the great man's fondness for rain on the roof, often went outside, unbeknown to Fields, and sprayed the roof of the house with a garden hose. With my support system atrophying almost entirely, I reflected, by the time I died there wouldn't be anyone around to spray a garden hose on the roof. There probably wouldn't be anyone around to even *hold* my garden hose. On the other hand, there was a somewhat positive note about the situation. If something in your life had to be atrophying, I thought, far better it be your support system than your garden hose.

About four potholes later, my meditation on the tragic life of W. C. Fields, along with the rain, I noticed, had stopped. My mind now was welling up with thoughts full of angry frustration, almost all of them aimed directly at my old pal McGovern. Whatever the nature of his personal problems, he'd picked a hell of an inconvenient time in which to be experiencing them. He's the last guy in the world you'd ever want in your support system, I thought, and he was just about the only one I still had in mine.

To be totally fair to McGovern, he had many rare, human, almost Christ-like qualities. How a guy like that ever wound up in New York was another question. He was not materialistic like Ratso. Of course, no one was materialistic quite like Ratso. Ratso had materialistic staked out. Stood to inherit slightly under 57 million dollars and didn't want to run up the phone bill calling his old friend over the holidays. Never true of McGovern. McGovern was there when you needed him. Unfortunately, McGovern was also there when you didn't need him.

I paid the hack and legged it up Jane Street past the place where the last windmill in the Village used to stand. As I climbed the steps to McGovern's place, I tried to imagine a guy as big as he was crouching in his bedroom and whispering hoarsely on the telephone so as not to alert the mysterious character who was lurking on his fire escape. It was a mildly humorous picture. Even when McGovern crouched he was bigger than anybody else.

I pressed the buzzer for apartment 2B.

The answering buzz came almost immediately. I jerked open the front door and moved quickly through the little foyer, down the narrow hallway, and up the short stairwell to the second floor. McGovern's place was at the far end of the second-floor hallway, and I could see that his door was slightly ajar. No light was coming from inside his apartment.

I pushed the door open cautiously and waited for my eyes to adjust to the dim light. After a moment or two, Carole Lombard's framed photograph gleamed at me from the brick wall beside McGovern's fireplace.

'MIT . . . MIT,' I said softly.

There was no answer.

MIT was a code word McGovern and I often used to remind each other that we were still alive. It was an acronym that stood for 'Man in Trouble'. The idea had come when McGovern had seen a story on the wire about a guy who'd died in his apartment in Chicago. It'd taken six months before they'd discovered the body and by that time it looked worse than anything the guy who discovered penicillin ever saw through his microscope, whatever the hell his name was. The legendary what's-his-name.

'MIT – MIT – MIT!!' I said again, this time a good bit louder.

'MIT,' came the almost grudging reply from a dark corner of the room.

I looked in the direction of the MIT and saw McGovern's large, familiar form slumped motionlessly in his ancient easy chair. In his hand there appeared to be a tall glass of something that my cowboy intuition told me was very likely a rather strong Vodka McGovern.

'Growing hallucinogenic mushrooms, are we?' I said, as I felt around for the light switch. It certainly would've explained McGovern's recent behaviour.

'Turn on the lights,' said McGovern bitterly. 'The party's over.'

'Good line for a country song,' I said. 'I'll see what I can do with it.'

'That fucker was there, I tell you, and now he's gone.'

'I'm not sure if *that* lyric is quite as commercial.'

I found the lights and glanced round McGovern's cluttered living room. It looked like it'd been hit by the Sunset Limited, but as far as I could tell everything was in its usual place, which, of course, was all over the place. McGovern could be criticized for many things but it was refreshing, for some reason, to find a man who was beyond any shadow of a doubt *not* an anal retentive.

'Fucker was right there on the fire escape,' said McGovern, like a small, petulant child, used to having the grown-up world not believe his stories.

He pointed stubbornly to the landing of the fire escape, which was plainly visible through the nearby window. It was also plainly visible that no one was standing on the fire escape. Apparently McGovern had already had more than a few Vodka McGoverns this evening. I was not, of course, in a really good position to be giving him a temperance lecture.

'Let's have a look out there,' I said.

'Be my guest.'

'I've been your guest, McGovern, on several rather memorable occasions, if you recall.'

McGovern laughed for a moment, but I could tell his heart was really not in it. It was a quiet, almost sad laugh, a rare thing indeed for the hard-living, fun-loving Irishman. Possibly, it emanated from the tall, proud Native American side of his family tree.

I walked past McGovern and over to the window that opened on to the fire-escape landing. I started to open it and found that it was locked. Not an unusual thing in New York.

'You normally keep this window locked when you're at home?'

'Only when there's a guy standing on the fire escape.'

'Could this guy see you?'

'I don't think so. I was kind of peeking at him through the blinds in the bedroom. He seemed to be looking here into the living room like he was casing out the place.'

'You told me on the phone you knew who this guy is. Who is he?'

'You know that old Indian guy we saw in Myers of Keswick?'

'The one with the receding turban?'

'Absolootely. I saw him following me yesterday morning without the turban. Then he shows up at Myers of Keswick that evening. Tonight I catch him looking in my window wearing a fedora.'

'Curiouser and curiouser.'

I unlocked the window and raised it up as far as it would go. I stepped out on the fire-escape landing and looked down at the little alley that ran behind McGovern's building. Not a soul down there. McGovern, like some kind of urban turtle, briefly poked his large head out of the window. As I turned towards him, I saw what looked like a man's wallet lying on the landing next to the wall. I picked it up and started to check its contents.

'What've you got?' said McGovern from back inside the apartment.

'Michael R. McGovern,' I said, reading the driver's licence by the lights of the city. I held the wallet up for him to see.

'Hey, that's great!' he said. 'I've been looking for that wallet for almost a week!'

'It's dry, you'll note,' I said, as I climbed back into the apartment. 'When did you first see this guy and when did he leave?'

'When I first saw him it was already raining.'

'That'd make it about half an hour ago.'

'Just after it stopped, I looked out again and he was gone. So he must've dropped the wallet right after the rain stopped as he was leaving.'

'Yes, Watson, but don't you find it quite singular that he

was able to steal the wallet in the first place, considering that the window was locked?'

'He might've taken it earlier in the week.'

'And now, like a good little New Yorker, he's bringing it back? I have my doubts about that theory, Watson.'

'At least he didn't take any money,' said McGovern as he looked through his newly reclaimed property.

'McGovern,' I said, as I carefully lit a cigar with the new phlegm-coloured Bic that had been in the family for about forty-eight hours, 'you and I are men of the world.'

'We are?'

'Ah, yes. We live. We love. We will, on occasion, take a drink.'

McGovern, I noticed was already freshening up his Vodka McGovern as I spoke. I continued in what I hoped he would perceive as a rather stern voice. 'McGovern, were you at any time tonight out on that fire escape?'

McGovern continued to stir his drink without looking at me, but I could feel him gearing up to drive off in a 1937 Snit. These snits didn't last long, but for their duration there was no use talking to him. If he responded at all he was usually quite childish, and that was a nice word for it. I puffed on my cigar a bit in the heavy silence, then moved towards the door.

'Say, McGovern,' I said, 'who was the guy who discovered penicillin?'

'Fleming,' he said, rather sulkily. 'Alexander Fleming.' It was amazing, I thought, that his mind could remember something like that and yet not be able to keep track of his own wallet.

McGovern drank a healthy slug from his tall glass, then turned his back on me to make eye contact with Carole Lombard. He was obviously still smarting from my implication that he might have dropped his own wallet on the fire escape.

'Why do you want to know about Fleming?' he said.

'No reason.'

He stared at Carole Lombard for a long while, and since I had nothing else to do, I stared at her, too. She smiled sensuously back at both of us. In fact, she smiled sensuously back at the whole damn world. She knew she met all the criteria. She was funny, beautiful, intelligent, and dead. If you had to fall in love, I thought, she was about the best you could ever hope for.

McGovern had now turned round and appeared to be getting ready to address me. First he took a generous swallow or two of his drink. Then he fixed me with what he felt was his version of a stern gaze.

'Can I give you some constructive criticism?' he said.

'Sure,' I said. 'Let's hear it.'

'Fuck yourself,' he said.

Then he laughed. This time it was the real thing.

TWELVE

The first thing in the morning I looked at the clock and realized it was noon. I'd slept relatively well for a change, not experiencing any wet dreams about McGovern's dry wallet, but I had to admit it was still on my mind. The fact of the business, I thought, as I went into the dumper and attended to my various morning ablutions, was that I had to prioritize my work schedule or nothing at all would get done. The whole situation with McGovern, I had come to realize, was merely a sideshow, but, like any good sideshow, it had stolen my attention away from the really important matters at hand: finding my battery-operated nose-hair clippers and finding Derrick Price.

Nose hairs are something you don't think about much until you reach middle age, and then they seem to take over your life. Looking at things from the other nostril, Derrick Price was going to be one tough little booger to find. I finally had a lead and I planned to start checking it out as soon as I'd fed the cat, jump-started the espresso machine, and set fire to my first cigar of the day. But I wasn't all that optimistic about it. Of course, I wasn't all that optimistic about anything.

I'd spent enough time playing cops and robbers with Sergeant Cooperman and Sergeant Fox and Rambam and my private-investigator friend in LA, Kent Perkins. From them I'd learned the conventional, and occasionally unconventional, wisdom about missing-persons cases. If you didn't find the person within the first week or so, you'd better be prepared to spend your lifetime looking for him. Somehow I didn't think Polly Price's retainer, or her patience, or even her new-found religiosity would last that long. As for my own beliefs, I did not think that God wanted me to spend my life searching for some mysteriously misplaced lawyer. I listened to the still, small voice within and suddenly, very possibly for the first time in my life, I heard clearly the Lord's commandment to me. I understood what He wanted me to do. God wanted me to find my battery-operated nose-hair clippers.

'God,' I said, as I went back into the dumper, cigar in hand, to take a large Nixon, 'a man's life may be at stake and I think I've finally got a hot lead to run down that may help me find him. Why in the hell would you want me running around looking for nose-hair clippers?' It sounded like a fairly reasonable question for a mortal to ask.

'Cleanliness is next to godliness,' said the still, small voice. The Lord was obviously no respecter of persons. Even persons trying to take a Nixon.

'Look,' I said, 'I'm kind of busy right now. One thing at a time. Let me finish laying some cable here and then I'll jump in the rain room for you. Be cleaner than the whole damn continent of Europe.'

Actually, I had no intention at all of taking a shower. For one thing, the cat's litter box was always kept in the rain room, and if I wanted to take a shower I'd have to move it out. This could prove mildly unpleasant, seeing as I hadn't changed the litter in so long that some of the turds had fossilized and now were beginning to resemble rare pre-Columbian artifacts. This, of itself, was not entirely bad. If things ever really got rough, there always existed the possibility of putting them on the market. I felt pretty sure some New York art dealer would snap them right up. This wasn't the time, however. There was all kinds of crap on the market right now and, whatever happened, I didn't want to sell short.

'Frank Sinatra washes his hands five times a day,' said the still, small voice, ever eager to make its point. Like a great number of biblical characters, I continued to smoke a cigar and take a Nixon and pretended not to hear the voice. This effort at normal daily behaviour on my part wasn't about to stop God, however. If anything, it only seemed to encourage Him.

'Stephanie DuPont takes three showers a day,' said the voice, becoming positively garrulous now.

'Why you ol' devil,' I said good-naturedly, 'you've been watching, haven't you?'

There are times when you feel close to God and times when you don't and there are times when the two of you need to get away from each other for a while. I finished my paperwork in the dumper, washed my hands one time, grabbed a cup of steaming espresso, and headed for the kitchen table to tackle my other paperwork. Maybe I was being a bit curt, but I didn't have time to sit around heaven all day watching every nose-hair clipper, sparrow, and Hutu machete. I felt fairly sure that God, once He'd had a chance to think about it, would understand that I needed to get busy being my brother's keeper. You never knew, I figured. One of these days you might just find that your brother's name is Derrick Price.

THIRTEEN

Like Columbus, it took me quite a while to reach the Bank of America. And that was only the beginning of the journey. I was working with a cancelled cheque that Price had written on his own local bank the week before he'd disappeared. It was made out to the Inter-America Trading and Finance Corporation to the tune of one hundred and fifty thousand dollars. The amount and the timing of the cheque made it stand out from the rest of Price's transactions like a Jew with an ant farm.

The basic method I planned to adopt in order to establish a paper trail was what Rambam often spoke of as his 'hard-boiled computer' approach. I didn't have a computer and Rambam was still in Tel Aviv, London, or Sri Lanka, but otherwise, I figured, the damn thing ought to work. So, from the information on the back of the cheque I called the local Bank of America office and asked for the location of their Branch 282. They spat it back to me with all due haste. It was in Fairfax, Virginia. I was on a roll.

Now I picked up the blower and called information in Fairfax, Virginia, for the local Bank of America branch, called the bank, and held on while I was shunted between under-lings until I reached a customer service corporate accounts type of individual.

'My name is Derrick Price,' I said, 'I'm calling from New York.'

'Gladys Hemoglobin,' she said. 'How can I help you?'

'I'm with Schmeckel and Schmeckel and I need to make a second payment to one of your corporate customers, Inter-America Trading and Finance. What I need is their mailing address. My secretary managed to leave the file in Hong Kong.'

'One moment, please, Mr Price.'

I winked at the cat and waited. This was so easy you could do it at home.

A short while later she came back on the line and gave me an address in Silver Spring, Maryland. I thanked her, hung up the blower, lit a fresh cigar, and restocked myself in the espresso department. Then I called information in Silver Spring for the Inter-America Trading and Finance Corporation.

There was no listing.

Now I had a mailing address for the corporation but no listing for their phone number. I could have someone in the area check out the address for me or, as Rambam would say, I could 'develop a new address'. The latter sounded like the way to go. I didn't know what kind of dark venture Derrick Price was up to or caught up in – blackmail, extortion, embezzlement. Any one of them might be enough to make your average American hop the next flight on Qantas, the Rainman's favorite airline, with a one-way ticket to Malabimbi. Provided, of course, that somebody hadn't already punched your ticket.

Whether you considered the 'hard-boiled computer' method of investigative work fascinating or tedious, or a little of both, it had one rather large advantage over the standard physical gumshoe approach. It was better for your health, education, and welfare to be smoking a cigar and sipping an espresso in your loft than it was to be lurking in a freezing, rainwept alleyway by some shipyard watching a warehouse door out of which at any moment might emerge a thousand clowns, all of them named John Wayne Gacy.

So it was an easy decision, if it was at all possible, to keep the long, long paper trail winding into the land of my dreams. Stymied temporarily by the lack of a phone number for the Silver Spring address, I set about developing a new address for the Inter-America Trading and Finance Corporation. I called the Maryland Secretary of State's Office, Division of Corporations. I had now assumed the identity of your basic everyday process server, an individual that, according to Rambam again, is 'very low on the food chain and will arouse no suspicion'. Indeed, the petty functionaries I spoke to at the Secretary of State's Office did appear to regard me as little more than a rather commonplace nuisance. A real process server probably gets used to this shabby treatment. For me, however, it was a hell of a step down from my secretary leaving the files in Hong Kong.

'An out-of-state service address,' remarked one bureaucrat, after I'd been passed around for ten minutes like an Olympic baton. 'Very unusual.'

'I've never seen anything like it,' I said – the most truthful words I'd uttered all day.

'I don't even know if it's legal,' said the bureaucrat noncommittally, a natural timbre of ennui beginning to return to his voice.

'That's what keeps me in business,' I said, trying for a little enthusiasm to further feed his lack of interest. It worked.

When I hung up the blower I had the name and phone number of a Washington, D.C., law firm that ostensibly served as the service address for the corporation to which Derrick Price had recently paid out one hundred and fifty thousand dollars. I kind of preferred blackmail, but by this time, fraud, extortion, or embezzlement all would've been fine. Anything to lead me to the king.

'We're closing in on this bird,' I said to the cat, using a metaphor I knew she could relate to. The cat blinked several times and seemed to be taking a renewed interest in the proceedings, which I hoped were finally leading somewhere, because by this time they'd become extremely tedioso.

I called the law firm in Washington as a representative of the Acme Process Service with a summons and complaint on the Inter-American Trade and Finance Corporation. I was transferred to somebody's administrative secretary, who seemed to have at least twenty seconds for me.

'Are you still the valid service address for Inter-America?'
I said.

'No,' she said. 'There's a new valid service address. Just a
moment.'

I waited. I put my boots up on the desk, puffed the cigar,
and took a little break like any tired cowboy along the old
paper trail.

'Any legal papers,' she said, coming back on the line,
'should be served on Roscoe West.' Then she gave me another
address in Washington.

I called information and got the phone number. Then I
called the number. It rang and rang and rang.

Repeatedly, for the rest of the day, I called the number in
Washington with no results. Nobody was home and I was
past developing a new address because probably nobody
would be home there either. There's very little flesh and blood
along a paper trail. You might meet a paper doll. She might
live beside a cardboard sea. And yet something told me
instinctively that I was getting fairly close to my target. I had
an address. I had a working phone number. Once I came
down from feeling like I'd spent most of my adult life
manning the phone banks at the Jerry Lewis Facial Tic Tele-
thon, I might well be able to move forward actively with the
investigation.

Later than evening I made one final phone call to Polly
Price. She seemed much more in control of herself than she
had earlier in the day.

'Any progress?' she wanted to know.

I filled her in as much as I thought was appropriate, which
was not too much, and I gave her a slightly more positive
spin on the thing than I, at the moment, felt.

'A lead's a lead,' I said, 'and it's the best we've got. So I'm
haulin' buns for Washington in the morning.'

'That's funny,' she said.

'Haulin' buns?'

'No,' she said tonelessly.

'What is it, Polly?'

'Derrick used to love Washington, but in the past year he's been avoiding it like the plague. These days we always seem to be getting together in New York.'

'That's interesting,' I said.

'Whatever you find out, Kinky – whatever trouble he may be in – I want to know. Promise you'll tell me. Whatever it is.'

'I promise. When I know something, you'll know.'

To be totally truthful, I thought I knew something already. What I knew was that Polly knew something. Why else would a distraught woman who'd mislaid her husband not want the police involved? Maybe she had dark suspicions of her own. Maybe she knew what kind of trouble he was in. Maybe she wanted to protect his reputation from his partners at the firm.

But for whatever the reason, not unlike many a bird in a gilded cage, Polly wasn't talking. If she had, it might've saved a handful of Americans from a worldful of grief.

FOURTEEN

The shuttle from LaGuardia flew low over the Potomac in preparation for landing in Washington, the city where William Henry Harrison steadfastly refused to wear his overcoat for his inaugural parade. He died about two weeks later of pneumonia. I wasn't about to make the same mistake. I wore a heavy blue peacoat that looked like it'd been handed down to me by Oliver Twist along with a bright red Sydney Swans Australian football scarf and a black cowboy hat. I might not blend in too well at some of the more upscale restaurants, but it's always better to look like a squirrel, I figured, than it is to freeze your nuts off.

Because of Washington Ratso's time-consuming job as news

cameraman for Channel 9 and my own time-consuming job of being an unemployed youth, I hadn't actually spoken to him since the moment Polly Price had first held my puppet head. I had left a few messages on his machine, he'd left a few messages on my machine, and that had been about the extent of both of our contributions recently to peace in the Middle East. Ratso was a Lebanese Druse, a tribe of people, not unlike the Jews, who only seemed to fit in where they didn't belong.

I'd first met Jimmie 'Ratso' Silman in 1978 when I was playing a gig at the Cellar Door in Georgetown. He was then performing with the great rockabilly legend Tex Rabinowitz and the Bad Boys. At the time, I was working with only a guitar player, so Ratso had consented, sight unheard, to sit in on bass. After the first set, I had apparently decided to jet the guitar player for some reason, so I told Ratso I didn't need a bass player. He moved over to guitar for the second set. After the second set I decided I didn't need another guitar player. Not too long after that, I realized I didn't even really need myself.

Yet Ratso and I had remained close friends. We'd performed together sporadically over the years, musically speaking, at Willie Nelson picnics, the Lone Star Café, the famous Mo & Joe's Steakhouse, and the occasional whorehouse or bar mitzvah. We never made the White House, but then again, neither did Adlai Stevenson.

Now, as I stepped out of the airport on to the cold chill of the sidewalk, I lit a cigar and scanned a stormy sea of agitated faces. It looked like the entire United Nations was waiting in line for the same taxicab, but I did not see Ratso among them. So I stood on the kerb and smoked the cigar and nodded as two friendly looking Sikhs walked by. Those are always the best kind.

'Kinkster!' came a loud voice from somewhere amongst my fellow-passengers to the grave. 'Over here!'

Once I saw him he was hard to miss. Ratso was wearing a

big black cowboy hat like my own and a thick, general-issue Iraqi-type moustache. Under the moustache was one of the biggest smiles this side of Watergate. He was driving a mobile media arsenal with antennae and satellite dishes all over it and Channel 9 News scrawled across the side in bright red letters.

'Your limo's here, sir,' he said, as I climbed into the front seat alongside him. 'And welcome to your nation's capital.'

'And all this time I thought it was Austin,' I said.

'That was before Ann Richards lost.'

Ratso put the van into gear and before I knew it, he was weaving the bold, yet intricate embroidery required to get out of any modern airport alive.

'Now if you'll just tell me where the hell we're going,' said Ratso, 'and possibly why.'

I tore the address out of my little private investigator's notebook and handed it to Ratso.

'Not my usual beat,' said Ratso, glancing at the address. 'It's in a nice neighbourhood.'

'Right. So what did Polly Price tell you?'

'Not a hell of a lot.'

'Funny. That's the same thing she told me.'

'Nice nay-nays, though.'

'Ah, your roaming Bedouin eye caught that, did it?'

'Roger. And I'd like to get the nose of my camel into her tent.'

'Cheer up. She thinks you're a fine, clean-cut, upstanding gentleman and you may get your chance as soon as I don't find her husband.'

'You'll find him, Kinkster. I've got faith in you.'

'Faith in me? I thought you were supposed to have faith in Allah.'

'Allah,' said Ratso dismissively. 'I gave up on Allah when the Redskins lost to Tampa Bay.'

As we headed towards the city, both of us wearing black cowboy hats and smoking big cigars, we looked, I thought, very much like the biblical brothers we no doubt were if anybody ever bothered to climb our family trees high enough to find the olive branch. Just as the traffic began getting more congested, Ratso's three police and fire scanners started speaking in tongues.

'*Motor Twenty-three*,' said one scanner.

'What's that?' I said.

'That's nothing,' said Ratso. 'It takes a while to develop scanner ears.'

'*Motor Twenty-three*.'

'*Respond to gunshots seven-hundred block of Eighth Street, NE.*'

'*Response?*'

'*Code one.*'

'What's code one?' I said.

'Lights and siren,' said Ratso.

'What's code two?'

'Lights only.'

'What's code three?'

'No anchovies,' said Ratso, as the van hurtled across the Fourteenth Street Bridge.

'What's that?' I said, pointing over to the left.

'Jefferson Memorial. Sorry there's no cherry blossoms this time of year. Japan's gift of peace and friendship to the American people.'

'I thought it was karaoke.'

As the neighbourhoods changed kaleidoscopically from Beverly Hills to Calcutta and back again in a heartbeat, Ratso and I drove through the mean streets of our nation's capital, smoking cigars, discussing the possible whereabouts of Derrick Price, and half-listening to the almost non-stop chatter of the scanners.

'*Gunshot wound in the lower back –* '

'That means his ass,' said Ratso.

'*What hospital is the victim going to?*' asked a dispatcher.

'*The victim is unconscious –* '

'That means he's dead,' said Ratso. 'We're getting close to our address. What's the name of the guy again?'

'Roscoe West. But I don't think he'll be there, whoever the hell he is. It'll probably be the Latvian embassy or something. More than likely, ol' podner, this is the end of our little paper trail.'

'Don't forget to recycle.'

As we closed in on our destination, Ratso slowed the van and we gazed around to see block after block of wide, peaceful streets, large expanses of lawns, and graceful Second World War era houses, many of them old mansions.

'Roscoe West appears to be farting through silk,' said Ratso, as he slowed down even further and began looking for the address.

'Not what I expected,' I said.

Suddenly, in stark contrast to our genteel and, qúite possibly gentile, surroundings, all three scanners exploded in terse commands, grunts, shouts, and raucous white noise. It sounded a bit as if the trio of communication devices had somehow achieved the effect of a ménage à trois reaching simultaneous sexual climax.

'What the hell is going on?'

'That's the code for officer in trouble,' said Ratso. 'All hell breaks loose, people running, total pandemonium, cars driving on sidewalks. We call that a ten thirty-three.'

'I've heard of that,' I said, 'but we have another name for it.'

'What do you call it?' said Ratso, pulling up in front of the address.

'We call it New York,' I said.

FIFTEEN

A freezing rain had started to fall as Ratso and I, like two friendly cowboy Jehovah's Witnesses, eased up the walkway to the old mansion. The dark, stormy weather added a bleak countenance to the place which had already been redlining in the Lon Chaney department to begin with. Ratso's TV news van was parked down the street, and with another tedious Christmas season already thankfully in the side pocket, there still did not seem to be a creature stirring in the immediate vicinity. But appearances, like people, could be deceiving. So, like good little Jehovah's Witnesses, we masked our zealous persistence with an infuriatingly patient demeanour.

We observed the three brass plates beside the door. One of them read: Roscoe West and Associates.

'Looks like the place,' said Ratso.

'It also looks like all the little lobbyists and lawyers are still on their holiday skiing trip to Upper Baboon's Asshole, Colorado.'

'Or busy being ugly Americans somewhere in the sunny Caribbean. How come you and I never go to those places, Kinkster?'

'Because some of us work for a living,' I said.

'You've never had a job in your life.'

'I said *some* of us work for a living.'

During the course of this little repartee we'd walked over to several of the front windows and observed that, indeed, the old place did seem rather void of human habitation. So, having rung the bell at Roscoe West and Associates with no apparent response, we turned the old knob, gave the big door a push, found to our surprise that it was open, and walked inside.

The wings to our left and our right were dark and silent,

but from the Roscoe West suite, which apparently was upstairs, there seemed to come faint scurrying sounds. It could've been rats, people, or my imagination, any of which had the potential to be rather unpleasant. Then the faint noises ceased and it was silent again all through the house.

'Up the stairs, Goldilocks?' asked Ratso.

'Lead the caravan on, my brave Arabian brother.'

'Oh no, my wise Hebraic elder. This is your gig.'

It certainly wasn't breaking and entering, since the front door had been unlocked, but as we climbed the darkened stairs, I felt an increasing sense of not belonging there pervade what little was left of my conscience. The mere possession of a conscience, I reflected, can be a somewhat severe handicap, both in the field of crime detection and, of course, in Washington.

At the top of the stairs we walked through an open door into a large suite of offices. No one seemed to be around, but the lights were on. I gave a few half-hearted shouts of greeting and we waited. Nothing. Empty bureaucratic canyons.

'Maybe somebody just accidentally left the lights on,' said Ratso.

'And the door unlocked?'

I walked into Roscoe West's office and did a bit of exploring as Ratso wandered further along the adjoining rooms. A quick search through West's filing cabinet revealed no Derrick Price file. That would've been too easy, I thought. But as I was leaving the office I heard a slight humming sound. It seemed to be emanating from a nearby desk. It was a typewriter left in the 'on' position. In the carriage was what appeared to be a half-written business letter of some sort. I was just beginning to check out the letter when I heard a shout from down the hall.

'Kinkster!' said Ratso. 'You better come over here.'

As I walked down the long hallway towards Ratso, I noticed something out of place. A phone had been left off the hook. I picked up the wayward blower and tried to listen over Ratso's persistent shouting. All I could hear were unintelligible background conversations that sounded vaguely like what I'd been hearing in Ratso's news van.

'Where in the hell did everybody go?' I said, as I entered the doorway of the small storage room in which Ratso was standing. 'Did someone declare World War Three and decide not to tell us about it?'

Ratso didn't answer. He was standing behind a small table staring down at what appeared to be a medium-sized half-open suitcase.

'We're certainly dealing with a rather forgetful crew,' I said. 'They left the lights on. They left a typewriter running. They left a phone off the hook – '

'That's not all they left,' said Ratso.

I walked around the table and gazed transfixedly down at a whole suitcase full of clear bags of white powder. Whiter than snowflakes. Shinier than fish scales. The ashes of my misbegotten youth.

'If that's cocaine,' said Ratso, 'there's enough there to send your penis to Venus.'

'Probably several times,' I said. 'As Mrs Henry Cabot Lodge once remarked: "If you took everybody who fell asleep in church and put them end-to-end in a line on the floor, they'd be much more comfortable." '

'Until you snorted the line,' said Ratso.

I stood over the white stuff like I was looking over my open grave. I didn't know whether to curse or pray as my mind went back a million years to a sometimes celestial sometimes nightmarish world that Nancy Reagan, for better or worse, would never know. Moments of magic, decades of destruction, fragile, tender, star-crossed, deathbound, heroic, beautiful, hopeless, immortal. From the Wichita Lineman to *Twenty Thousand Leagues Under the Sea* and back again, before the time of my first Black Mary, which is a fairly degenerate drink consisting of one part vodka, one part Bloody Mary mix, and one part Worcester sauce. Dancing with angels, struggling with demons, understanding finally the wisdom of the Roger Miller song my friend Captain Midnite once sent me: 'Don't Write Letters to My Dog'. If this shit was Peruvian marching powder, it could make the whole city of Los Angeles so high that it'd start to get lonely. If this shit was heroin, there was enough here to create a whole new galaxy of dead rock 'n' roll stars. Whatever this shit was, its street value was just about whatever you thought your life was worth. If this supply ran out before you did, the only possible greater high would be for you to chop up and snort Nancy Reagan.

Without even touching the stuff in the suitcase I was now seeing vague flashes of red and blue light on the far wall of the storage room.

'We've been set up!' shouted Ratso, running to the nearest window, then scampering back at twice the pace. 'There's a sea of squad cars down there with their lights flashing. How in the hell did they slip up on us like this?'

'Obviously code two,' I said.

SIXTEEN

From a frozen fire escape in the back, through the open window, we could hear the sounds of the cops storming the stairs. The whole experience still seemed like something from a movie. The kind you wanted to get up and walk out of. In this case, run. Of course we'd been set up. How and by whom I'd try to figure out later. If there was a later.

Just as most of us operate our brains on about one cylinder much of the time, our true athletic prowess is a component of our being that is also often unknown to us. Ratso and I scooted down that fire escape faster than God makes fat ladies at the supermarket. We ran across the sprawling back lawns of the mansion, across the little delivery drive, and through a thick hedgerow of bushes that had, almost miraculously, retained their green foliage. Maybe God had had something to do with that, too, foreseeing Ratso's and my need for concealment as we wandered rather quickly through the spiritual desert of Washington. If God had indeed been busy creating fat ladies in the supermarket and leaves on this hedgerow, it could account for why the rest of the world seemed to be going inexorably to hell. Yet we needed a God, I thought, in passing yet another yard and another hedgerow. Without Him there would be no one to curse. And I certainly wasn't about to deny His existence at this time. No man is an atheist when he's running for his life.

The body runs fast, but the mind runs faster. Why leave the phone off the hook, I wondered? Had somebody set us up by placing a call to the cops or by dialling 911? If so, leaving the blower off the hook would be an effective way to make sure the lead was followed up. Maybe we had been set up. Maybe I was closer than I thought to finding Derrick Price. But why would it be so important for someone to try to hinder my investigation in this matter? And who could possibly afford to leave that ungodly amount of Irving Berlin's White Christmas lying around in a suitcase merely to attempt to implicate me?

It was quite ridiculous. Of course, it was also ridiculous to be running blithely through the grounds of neighbouring estates in an effort to elude the division of cops who were now streaming on to the fire escape. I heard them shouting but I didn't stop. I was on autopilot and I suddenly felt a giddy flash of childhood clotheslines and garbage cans and forts made from discarded Christmas trees. Ratso had swiftly metamorphosed into my long-ago friend Steve Worchel, and the two of us were speeding through the backyards of the 1950s and of summertime in Austin, Texas. We'd just thrown some rocks at a yellowjacket's nest and were running for our lives much in the manner that one part of my mind still knew

Ratso and I were running for our own lives. No matter who you are, running for your life can be dangerous, stressful, tiresome work, I reflected very briefly, but it sure beats jogging.

'Are you OK?' Steve Worchel was asking me.

But I wasn't. My right arm was hurting terribly. Six years into the charade of life and nothing had hurt this bad.

'You got bit!' Steve shouted in total six-year-old panic.

'What?' I said, in total six-year-old confusion.

Then the veil of childhood was suddenly lifted and Steve Worchel became Jimmie 'Ratso' Silman and more than forty years had gone over the goddamn dam and I was leaning against a rock wall and men were shouting somewhere on the other side.

'You got hit!' said Ratso. 'But I think we can make it to the truck from here. Rest a moment and then we'll make a break for it.'

Blood was now beginning to stain my Oliver Twist coat, but I felt strangely at peace.

'How do you feel?' asked Ratso, with what seemed like six thousand years of biblical brotherhood in his brown eyes.

'As the Spider Woman whispered to Raul Julia,' I said, ' "This dream is short. But this dream is happy." '

SEVENTEEN

What had stung me this time was a hell of a lot worse than what had stung me forty years ago. This time it was a cop's bullet. Or maybe you could call it a modern, grown-up, technological yellowjacket. But somehow Ratso and I made it up a narrow driveway and into the news truck. Ratso tied a strip of cloth tightly and quickly around my arm, which, fortunately for me, the bullet had gone right through. I was taking a little power nap in the back seat when I heard Ratso's voice drifting through the hole in the ozone layer around my brain.

'Goddamnit, they've surrounded the whole neighbourhood. They've set up some kind of a perimeter.'

'How do you know?'

'They're talking about it on the scanner. The only reason we got to the truck was that some homeless guy was stumbling around in the vicinity and they went after him by mistake.'

'Possibly Lazarus,' I said, wincing with a sudden jolt of pain as I tried to sit up.

'Stay down in the back seat,' said Ratso. 'They know they've got the wrong guy now. But I've got an idea and if it works we'll be out of here quick.'

'And if it doesn't?'

'I think it'll work. It's always worked in the past.'

'What if I bleed to death while we're finding out?'

'Then we may need Allah's services after all, but I don't think it's going to happen. I've seen a lot of wounds before on this job. Yours looks fairly clean and I know a nice little Lebanese doctor.'

'I hope he has some magic rocket beans,' I said, holding my arm. 'It feels like I've just been crucified by Mr Magoo.'

'Just cover yourself with that blanket and stay out of sight. The Rat Man's in charge.'

This declaration of bravado did not particularly instil great confidence in me, but I was not in a really good position to argue. In fact, from my recumbent locus in the back seat under the blanket, I couldn't see what Ratso was doing or even begin to guess what he had in mind. Probably that was just as well.

'Hold on to your yarmulka!' shouted Ratso, as the vehicle careened over the kerb, sending hot arrows of pain up my right arm.

I grasped the seat as best I could and prayed to whatever

gods resided in the sullen skies above Washington, D.C. From my somewhat limited vantage point it appeared as if Ratso was attempting to perform a U-turn and aim the van back in the direction of the old mansion we'd just narrowly escaped from and which now, no doubt, would be swarming with angry cops, one of whose belt was now one bullet lighter.

'Don't go anywhere!' shouted Ratso.

'That's what they told Emily Dickinson.'

Ratso accelerated, then skidded to a sudden stop, and before I could grit my teeth, he was out the door and running towards the house with the television camera on his shoulder. It was pure genius. I couldn't see anything, but I could hear the cops very aggressively giving him the bum's rush out of there. In no time at all, Ratso was back behind the wheel feigning great disappointment as the cops unceremoniously escorted us down the street and out of the neighbourhood. There were, after all, I reflected, some advantages to being with the media.

'Not only were we lucky to get *out*,' said Ratso, some hours later as we relaxed at his apartment, 'we were also quite lucky that Dr Fouad was *in*.'

'It certainly was preferable to loitering around some hospital emergency room with cops checking us out and then being slowly done to death by skinny Jewish doctors and fat black nurses like the ones who killed Libby Zion in New York.'

'Be careful what you say here in our nation's capital,' said Ratso. 'Your remarks could be construed as being politically incorrect.'

'So could the COLOURED MEN sign over the door of your dumper.'

I looked around the place and realized that not only was I a two-Ratso man, but both Ratsos inhabited extremely eccentric apartments. Of course, Washington Ratso still had a way to go before catching up with New York Ratso, but that didn't mean he wasn't trying. Maybe if your name was Ratso you just liked to collect weird things and live like a pack rat. On the other hand, if your name was Kinky, what did that indicate that you might like to collect? Always excluding grief, of course. I did not want to ponder too hard on these theories, and, thanks to Dr Fouad's rocket beans, I didn't have to. My mind, like that of a television talk show host, didn't seem to stay on any one subject for very long.

'How many guitars are in this apartment?' I asked.

'Twelve,' said Ratso. 'I had to sell two.'

'Sorry to hear that. How many snakes do you have?'

'Seven,' said Ratso, standing proudly beside a number of nearby glass cages. 'They're American king snakes and I've given them all names that have something to do with the King.'

'King Herod?'

'No. The American king. Elvis.'

'Very nice,' I said, watching the large creatures weave their bodies against the other side of the glass.

'This is Elvis,' said Ratso, pointing out the largest snake. 'This is Priscilla. This one's Lisa Marie. This is Colonel Tom. This is Scotty Moore, Elvis's guitar player. This is D. J. Fontana, Elvis's drummer. I haven't named the seventh one yet.'

'Well,' I said, 'there's time.'

'Right now it's time for you to get some rest. Do those painkillers seem to be kicking in yet?'

'They're working kind of slowly,' I said, as I lay back on the couch. 'Of course, they don't have much of a pension plan.'

I watched the snakes for a while. Then I watched the guitars. Then I wondered who could afford to leave behind half a million bucks' worth of marching powder just to try to keep me from finding Derrick Price. Just before the rocket beans took my head into orbit, I thought I had the answer. But when I woke in the morning, it was gone. A few hours later, so was I.

EIGHTEEN

For a Lebanese Druse, I reflected on the shuttle flight to New York, Ratso was certainly a fine American. He'd risked his very life for me and had not complained once about all the tedium and trouble I'd dragged him into. He'd been a wonderful Dr Watson, and, possibly more importantly, he'd been a wonderful friend. Why was this Ratso different from all other Ratsos, I wondered? And what else can you give a guy who already has twelve guitars and seven American king snakes?

I took a few more of Dr Fouad's rocket beans on the plane and the pain in my arm settled down to a dull throb. I could live with that. I just wasn't sure I would be alive much longer if I kept aggressively investigating the disappearance of Derrick Price. Again and again I came back to the perplexing question of why someone had gone to so much trouble to try to set me up. If I'd been getting that close to finding Price, I wished someone would tell me about it. Maybe, I thought, that was exactly what somebody was trying to do. Whether Price was alive or dead I still didn't know, but I was beginning to plunk for alive.

With my head swirling in confusion and my arm beginning to ache again, I hailed a hack at LaGuardia and rode it all the way to Vandam Street. I kept my eye on the blurry big-city scenery and tried not to think too much. I hated to admit it, but it felt good to be back in New York. Now all I had to do was make a report to Polly Price and decide how best to proceed with the investigation, provided she didn't want to take me off the case and replace me with McCloud.

I paid the driver, opened the door of the building, and rode up to the fourth floor in the old freight elevator with the one exposed lightbulb. I slipped my arm out of the little sling that Dr Fouad had provided and observed it carefully. The arm was still there, all right. It just felt like it belonged on the freight elevator. I put it back in the sling and did a pretty fair one-handed job of opening the door to the loft and carrying my suitcase across the threshold.

'Honey, I'm home,' I said.

The cat did not look particularly pleased to see me. Cats rarely do, of course. As young kittens, they were probably never allowed to laugh or cry or to express other intrinsically sensitive feline emotions. This, no doubt, was the main reason why most cats, as well as most people, once they grew up, seemed to turn into assholes. Or, very possibly, they were just born that way.

In stark contrast to the cat, I noticed, the puppet head on the top of the refrigerator was smiling broadly at me from the moment I entered the doorway. This was a bit peculiar, I thought, because, to the best of my knowledge, I'd left the puppet head facing the far wall looking away from the door of the loft.

I got out a can of Southern Gourmet Dinner for the cat, who now seemed to be warming up a bit to my presence in the loft. Then I looked more closely at the puppet head, which now stood almost in profile to me. I glanced around the loft for a moment, but everything else seemed to be exactly as I'd left it. Only the puppet head had changed its position. Maybe it had gotten bored with the view of the far wall. The wall was covered almost entirely with a huge American flag that had been given to me years ago by Vaughn Meader. Possibly the puppet head's actions could be construed as unpatriotic.

Now I took the puppet head from the top of the refrigerator and stood by the window holding it in my hand like Yorick's skull. Gazing at its friendly countenance more closely, I remembered that the puppet head had been wounded, too, some years earlier, when a stray bullet from a Colombian drug cartel member had struck it during a late night shootout in the loft.

None the less, I'd painstakingly glued it back together and, with the passage of time, the wound was now visible only upon very close inspection. I wasn't sure if it was a healthy thing to empathize with a little black puppet head, but at the moment, the two of us seemed like blood brothers. After all, we had a lot in common. We both had spent a great deal of time alone. We both continued to face the cold world with a brave smile. And for the many good works performed by the puppet head and myself, all either of us had to show for it was that each of us had caught a bullet. Of course, I reflected, his had only been a head wound.

I took a few more of Dr Fouad's rocket beans and washed them down with some Irish whiskey to possibly give myself a little buzz. Then I went over to the desk and checked out the blower traffic for the past twenty-four hours. There were five messages on the answering machine. One was from Rambam, who was now back in town but was sleeping it off and didn't want to be disturbed for forty-eight hours.

'Reinforcements!' I shouted to the cat.

The cat looked at me as if I were clinically ill.

The next message was from Stephanie DuPont, who was calling from the Concorde as she was coming into Kennedy. There was a lot of static in the background, but it sounded promising.

'The love interest returns!' I shouted to the cat.

The cat absorbed the exciting news and then began licking herself repeatedly in a rather intimate area.

'Anything's possible,' I said.

The remaining three calls were from McGovern. All three were MIT calls and each one seemed to become progressively more frantic. Apparently McGovern had been receiving more, and increasingly threatening, phone calls from Leaning Jesus.

I planned to call him back, of course, but first I felt compelled to report in, regardless of the unresolved nature of my findings, to Polly Price. She was, after all, my client of record. My real client. My paying client. McGovern and whatever madness, real or imagined, he was involved in, would have to take a backseat in the family Desoto.

I dialled Polly's number, and while her phone was ringing, I reached over with my good arm to open the side drawer of the desk. I accomplished this without too much difficulty, but when I looked down into the drawer there was a little surprise waiting for me.

All of Derrick Price's bank statements, records, and papers were missing.

'Hello,' said Polly Price.

'I'm glad I got you,' I said. 'I was afraid I'd misplaced your number.'

'What happened in Washington?' she wanted to know. All business now.

'Look, I was wondering if we could get together tonight. You know, socially. Maybe have a few drinks – '

'Listen,' she said. 'My husband's missing and I don't know if he's in danger or what harm has come to him. I believed in you and put my faith in you to find him. And you want to get together *socially* and have a few drinks? Just what kind of a woman do you think I am?'

'I'll pick you up about eight,' I said.

NINETEEN

Maybe I was missing something, I thought. Besides Derrick Price's papers, which had been recently removed from my loft, and the ounce of flesh, which had been recently removed from my right arm. If there was something Polly Price wasn't telling me, it was about a quarter past time to find out. Someone had set Ratso and myself up in Washington. Someone who knew or strongly suspected I was coming to the address of Roscoe West and Associates. That was why the cocaine had been left there. That was why the phone had been left off the hook after someone, no doubt, had called in the tip to 911. By leaving the blower off the hook, they'd ensured that the 911 operators, who, according to Rambam, were even lower on the food chain than process servers, would get the message and eventually send someone to the address.

After flipping the thing over in my brainpan for a while, I concluded that was how the setup was set up. Now all I needed to figure out was why. Aside from myself and the cat, only two people knew I was even going to Washington – Ratso and Polly Price. But neither of them could've known the details of my visit. Ratso only learned the address I was going to once I'd gotten into the van at the airport. And Polly had known almost nothing of my plan of action in the nation's capital.

The logical explanation for the setup was that someone I'd talked to along the paper trail had gotten wise and alerted someone else who'd alerted someone else and if Ratso's aggressive on-camera media approach hadn't worked, we'd both probably still be sitting in the calaboose looking for our shoelaces. It is one of the unfortunate aspects of being a private investigator that you must suspect everyone, whether he or she may be one of your oldest friends or even your recently grief-stricken client.

As an amateur detective, you almost have to make it a way of life to suspect everyone around you. This pattern of behaviour may not prove to be brick and mortar to your interpersonal relationships, but it is an ancient, trusted, Holmesian method of crime solving that is almost as infallible as a pope on a bloody rope. You probably won't be left with many friends, but at least you'll be left with the truth. The truth, of course, can often be the world's most tedious, stultifyingly dull companion, but such is the lonely, monastic life of the amateur detective.

After meditating on these matters for a while, I finally got off my buttocks and carefully checked out the door and the windows of the loft. I noticed no new marks on the locks and no signs of entry anywhere. A very professional job. And its only purpose appeared to be to steal the papers my client had recently given me. Tonight I would have to find out if Polly had spoken to anyone about Derrick's papers, or even told anyone that she'd hired me to investigate.

'You didn't see anyone?' I said to the cat in a semi-accusatorial manner. 'Maybe somebody who came in here late last night, looked around carefully, went through the desk, and removed a big yellow envelope? Then the person went over to the refrigerator and examined the puppet head? Did you see anyone like that?'

The cat did not respond and obviously did not care. She was quite used to seeing wayward human beings drifting purposelessly in and out of her field of peripheral vision. To a cat, all human beings are relegated to the peripheries of life. This is also the way most human beings look at other human beings. Unfortunately, our fields of peripheral vision are not as large or as well developed as those of the cat.

I set fire to a cigar and paced back and forth a bit while the cat watched from her rocking chair. On about my seventh crossing of the dusty wooden floor I noticed something else that was out of place in the loft. The blue down sleeping bag that had been left at camp many years ago by Ryan Kalmin had been folded neatly on the sofa when I'd left for Washington. Now it was unfolded and lying on the floor next to the window by the fire escape.

The significance of the sleeping bag was something that did not escape me, but I wanted to confirm my theory with Rambam, who would still be in hibernation for another forty-three hours or so. Possibly I'd have to call him and cause him to leap sideways. I studied the window by the fire escape again. It did not appear to have been tampered with.

I planned to take Polly Price to Asti's, which was not a particularly quiet place, but what I had to tell her wasn't going to take long. Maybe I'd invite McGovern to join us there a little later as well. Polly said she had wanted to meet him before they took him away to the mental hospital and, judging from his recent messages on my machine, this might be her last chance. Might as well make it one big, unhappy family, I thought, as I reclined upon the sofa for a brief power nap before the evening's entertainment.

Of course, I'd probably want to take a few more of Dr Fouad's rocket beans before I picked up Polly and we got together with McGovern. Like I always say, if you're going to kill two birds, you might as well get stoned.

TWENTY

The fat lady was already singing by the time Augie had shown Polly and me to our table at Asti's. Of course, the fat lady was always singing at Asti's. Or else somebody was acting out some opera dressed up as a bullfighter. Or playing the cash register and the bottles at the bar along with Eddie on the piano. It was not a particularly quiet or romantic table, but the mood of its two occupants was, alas, far from quiet or romantic. Indeed, somewhere between the time we'd ordered drinks and the time the Asti's Deluxe Antipasto had arrived, Polly and I had set about openly bickering. This did not upset the other diners, who probably thought we were part of the show. It did not, however, serve as a digestive aid for the lavish meal that I knew Augie always provided his patrons.

'What I want to know,' said Polly while waiting for her second Scotch, 'is what happened in Washington, how did you manage to get yourself shot, and what does all this have to do with finding Derrick?' In her blue eyes I could see a chill wind blowing.

'I'll be happy to report it all to you,' I said, 'but then you have to promise to tell me the truth about something I want to know.'

'Agreed,' she said, nodding as the waiter brought her another Scotch. Polly, I noticed, was the kind of woman who would take a drink. Of course, there were circumstances, and, in this case, I suppose I was part of them.

'Not "agreed," ' I said, pinning her with my best vulnerable-tough-guy look. 'I want you to promise you'll tell me the truth about something.'

'I promise,' she said icily.

'Good,' I said. 'We should get together socially more often.'

'Keep dreaming,' she said.

I looked round in the vain hope that McGovern would be arriving earlier than planned. If things continued like this, we were going to need a buffer before our menus arrived and I had to order my client to leave the restaurant.

'There's nothing wrong with dreaming,' I said, in the way of small talk. 'Lawrence of Arabia spoke of the dangerous men who dream in the daytime.'

'If that's what you've been doing,' she said, 'I want my retainer back.'

We bantered in this fashion for a while, as I continued to drink in her good looks, which only seemed to increase with her anger and impatience. I was also killing time, trying to decide exactly what to tell her. Finally, I decided to tell her everything just as it happened. I could only hope that Polly Price would be as forthcoming with me. If not, it was her funeral, I figured. Of course, in light of recent events, it could also be mine.

Between the time we ordered and the time the food arrived, I was able to regurgitate almost everything that had occurred in Washington. While Polly was picking at her salad, I filled her in on the break-in at the loft and the theft of Derrick's papers. Except for a brief moue of something akin to pity, when I described how I'd gotten winged by the cops, Polly seemed to take it all in rather stoically.

'So somebody doesn't want you to find Derrick,' she said.

'Or Derrick doesn't want me to find Derrick,' I said.

Polly didn't seem to like that idea much, but that was the way the breadstick crumbled. We never are who we think we are and the people we think we know are never the people we think we know and the little country station never stays in one place long enough for us to hear the end of the song. Every time Cinderella marries Rockefeller, here comes Jesse James.

'Which segues nicely into what I want to know. If you're so concerned about finding your husband, why not call the police? The truth, Polly. You promised to tell me the truth.'

Polly looked down at her lobster Fra Diavolo. The fat lady was now singing 'Happy Talk' from *South Pacific*. 'You've got to have a dream / If you don't have a dream / How you gonna have a dream come true?'

Polly had a dream, all right. But, as often happens in this grainy old black-and-white world, her dream was turning into somebody else's nightmare. And as I watched a blue teardrop make a tiny little splash into her Chivas, I began to realize that the somebody else was me.

'Derrick's been in trouble before,' she said softly. 'Some financial discrepancies arose. But some of his partners stepped in and smoothed it over. I didn't think it would happen again. He promised me it wouldn't. Now I don't know what to think. I can't go to the police. Will you still help me find him?'

I took Polly's hand and gave it a little squeeze. Her eyes were the colour of bluegrass mountains after the rains.

'Wherever he is and whatever he's done,' I said, 'I'll help you find him.'

Polly squeezed my hand in the heartbreaking manner of a child who now believed that everything was going to be all right.

Then a large man squeezed himself into the chair beside me. It was McGovern, and judging from his rather ebullient demeanour, he'd already had a few of the tall vodka drinks that bore his name.

'Let me guess what happened to your wrist,' he said, in a voice loud enough to make a number of nearby tables pause over their pasta. 'You were jerkin' off and your *balls* blew up!'

TWENTY-ONE

McGovern, however, was not without charm. He'd come into contact with many fascinating people in his life, not the least of which was himself. And now that was part of the problem, I thought: how well he was in contact with himself. I wasn't a psychiatrist and I didn't know. All I knew for sure was that if I were a psychiatrist I probably wouldn't have many patients, because I wouldn't be forever sipping a cup of tea and constantly asking them how something made them feel. I'd be kicking their asses out of my office for feeling sorry for themselves and then reminding them that a kick in the ass can be a big assist in helping them take that first big step forward. Then, after kicking their asses, I'd bill their asses. It sounded like a pretty good racket. Of course, there were people in this world who did need help, no doubt more than I could provide. Unfortunately, at least two of them were sitting at my table.

But they weren't alone. I was having problems of my own at the moment. Cutting a cognac-covered, peppercorned, big, hairy steak with one arm in a sling is harder than Japanese arithmetic. Somehow, I managed. It was heartening to see that McGovern's Irish charm seemed to be working on Polly Price. As he recounted his own troubles in self-effacing, humorous, colourful anecdotes, some of the tension appeared to go out of Polly's well-constructed body. Whereas, moments ago she'd been crying, now she was smiling sympathetically, laughing and shaking her pretty head in disbelief.

McGovern's intrusion, as well as giving me a chance to eat, also provided me with a little time to digest what Polly had revealed about the chequered character of her husband. It confirmed the feeling I'd had for some time now that Derrick had been the architect, or one of the architects, of his own disappearance. It didn't mean that Derrick was out of danger, but it did serve to take a bit of the life-or-death urgency out of the case, maybe buy a little more time for me and possibly shed some light on a few new angles and areas to explore.

Derrick, it now seemed quite clear, was not the good little church worker that Polly had at first described. He obviously had perpetrated some sort of fraud or scam and now, quite possibly, had got himself in over his head. I'd find him, all right, I thought. I just hoped it wouldn't be in the trunk of a rent-a-car at JFK. But at least I now knew pretty damn well what it was I was looking for. That was more than most people could say.

'Tell me more about this Leaning Jesus character,' Polly was saying.

'He should've been dead by now,' said McGovern. 'Of course, so should Kinky.'

'So should you,' I said a little testily. 'We've both just struggled with slightly different demons.'

'Leaning Jesus?' said Polly, like a small child asking if you'd brought her something.

'That's why I wanted to talk to Lord Peter Wimsey here,' said McGovern. 'I've had three more calls from Leaning Jesus since you left town.'

'According to your chronology,' I said, 'he's got to be about a hundred and seven years old.'

'Not really. I met him when I was sixteen. A mere slip of a lad. He taught me how to cook, how to play Hollywood gin, and he introduced me to an older woman who taught me the ways of the world.'

'You've still got a lot to learn, McGovern,' I said, already growing bored with the conversation. Polly, however, was hooked.

'And he really was Al Capone's personal chef?' she asked.

'I suspect he probably had some other duties, as well,' said McGovern. 'But that's how I knew him.' McGovern conferred with a waiter and, magically, a Vodka McGovern soon materialized before him.

'Did you ever meet Capone?' Polly wanted to know.

'No. In 1932, Capone went to prison for eleven years, the last nine he served in Alcatraz. When he got out he went to his estate on Palm Island, Florida, where he died in 1947. So he was a little before my time.'

'Just a *little* before your time,' I said.

'Anyway, I was only sixteen and Leaning Jesus seemed like an old man to me, but he could've been younger. It's possible he's still alive and in his mid-eighties.'

'It's possible,' I said, 'that these calls are emanating from the area code of Jupiter. What does he say when he calls? "Hi. I'm Leaning Jesus and you may be the next recipient of big prizes from Publishers' Clearinghouse?" '

'Stop, Kinky,' said Polly, already siding with McGovern. 'Let Mike tell us what he said.'

'Well,' said McGovern, finishing his drink and warming up to the feminine interest, 'it's really strange. The last call sounded angry. Kind of threatening in a way.'

'What'd he say?' I asked, beginning to feel a little uneasy in spite of the ridiculous nature of the situation.

'He said: "You've got it. I know you've got it. Give it up, kid." '

McGovern had recited Leaning Jesus's words in his own version of an old mobster's voice. Polly listened in rapt attention. Then she shivered slightly.

'OK, McGovern,' I said, 'let's assume for the sake of argument that Leaning Jesus really is calling you. What the hell could you possibly have that he wants?'

'I don't know,' said McGovern. 'I just know what *I* want.'

'What?' asked Polly.

'Another Vodka McGovern,' he said.

TWENTY-TWO

In 1953, when I was about seven years old, my parents took me to see Shoshone the Magic Pony. That was also the year that Tom and Min Friedman bought Echo Hill Ranch and turned it into a children's camp, providing thousands of boys and girls with many happy, carefree summers of fun. Echo Hill also provided the setting for one of my more successful cases, recorded in *Armadillos and Old Lace*. But although 1953 might've been a good year for the Friedmans and a good year for wine, it'd been a bad year for almost everybody and everything else. Hank Williams, along with Julius and Ethel Rosenberg, had checked out of the mortal motel that year, quite possibly unaware that the other party had been there to begin with. Hank fried his brains and heart and other internal organs for our sins, using eleven different kinds of herbs and spices. Julius and Ethel, charged with spying for Russia, many thought falsely, were fried by the government and died declaring their innocence and their love for each other. Hank's songs declared his innocence and his love, inexplicably, for people. It is doubtful whether Hank and the Rosenbergs had anything in common at all, except that a small boy in Texas had cried when each of them died.

The boy also cried the year before when Adlai Stevenson had lost the potato-bag hop at the company picnic to good ol' Ike, the Garth Brooks of all presidents, who turned out to be the most significant leader we'd had since Millard Fillmore and remained as popular as the bottle of ketchup on the kitchen table of America, even if Lenny Bruce and Judy Garland, who were both destined to die on toilets, like Elvis, remained in their rooms for the entire two terms of his presidency.

The kid had seemed to cry a lot back then, but fortunately, human tragedies of this sort never cut into his happy childhood. When he grew up, he continued to cry at times, though the tears were no longer visible in or to the naked eye, for he never let human tragedies of this sort cut into his cocktail hour. But during his childhood, it is very likely that his parents noticed the tears. That may have been the reason they took him to see Shoshone the Magic Pony.

Now, on a grey afternoon, on the day following the dinner at Asti's, I found myself looking out over Vandam Street and dreaming in the daytime like Lawrence of Arabia. I could afford to dream in the daytime, I thought. Last night had gone well with Polly, and it didn't even bother me when she and McGovern exchanged phone numbers and hobbies, thereby slightly enlarging their own support groups, while mine continued, almost inexorably, to atrophy. I wasn't jealous of Polly's apparent fascination with my favourite Irish poet. Not yet.

I'd also gotten through to Rambam finally and was expecting him to drop by sometime this afternoon. There were things he could be very helpful with, I felt, pertaining to the whereabouts of one Derrick Price. And, if there was any time left over, maybe I'd take a whirl at straightening out Leaning Jesus.

I looked out over the cold, listless afternoon, and my mind went back again to the summertime of 1953. Shoshone the Magic Pony had just been announced over the loud speaker at the little rodeo arena near Bandera, Texas. My father and mother, Tom and Min, were sitting on the splintery wooden bleachers next to me and my little brother, Roger. And suddenly, all our eyes were on the centre of the arena.

Shoshone came out prancing, led by an old cowboy with a big beard. He took the reins and bridle off Shoshone and the horse bowed several times to the audience. Shoshone had a beautiful saddle and a large saddle blanket that seemed to glitter with sequins of red, white and blue. Then the old cowboy stood back and the music began. It was 'The Tennessee Waltz'. And Shoshone the Magic Pony started to dance.

It was apparent from the outset, even to us children in the crowd, that there were two men inside the body of Shoshone. You could tell by the clever, intricate soft-shoe routine she was performing, by the fact that she often appeared to be moving hilariously in two directions at once, and by the funny and very unponylike way she now and again humped and arched her back to the music. I was laughing so hard I forgot for the moment about Hank Williams, Adlai Stevenson, the Rosenbergs, and myself. Whoever was inside there was so good, I even forgot that they were inside there.

Then 'The Tennessee Waltz' was over.

Shoshone bowed a deep, theatrical bow. Everybody laughed and clapped and cheered. The old cowboy took off his hat. Then he took off his beard. Then he took off the old cowboy mask he was wearing and we saw to our amazement that the old-timer was in reality a very pretty young girl.

She took off Shoshone's saddle. Then she took off her saddle blanket. And there, to my total astonishment, stood only Shoshone the Magic Pony.

Shoshone was a real horse.

'And so you see,' I said to the cat, who during the childhood reflections had been gazing at her own reflection on the windowpane, 'there is a lesson in all this.'

The cat did not seem to see the lesson. She was so self-absorbed that all she appeared to care about was her reflection. I plodded on.

'The lesson,' I said, 'is that nothing is what it appears to be. And no one is *who* they appear to be. It can be a rather useful spiritual tool for private investigators, people in general, and some cats.'

At almost precisely that moment, there came a soul-wrenching, rather primitive, vaguely Palestinian keening noise from somewhere on the street below. I looked down to observe that Rambam had parked his car on the sidewalk and was standing there with one hand lifted in what appeared to be a somewhat arcane gesture of somewhat intense Middle-Eastern obscenity. I opened the window.

'I'm freezing my ass off down here!' he shouted. 'Throw down that fuckin' puppet head!'

'And sometimes,' I said to the cat, as I walked over to the refrigerator, 'a Rambam is simply a Rambam.'

TWENTY-THREE

A short while later, Rambam and I were sitting at the kitchen table drinking espresso. The cat was sitting on the kitchen table watching Rambam drink espresso. I had to admit that it did look rather ridiculous for a big, tough guy like Rambam to be drinking from such a dainty little thimble, but it was one of the few gifts I'd received from friendly, misguided gentiles that year and I was determined to use it for something besides housing dead cockroaches.

'Don't you have something to drink from besides this little fucking demitasse?' said Rambam, always the gracious guest.

'The Dowager Duchess of New Jersey found it quite lovely,' I said. 'Stephanie DuPont gave it to me before she left for St Moritz. Would you care to see the whole set?'

'Not really,' said Rambam, 'but you could always break it out if you have the Gay Men's Choir of Manhattan as your next client.'

'How about I pour some espresso in the bull's horn? It's a rare privilege to drink from the Kinkster's bull's horn.'

'Don't you have a goddamn coffee cup in the house?'

'Not that you would enjoy drinking from. They're all being used for laboratory experiments by Alexander Fleming. The only functioning coffee cup in the loft is the one I'm drinking from, my official Imus in the Morning coffee mug. And it's not in particularly great shape.'

'Neither is Imus,' said Rambam, getting up to refill his demitasse.

'The I-Man's doing all right,' I said. 'He's hauling down about three mil a year, he's got a beautiful new wife who's about ninety-seven years younger than him, and he's got a huge country estate in Southport.'

'But he doesn't have a little black puppet head,' said Rambam, standing by the refrigerator and patting the puppet head several times, a little harder than necessary. 'Which reminds me, why don't *you* move somewhere a bit more upscale? Say, any place that doesn't directly abut the city's main garbage truck depot?'

'And they still don't pick up the garbage.'

'I noticed,' said Rambam, getting up again rather irritably to refill his demitasse.

I sat back and lit a cigar and thought about how best to handle Rambam. All I'd told him on the phone was that I'd gotten a new client and a hefty retainer, that I was looking for a missing husband, and that I'd already managed to get myself winged by a cop in our nation's capital. He was a working PI, and this was not his case. I didn't want to take advantage of his friendship. I just wanted to pick his brains thoroughly enough so that somebody wouldn't blow away mine.

Thus it was that two cigars later, with Rambam having jumped up intermittently, and, at least to me, quite entertainingly, to refill his demitasse, I'd told him the whole story. He'd made a number of rather insightful observations already. One had been to stop the next time a cop yelled 'Freeze!' or I might get a warning shot right between the eyes. Another had been that the wayward sleeping bag had probably been placed over the windowsill during the break-in to avoid leaving evidence and indicated a rather surprisingly sophisticated job. Another one was something I'd already figured out for myself. That the setup in Washington and the break-in in New York had occurred in basically the same time frame and might indicate that I was up against some kind of large outfit.

'But how did they even know that Polly had hired me?' I said.

'She's your basic woman client. She probably told her best friend and *she* told *her* best friend and the next thing you know you've got a sleeping bag over your windowsill and a bullet through your arm. How is your arm, by the way?'

'I'll be able to play,' I said.

'You'd better be careful. Whoever these guys are, they seem to be going to a lot of trouble to stop you.'

'You think Derrick's alive, then?'

'Until they leave his dead body on your doorstep, assume that he is.'

'Maybe they're waiting for Derrick to strike oil,' I said, 'and then they'll cap him.'

Rambam laughed very briefly. More of a bark, really. From a dog you didn't want chasing you.

'I'll do some checking for you,' said Rambam. 'How the cops showed up so fast in Washington. And how somebody could afford to lose that much cocaine. It does suggest some possibilities and none of them are good. In the meantime, you should sit tight. It's safer for you, and besides, I don't really see any active leads for you to follow.'

'There's got to be something I can do.'

'You can practise masturbating with your left hand,' said Rambam, as he headed for the door.

'I'm afraid that's impossible,' I said to his large, retreating back. 'My penis sloughed off when I was working with the Peace Corps in the jungles of Borneo.'

'That would explain a lot of things.'

'Well, before you leave, I'd like you to explain one thing to me. What do I do about McGovern and this Leaning Jesus business?'

'You follow the number-one rule of all good private investigators: Don't work for clients without a fee.'

'Yeah, but do you think there's anything to it?'

'I don't know,' said Rambam, as he opened the door. 'Sometimes even paranoids have real enemies.'

TWENTY-FOUR

'That's a good bit of deductive reasoning on Rambam's part,' I said to the cat by way of explanation. 'He knows I'm left-handed. He knows I've injured my right arm. He knows if you bat left you masturbate right. And vice-versa. That's why he said I should practise masturbating with my left hand.'

The cat appeared to be appalled by my rather lascivious sermonette.

'Don't worry,' I said. 'I'm not going to indulge in self-gratification with my left hand. Not even to fantasies of Polly Price. Do you know why?'

The cat did not appear to know why. I wasn't sure I knew why either. Spanking my simian seemed like a fairly appropriate action at this stage of the game.

'Look, it's not such a big deal in the whole spiritual scheme of things. Say I break two of the top ten commandments. I cast my seed upon my loft. And I covet my client's ass. What's the worst thing that can happen? God'll ground me?'

The cat was rapidly losing interest in the subject and, quite frankly, so was I. I walked over and shook hands with the

Jameson bottle and poured a long shot into the bull's horn. The whole damn thing's a long shot, I thought. How am I going to find this bastard with such a large, Hydra-headed forcefield of evil arrayed against me and this bastard I'm looking for is part of it?

I remembered something my father had once told me. It was something to the effect that a person can be characterized by the size of the enemies he fights. Small battles are indicative of a petty mind. Large battles are in keeping with being possessed of a big spirit. My father, I recalled, had two rather unusual heroes of the last half of the twentieth century: Natan Sharansky and Rosa Parks. According to my father, they both took on the system and they both beat the system and they're both still alive. I toasted my father for being the kind of man who could have two heroes like Natan Sharansky and Rosa Parks. Then I poured the shot down my neck.

The cat, like many Americans, probably had never heard of Natan Sharansky, but as far as I was concerned, they could all look it up when they got home. Ask the man at the Greyhound station. Of course, I had my own two heroes of the twentieth century. Hank Williams, the Hillbilly Shakespeare, and Anne Frank, the Jewish Joan of Arc. They didn't take on the system, they didn't beat the system, and they were both dead. What the hell. Different windmill strokes, I suppose.

I set fire to a cigar and went over to the little table where my unused chess set stood waiting in dust and cobwebs to be touched by the hand of man or God. I sat down and studied the board. Patterns are always interesting even if they're not there yet. I filled the bull's horn again and tried to remember something Polly Price had said that had vaguely bothered me at the time. I couldn't remember. It would come to me. I looked at the chess pieces and they looked at me and it started to get darker outside. I meditated on the board for a while, thinking of the legendary game Abraham Lincoln once played with a rather saturnine Supreme Court justice.

As they played, Abe's young son, Tad, kept pestering his father for attention. This did not faze Abe but irritated the judge enormously. Abe smoked his pipe and told Tad to pull his lips together and he'd be right with him after the game. But Tad, in childish anger, at last reacted by suddenly sweeping all the pieces off the board. This action caused the Supreme Court justice to become highly agitato. Abe, however, calmly continued to smoke his pipe and study the empty board as if he was still searching for his next move. Finally, Lincoln stood up and looked across at the apoplectic old judge. 'That's Tad's game,' he said.

But this wasn't Tad's game, I thought. It wasn't Rambam's. It wasn't even Polly Price's any more. It was my game to win.

I was still staring at the board when the phones began ringing. I got up and ankled it over to the desk and collared the blower on the left.

'Family counselling services,' I said.

'Kinkstah!' said a familiar, rodentlike voice.

It was Ratso. Not Washington. New York.

'Kinkstah!' said the voice again, several decibels louder. 'I got to talk to you.'

'OK, Rat. Start talkin'.'

'I just got a very strange phone call from somebody named Leaning Jesus.'

TWENTY-FIVE

This was exactly what I didn't want to happen. To become sidetracked. To lose focus. To get caught up in the sideshow. To forget what side my bread was buttered on. To use a large number of clichés. But in light of the fact that the search for Derrick Price had virtually slogged to a standstill, this appeared to be as good a time as any to become sidetracked. Rambam was right. The Price missing person investigation was *the* case. But if I encountered any significant dead time, pardon the expression, I might as well follow out a lead for McGovern. It was at least as efficient a use of time and energy as talking to a cat or playing chess with Tad Lincoln.

I waited for Ratso out on Mott Street that evening, smoking a cigar and making small talk, no pun intended, with the Chinese dwarf who used the same corner to paint pastels on a makeshift easel. The guy was very good, now that I, unlike millions of other people in the city, had at last slowed down to notice. Might even be the Toulouse-Lautrec of Chinatown. I'd buy some of his work sometime, I figured. Of course, the only art that I'd managed to acquire so far in my life was my pre-Columbian cat-turd collection, which I still had high hopes for. On the other hand, diversification into Chinese-dwarf pastels might make a rather sound investment. I was still weighing the possibilities when I heard a macawlike voice calling from somewhere up the street.

'Kinkstah! Let's go, baby! Kinkstah! Big Wong's!'

It was Ratso, and it didn't take me long to realize that rumours of his sartorial improvement had been greatly exaggerated. He still looked pretty much like Ratso. Pink trousers with Elvis Presley song titles scrawled all over them in hot purple. Unfashionable and unpleasant-looking racoon coat and coonskin cap with the creature's head attached, eyes sewn shut. Antique red shoes which, I knew from past experience, had once resided on the wheels of a man who had gone to Jesus. The only new affectations, in fact, that would seem to indicate an impending influx of bucks, were an expensive-looking Burberry scarf and a cigar that I now noticed was a very nice torpedo-shaped Habana Montecristo No. 2.

'Kinkstah!' said Ratso again, like some form of annoying modern urban mantra. 'Kinkstah!'

'I see you've upgraded your taste in cigars,' I said, as we walked up Mott Street toward Big Wong's.

'Yeah. These are top-drawer. Sorry I don't have another one to give you. My lawyer got this out of a special humidor that was given to him by a former client.'

'I'm glad to see they're good for something.'

'Humidors?'

'No,' I said. 'Lawyers.'

It was almost like old times as Ratso and I walked into Big Wong's together. It wasn't clear whether there was any truth to Tom Baker's theory that the waiters thought I was a Mafia don because I tipped so extravagantly. Ted Mann's notion that the waiters regarded Ratso and myself as two friendly homosexuals because we'd never come in the place with a broad was also a possibility. Whatever their motivation, the waiters and busboys dropped whatever they were doing and came forth to greet the two of us like long-lost brothers.

'Oooh-lah-lah! Oooh-lah-lah!' Ratso and I offered as part of the intercultural mating call.

'Kee-kee! Chee-chee!' shouted the waiters in return.

Other diners, almost all of them of the Oriental persuasion, looked up briefly, with maddeningly inscrutable expressions. Then, just as quickly, they returned their attention to their pork gruel. Ted Mann's addendum to his theory was that 'Kee-kee' and 'Chee-chee' meant 'crazy' and 'smelly' in Mandarin. From the reaction of the house tonight, this could not be ruled out as a possibility either.

'Kee-kee,' said the waiter, as he placed a glass of hot tea in front of me. 'Chee-chee,' he said, as he performed the same action for Ratso.

'Kee-kee,' I said, 'is obviously a bastardization of "Kinky."'

'If that's the case, where does "Chee-chee" come from?'

'Lower Baboon's Asshole,' I said. 'For the present, how about telling me about that phone call you got from Leaning Jesus?'

Ratso quickly looked at his menu in a vain effort to hide a mischievous little smile. I knew at once that there'd been no Leaning Jesus phone call to Ratso. Surprisingly, I was not even angry about his little prank. I took it rather philosophically. It was a small disappointment, I reflected, in a lifetime of disappointments.

'So you've been talking to McGovern?' I said.

'That's right, Sherlock. And I've evolved a little theory that's quite fascinating.'

'Let others be the judge of that,' I said curtly.

The waiter took our orders. I ordered the soy sauce chicken chopped Chinese style and a bowl of wonton mein soup, the best soup in the world, I had to admit, including the matzo-ball soup at the Carnegie Deli. Ratso was enormously disappointed to learn that the restaurant had run out of roast pork. He took it well, however, and made do with three other dishes, including the ever-popular squid with sour Chinese vegetables.

'This is a classic case,' Ratso said, before the waiter had even turned his back, 'of MIBs.'

'MIBs?'

'You know. MIBs. Men in Black. The otherworldly creatures that always appear in the life of anyone in the weeks after they claim to have seen a UFO. It's all in John Keel's book, *The Mothman Prophecies*.'

I remembered the book vaguely. What I remembered most about it was that it had scared the hell out of me at the time. It was not a work of fiction. Keel, who was a rather eccentric, scholarly friend of Ratso's, had painstakingly chronicled the subsequent almost invariable deterioration that had occurred in the lives of people who had reported seeing UFOs. Fortunately, he did not record the deterioration that had occurred in the lives of those of us who have not seen UFOs.

'It all fits,' Ratso was saying. 'By the way, you seem to be favouring your right arm. You didn't get hit by another tranquillizer dart like that time at Madison Square Garden, did you?'

'No, I was – uh – jerkin' off and my *balls* blew up.' Ratso might, indeed, be helpful with the McGovern matter, but the charming naïveté that he occasionally lent to a case was not going to help plunge the plugged-up commode that was also known as the Derrick Price investigation.

'Common household accident,' Ratso was going on. 'You're sure you weren't trying to hang yourself while you were spanking your monkey? Autoerotic death syndrome is quite common among teenagers these days.'

'Not common enough,' I said grimly. 'Back to McGovern.'

'It all fits,' Ratso said again. 'McGovern sees a little green man. Then electronic devices start fucking up in his house. The television turns on and off mysteriously. The telephone starts disconnecting, echoing, clanging, beeping. The blender turns on by itself – '

'Hold the weddin'. He never told me about the blender.'

'Yes, the blender, the television, the telephone. These are classic electronic interruptions that always occur after the subject sees a UFO, according to Keel. Of course, if you're a cynic you could also say there's probably some loose wiring in McGovern's apartment.'

'Or you could say there's probably some loose wiring in McGovern's brain.'

At this point, the waiter arrived with the food. Ratso paused briefly to order duck sauce, ginger sauce, soy sauce, and hot red oil chilli sauce. I thought about what the great Frog philosopher Voltaire said about the British: 'The English have 365 different religions and only one sauce.' Then I thought about the H.P. Sauce that McGovern had railed against at Myers of Keswick. Then I thought about McGovern. Then Ratso was talking again, this time with his mouth partially full of squid and sour Chinese vegetables.

'According to John Keel, the Men in Black, or MIBs, who may be from the government or may be supernatural creatures, begin to appear shortly after these electronic phenomena occur. The MIBs are often said to wear clothing that's decades out of fashion.'

'Much like yourself.'

'No. Their clothes are new and they frequently are seen to drive mint-condition Cadillacs from the fifties and sixties with their headlights off at night.'

'New Jersey plates?'

'You can poke fun at it all you want, but Keel has interviewed thousands of people who've reported close encounters, and McGovern fits the profile perfectly. The guy he claims he saw on his fire escape sounds a hell of a lot like a typical MIB. The little supernatural trick of a dry wallet left outside a locked window in the rain also fits perfectly.'

'So does a drunken McGovern losing his wallet on the fire escape.'

'But the wallet was dry.'

'So's the soy sauce chicken.'

'Then you've got the paranoia factor. McGovern thinks he's being followed, thinks he's being spied upon. No one believes him. Not even some of his best friends.' Here Ratso stopped his chopsticks in midair to eye me coolly. I met his gaze, then returned to slurping my wonton soup.

'Don't you see, Sherlock? Not everything can be explained by deductive reasoning. McGovern's like the high school football coach Keel interviewed in Alabama. Crew-cut, redneck, total cracker. An average Joe until he makes a sighting. Then come the electronic phenomena, the Men in Black, the paranoia, the disbelief of friends and family, the disruption of normal life, the obsession with the situation, the divorce, the alcoholism, and before long you have – '

' – the typical American?'

We finished the meal in thankful silence. Obviously, McGovern had done quite a fair bit of yapping to Ratso about his situation. There was nothing wrong with that, I thought. Ratso was a friend, McGovern needed friends, we all needed friends. McGovern already believed an old man with a turban was following him around. What further harm could Ratso cause by getting involved? Meanwhile, maybe McGovern would leave me alone long enough for me to justify the confidence Polly Price had placed in me.

Eventually, the waiter returned to drop the hatchet. Ratso made a feint or two for his wallet but I ended up paying the bill and leaving an extravagant tip because I wanted people to like me. It didn't always work.

Ratso hadn't mentioned his impending inheritance, so I assumed it was still impending. I hadn't mentioned the money he still owed me for services rendered. He'd pay me one of these days. I'd find true love. I'd live happily ever after. The world would be at peace. Big Wong's would continue to be a killer-bee restaurant until some nerd from *The New York Times* walked in with a bow tie and an umbrella and wrote the place up and gave it a couple of stars and soon they'd be serving sweet-and-sour veal and giving fortune cookies and nobody'd ever say 'Kee-kee' or 'Chee-chee' again.

When I got back to the loft that night there were three messages on my answering machine that torpedoed my little sabbatical from crime solving and caused me to become highly agitato. The first was from McGovern, who'd just had a visit from two men all dressed in black. The second message was from Polly Price, who'd just found a message on her answering machine confirming Derrick Price's meeting the next day in Chicago at Merrill Lynch to 'prepare trust documents'. The third message was from Rambam. It was, like Rambam, rather terse and to the point. Derrick Price's automobile registration papers had expired seven years ago. And so, according to Rambam, had Derrick Price.

I took a fresh cigar out of Sherlock Holmes's porcelain head. I studied it thoughtfully for a moment, then lit a kitchen match and set fire to the end of it. I puffed until it glowed like a gypsy campfire in the distance. Then I got up and walked over to the counter and stroked the cat.

'It's time,' I said, 'to reach out and touch somebody.'

The cat, of course, said nothing.

TWENTY-SIX

As the big jet vectored tediously above O'Hare Airport, many loose thoughts vectored equally tediously around my some-what frazzled mind. I'd chosen not to tell Polly Price yet about Rambam's discovery that her loving husband had been dead for seven years. That kind of sudden news can be hard on a wife. Besides, Rambam was hardly infallible and I never did much believe in computers. Also, somebody thought Derrick Price was supposed to be at a meeting that would be taking place very shortly at Merrill Lynch to prepare trust documents. That sounded like a euphemism for stashing some of the money Price may have been routing through Roscoe West and Associates in the nation's capital. If I could catch Price at that meeting it would be living proof that he wasn't dead. If this plane ever landed at O'Hare it would be living proof that I wasn't dead.

As we continued to turn and circle over the Windy City I stared out of the window into the grey, viscous soup that provided such an apt metaphor for the direction, or lack of it, the case was taking. Why, I asked myself, was this flight different from all other flights? Why was I going to Chicago if Derrick Price was dead? The answer was that I had what we big private dicks called a hunch and fortunately for me it wasn't on my back. This, I believed, was one of the rare occasions when Rambam and his hard-boiled computer were wrong.

My decision to come to Chicago had been so sperm of the moment that I hadn't even told my client. When Polly had informed me about the message regarding Derrick's meeting, I'd left her with the impression that I planned to sit on my buttocks and take it under advisement. I did not share Rambam's male-chauvinist view that a female client always tells her best friend who tells *her* best friend who tells *her* best friend and you wind up having to vigorously employ your getaway sticks to avoid being set up with half of Peru. It was much more likely, I reflected, as I gazed out into the unnerving, unending goo, that my own barrage of telephone calls had stirred up the nest of yellowjackets. Getting winged once a week was about all I could handle, so I'd made no advance calls to Chicago.

'Can you see anything yet?' asked the woman on the aisle seat as she nervously fingered a cross that was big enough to drown a horse.

'I can see we're in for a rather unpleasant experience,' I said. If anything, the grey goo was getting thicker outside the window.

'You can't see *anything* down there?' she asked again, her rather hirsute upper lip breaking out in a sweat.

'Wait a minute,' I said, with my eyeballs aimed downward as close to the window as my hat would allow. 'I thought we were passing over the River Jordan, but I guess it's just a cloud formation.'

'Folks,' said the pilot over the intercom. Then he paused and all of my fellow passengers to the grave waited on the edge of panic. It's always a bad sign when a pilot pauses after 'Folks'.

'It looks like traffic is heavy into O'Hare,' he continued after a brief eternity. 'The tower hopes to give us landing clearance in about thirty minutes – '

A collective groan went up. It seemed not dissimilar to the sound you might have heard if all the air had suddenly gone out of God's basketball. Kind of like the sound the crowd makes at a Rolling Stones concert when Mick Jagger announces they're going to perform a new song.

Now some turbulence began to inject itself into the little equation and this had the rather disheartening effect of pro-voking the lady next to me into dragging out her Bible and murmuring madly to her Lord. I wasn't sure where my Lord was at the moment. Maybe He was sitting in Carnegie Deli eating a salami sandwich. Maybe He'd gone to the country for the weekend.

Only two Americans knew where I was. To get my mind off the present tedium, I thought about them now. Rambam had been against my coming to Chicago. He'd wanted more time to run down information on Derrick Price. Whether Price was alive or dead, he felt I should approach the Merrill Lynch meeting with great care. If a party professing to be Price showed up, something was definitely going on, Rambam felt, that was not in your kosher area. On the other hand, why would the non-spiritual corporate denizens of Merrill Lynch want to hold a seance for a dead guy? Obviously, others beside myself believed Price was still lurking around somewhere along this mortal coil. How I was going to get into the meeting was another problem, but I could deal with it once we landed. I hoped that would be soon, because the lady on the aisle was now holding her cross up to me and talking in tongues.

The other American who knew my whereabouts was McGovern. Unlike Rambam, he'd been very excited about my rather abrupt plans to go to Chicago. He'd hoped that after I'd located Polly Price's wayward husband I'd be able to take a little time to lean on Leaning Jesus.

Suddenly, we heard the thump of the landing gear coming down and locking in. The lady on the aisle looked up from her Bible in shock.

'What was that?' she demanded.

'Can't see a thing,' I said. 'Maybe we just T-boned a band of angels.'

'Lord help us!' shouted the lady.

'Amen to that,' I said conversationally.

It was quite an unusual case, I thought to myself. It was quite an unusual client–investigator relationship. There was no way to round up the usual suspects. There weren't any. There was only the shadow man, Derrick Price.

Just as I was thinking these dark thoughts, the plane

descended through the last layer of the soup that so long had surrounded us. And for the first time in what seemed like weeks, I thought I could see the light of day.

TWENTY-SEVEN

The Merrill Lynch offices were located in downtown Chicago just inside the Loop and very near the area where Abbie Hoffman led his Yippie Charge of the Light Brigade against the Chicago police in 1968. I was eating monkey brains with the pygmies in the jungles of Borneo at the time, so I missed out on the action in that particular theatre of the war. I didn't meet Abbie until some years later at the Chelsea Hotel in New York in room 1010, Janis Joplin's old room. It was while Abbie was underground and on the run from the feds that I first really became his friend. It was after he died like a disillusioned Jewish dinosaur that I realized how very little people truly ever change. Mankind plods on from millennium to millennium in a cruel, pathetic, often stultifyingly dull Bataan Death March of the ages. Not that people don't try. It's just that you walk for thousands of years towards what you think is a beacon of light and when you get there, it's only Joan of Arc with her hair on fire.

I stepped out of the hack on Michigan Avenue and looked at my watch like any good little constipated, humourless junior executive on his way back from Bennigan's. It was two-thirty. The much-awaited Derrick Price meeting was at three. Always nice to be punctual, I thought, as I set down my leather Australian bookie's bag on the sidewalk next to the shivering skeletal remains of a man selling pencils.

'Sooner or later,' he said, 'you're gonna need a pencil.'

'I see your point,' I said, as I took a pencil from his coffee can and stuffed in a double sawski. I hoped God was watching.

I shouldered the bookie's bag and ankled it up Michigan, lighting a cigar and looking for the right skyscraper. I was travelling light in the dead of winter, but not as light as the guy selling pencils. All I had in the bookie's bag was a box of cigars, one change of clothes and a hand-tooled toilet kit that I'd picked up twenty years ago in Juarez. You never know when you might have to leave town in a hurry.

I found the address on Michigan Avenue, bootlegged the cigar past building security, and located the Merrill Lynch offices in the building directory. At the bank of elevators I watched one particular Otis box spit out a large assemblage of the species and, quite miraculously, stand empty for a moment. I hopped in, pushed thirty-three, watched the doors close, and headed for the heavens. It was kind of a lonely ride and I found myself singing a line from an old Flying Burrito Brothers song: 'On the thirty-third floor / a gold-plated door / won't keep out the Lord's burning rain . . .'

It wasn't going to keep me out either. By the time I descended back into the bowels of the city, I planned to be packing a few more pieces to the puzzle that was Derrick Price. If Price was here in person, of course, I could strike the tent and my one-man caravan could wing its way back to New York in triumph, suffering only a mixed metaphor and a few mixed emotions. I had to admit that I'd be surprised and probably a little disappointed if I nailed Price at this meeting and he turned out to be some run-of-the-mill white-collar criminal. The truth was, I wanted more. After what had happened in Washington and the burglary of my loft, I felt I deserved more. On the other hand, finding a missing person is finding a missing person. Or, as they say in Hollywood, a lay's a lay.

I puffed the cigar peacefully in the empty elevator and pondered Rambam's notion that Price was dead. If that were the case, there was a Derrick Price impersonator at work and he was doing a pretty damn good job. But now, with a misguided confirmation call from a colleague, he might finally have tripped himself up. Whoever the hell he was. Identities, according to Rambam, were fairly easy things to create if you were methodical and spread a little money around. There's McNerd's car. There's McNerd's office. There's McNerd's company. There must be a McNerd. But quite often there isn't. Of course, in those cases you don't usually encounter a Mrs McNerd.

The doors opened before I got any further with the idea. There wasn't an elevator boy to say 'Nice ride' to, so I legged it out into the hallway just as a young, upwardly mobile couple got in to go down. They immediately popped back out of the elevator with the woman making exaggerated fanning gestures in front of her beak.

'That's beautiful, man,' the guy hollered down the hallway at me. 'That's beautiful.'

I just kept walking. There was no point in getting my bowels in a twist over the matter. They'd just have to wait awhile and then they'd find another elevator. People like that always do.

The receptionist at Merrill Lynch looked up from her space console long enough to give me the fish-eye.

'Can I help you?' she said.

'I'm here for – '

'There's no smoking in the building.'

'There's no ashtrays in the building either,' I said, looking round at the plushly antiseptic ambience.

'You'll have to leave with that cigar,' she said, obviously enjoying the chance to exercise what little authority she had.

'I'll be right back,' I said needlessly. The woman's focus was clearly on my leaving. She did not care a fig whether I returned or merely jumped down an open elevator shaft. She did not care if the entire corporate holdings of Merrill Lynch came crashing down on the world market. All she wanted out of life was for a man with a large hat to take his cigar out of the reception area immediately. It was sad, really.

I walked out into the hallway like a biblical leper looking for an empty cave. There were no ashtrays. No one had ever been crazy enough to smoke a cigar in the building before and no accommodation had been made for that unlikely circumstance. So I killed the cigar as best I could with the heel of my boot on the marble floor of the hallway. It lay there like a steaming turd. I walked back into the reception area with renewed determination.

'Can I *help* you?' said the receptionist, not bothering to conceal her irritation.

'Yes, little lady,' I said, affecting a somewhat more forceful Texas accent. 'I'm Billy Bob Bullock, the lawyer from Dallas. I'm up here for the Derrick Price meetin'.'

'The what?'

'Derrick Price meetin'. Three o'clock. Would've been here earlier but they wouldn't let my horse into the parkin' garage. Heyeugh-heyeugh-heyeugh!'

'Take a seat, please. I'll call Mr Beadleheit.'

There were lots of couches and lots of glass tables and lots of financial and investment-oriented magazines. You could just sit there and browse for ever and after a while that's what I thought was going to happen to me. Then Mr Beadleheit walked in.

'I'm Mr Beadleheit, the assistant office manager.'

'Billy Bob Bullock. Come up from Dallas.'

'How nice. How can we help you, Mr Bullock?'

'I'm here for the Derrick Price meetin' at three o'clock. Should be about now unless my watch is slow.'

'There is no Derrick Price meeting scheduled for three o'clock. There is no Derrick Price meeting scheduled for any time. Brenda, do you have a Derrick Price on our client list?'

The receptionist consulted her computer briefly, then looked up and smiled.

'No Derrick Price,' she said cheerfully. 'In fact, no one named Price at all.'

'Mr Price is not known to us,' said Beadleheit.

'Well, I'm a one-legged man at a butt-kickin' contest,' I said.

I walked out of the reception area and down the hallway to the elevators feeling almost as stupid as Billy Bob Bullock. I wasn't totally surprised, however. In this business if you don't feel stupid a lot of the time you're not very smart.

Rambam was right, I thought, as I hurtled thirty-three storeys downward in the elevator. Everybody was right but me. Either Derrick Price no longer existed or he'd somehow vanished completely from the face of the earth. The trip to Chicago had been a waste of time. My whole life had been a waste of time.

When I stepped out on to the freezing sidewalk of Michigan Avenue, the first thing I did was fish out a fresh cigar and fire it up. I had just raised my head and was starting to puff rather stoically on the stogie when I noticed a shiny black limo parked just to the left of the main entrance to the building. A uniformed driver was standing next to the limo on the sidewalk looking mildly bored and holding up a little sign.

I took a few more patient puffs on the cigar and walked a little closer. Maybe, I thought, my whole life had not been a waste of time.

The sign read: DERRICK PRICE.

TWENTY-EIGHT

It is a rather tedious fact of life that most of us who are confined to the human condition spend a great deal of time wishing to be something we're not. Or someone we're not. The proctologist, scrupulously washing his hands before and after each patient, dreams of being Dr Albert Schweitzer. The rock star, as he worries whether to leave the Porsche with valet parking, dreams of saving the rain forest. The bank clerk dreams of embezzling a million dollars and moving to Costa Rica. The average Costa Rican dreams of moving to Akron, Ohio, and becoming a bank clerk. The many people who lead anonymous little lives long for fame. The handful of people who've become truly trapped in the thing that fame is, invariably long for anonymity. As far as the rest of us go, we have to deal with so many assholes every day we figure we probably should've been proctologists and at least get paid for it.

'I'm Derrick Price,' I said to the limo driver.

'Your office has given me your itinerary, sir,' said the chauffeur, touching his cap. 'I'm to take you to your next meeting, then back to your hotel.'

'Sounds fine,' I said. 'One of these days my office is going to tell me where I'm going.'

The limo driver chuckled politely. Then he stepped over to the back door and opened it for me. Somebody was conning somebody here and I might as well find out if it was me. Besides, there's very few chances in life to walk in another man's shoes, unless, of course, you're Ratso and your closet floor is covered with other men's shoes, the owners of which have previously gone to Jesus.

I got into the limo.

The driver smiled and shut the door, reassuringly touching his cap again. As he walked round to the driver's side door, I settled back for the ride. I wondered briefly how I was able to do what I was apparently doing. It was a bit like voluntarily flying off with the extraterrestrial crew of a UFO, and it isn't always courage that enables you to proceed with that kind of mission. It is often only a rather heady mix of stubbornness, and maybe something else, I thought: a little thing called emptiness. The Plexiglas partition was not only up between myself and the driver, it was up between myself and the rest of the world.

As we smoothly wound our way through the windy canyons of downtown Chicago, I was aware of being very close to the resolution of the investigation. One way or the other. If this was a trap, I was ready. If the driver truly believed I was Derrick Price, then I had successfully, albeit by dumb luck, infiltrated myself into the heart of the operation. I was ready for that, too.

I thought of something Karl Wallenda, the father of the Flying Wallendas, had once said. It was on the day immediately following the worst tragedy that had ever befallen the famous circus high-wire act. Less than twenty-four hours earlier, three members of his family had fallen to their deaths before thousands of horror-stricken onlookers when the seven-man pyramid had collapsed. Reporters had asked Wallenda how he could go back out on the wire so soon after the accident. 'Life,' replied Wallenda, 'is always on the wire.'

Yes indeed.

From the direction of what sun there was, we seemed to be heading in a vaguely south and westerly direction. Chicago, of course, has always been a city of neighbourhoods, and a great many of them seemed to be flashing by the window of the limo. The faces were now predominantly black and brown and yellow but in one of these neighbourhoods about sixty-five years ago, my father had been a little boy. When he was about ten he'd spent the summer working for a Polish man selling vegetables to housewives. The Polish guy rented a horse and cart and loaded it up at the market, then proceeded down the streets and alleyways of the West Side, shouting his wares in at least five languages. My dad rode on top of the cart. It was the first horse he'd ever seen in his life.

Clotheslines stretched like medieval banners across every dark, sooty alley as the horse and cart plodded along, the vegetable pedlar screamed his wares, and my father ran the purchases up to the housewives living on the higher floors. To this day, my father remembers his employer shouting one word much more often than any other. The word was *kartofel*. It means 'potato' in Polish.

Sixty-five years later, my father's son was riding in a sleek limo down the same streets, looking, no doubt, at some of the same old brick buildings now boarded up, clinging to each other for dear life. The vegetable pedlar was gone. The horse and cart were gone. The housewives were gone. Their omnipresent clotheslines were gone. All that remained were some trashed-out vacant lots, a few sad old buildings and an occasional dark, sooty alleyway leading from nowhere to nowhere.

I put the window down for a moment. The back of the limo filled up with an almost primordial cold that seemed to come from somebody else's ice age. I stared out at the desolate landscape where every now and then the dull glint of an old streetcar track became visible just below the surface of the worn-out road like the scarred, submerged, hard-to-find veins of a dying junkie.

'*Kartofel*,' I said.

No one was there to hear me except the driver and he just kept his eyes on the road. Either he wasn't Polish or he didn't want any potatoes.

TWENTY-NINE

The limo pulled off to the left across a potholed patch of asphalt that looked like runway number three at Sarajevo International. Taking a meeting of this nature, I reflected, not for the first time on the journey, was like taking your life in your hands. Of course, you had to do something with your hands. It was also a good idea, occasionally, to do something with your head.

The sun was now breaking through the cloud layer, but things did not seem to be measurably warming up. If anything, a cold chill appeared to be moving through the limo, though I'd put the window up some time ago. I thought about asking the driver to adjust the thermostat, but decided to let it slide. Is it cold or is it me is a question that few of us ever truly resolve during the course of our lives. Anyway, he was slowing the limo down now and looking intently towards the side of a nearby warehouse. I didn't want to disrupt his driving patterns this late in the game.

Obviously, the driver thought we were supposed to be meeting someone, but nobody seemed to be around. Just a few rats running along in a ditch, and even they appeared to be only of the four-legged variety. The driver pulled up closer to the warehouse. Then he stopped the car.

'Terribly sorry, Mr Price,' he said, without turning his head. 'They should be along any moment now. They probably got held up in traffic.' This was a long speech for the driver.

'Very possibly,' I said. On this trip, it was a rather long speech for me, too.

The limo driver and I sat in our respective seats and waited. I looked bleakly through the window at the desolate patches of dirt and weeds. If there was going to be a meeting out here it wasn't going to be the kind where the young executive stands up and shows off his multicoloured pie charts from Kinko's. But I'd known that long before I'd got into the limo. That was why I'd come to Chicago. To make something happen. Everybody's got to die sometime, I figured. Either you die suddenly at the hands of strangers near an abandoned warehouse or you die of ennui sitting around your house wondering how you're going to die. I tell you, it's no way to live.

A dark blue Lincoln Town Car pulled slowly into view from the far corner of the warehouse. It stopped about half a shopping mall away. There were two men sitting in the front seat. Suddenly the city seemed very quiet, distant somehow, though it was everywhere around me. Like the fly that buzzed when Emily Dickinson died.

'One moment, Mr Price,' said the driver, as he opened his door. Then he himself buzzed off in the direction of the newcomers.

I watched. I waited. I worried. There wasn't a hell of a lot else I could do. Since no one had known I was coming to Chicago, except Rambam and McGovern, it seemed unlikely that this meeting, or trap, or scene from *The French Connection*, was being played out for my benefit. Whatever was meant to happen was meant to happen to Derrick Price. Whether or not he existed was something for fans of Kant and Kierkegaard to kick around when they got through discussing whether or not the tree falling in the empty forest makes any noise. The point was, somebody *thought* there was a Derrick Price. If Rambam was right and Price had died seven years ago, how would they ever know he wasn't me?

It was all very confusing, so just for the fun of it I reached for the door handle. My driver, I noticed, was now talking to the guys in the Town Car, and none of them seemed to be too interested in me. If I was going to use my getaway sticks, now was the time. I pulled the door handle. Nothing happened. I pushed every button and turned every switch I could find and pulled the door handle again. No joy for Derrick. The Plexiglas shield was up. The driver had locked me in.

This was not a particularly good sign, but, as events transpired, there wasn't a lot of time to ponder its implications. My driver got into the back of the Town Car and off it sped in the direction it had come. No 'Terribly sorry, Mr Price.' Not so much as a wave.

I have often contended that it's a small step from the limo to the gutter. Rarely, however, have I articulated the corollary to that notion. That being, if you never take that small step from the limo to the gutter, something even more tedious inevitably happens.

Tedium on this occasion manifested itself in the form of two men wearing ski masks whom I could now see approaching the limo from the back. They moved methodically up to the limo in the frozen sunlight like two guys coming to work at a carwash. They emptied the contents of two large gasoline cans on to the limo. Then they stood back and one of the ski masks took out a pack of cigarettes and a book of matches. He cupped his hands near his face and lit the cigarette like the Marlboro Man. Then he tossed the match on to the limo.

At least I would be going in style, I remember thinking in the split second before the entire landscape seemed to ignite with a rather singular swooshing sound. Through the flames, I scanned the near horizon just in time to see the two ski masks scurry into the distance, jump into a station wagon, and fishtail it out of there. I fought down a cold, visceral fear as I pounded on the windows and tried and failed repeatedly to open the doors. Not a living soul seemed to be stirring anywhere in the vicinity. Even the rats in the ditches had headed for safer ground.

It did not look as though I was going to find Derrick Price on this trip. Leaning Jesus, as well, would have to wait for another incarnation. Like Nellie Fox, the great second baseman for the Chicago White Sox who should've made it into the Hall of Fame but never did because he died at the wrong time, I was oh-and-two. If I couldn't get out of this limo pretty damn fast, I'd be oh-and-three. Out of there. Grab some bench. Die at the wrong time. Like Nellie Fox. Like Lefty Frizzell. Very important in baseball, as in country music, to die at precisely the right time. Otherwise, you might as well drive your car into a tree in high school. Nobody's ever going to remember you except for a few purists and if there's one thing the world doesn't need it's a few purists. But baseball and country music are not life. They are more fun, more colourful, and often more meaningful than life, but they're not life. In the game of life almost no one comes out a winner and, even if you're a saint or a martyr, it's always the wrong time to die.

I stared, mesmerized, at the window to my right. As the flames danced across the glass to lick the limo, the dark window tinting was beginning to bubble and melt and drip. A strange pattern seemed to be forming there that did little to assuage my fears. It was Joan of Arc with her hair on fire.

THIRTY

On the first day of classes in the second grade at Edgar Allan Poe Elementary School in Houston, Texas, it became apparent to me and my little classmates that something was terribly wrong. Larry Duckworth, the fat kid with ringworm and the Hopalong Cassidy lunch kit was not in his front-row seat. From what us kids could piece together later, considering our ignorance at the time of both death and geography, he'd managed to drown on the last day of summer vacation at some place called Lake Stupid along the Texas–Israeli border. The second-grade teacher, Mrs Necrophiliac, never explained what had happened to the kid. As the whole class stared in wonderment and confusion at the empty chair, all she said to us was that Larry Duckworth had stepped on a rainbow.

Now, almost half a century later and just within sight of the pot of gold, I felt with a dead certainty that I was as perilously close as I was ever going to get to stepping on a rainbow myself. Being trapped inside a burning limo in a desolate area of a strange city will do wonders for speeding up your thought processes. Not that I'd completely solved the case or anything. But shards of information and snippets of conversation were powering through the tiny Tokyo subways of my brain at such a rate as to make me at last realize that I'd been searching for the wrong man.

There'd been a multitude of little red flags all along the parade route, now that I thought about it, and it was just a damn shame that it'd taken a multitude of little red flames for me to finally see the little red flags. Maybe it was something Polly Price had said about McGovern. She'd known he was a journalist yet she wasn't even from New York. Maybe it was the whole style and scale of the adventures that had befallen Washington Ratso and myself in the nation's capital. Maybe it was what Rambam, the world's greatest hard-boiled computer expert, had turned up on Derrick Price. Maybe it was what he hadn't been able to turn up. Maybe it was the close proximity of McGovern's problems, Polly Price's problems and my own problems. Everybody had problems, of course, but this was ridiculous. When the driver came back I'd really have to tell him to turn down the damn thermostat. I felt like I was burning up. Maybe it was the almost predatory way that Polly had looked at McGovern that night at Asti's. Maybe it was the fact that if you're sure you're going to kill a guy who's trapped inside a limo and you know he'll never be able to identify you until he sees you in hell, the party is usually ski-mask optional.

It all added up to a whole wagonload of maybes, and now, as near as I could calculate before my own personal computer became hard-boiled, there was only one maybe left. Maybe I could kick out that Plexiglass divider before I was transformed irrevocably into fricassee of Friedman. Plexiglass is not really plastic and not really glass and not really what you'd like to have blocking your last exit to Brooklyn. It has been known to bend slightly, however, and eventually, if the proper force and rhythm are applied, to buckle. It has also been known to melt, but so have cowboy hats and amateur private investigators and I wasn't planning to stick around for that particular chemistry class if I could borrow somebody's notes and make it up later.

You've got to get your kicks in life while you can, and in my corner I had a sturdy pair of brontosaurus foreskin boots and six months of repressed karate classes that I'd taken years ago along with my pal Sal Lorello from the talented black belt Neil Davino in Mount Kisco, New York. Neil was such a great karate expert that he couldn't even join the army. He was afraid if he ever saluted he might kill himself. Neil Davino could've kicked out the partition in a New York second and, judging from the heat inside the limo, there was only a handful of them left. Neil wasn't around, however, and I was, and it was undeniably time to drop-kick me Jesus through the goalposts of life.

My first few efforts were rather disappointing but as the crackling and hissing noises grew louder and the interior of the limo began to resemble the smoking car on the *City of New Orleans*, I started to get the hang of it. It might've been my imagination but the partition seemed to be giving a little more each time I kicked. I was no longer sure what was happening. Possibly the sea was playing tricks on me. But I continued to attack the divider with a series of measured, if somewhat frantic, kicks, all of them focusing on follow-through. By the time the damn thing buckled I felt like a Rockette on angel dust, but I knew Neil Davino would've been proud.

It didn't take Huey Long to build a bridge in Louisiana and it didn't take me long to collect my belongings and leapfrog over the seat and out of the unlocked front door of the limo. In no time at all I was out on the windswept, frozen corner of Nightmare Alley and Desolation Row looking for a working pay phone to call my cousin Rachel Samet. It was a close call, but I made it. Then all I had to do was wait around and try to blend into the rotten woodwork and terrifying twilight of cosmic confusion and post-traumatic stress from my near-death, out-of-limo experience.

By the time Rachel's car pulled up to the kerb I was a half-frozen, spinning ghost, half-heartedly hoping that somewhere amongst the ruins of the city I'd run into Leaning Jesus. Hell, I thought, *any* Jesus would do.

Rachel leaned across the front seat and held the door open for me. I got in, slightly feverish and still shaking from the cold and the heat, and gave her a quick hug. Then she pulled away from the kerb and we headed out to her apartment.

'So what brings you to Chicago?' she said.

THIRTY-ONE

Rachel Samet's apartment was north of the city and provided the perfect sanctuary for me to soothe the singed feathers on my cowboy hat, make a few phone calls to New York, and try to decide how to answer the question 'So what brings you to Chicago?' It wasn't really a hard question, but the answer, rather maddeningly, seemed to be in a state of continuous evolution. A strange sense of foreboding and a somewhat persistent, prickly sensation along the back of my neck kept convincing me that I'd come to the right place for the wrong reason.

Rachel was twenty-six years old, very bright, very pretty, and an interior designer by trade, who'd made her apartment just beautifully appointed enough to make a guy like me feel slightly uncomfortable. Rachel's father, Dr Eli T. Samet, a brilliant surgeon, had been my mother's younger brother until both of them had stepped on a rainbow. Eli had been the 'doctor in Chicago' that I'd made reference to in the song 'Rapid City, South Dakota,' which, to my knowledge, was the first pro-choice country song. It is also, to my knowledge, the only pro-choice country song.

'Here's a little bit of spiritual trivia for you,' I said, trying to make the best out of my scattered thoughts and sordid appearance. 'What is the only bird in the world that has two feathers for every quill?' I took off my cowboy hat and showed Rachel the two feathers. They were only very slightly singed.

'I'm stumped,' said Rachel, who obviously didn't give a damn but was trying her best to be an accommodating hostess to her elder cousin, who was shaping up to be a rather troubled, tormented house pest. She walked over to the cabinet and came back with a large unopened bottle of Wild Turkey, which she placed on the table before me.

'There's another bird I like,' I said, as Rachel brought some glasses and sat down across from me at the table.

Sometimes, when you're in a confused state of mind, it's hard to talk to a friend or relative that you haven't seen in a while. But as the snake piss started flowing, so did the conversation and soon we'd covered Rachel's two cats and my cat, whom Stephanie DuPont had agreed orally to take care of in my unexpected absence. Stephanie had not been ecstatic about the arrangement, but somehow I trusted her, which was more than I could currently say about clients or limo drivers, or just about anyone else in the world.

Except possibly cousin Rachel. I don't know if it was just the Wild Turkey gobbling or whether I badly needed to talk the situation over with a fairly objective friendly human being, but in the next two and a half hours I rolled out the whole megillah for Rachel, her two cats, and a life-size wooden Indian that stood stolidly in Rachel's apartment and vaguely resembled Kawliga's smarter older brother. I also wanted to hear myself tell the story again just to see if I'd been as careless, blundering, and unobservant as I thought I'd been. Apparently, I had.

At one point in my dissertation I got up to make three phone calls and then to visit the little detective's room, where evidence of Rachel's designer talents made urinating mildly uncomfortable. Give me a brick wall in an alley, I thought. Give me a field in Texas under a starry sky. Give me a chance to sort this craziness out in my brain.

Rambam's computer had kept burping every time the name Derrick Price came up. He'd never seen anything like it, he said. He also commented that anyone who really wanted to burn a vehicle burned it from the bottom up instead of the top down. 'Either they weren't trying to kill you or they fucked up,' he added. I told him either one was fine with me. McGovern's line was busy. So was Polly Price's. I flushed the dumper and went back to finish my story without washing my hands as all employees must. It was one of the small advantages to being your own boss. Also, I didn't want to soil cousin Rachel's beautifully mounted hand towels. At any rate, I doubted seriously if a germ from my penis would jump on to my hand and wind up killing me. It hadn't happened yet and there'd been lots of opportunities. Or, if it had happened, I didn't know about it. The disease had been very slow in developing. Even slower than I'd been in figuring out what had brought me to Chicago.

'So that's the whole turbulent, sometimes rather tedious affair,' I said, a short while later as I noticed the bottle was nearing the midway mark. 'As a polite, but disinterested observer, I've told you everything from the original phone call from Polly Price to the call I made to you earlier this evening when I popped out of the burning limo like a gourmet scion of Orville Redenbacher. What do you make of it, Rachel?'

'Well, Kinky, I've never been involved in anything like this before, searching for somebody's husband. All the weird things that've happened to your friend McGovern. The close scrapes you got into in Washington and now here in Chicago. You've had a lot more experience than I have at – '

'C'mon, Rachel, don't massage my wilted ego at a time like this. Get to the chorus, Boris. What do you really think is happening?'

'Sounds like someone's sending you on a wild goose chase,' said Rachel.

'There's a bird I *don't* like,' I said.

THIRTY-TWO

Rachel steered me steadily to the spare bedroom so I could take a short power nap, but I didn't sleep. I kept empathizing rather heavily with a fictional character named Jabez Wilson. Jabez Wilson had red hair and I didn't, but otherwise it seemed that the two of us had a hell of a lot in common. For those of you who may feel fairly foggy in your Sherlock Holmes area, Jabez Wilson was the owner of a pawnshop who came to the great detective with a strange story. Wilson's shop assistant, a man named Vincent Spaulding, who'd taken a job at half wages, had approached his boss several months before with a hot news item. Ezekiah Hopkins, an extremely eccentric American millionaire, had recently croaked, leaving his loved ones, after they'd carefully perused his will, in somewhat of a snit.

Apparently, Hopkins, being a redhead himself, and very possibly having very little inside his head, had left his vast fortune in the hands of trustees along with a set of somewhat peculiar – especially to the minds of the greedy, rather repellent relatives – instructions. The money was to be reserved expressly to provide easy berths for men all over the world who had hair of a colour similar to Ezekiah Hopkins. Thus was born one of Sherlock's most convoluted and baffling cases, that of 'The Red-Headed League'.

Jabez Wilson had dutifully gone to a certain address where he was informed that if he remained at that address each working day copying the *Encyclopaedia Britannica*, he would indeed find it to be a financial pleasure. He had and it was. Unfortunately for Mr Wilson, however, Ezekiah Hopkins's largesse did not continue for terribly long. About two months after beginning the monumental and somewhat ludicrous task, he came to work one morning to find a rather unsettling notice tacked to the door. It read:

The Red-Headed League
Is
Dissolved
October 9, 1890

Jabez Wilson was, to say the least, extremely irritated. He'd only gotten as far as 'asshole'. That was about as far as I'd gotten, too. I just wasn't quite certain who the asshole was.

As I lay in Rachel Samet's spare bed with a strange cat, it became glaringly apparent to me that my actions and efforts of the past few weeks had been equally meaningless as those of Jabez Wilson in copying the *Encyclopaedia Britannica*. If anything, Wilson had probably learned more. But what seemed truly disturbing to me was my growing belief that both Jabez Wilson and I had been sucked, fucked and cajoled into our various fruitless endeavours for precisely the same reason. Somebody had clearly wanted both of us out of the way.

In Jabez Wilson's case, the Red-Headed League itself had merely been a clever device to lure him away from his own office so he wouldn't lamp on to the fact that tunnelling was occurring directly beneath him to the bank vault next door. For Sherlock Holmes, the whole affair had hardly amounted to a three-pipe problem. In the pale light of the twentieth century, however, life is quite another story. Our lives today come very close to being defined by something Edgar Allan Poe, even before Sherlock, had once observed about the game of chess: 'Complex without being profound.'

Sherlock, of course, was not here to help me. He was sitting on my desk in New York, surrounding a precious handful of Habana Montecristo No. 2 cigars Ratso had belatedly sent over, and doing his best to keep the dust and cat hair out of his timeless, all-knowing, penetrating porcelain eyes. It fell entirely to me to figure out what it was that had piqued someone's interest about my somewhat bohemian, often rather melancholy, existence to such a degree that they'd find it important to try to lure me away from New York. In my life and my loft, both figuratively and literally speaking, and much to my own private disappointment, there did not appear to be any bank vault. My life lately, at least before Polly Price had strolled into it, could be fully captured in one word. It was the same word that Captain John Smith had used to describe his forty years at sea in his last interview before sailing off at the helm of the *Titanic*. The word was 'uneventful'.

Yet I suspected that Cousin Rachel was right. Chicago had been a wild goose chase. Now that I thought about it, so had Washington. There I'd been winged. Here I'd been slightly defrosted in an extremely expensive microwave on wheels. In both instances, money was clearly no object for these people. Torching a new limousine or leaving around a busted valise full of Irving Berlin's White Christmas meant nothing to these folks. Nor – and this was significant – did they particularly seem to want to croak me. Lord knows they had had plenty of opportunities. 'Either they weren't trying to kill you or they fucked up,' Rambam had told me on the phone. After that, he'd launched into a rather laborious technical treatise on how to make your own napalm by dissolving Styrofoam cups in gasoline and then laying out this little jellied dessert underneath an unsuspecting vehicle. I'd nodded off about halfway through Rambam's tutorial, but I'd effectively grasped the subject matter. They wanted to frighten me maybe. They wanted to send me on my merry way looking for the next clue in some mindless scavenger hunt. But they weren't trying to croak me. If they'd wanted to croak me, they would've already croaked me. This kind of people did not fuck up.

Now I thought back to the break-in at my loft that had occurred when I was out playing with Ratso in my nation's capital. Maybe they'd only lifted Derrick's papers to cover for what they were really after. The bank vault had to be somewhere in my loft or in my life. Had to be. These guys operated like pros. One could only assume they knew what they were searching for. If that was indeed true, the bastards were ten steps ahead of the rest of us.

If I was going to follow Sherlockian dictum, my task was to offload that which was impossible, and whatever was left, no matter how improbable, had to be the truth. It was improbable, all right. I'd most likely suspected it for some little time, but it was only now, as I lay in Cousin Rachel's guest room counting flowers on the wall that I admitted finally to myself what that improbable thing was that had to be the truth. Had to be what these mysterious people were really after.

It was not me they wanted. It wasn't even Derrick Price. It was McGovern.

It was a wildly improbable idea, but it explained a lot of things. Why I couldn't find Derrick Price. Why McGovern was being followed, spied upon, and harassed. Why they wanted me out of the way so they could get to him more easily. Maybe it all had to do with Leaning Jesus and whatever he'd once given to McGovern that he now evidently wanted back. Of course, Leaning Jesus was almost certainly dead, but that made things only a little more improbable than they already were.

I got out of the little bed and walked over to the antique-style designer telephone. I dialled McGovern's number. It was still busy. I hesitated for just a moment and then I called Polly Price's number. Her number was also still busy.

I walked out on to the little patio and looked across at the North Shore. I lit a cigar and watched as people painted lights on to the dark velvet of the city night. It was time for me to get busy, too.

THIRTY-THREE

It was crowding Cinderella time when Cousin Rachel and I pulled over to the side of the street to look at the map again. It wasn't the kind of neighbourhood you'd really want to be in at Cinderella time or at any other time for that matter. But it hadn't always been this way. There was a time, back in the forties and fifties, when guys like Redd Foxx played Negro clubs in this neighbourhood. It was a very happenin' place in those days. According to the notes I'd made from my earlier conversations with McGovern, one of the hottest venues here on the South Shore had once been a place called the Ambassador Club. The old Ambo, as it was called, had been located at the corner of 79th and Kingston. It had been owned by a man named Leaning Jesus.

'Rachel, I've got a bad feeling about dragging you into all this. I'm not certain exactly what it is but I do know it could be hazardous to your health.'

'Don't be silly. Give me the map.'

'I'm not kidding. Someone's been tailing me around New York. Then they show up in Washington. Now they're here in Chicago.'

'You sure you're not just getting paranoid?'

'The only thing I'm sure of is that I left my fucking reading glasses in the limo.'

'So give me the map.'

I gave her the map. She studied it for a moment with the small flashlight that we'd picked up at the last convenience store before we'd left civilization as we knew it. It didn't take long for her to pinpoint our current location and the location of 79th and Kingston. It was only a bad dream away.

I looked into the rearview mirror again but saw no sign of any vehicle in the vicinity. All I saw was a ragged old man with a bottle in his hand vomiting in the gutter. Could've been

Edgar Allan Poe or Ira Hayes or Stephen Foster. Could've been me, I thought, given the wrong bloodlines and the right heartbreak.

'Listen, Rachel, I just have a feeling your mother wouldn't want you to be involved in this.'

'Mom doesn't have to know,' she said, sounding suddenly very young.

'That's true.'

'Besides, something tells me that my dad approves.'

I suspected she was right. If things went wrong, of course, I might be catching hell a little sooner than I'd planned.

'Drive on,' I said.

As we closed in on the area of Leaning Jesus's old haunts, the street seemed to become a little more populated, if you wanted to call it that. The people seemed to cling to the shadows and the shadows seemed to cling to the people. Like lepers or whores or other biblical types, they huddled together beneath burned-out streetlights waiting for the sun to take them away.

'Kind of gives you the creeps,' said Rachel.

'That's correct,' I said. 'And just to get your mind off it, this might be the time to tell you that the only bird with two feathers for each quill is the emu.'

'I thought the emu was extinct.'

'Not yet, but we're working on it.'

By the time we got to the corner where the old Ambo Club had been, the people and the shadows had gone away and so had just about everything else. The corner was as quiet as a country graveyard with nothing and no one stirring anywhere, and that was fine with me. The old building on the corner might've once been a jumpin' joint but now stood sombre as a shipwreck on the forgotten floor of some unchartered sea Columbus missed on his way to discovering the Bank of America.

Rachel parked the car across the street from what had once been the Ambo. At least I hoped it had once been the Ambo.

Everything else in the area looked about as promising as a lunar landscape. I told Rachel I was only going to pop inside the place for a moment and she was to wait inside the car with doors locked and lights off.

'Can I play the radio, Daddy?'

'NO. And if you see anyone at all come near the car I want you to make this place sound like rush hour in the Loop.'

'Don't worry,' said Rachel. 'I'll honk if I love Leaning Jesus.'

I took my little flashlight and headed for the door of the dark, godforsaken, old structure. It didn't look like a major B & E job, because the front door was standing open off its hinges. Forty, fifty, maybe sixty years ago this place might've been brimming with guys and dolls and machine-guns and money and laughter and liquor and excitement and intrigue. You might've even had to say 'Joe sent me' to get in. I wasn't sure who had sent me, but whoever it was had a pretty sick sense of humour. It was a stretch to imagine that there could be any relic of the past in this old house that could help explain the events occurring in McGovern's life or my life today. It was a long shot but it was the only shot I had. I knew what I was looking for. I had to give Leaning Jesus a name.

I quickly moved through the front of the house, shining the flashlight around enough to show me that it'd been totally trashed through decades of disuse. It looked like a crack house that had seen better days. On the floor, in the place of furniture, were old boxes, blankets, broken wine bottles, used butane lighters, pads of dirty steel wool to smoke crack through, and an old shopping cart that stood in a cobwebbed corner. It was asleep. Waiting for its happy suburban shopper to come.

I wasn't sure yet if indeed this had ever been the old Ambo Club that McGovern had talked about so glowingly. If it truly was the place, generations of life's refugees had come here since Leaning Jesus had lurched off the screen. From the look of the place, I doubted if Joe had sent any of them. Maybe another Jesus had.

I didn't want to leave Rachel in the car too long and I didn't want to stay in this hellhole of a house too long so I worked my way towards the back of the place, where McGovern had said the bar and kitchen used to be. I found what must've been the cooking area, but there was no one in the kitchen with Dinah strummin' on the ol' banjo. I had to duck round and under old rusted pipes everywhere, some of them still dripping on to places where the floor was rotting away. It was like watching ancient gnarled limbs leaking the life-blood of a bygone era.

On a dusty shelf near by was a rain-soaked makeup and cosmetics kit, possibly left by street prostitutes who'd come here to get high between tricks. Then I shone the light in the far corner and saw the old beauty herself. She'd probably been too heavy for looters to take away like almost everything else that had once been in the place. I could almost smell the old Italian pasta sauces cooking. I could almost see Leaning Jesus himself coming by at regular intervals to stir the pots with a wooden spoon as they simmered away for ever. Well, almost for ever. It was a huge, old-fashioned gas stove with iron feet like you used to find on some old bathtubs.

My gaze wandered to the black, greasy wall just behind the big gas stove. That was where I found them. The food and liquor licences for the Ambassador Club. They looked like a museum display of the Magna Carta, faded like the years themselves, but still legible enough to reveal a name. Here was something very few people, including McGovern, had known.

Leaning Jesus's name was Jim Pollard.

There was even a legible home address on one of the tattered yellow documents. Leaning Jesus was almost certain dead, according to my calculations, but surely there must be friends or family still loitering around where he'd once lived. And it wasn't easy to forget a guy named Leaning Jesus.

Suddenly, I was very excited. I felt almost sure Polly Price had set up wild goose chases for me in Washington and Chicago so that she could get at McGovern. She'd hired me to pursue her imaginary husband because she knew McGovern was confiding in me about Leaning Jesus. Did that make sense? No. But it got worse. She'd hired me before I'd even told her about McGovern or Leaning Jesus. What did that suggest? And Leaning Jesus had been Al Capone's chef. *Bon appétit* and curiouser and curiouser.

I was scribbling Pollard's name and his home address in my little private investigator's notebook when I heard a voice in the darkness behind me.

'What up?' it said.

Then I heard another voice from somewhere a little closer. 'Hey, white boy,' it said. 'Got any money?'

All the flashlight was doing was revealing my location, so I killed it and tried to move away into the semi-darkness. I could see the afterimages of two large, dark forms lumbering towards me. From the way they moved and sounded they were obviously sprung on crack. I slid quickly into the side room where the prostitutes had maintained their little vanity. I grabbed a half-full can of Aqua Net hairspray, took out my Bic lighter, and waited. I wasn't going to fire until I saw the whites of their eyes.

They came at me a little faster than I'd thought. I got off one strong shot of aerosol over the tiny lit flame of the Bic, which roared through the little room like a fire out of hell. But crack addicts are used to fire. I was stumbling round in the darkness, hoping that the exits were well lit when a large figure loomed up in front of me and hit me over the head with what appeared to be a table leg.

The last thing I remember hearing before I became totally out where the buses don't run was a car honking somewhere out in the street.

THIRTY-FOUR

I woke up in a strange room with a strange woman. It wasn't the first time, but it felt like the worst time. My orbs were having some difficulty focusing, and it sounded like some chubby little kid was inside my head warming up for his bassoon recital. Then my eyes and ears began to clear and I realized I was flat on my back in the Ambo Club with celestial light shining on my face as I listened to the voice of an angel. The angel had a slight Chicago accent.

'They took your wallet and your watch,' she said, 'but they left your cowboy hat and this little notebook you were scribbling in.'

'Rachel?'

'I thought I saw a fire inside, so I started honking my horn, and a few moments later two men started running south down the street.'

'We'll head north.'

'How many fingers am I holding up?'

'Very funny, Rachel.'

'Well, it's what you deserve for coming in here alone and almost getting yourself killed. If it hadn't been for you wearing this cowboy hat and me honking the horn –'

'Maybe God protects middle-aged Jewish amateur detectives,' I said, sitting up painfully and putting the cowboy hat gently back on my head.

'And children, drunks and fools,' said Rachel disapprovingly.

'Yep,' I said, looking at my little notebook, 'He keeps Himself pretty busy, but so do we. And we ain't through yet tonight.'

'What?' said Rachel. 'You've got to be crazy.'

'As Willie Nelson once told me: "If you ain't crazy, there's something wrong with you." '

I got up a little less gracefully than I would've liked and showed Rachel the address where I believed Leaning Jesus had once lived. She took the notebook a bit reluctantly but, after a brief hesitation, shone the flashlight on the page.

'I remember McGovern saying that Leaning Jesus used to walk home from here after the bar closed, so it couldn't be too far. He used to carry a sawn-off shotgun inside a brown paper bag and everybody knew it, so nobody fucked with him. Pardon my Shakespeare.'

'You *are* getting middle-aged.'

'Anyway, he gave a whole new definition to brown-baggin' it. Let's check out this address on the map and go for a little late-night ride, baby.'

'Right away, General Custer.'

A few moments later we were safely inside the car, studying the map together. One headache more or less didn't bother me much if I was as close as I thought I was to untangling the enigma that was Leaning Jesus. A lot of ideas were beginning to flow in and out of my mind, no doubt shaken loose by the contact between my head and the table leg. Sort of like the time Isaac Newton was sitting under a tree and got hit on the head by a gravity-driven apple. Some of the ideas were quite preposterous, even to my own currently mildly amphibious thought processes. But some of them were starting to make an eerie kind of sense to me. I thought I'd try one of them out on Rachel as she drove the little car warily through the silent, desolate streets.

'Think about this, Cousin Rachel. Al Capone went away sometime in the thirties – '

'Went away?'

'To prison. Tax evasion. Don't interrupt your elders.'

'You got that right.'

'I'm a little rusty on the time lines, but I remember he was stabbed but only wounded at Alcatraz by a Texas bank robber named James Lucas who was no relation to Old Ben Lucas who had a lot of mucous – '

'That's disgusting.'

'That's what Al thought. So anyway, McGovern left Chicago in 'sixty-seven to go to New York. The only possible connection between Al Capone and Mike McGovern was Leaning Jesus. Now what does that suggest to you?'

'That Al Pacino may play McGovern in *Godfather Part Five*?'

'No, dear – '

Suddenly Rachel swerved the car to the kerb with an enthusiasm that almost sent my head spinning again.

'That's it,' she said excitedly. 'That's the address. It's two o'clock in the morning and all the lights are on. Do you think Leaning Jesus could still be living there?'

'It's either him or Tom Bodet,' I said.

THIRTY-FIVE

On the South Side of Chicago, as in almost every other urban centre of America today, even a Jehovah's Witness knows it's not particularly best foot forward to knock on someone's door at two o'clock in the morning. Nevertheless, it was mildly frustrating to have been parboiled in the back seat of a limousine and then bopped on the head by some australopithecine, all so I could sit out at the kerb and gaze at a house that was lit up like a Christmas tree in Las Vegas. If someone inside had some answers I wanted them now. The more I thought about it, the more concerned I was becoming about the uneasy state of McGovern's health, education, and welfare.

As somewhat of a past expert on various forms of substance abuse myself, I knew that different drugs produce different perceptions of what for most normal, non-using, good little church workers remains the same hideously boring, stultifyingly dull workaday treadmill of an existence. Not only will those who freely partake of drugs and alcohol see reality differently, but their perceptions may vary greatly from one individual to another depending upon precisely how they mix their John Belushi cocktails. For instance, it is not at all uncommon for the speed freak to look repeatedly out between his venetian blinds in the middle of the night and think he sees the deputy sheriff lurking in the backyard. No one on cocaine has ever looked through the venetian blinds and seen a deputy sheriff. For the children of the snow it has to be the CIA, Interpol, or maybe a crack Gurkha unit, and I do mean crack. And when you pour alcohol on top of all of this, things can really start to get a little wiggy.

But what was bothering me went far deeper than the blurred edges of reality and the perceptions of man or the lack of these perceptions. McGovern was a veteran of the fifth estate. As a seasoned journalist who'd travelled the world and plumbed the minds of men to record what he'd observed, he wasn't all that likely to be this far off the tracks. What if all the things McGovern thought were happening to him were really happening to him? If that were indeed the case, McGovern might currently be in some rather deep, dangerous waters. Far deeper than the denizens of California hot tubs ever dream of.

'We're going in,' I said.

'I don't know, admiral,' said Rachel, 'but don't you think we should wait till the first light of dawn?'

'By the first light of dawn,' I said, 'I plan to be drinking a Bloody Mary on an aircraft headed for New York.'

'That's better than flying back to Texas in a pine box.'

'I'll mention it to my travel agent,' I said, as I got out of the car. 'You can come with me if you like.'

'I think I'd better,' said Rachel.

The path to Leaning Jesus's old residence was well kept and well lit, with the door and the windows of the place being protected, of course, by heavy bars. It almost made me a little homesick for New York.

I didn't have a prepared Rotary luncheon speech in my

mind. I just hoped, as we stepped up on to the little front porch, that the name Leaning Jesus would mean something here. If it didn't, I could always try pissing up a rope for an encore.

I knocked on the door.

After a moment or two, steps could be heard inside the house. Then a shadow moved across the windowshade in the direction of the front door.

'Who is it?' came a wary voice from the other side of the door.

'Friends of Leaning Jesus,' I said. Sometimes you have to stretch the truth a little to find out what it is.

We waited.

Soon we were rewarded by the sounds of bolts being unlocked and a chain being removed. Then the door opened to reveal the figure of a man. He appeared to be a gentle soul with grey hair and a smooth, youthful-looking face. I guessed he was about my age.

I introduced myself and Rachel and gave him the briefest of bumper stickers about my search for Leaning Jesus and how I found this address at the old Ambo Club.

'I'm James Pollard Jr,' he said. 'Leaning Jesus's son.'

THIRTY-SIX

'My father died in 1962,' he said, as the three of us sat round the kitchen table like the old friends in 'Bob Dylan's dream.' 'He was hit by the last working streetcar in Chicago. It was sort of a tourist attraction. A real dinosaur. But then again, in many ways, so was my dad.'

'Thirty-four years is a long time,' I said.

'So they tell me,' said Pollard.

As I watched him diligently measuring out coffee for the

three of us, I thought that James Pollard Jr was a lonely man. I wondered briefly whether he was gay or not and decided that it didn't matter to a tree. He had a cute little black dog named Perky, who was currently sitting in Rachel's lap. He had apparently been up at two o'clock in the morning reading. Right now he seemed to be reading my thoughts.

'Perky and I don't often get visitors at this hour of the morning,' he said. 'In fact, we don't often get visitors much at all these days. It gets a little lonely sometimes, but it's fine with us. Makes up for all the years when my father was alive and the feds wouldn't leave us alone. One of the reasons I let you in tonight is that you look like one of the colourful characters my father would've liked.'

I took that as a compliment and found myself starting to like this guy. In many ways, of course, he wasn't so very different from myself.

'If you don't mind,' I said, 'tell us a little about the feds. Why wouldn't they leave your father alone?'

'How much do you really know about my father?'

'Very little really except that he owned the Ambassador Club, he was Al Capone's chef, and they called him Leaning Jesus.'

'He was much more than Al Capone's chef,' said Pollard as he brought the coffee to the table on a little tray. 'Capone, at the height of his reign, was such a powerful man that he trusted almost no one. He was like the king of the gypsies. He had a huge extended family, some of whom were even related to him. He was like Napoleon. He had a vast army of soldiers awaiting his every command. Yet he never was able to be very close to these people. He never trusted them. He trusted my father.'

Pollard was giving his account with almost no pride or approbation. He spoke dispassionately, as if he were a kindly professor giving a lecture on Pharaoh Esophagus's reign in Ancient Egypt, now all but forgotten within the dusty book jackets of what we call history. Of course, yesterday's triumphs and tragedies may well be today's trivia. But as my own father often reminds me, there is no trivia.

'In 1931, just before Capone was convicted on income-tax charges, he summoned his tailor to measure him for several lightweight suits to wear in Miami. Leaning Jesus was there, along with Frankie Rio, one of his many cohorts. "You don't need to be ordering fancy duds," said Rio. "Why don't you have a suit made with stripes on it? You're going to prison." Then Capone winked at Leaning Jesus. "The hell I am," he said. "I'm going to Florida for a nice long rest and I need some new clothes before I go."

'Capone never really believed it was over. Leaning Jesus never believed it either. But it was. By that time the gang wars had taken over seven hundred lives, including the notorious St Valentine's Day Massacre in 1929 when seven survivors of the O'Bannion Gang were lined up and mowed down with machine guns in a North Side garage. I'm sorry. Do you take sugar?'

Rachel and I shook our heads. For whatever reason, possibly his insular lifestyle, Pollard seemed to be opening up to us in an almost cathartic fashion. I didn't want to stop him if he was on a roll. Soon he continued.

'When Capone walked into the Big House in Atlanta in May of 'thirty-two, for all practical purposes he was washed up as a mob boss. Two years later, he was transferred to Alcatraz. Four years after that, the authorities there announced he was a mental patient. He died in 1947 in Miami at his Palm Island estate. Doctors said he had the mentality then of a child of twelve. But my father had been in touch with him over the years and also just prior to his death. He said the doctors were crazy, Capone was as sharp as ever.'

At this point Perky jumped off Rachel's lap and Pollard seemed precariously close to jumping off the tracks himself for a moment.

'Wait a minute,' he said, 'this isn't for publication or anything? You're not writing a book, are you?'

'Of course not. I'm just interested in why someone is invoking Leaning Jesus's name to harass and intimidate a friend of mine and why his problems seem to be spilling over on me.'

'Leaning Jesus never killed anyone, you understand. That wasn't why the feds hounded him. They knew he was more than a chef. They knew he was Capone's confidant. And they suspected Capone might have transferred a certain vital missing document of his to my father. But the feds never would say exactly what it was, and if it existed at all, Leaning Jesus took its nature and its whereabouts with him when he died. After Capone went away and especially after his death, they interrogated my father unmercifully. Tape recorded interviews with him for hours at a time. Searched this house on many occasions. But by the fifties it had all stopped. Then there was one last gasp in 1962 after he died. They went through this place from top to bottom, but they found nothing. They asked me a lot of questions, but there was little I could tell them. Dad never talked to me about his business. Just as well, I suppose.'

Tape recorded interviews, I thought. Getting warmer.

Pollard got up and poured us all a fresh cup of coffee. I asked if I could smoke a cigar. He said he'd like that. It'd remind him of the old times. He went to get an ashtray and I shrugged at Rachel. The guy might not have all the answers but at least he was an accommodating host. God knows, there was a shortage of those these days.

'So when Leaning Jesus died in 1962,' I said, as he came back with the ashtray, 'that was the last you saw of the feds.'

'Until about two months ago,' he said.

I stopped my cigar in mid-flight to my mouth. A big piece had just fallen into place here and I knew it. I also knew, somewhat to my discomfort, that we were dealing with a very big puzzle. One that had just spanned eight decades in the time it had taken to drink two cups of coffee.

'This is getting too close for country dancin',' I said. 'What was their excuse this time?'

'Somebody'd finally retired at headquarters. They said they were closing the file.'

'Did you get the names of any of the agents involved?'

'I'm afraid not. Of course, they didn't get anything either. I don't really believe there's anything to get.'

I leaned over and patted Perky for a while. The dog looked smarter than many people I knew. I wasn't feeling too bright myself at that moment. Like a character in a long-ago children's story I half remembered, I was leaving Chicago an older but not a particularly wiser bear. The smart thing to do, I thought, would be to hibernate until spring. Bears slept for months at a time in their caves, why couldn't I? Of course, bears didn't have to get up to urinate or feed the cat. And they probably didn't have nightmares unless they were scared of mice. No, that was elephants. Bears probably had nightmares about men. Between mice and men, we could no doubt scare the shit out of anybody. I didn't plan to be having any nightmares, however. As Warren Zevon once recommended: 'I'll sleep when I'm dead.' And that, if I wasn't very careful, could well be sooner instead of later.

I was still patting Perky and now, half consciously, I suppose, I began singing to him. It was a little thing I'd picked up from the old Big John and Sparky radio show, a programme I listened to often as a child. Quite possibly, if what the doctors said was true about Capone, he and I might've been listening at the same time.

' "If you go down to the woods today you're in for a
   big surprise,
If you go down to the woods today you'd better go
   in disguise . . ." '

Perky seemed to be listening to the song rather intently. James Pollard Jr appeared to be staring at me rather intently.

' "Dah-dah dah-dah, dah-dah dah-dah-dah
Dah-dah dah-dah, dah-dah dah-dah-dah
Today's the day the teddy bears have their pic-nic . . ." '

'Well,' said Rachel, 'I think it's about time for us to be going.'

'I just have one more question,' I said. 'Suppose for just a moment that this mysterious document did exist and that Capone did actually entrust it to Leaning Jesus before he went away. Now, cast your mind back, Mr Pollard. Did your father ever allude to anything like that, possibly in a seemingly rather cryptic fashion?'

Pollard thought about it for a moment. Rachel began readying herself for departure. Perky wagged his tail beside my chair, more than likely hoping for another verse of the Big John and Sparky theme song.

'Not that I remember,' said Pollard, with a bit of hesitation. But there was something in his manner that was keeping me in the game.

'Was there anything he ever said, that comes back to you now, that you didn't understand? Anything peculiar that didn't make sense?'

Rachel and I were standing now. So was Perky. Pollard was standing by his coffee cup, leaning against the counter, possibly debating whether or not to spill it.

'Actually,' said Pollard, 'there was something my father said after the streetcar accident that I didn't understand. It was later that night in the hospital just before he died. Of course, it's possible that his mind had been affected by the accident, because I'm his only son and I know he had a girlfriend for a while, but I would've certainly known if he'd had an illegitimate child.'

The kitchen had become very still. In fact, the whole world seemed to have become very still. Pollard, appearing to be half in a trance, looked like he might be prepared to stand there like that for ever. After another moment or two I gave him some gentle encouragement.

'Try to recall,' I said, 'the exact words Leaning Jesus said to you.'

Pollard's eyes looked into that hospital room. Perky tried to follow his master's gaze, but, like the feds over the years, he came up short.

'The last words my father spoke made no sense to me whatsoever. He looked up at me from the hospital bed and grabbed my arm tightly. All he said was: "The Kid. Where's the Kid?" '

THIRTY-SEVEN

My flight back to New York was, to quote Captain John Smith of the *Titanic* again, 'uneventful'. Unlike James Pollard Jr, I felt pretty sure I knew who the kid was. I kept asking myself, however, the same question Leaning Jesus had asked on his deathbed: *Where* is the kid? I'd called McGovern's number from O'Hare earlier in the morning, and then again when I landed at LaGuardia. The phone rang and rang and rang. No busy signal any longer. No answering machine. No kid.

Not only did I call McGovern's number, but, for good measure, I called Polly Price's number from both airports as well. The results of these efforts were, not terribly surprisingly, the same. Not only was there no kid, there was also no client. It was shaping up to be one honey of a case.

In the cab, on the way over to Vandam, I thought once again of Rambam's rather chauvinistic advice: Never trust a female client. That credo was certainly out of sync with the prevailing attitudes of the times – *The New York Times* or any times, but that didn't necessarily mean it was without merit. A little chauvinism today, quite possibly, might prevent a little tedium tomorrow. But not only was I feeling very distrustful of female clients at the moment, I also was developing a rather low regard for large Irish journalists. In fact, my attitude was strikingly similar to that of Al Capone's towards the end of his life when, like a bloodthirsty, psychotic, paranoid, stubborn, diabolical twelve-year-old, he refused to trust anyone. That attitude may never win you a lot of friends, but it's not a bad one to have if you know you're coming to New York.

'I don't believe it,' Rambam was saying later that afternoon as both of us were busy pacing the loft at different diagonals. 'The last time I spoke to you, when you were in Chicago, you had *two* clients. Now they're *both* missing.'

'Well,' I said, 'it's easy for something like that to happen. I've been quite busy, you see, copying the *Encyclopaedia Britannica* for the Red-Headed League.'

'Did you get as far as the word "fuckup"?' said Rambam.

'No,' I said, 'I was waiting for you to help me.'

'Well, here I am. Of course, you've already broken the first two rules of the private investigator: Never trust a woman client, and never take on a non-paying client.'

'I guess it's just that Christ-like streak in me that keeps coming out.'

'If it comes out again,' said Rambam, 'don't be surprised if somebody takes three little nails and puts you up for the night.'

Rambam was very frustrated. I was rather highly agitato myself. And none of this was going down very well with the cat. Cats do not enjoy hearing acrimonious conversations and seldom if ever take part in them. In this case, the cat was hunkering down rather pathetically beside the gurgling espresso machine, partly because the loft was cold, but also, I felt, because she was disappointed by the general absence of human warmth in the place.

'Now look what you've done,' I said to Rambam. 'You've upset the cat.'

'Fuck the cat,' said Rambam.

He advanced upon the cat and myself rather angrily, stopping only to pick up a small piece of perfume-scented, pink pastel stationery on the counter. I tried, unsuccessfully, to grab it away from him.

'What do we have here?' said Rambam tauntingly.

'It's nothing,' I said. 'Just a little love note from Stephanie DuPont. She's back in town and she was taking care of the cat for me while I was in Chicago. Give it to me.'

Rambam sniffed the stationery.

'Very nice,' he said. Then he shot his cuffs back in an exaggerated preparation to read the letter. The gesture bore an uncanny resemblance to that of Ed Norton in *The Honeymooners*.

'Let's see what she says,' said Rambam, easily frustrating any efforts I made to snatch the paper from him. He cleared his throat several times. Then, much to my chagrin, he read the note out loud.

'You need more cat food, turbo dick. And while you're out shopping, get a life.

Stephanie

'I like a girl who's not afraid to express herself,' said Rambam, with a sarcastic smirk.

'She's got a rather caustic sense of humour,' I said.

The cat merely closed her eyes in mortification.

A short while later, peace and harmony and a growing feeling of excitement reigned throughout the loft. Cooler heads were definitely prevailing, though none, of course, was quite as cool as the little black puppet head that resided on top of the refrigerator flashing that heartfelt human smile you rarely see around New York these days.

I'd taken Rambam step by step through the events in Chicago, and he seemed quite impressed with my insight in divining the parallels between my own experience and that of Jabez Wilson in the Red-Headed League. He seemed

troubled when I explained the roles I believed Polly Price
and McGovern were playing in the whole sordid affair. Most
of all, he appeared to appreciate the linkage I felt had been
established between Al Capone, Leaning Jesus and the kid,
who, of course, was McGovern, though he was much too
large to be appropriately labelled as such today, even if he
often acted like one. Most important, Rambam seemed to
understand the gravity of the case and where I was going
with it, from one private investigator to another.

'I've got a more practical idea,' said Rambam, after I'd
brought him up to speed on the investigation. 'Why don't
the two of us just saddle up and go out in search of the Lost
Dutchman's Mine?'

'This could be bigger.'

'This could be a bigger pain in the ass.'

'Everyone from Eliot Ness to Geraldo Rivera would love
to be in our shoes.'

'As long as they don't try to get in our pants.'

'I'm serious, Rambam.'

'That's what I was afraid of. Look, I'll go along with this
for two reasons. One, you're my friend. And two, it does
have some entertainment value. But there's not one shred of
real evidence for what you're suggesting, and there are other
more mundane, but far more likely possibilities.'

'Such as.'

'Such as Polly Price likes McGovern. Maybe your ego can't
accept that she fell for his not inconsiderable Irish charm.
He's not my type, but who knows? Maybe the two of them
just decided to take off for Atlantic City for a few days.'

'It is difficult to imagine, but I suppose it's possible.'

'Of course it's possible. And it's also possible that your
Red-Headed League scenario is just a big red-headed herring.
Maybe these two investigations are not related, and neither
of them is going very well for you and you've made the
classic mistake that amateur private investigators often fall

prey to. You've tried to combine two as of yet unsuccessful efforts into one grandiose, self-concocted scheme.'

'All right, let's go over to McGovern's and find out.'

'I'll go along with you that far, but unless there are seven bullet-riddled members of the O'Bannion Gang lying on McGovern's living-room floor, I'm going to have a hard time believing Al Capone's got anything to do with this.'

'Would you go for seven days of dirty laundry?' I said as the two of us headed for the door.

THIRTY-EIGHT

I knew something was terribly wrong from the very moment Rambam and I had broken and entered McGovern's apartment. For one thing, it was clean and neat as a pin. In all the time I'd known McGovern I'd never seen the place to rise above the level of total disorder. He'd always contended that he had a system for finding things, and quite possibly he did, but no one in the civilized world had ever been able to decipher what it was. Now the place was so clean, spotless and well ordered you could eat Chicken McGovern off the floor. It looked like the model apartment the builder sometimes furnishes for prospective buyers to look round. But I, for one, wasn't buying it. Somebody had been through this place with a methodical vengeance. Somebody who was looking for something.

'Notice anything wrong with the picture?' I said to Rambam as we viewed the neatly stacked piles of newspapers and anal-retentive bookcases and closets.

'Yeah,' said Rambam. 'The place usually looks like shit.'

'At least McGovern's not as big a slob as Ratso,' I said.

'That's because *nobody*'s as big a slob as Ratso. OK, so somebody's been through here. Maybe McGovern hired one of those Beverly Hills mobile maid services where fourteen Guatemalan women jump out of a van and clean your house in eleven seconds.'

'Or,' I said, 'he might've just had Hercule Poirot over for a few days as a housepest.'

'I'll admit,' said Rambam, 'that when McGovern's place looks this neat it's comparable to any normal person's place being tossed. But that hardly establishes your Al Capone connection.'

'That notion was set in motion by the MIBs.'

'McGovern's an MIB?'

'No. McGovern's an MIT.'

'Which is?'

'Man in Trouble.'

'That's for sure. Now what's an MIB?'

'MIB stands for the mysterious Men in Black who routinely show up, presumably to investigate, after a UFO sighting.'

Rambam looked at me as if I were a prime candidate for the Bandera Home for the Bewildered. As with many Americans, the abstract often became too abstract for him. He wanted some hard evidence and I could see that he was running out of charm.

'You've heard of UFOs,' I said. 'Unidentified Federal Organizations?'

'I've had dealings with almost all of them, and sooner or later they all turn into MIBs and you wind up an MIT. If you're lucky.'

'How can you tell if you're dealing with one of them? It feels like I've been for the past few weeks. Large invisible tentacles and testicles are waiting for me around every corner.'

'They are large mammals,' said Rambam, as he made a careful tour of the room, stopping near the window by the fire escape. 'But they do sometimes leave little tracks in the snow for the discerning eye. Is this the fire escape where McGovern saw his MIB?'

'McGovern's been seeing a lot of MIBs lately. That's why he's an MIT. But yes, that's the fire escape. Why do you ask, chief inspector?'

But Rambam did not answer. He appeared to be staring through the curtains at something in the alley. I waited patiently.

'Holy Christ.'

'What is it?'

'I don't believe it.'

'What is it?'

I moved closer and saw that he was looking at a peculiar little burned circle in the curtain. I'd never noticed it before, but then, I suppose I could be forgiven. Thin curtains are a bit like freaks or bad automobile accidents. You never really look at them so much as you look through them.

'Does McGovern smoke?' asked Rambam grimly as he squatted down to take a better look. The marking was about at scrotum level.

'He hasn't smoked in years,' I said.

Rambam continued to examine the thing. Then he gazed up at the building across the alleyway.

'Of course, he probably hasn't changed these curtains in years either,' I said.

But Rambam wasn't listening. His face had taken on a very serious, intense countenance. He stood up again.

'Do you know what caused this burned place on the curtain?' he said, gesturing towards the window.

I took another look at the small spot. The burned place, or whatever it was, appeared to be not dissimilar to the kind of marking you might leave on the curtain if you aimed a cigarette at an upward angle and gently grazed the fabric just enough to barely burn through it.

'How the hell do I know what caused it?' I said. 'A midget with a long cigarette holder.'

'That's very funny, Kinky, but unless I'm very far off base this curtain was not burned from the inside. And, as you can see, there's a window behind it that probably remains closed most of the time. And there's not even room for a midget with a long cigarette holder to get between the curtain and the glass.'

'So where does that leave us?'

'With a laser.'

'A laser?'

'You wanted a UFO,' said Rambam. 'Now you've got one.'

THIRTY-NINE

It was getting dark by the time Rambam and I ankled it up Jane Street to Eighth Avenue and navigated our way to the fourth floor of the building across the alley behind McGovern's place. Rambam had narrowed what he felt was the laser site to two apartments with windows opening on to the alley side of the building. He knocked on the door of the first apartment.

'What are we looking for?' I asked, as the door swung open to reveal a happy homosexual couple just sitting down to a romantic candlelit dinner.

'Not this,' he said.

We walked down the hall a bit until we came to the door of the other apartment Rambam felt could be a candidate for the laser site. I was beginning to have my doubts about the whole deal.

'What does a laser do anyway?' I said.

'If shot properly on to the window of an apartment like McGovern's, it'll pick up vibrations that can go directly to a computer or be taped and later taken over to a lab.'

'And I take it they can glean something from these vibrations?'

'Glean, my ass,' said Rambam. 'They could've been

listening to every fart, belch and, possibly more importantly, every word that's been spoken in that apartment for the past month.'

Rambam knocked on the door and somewhere in the back of my mind a door opened. If McGovern's place had been bugged by a laser, it would explain a lot of things. Whoever was behind the whole setup would've heard McGovern talking to me on a number of occasions, both on the phone and in person. They'd have heard that the great detective, myself, of course, had taken McGovern on as a client. They'd have heard us discuss Leaning Jesus. They'd have known I was going to Chicago.

Rambam knocked on the door again.

Nothing.

'Two B & E's in one evening,' he said. 'It's not my record, but it ain't bad. Let's just hope there's a laser operation behind this door.'

'It'd be quite a letdown,' I said, 'if all we find in here's a midget with a long cigarette holder walking around burning people's curtains.'

'There'd be one less midget,' said Rambam grimly, as he started to work on the door.

'You wouldn't pick on somebody half your size, would you?' I said, as the door came open.

'If this is what I think it is,' said Rambam, 'it's very, very big.'

'That's what she told me last night,' I said to the back of his head as we entered the apartment.

The place was dark and smelled of dust and disuse. Then Rambam hit the lights and I saw something that seemed out of place. In fact, I saw many things that seemed out of place. Most of the furniture in the place appeared to be jammed into the hallway between the front door and the living room.

'This is what they do,' said Rambam, as we performed a two-man country line dance in between a chest of drawers, several table lamps on the floor, and a rocking chair for a child. It could've been for a midget but I now realized the midget wasn't here. Whatever was here, I didn't think I was much going to like.

'They find an apartment,' Rambam was saying, 'where they know that the occupants have gone on a photo safari to Botswana for seven months and they move the equipment in for the time of the operation. By the time the people who live here get back, everything'll be just like it was when they left. They've very good at this.'

'Who's they?'

Rambam didn't answer. He'd emerged from the clutter in the little hallway and was now moving like a power walker towards the window. As I rounded the turn myself, I saw that the living room was entirely bare of furnishings.

'Holy Christ,' said Rambam.

'What?'

'Look.'

He was pointing at the wooden floor by the window, which featured a fairly solid coat of dust, broken only by three dark smudge spots directly in front of the glass.

'Laser tripod,' he said.

'I'd recognize the tracks anywhere.'

'This window also provides perfect access to McGovern's apartment.'

'Is it possible that there are other explanations for these smudges on the floor?'

'Of course,' said Rambam, 'but there's no other possible explanation for this little item.'

Just against the nearby wall was a small sleek black object that looked dangerously similar to the common ballpoint pen. He picked it up, glanced confirmationally at it, and handed it to me. It read:

US Government
Skilcraft

'You've seen the tracks of the monster,' said Rambam. 'That's the droppings.'

'I just want to live long enough,' I said, as I looked across to McGovern's innocent little apartment, 'to see technology fail.'

'When it does, I'll fax your E-mail.'

We both got out of there a lot faster than we'd gotten in. Paranoia, I suppose, had begun to raise its large, ugly head. It was clear to both of us that there was a UFO involved along with lots of MIBs. We hailed a hack on Eighth Avenue and headed uptown. Polly Price's penthouse might provide some more answers, I thought. I told Rambam about the special elevator to the penthouse and the large number of doormen, and he said no problem. I didn't ask any questions. In the B & E department, Rambam was king.

'So who were those masked men?' I said, checking out the cab driver before I spoke. He was an Israeli, but he didn't look like he worked for Mossad.

'Process of elimination,' said Rambam. 'NYPD doesn't have this kind of equipment. DEA doesn't have the manpower to monitor a little place like McGovern's apartment unless they have good reason to suspect a hundred thousand kilos are moving through it every hour on the hour, which they don't. The CIA has no authority over internal matters unless they have good reason to suspect terrorism is involved, which they don't. That leaves the good ol' FBI.'

'Which, from your warm tone of voice, I gather is your least favourite.'

'You could throw in the KGB,' he said, 'and it'd still be my least favourite.'

I felt a slight shiver as I watched the grimy, neon New York night slide by my window. There had to be safer places to be. More practical things to do with my life. I meditated on the subject for about twenty blocks, and the only two possibilities that came to mind were starting up a kosher nudist ranch in Texas or being the friend that Janis Joplin never had.

So I sat back with a slight shiver as I watched the grimy, neon New York night slide by my window.

FORTY

'Maybe,' said Rambam, as we got out of the hack, 'you ought to start thinking about a less dangerous, less stressful line of work. You could settle down with that tattooed lady you were telling me about. Where's she from?'

'San Diego.'

'Does she have any kids?'

'Yeah. One boy. Ten years old.'

'Well, Kinky, are you prepared to be a stepfather?'

'I'm prepared to be a stepladder,' I said.

'Good,' said Rambam. 'We may need you to get us into this penthouse.'

We took a casual Upper West Side walk round the premises to get ourselves acclimatized to the situation. The doormen were swarming along the sidewalk and street in front of Polly Price's building. With their snappy uniforms, it looked like either the circus or the Prussian army had come to town, and I wasn't a fan of either one of them. The only army I believed in was the Salvation Army. As far as the circus was concerned, I had three reasons for disliking it. One, my own life had become such a circus lately that I didn't really need the distraction. Two, all the clowns these days seemed to vaguely resemble John Wayne Gacy. Three, ever since the elephant stomped the trainer, broke away from the circus, and had to be killed by police in Honolulu, I've begun to have my doubts about the big top. The owner of the circus was scratching his head about the elephant, who happened to be a mother elephant, and asking the question of the day: 'Why did she do it?' The answer is quite simple really. If you were flown back and forth every day and every night across the world in a hot, stuffy, frightening cargo plane and then paraded in front of thousands of screaming idiots with a stupid tiara stapled to your head, you'd run away from the circus, too. Maybe she was looking for Dumbo. Who knows? There's very little we can do about it, at any rate. Everybody's either running away *from* the circus or running away *with* the circus, and the circus keeps ruthlessly, relentlessly rolling until it superimposes itself upon all of our lives, most of which could've used a little grease paint and peanuts anyway. Occasionally, however, the circus hits a little snag, for example the circus train that derailed recently in Florida. All of the animals survived. The only fatalities were a lion tamer and a clown. Maybe God *does* have a sense of humour. If there is a God.

'How the hell are we going to get past all those doormen?' I said, as we walked further away from the building.

'You won't even see 'em,' said Rambam, as he turned left into a dark alley alongside the building. 'Just follow me.'

'Into the Valley of Death.'

'There's always that possibility.'

'I doubt if my number's up yet. I'm not that happy.'

'You're not making me very happy either,' said Rambam. 'I'm used to bucking the odds, but me and you against the FBI isn't anything I'd want any action on.'

'Well, as Damon Runyon once said: "All of life is six to five against." '

'I wonder if he's ever broken into a penthouse.'

'Not lately.'

We took another left at the back of the building and walked over broken glass, trash and other crap along the not-so-attractive backside of the beautiful building. At last we arrived at a poorly lit, rather dingy door marked EMERGENCY EXIT – IF DOOR IS OPENED, ALARM WILL RING.

'Notice that alarm bell in its casing?' said Rambam. 'It's the good old-fashioned kind. I'm going to look around back here for a while. Meanwhile, I've got an errand for you.'

'Yes, Mother.'

'You know that drugstore we passed on the corner? Get us a can of shaving cream. Economy size.'

'This is no time for practical jokes,' I said to the back of Rambam's head, as he walked further off into the gloom.

I'd already had a couple of pretty close shaves, I thought, as I headed rather grudgingly for the drugstore. Probably, I'd been lucky to get out of Washington and Chicago alive. I'd have to be more careful on future field trips. Maybe these guys hadn't really intended to kill me, but the whole experience wasn't doing much for my mental health. And if you keep messing with somebody, even if they don't want to croak you, they could change their mind. I was certainly changing mine.

What had once seemed like a perfectly straightforward missing person investigation now was pointing the fickle finger of suspicion directly at the person whom once I'd thought of as my client. The frivolous, quirky, nuisance investigation into the goings-on both inside and outside of McGovern's large head had now escalated into what was shaping up to be a personal confrontation with the Federal Bureau of Investigation. And on top of all that, McGovern could quite conceivably be perched on top of my client right now in some hotel suite while I'm busy here fetching a can of shaving cream for Rambam. Economy size.

It was just like Shoshone the Magic Pony, I reflected, as I put the bag with the can of shaving cream under my arm and called Polly Price's number one more time for good measure from a pay phone on the corner. Nothing in life is what it appears to be. And, as in the case of Polly's telephone, there didn't appear to be any answer. You just had to keep shopping for shaving cream and drinking coffee and following the tedious trail of the bad guys until you couldn't tell the difference between them and everybody else and anyway you didn't give a damn any more. Maybe you'd find someone who'd been missing. Maybe you'd find what you were looking for. Maybe you thought that you'd been following your star and then one dark, lonely night you found that it was none of the above.

Just for the hell of it, I dialled the number of my favourite member of New York's finest. Detective Sergeant Mort Cooperman. He wasn't in but his executive butt-boy, Sergeant Buddy Fox, was.

'How lovely to hear from you, Tex,' said Fox somewhat facetiously. 'Haven't seen you since we found that dead meat in the trunk of that car.' He was referring to a lawyer named Hamburger that Kent Perkins and I had indeed found croaked in the trunk of a Lincoln in an underground parking garage.

'I need a quick favour, Sergeant.'

'We're here to serve, Tex,' he said, in a bored monotone that might've been an indicator of his level of enthusiasm for the project.

I gave him Derrick Price's name and the licence number of his car. Rambam had already run this information through the DMV and his hard-boiled computer and learned that Derrick Price had stepped on a rainbow seven years before. But rainbows were funny things. They came and they went and not everybody saw them the same way. If Price was who I thought he was, I wanted NYPD's read on this. Not that I thought they'd bust their hump to help me, but their reaction might be interesting.

'We'll jump right on it,' said Fox, with a smirk I could almost hear. 'Priority one, for sure.'

I started to thank him, but he'd already hung up. So I took the bag with the shaving cream back to Rambam, who'd managed to cut a little hole in the bell casing and now proceeded to fill the insides with enough lather to shave and groom every poodle in Central Park. Then he opened the door to a barely audible buzz that sounded more like a bee than a bell.

'So much for building security,' he said, as the two of us stepped quickly into the dank basement.

'You know there's a problem here,' I said. 'The elevator won't take us all the way. You need a special key to take it up to the penthouse.'

'No problem,' said Rambam. 'We're taking the service elevator and I'll bet you anything it isn't rigged with a special key to get us to the penthouse. It's a funny thing, but people who live in penthouses or even plan to visit them would never dream of riding up in a service elevator.'

'They probably think it's beneath them,' I said, as we wandered down a long dark hallway.

We located the service elevator and I saw that Rambam had been right. We rode all the way up to the penthouse with a cartful of dirty linen. Moments later, Rambam was working on Polly Price's penthouse door, his third B & E of the night – fourth, if you wanted to count the building's emergency exit. Maybe one alarm bell had been muted, but another had started to sound somewhere in the back of my own penthouse, and somehow I didn't believe shaving cream was going to silence it. It was a voice, actually. Far away, frantic, and frighteningly familiar.

It said: 'MIT! MIT! MIT!'

FORTY-ONE

Polly Price's penthouse proved to be a more daunting adversary for Rambam than McGovern's apartment or the spy nest across the alley. After a full five minutes of knocking, ringing the bell, and Rambam's having taken from his pockets virtually every device known to man for getting oneself on the other side of a locked door, we were still standing in the hallway.

'What do we do?' I said. 'We can't stand here for ever.'

'Grab a mop,' said Rambam. 'Be a janitor.'

'What,' I said, 'and give up show business?'

'Especially when we're getting ready for our big opening,' said Rambam, as he extracted a strange-looking device from his pocket. The thing resembled a small flashlight with a prong-type mechanism on one end of it.

'What the hell is that?'

'Electric lockpick. It was developed by the feds. The probe on the end vibrates about one thousand times a minute.'

'I imagine female federal agents are very fond of it.'

'If we ever see your client again, we can ask her,' said Rambam, as he inserted the dingus into the keyhole and turned on the switch.

The operation was over very quickly. The whole thing required just about as much time as it takes for a heart to break. Rambam turned the knob and the door swung open silently. He held out his hand magnanimously for me to enter.

'Age before experience,' he said.

'Fools before angels,' I said, holding back.

'She's your client,' said Rambam.

'OK,' I said, 'watch my back.'

'Not if there's anything else on.'

I entered the foyer of the penthouse with Rambam close behind me. The place was dark and silent as a tomb. I had by now come to the firm conclusion that the fine feminine hand of Polly Price was behind a great deal of my recent aggravation. I felt fairly certain that she'd been interested in McGovern long before she'd even known of my existence. As for Derrick Price, finding him was about as unlikely as Jesus coming back as the Easter Bunny.

I was listening for a moment and letting my eyes adjust to the gloom when Rambam turned on the lights.

'So much for letting our eyes adjust to the darkness,' I said.

'Adjust away,' said Rambam. 'There's nothing to see. So let there be light.'

'And the Lord said: "This sucks." '

Indeed, it did. The place had been totally cleaned out. An empty penthouse in an empty world. All that remained were the chandeliers and, I noticed as we walked out on the balcony, the strange piece of sculpture upon which I'd not so long ago louvred my buttocks.

'Don't sit on that,' I said. 'It's a piece of art.'

'And your client's a piece of work,' said Rambam, as he wandered back along the empty hallways.

'What client?' I said.

'What client is right. Forget about finding her. The beast covers its tracks too well. We could search for the rest of our lives and never find a trace of them. Never be sure what they were really up to.'

'What do we do about finding McGovern?'

'We just hope he comes home,' said Rambam, 'wagging his tail behind him.'

'Some tail,' I said.

'Some home,' said Rambam.

We decided to leave the building through the front entrance and as we walked across the lavish lobby we encountered yet another surprise. One of the doormen came running up to us in a state of mild excitation.

'Mr Friedman! Mr Friedman!' he said. 'I just came on my shift. I didn't see you come in.'

'I thought I'd come in the emergency exit,' I said. 'I figured if I filled the bell full of shaving cream nobody'd get alarmed.'

I laughed. Rambam laughed. The doorman, whose name tag read 'Carlos', laughed. I'd never seen the man before in my life.

'That's a good joke, Mr Friedman,' said Carlos, continuing to laugh. Some Latin cultures tend to find more humour than many situations often merit.

'He's a killer,' agreed Rambam.

'How did you know my name, Carlos?' I said.

'Miss Price left an envelope for you. She said if a man with a big black cowboy hat comes in here smoking a big cigar, give him this envelope.'

Carlos handed me the envelope. 'Mr Friedman' had been typed on the front. The envelope was sealed.

'Where is Miss Price now?' I asked.

'Miss Price,' said Carlos, shrugging his shoulders extravagantly, 'she's gone away.'

'You can say that again,' said Rambam.

I thanked Carlos, and we walked outside, past the phalanx of doormen and down the sidewalks of New York. I stopped under a streetlamp and opened the envelope and read Polly Price's brief letter to me. Then I handed it to Rambam and he read it and handed it back to me.

The note read:

> You're a nice man, Kinky Friedman. In another time and another place, who knows? I'll never forget you.
>
> Love,
> Polly

'You really have a way with women,' said Rambam.

FORTY-TWO

Like a childhood accordion collapsing, all the air seemed to have gone out of the case at once. I admit to mostly feeling a pervading sense of relief as we walked along the thoroughfares of the Upper West Side. Trendy places were everywhere, often right next door to more authentic places populated by last year's people. I liked last year's people, I decided. But then, I suppose, I always had. I could live without ever seeing Polly Price again, without even ever knowing exactly what her game was. As far as her retainer went, which wasn't all that far considering what I'd recently been through, I could just hang on to the money or earmark it for some worthy charity. For the Benefit of Mr Kite sounded about right.

The only dark cloud on my horizon now, and it was a rather large one, was the curious absence of McGovern. He was very indestructible, very loyal, and very stubborn, but he was also, I reflected with a glint of guilt, very vulnerable. I just didn't know where to take it from here. The trail, if that's what it indeed was, had come to an end. Not for the first time in my life, I'd hitched my wagon to a falling star, and now I simply wished that McGovern would come safely back home.

Rambam seemed subdued and introspective himself as we walked along Amsterdam to 87th Street and stood outside Barney Greengrass, one of the oldest and greatest delis in New York.

'Joel Siegel took me here years ago,' I said. 'The place is really killer bee.'

'Lox specialist to the world,' said Rambam. 'Too bad it's closed.'

'Like the Polly Price file.'

'Just as well,' said Rambam. 'Messing with the FBI is like taking a picture of an Indian. Every time you do it it sucks out a little bit more of your soul.'

We walked round the corner to a little bar that was open and found an empty table and ordered a round.

'Obviously,' I said, 'the feds were using me to learn more about McGovern. Now that they've got McGovern, they don't need me. And for all the enormous amount of effort, expenditures and subterfuge they involved themselves with, it's got to be something big they're after.'

'Like what?'

'Like the same thing Geraldo Rivera thought he'd find when he went into what he hoped was Al Capone's secret vault on live television.'

'The money and manpower the feds put into something has nothing to do with anything. Look at what they did a few years back to Randy Weaver, the survivalist in Idaho who lived in an isolated cabin and was guilty of the heinous crime of selling someone a gun of a prohibited length. They spent about ten million dollars, killed Weaver's son and dog, and then shot and killed his wife as she stood in the cabin doorway with her baby in her arms. They weren't looking for Al Capone's treasure. They weren't really looking for anything. They were just a deadly, mindless swarm of hornets somebody'd stirred up. I don't want you to be another Randy Weaver.'

'They did a nice job recently in Waco, too.'

'And those are just the ones everybody knows about,' said Rambam, warming to the subject. 'J. Edgar Hoover ran that outfit like an American Gestapo for almost five decades, and believe me, since the bastard croaked it hasn't changed all that much. Hoover was a vicious anti-Semite as well as a fag basher, even though he and his lifelong companion, Clyde Tolson, were closet queens the whole fucking time, and I do mean the whole fucking time.'

'Can I push your stool in for you?'

Rambam ignored my effort at lightening the mood. He continued his clinical recall on the evils of the FBI, stopping only to order another round.

'Hoover burgled the offices of a lot of Jewish organizations. He had a room called the Jew Room loaded with files on prominent Jews from all walks of life. He believed all Jews were either spies or communists.'

'He forgot doctors.'

'The FBI was the home of the original dirty-tricks boys long before Nixon ever had his first erection. They burgled Dustin Hoffman's shrink's office and stole his private files to help protect America. They spent millions of taxpayer dollars and man hours hounding and harassing and spying on dangerous enemies of our country like John Lennon, Leonard Bernstein, Arthur Miller and Martin Luther King.'

'Don't forget Burl Ives.'

'Burl Ives? How'd you know that?'

'The Friedman of Information Act.'

'OK,' said Rambam, pausing in his monologue to chuckle briefly. 'Burl Ives. Where was I?'

'Hoover and the Hebes.'

'Right. The FBI tried to foment trouble and dissension between Abbie Hoffman and Jerry Rubin by sending phony letters and starting false rumours in a campaign of disinformation worthy of the KGB –'

'A little piece of spiritual trivia,' I said. 'Did you know that Jerry Rubin's death certificate lists his occupation as "Jewish Road Warrior"?'

'That's one of the things they all had in common. A huge number of people the FBI hounded were Jewish.'

'Not Burl Ives.'

'OK, Kinky. Not Burl Ives.'

'Not Martin Luther King either.'

'I won't argue that one. But what they did to him was really amazing. Martin Luther King was given to fooling around a bit, apparently, in his extramarital area. So these fuckers pursued him relentlessly and got his whole life on tape. They'd bug his hotel rooms when he was on the road and come up with some gem like: "Oh, Martin, your dick is so big!" Then they'd call his wife and play the tape into the phone. They'd get some white agent to imitate a black accent – they didn't have any black agents back then – and he'd do a half-assed Amos 'n' Andy impersonation. Say something like: "Miss King, I wants to play you this tape out of concern. Looks like your husband's in Wisconsin and he's taken his johnson." Then they'd play her the tape: "Oh, Martin, your dick is so big!" That's the kind of shit the FBI did.'

'Then God punished J. Edgar Hoover,' I said. 'He gave

Martin Luther King a holiday and he didn't give J. Edgar Hoover dick.'

'And that's what he'd always wanted. Of course, by that time, Martin Luther King was probably ready for a holiday.'

I was ready for another shot of Old Granddad and I decided to try a Guinness to back it up. It was an interesting combination and it was starting to give me a little buzz. Rambam was dipping his nose into some kind of obscure, very expensive brandy that smelled like somebody's feet. I didn't know what it tasted like, but it had Rambam rolling along full throttle on the FBI.

'Another thing. They have about nine thousand agents in the field. Multiplying like rabbits with very big ears every time you turn around. And they never let them work in the area they're from. This is different from cops. Cops live in a neighbourhood, raise families there. They know the people. They want to retire there usually. But the feds are different. They parachute them in from as far away as possible. So you got a fed from Alabama and they put him in New York and he's walking around among all these strange-looking, foreign-sounding people, orthodox Jews, Puerto Ricans, Orientals, and he hates everybody and comes to see himself as an enemy force. He wants to fuck *everybody*.

'I've had personal experience with the feds, too. They came to me once and wanted me to help them with some murder investigation they were working on. I met with them a few times and came to the conclusion they were going after the wrong guy. So I told them what I thought and that, under the circumstances, I wouldn't be able to help. That didn't go down very well with them. So they sent agents to talk to my landlord, my clients, my friends and they said "We'd like to talk to you about Rambam. It's in connection with a murder investigation." Well, when the FBI comes to you and says something like that, you immediately jump to the conclusion that Rambam is the murderer. My landlord freaked. I lost clients. My friends were all calling wondering what the hell was going on. And once that kind of damage is done it's hard to undo.'

'Ask Randy Weaver.'

'At least I didn't have a wife, a kid and a dog. All they managed to do was to temporarily destroy my reputation.'

'Which wasn't the best when they started.'

'The point is I've been through a hell of a lot of shit with the FBI and never again do I want to have anything to do with them. I've worked *with* them and I've worked *against* them and I definitely prefer against. Of course the secret service are pretty good guys. Unless you're goin' after the President.'

'OK, so what do we do about McGovern?'

'If he's in the clutches of the feds, there's nothing we can do about it. They'll get what they want from him – if they even know what they want – and then they'll let him go. He'll be fine. Besides, look at the positive side of the situation.'

'What's that?'

'Somebody finally cleaned up his apartment.'

FORTY-THREE

I couldn't sleep that night, but it wasn't because I was lonely. After having listened to Rambam's oral dissertation on the FBI, I had my doubts if I'd ever feel lonely again. Or alone, for that matter. As I paced back and forth across the living room of the loft, smoking a cigar, listening to the lesbian dance class overhead, I wondered if somebody else wasn't listening, too. Maybe somebody had tapes of my conversations with the cat. Maybe somebody besides myself and God knew that Stephanie DuPont took three showers a day. Everything Rambam said, of course, was not the gospel. The FBI, no doubt, had performed many good and valorous acts for my country over the years. The problem was that also over the years, great power had accrued to the organization, most of it centred in one man, J. Edgar Hoover. If power tends to corrupt, it didn't have far to go with old J. Edgar. He spied with an iron hand on anyone who had ideas different from his own. And he set the standard for the mentality of the FBI agent to be a control addict.

Like taking pictures of an Indian, Rambam had said. Somebody was watching Arthur Miller who never would appreciate *Death of a Salesman*. Another somebody was closely monitoring John Lennon. Somebody who could never imagine 'Imagine'. And the whole world remembers Martin Luther King for 'I have a dream'. Only J. Edgar Hoover and his pathetic acolytes would remember him for 'Oh, Martin, your dick is so big!' Maybe that was what Hoover had really wanted all along.

I went over to the desk and dialled McGovern's number. I got no answer. I'd called him four or five times already this night and always I'd gotten no answer. Always I'd hung up the blower and walked over to the bottle of Jameson on the counter. Always I'd poured a shot into the old bull's horn and fired it straight at my uvula. Always the cat had watched with thinly veiled disgust in her eyes.

'I miss McGovern,' I said.

The cat said nothing. She did not miss McGovern. She did not miss anybody. I looked closely into her roulette eyes and for a moment I wasn't even sure if she missed me when I was away from the loft. Maybe that was the way to be. Cold-blooded. Protect yourself. That was fine, unless you were the Indian someone was taking pictures of. Unwanted visions of McGovern's clean apartment ransacked my mind. Were they holding him prisoner somewhere? Interrogating him? Giving him lie-detector tests? Shooting him up with truth serum like they do in spy movies? Could whatever Leaning Jesus had given him be that important to anyone? And why did McGovern insist he couldn't remember what it was? Just tell them,

McGovern. Get it over with. Otherwise they'll hound you to your grave. If they don't decide to put you in it first.

At three o'clock in the morning, dressed in my Borneo batik sarong and old purple bathrobe, I found myself standing at the kitchen window looking out on Vandam Street as I had done many weeks ago on New Year's Day, the day Hank Williams had died. That was before I'd met Polly Price. Before I'd taken the bait to find her missing husband. Before I'd gone to Washington. Before I'd gone to Chicago. Unfortunately, I didn't know a hell of a lot more now than I had then. All I knew was that the world outside the window looked cold. Colder than a cold, cold heart.

I was smoking a Cuban cigar as I gazed numbly into the frozen darkness, sipping a cup of Hawaiian coffee, half-consciously stroking the cat on the windowsill. Business as usual. My mind was still at work. In its troubled, churning, confused state it was processing the recent past, looking for an answer from a world that didn't give a damn.

In many ways, I reflected, as I watched the tail-lights of a taxi vanish into the gloom, this had been one of my least satisfying cases. In fact, the Derrick Price investigation, much to my chagrin, had probably never really been a case at all. A bad joke was more like it. A red herring on an endless loop. A charade. A façade. A shadow game. A well-timed, trivial, rather tedious treasure hunt.

I looked in the cat's eyes and caught a glimmer from a car's headlights somewhere down the street, shyly shining like the moon reflects the sun. Maybe there was a treasure after all, I thought. Maybe Leaning Jesus had never revealed to McGovern the precise nature of the gift he had given him. Maybe it was something that a person would never think of as important. Maybe, just maybe, all this time, McGovern had the map to the Lost Dutchman's Mine and hadn't even known it.

The certitude that I now seemed to feel about the existence of this treasure, for no good reason at all, was suddenly making me feel rather fey. For those of you who don't believe in leprechauns, fey is a word of Irish derivation that has about as many shades of meaning as there are colours in the rainbow. It can mean 'enchanted', 'clairvoyant', or 'in touch with the higher powers'. It can also mean 'in touch with the fairies', or 'in touch with the leprechauns'. It could also mean, I thought hopefully, in touch with McGovern, who, though ridiculously large for a leprechaun, shared a great many of their behavioural and character traits.

But, as my kid sister, Marcie, sometimes delights in pointing out, there is yet another definition for the word 'fey'. It is somewhat less well known in terms of usage, and, of course, it is not particularly the kind of emotion you'd want to possess if you can help it. Fey can also mean 'to feel inexplicably happy before impending doom or, possibly, death'.

I did not intend to discuss the shades of meaning of the word 'fey' with the cat at this or any other time. Cats are not Irish. They are usually French, Jewish or Siamese. Dogs, however, are almost invariably Irish, with a few notable exceptions such as my father's dog, Sambo, who has been well-documented to be a Jewish Shepherd. None the less, I attempted to share my feelings with the cat.

'I feel strangely hopeful,' I said, 'for no reason at all. But it feels like somebody might come along and pull the rug out from under me at any moment.'

I looked around at the lunar landscape outside the window, the mildly bored cat, the stark, almost impersonal, gloom-gathering living room. There wasn't even a rug for somebody to come along and pull out. I walked over to the percolator and poured a new head on to my semi-luke coffee. In my old head, however, the same old thoughts seemed to be percolating, like little coffee grains of doubt ebbing and flowing with the tide almost invisibly across the black sand beaches of some Kona of the heart. I could almost feel the fey slipping away. Yet I vowed to remain upbeat, if only for the cat.

'Before we can look for the treasure,' I said, 'first we've got to find McGovern.'

With an expression of supreme disbelief bordering upon exasperation in her eyes, the cat gazed up at the ceiling where Winnie Katz and her lesbian dance troupe were, thankfully, silent, whatever that portended. Then the cat turned and padded without guilt or hesitation into the bedroom wherein she gracefully leapt upon the bed and curled up into what appeared to be the instantaneous slumber of the innocent. It was clearly one of the reasons, I reflected in the kitchen window, why many people hated cats.

It's a cold, uncaring world we live in, I thought. And that's in the best of times. Nobody had heeded McGovern's frantic and persistent MIB reports. Even his closest friends, I remembered with a pang of guilt, had deigned to turn a deaf ear. Hell, nobody would believe me now if I tried to tell them what I thought to be the truth. Not the cops. Not the newspapers. Not the cat.

I stared out into the New York nothingness that was not dark and not dawn but possibly only the mere absence of the human spirit.

'God bless you, J. Edgar Hoover,' I said grimly to myself. 'You're the only one who listens any more.'

FORTY-FOUR

'It's been five days since Rambam and I broke into his apartment,' I said, 'and he's still not back.'

'Maybe it's something as simple as boy meets girl,' said Stephanie DuPont.

'Kind of like us.'

'Don't make me sick, Friedman.'

In the low, romantic lighting of the little Indian restaurant in the East Village she looked, if possible, more radiant and ravishing than ever. Two weeks of helicopter skiing in Switzerland certainly hadn't hurt the girl. Not that I especially knew what helicopter skiing was. I did not have a particular fondness for skiiing or for helicopters, or for Switzerland, for that matter. But I did have a particular fondness for Stephanie DuPont.

'Look,' I said patiently, 'I've told you everything that's happened since you've been gone and surely you've reached the conclusion that Polly Price is not just a girl. She's a federal agent. Possibly worse. She may be some kind of counter-espionage rogue terrorist – '

'Waiter,' said Stephanie sweetly. 'Please bring my father some of those little cheese balls for dessert.'

'And the boy didn't meet the girl,' I continued, unruffled. 'The girl arranged through my good offices a method of gaining his confidence and then proceeded to seduce him in order to find out about Leaning Jesus.'

'We're not sounding a little jealous, are we?'

'The only ones I'm jealous of are Pyramus and Thisbe.'

'I *told* you I'm making a leash for you,' said Stephanie, in a voice a little louder than necessary. A number of our fellow diners looked over with gazes of mildly prurient interest. 'By the way, your face is now the colour of mulligatawny soup. I'm warning you, Friedman. Don't push me. I'm only twenty-two. Let me grow up. I'm just a kid.'

'Tell that to the guy at the far table whose turban just popped off.'

I poured us both another glass of Taj Mahal beer, which comes in a bottle a little larger and almost the same shape as an old-fashioned wooden bowling pin. When you drink three or four of them it feels like you've been hit over the head by an old-fashioned wooden bowling pin. But the vindaloo dishes tend to work like a spicy culinary form of speed and you don't get as heavily monstered as you might've. Usually.

'I'm telling you,' I said, 'if McGovern's not back or I haven't heard from him by the end of this weekend I'm going to the cops. I'll tell 'em the whole story. I'll file a missing person report.'

'Don't make me laugh,' said Stephanie with mild disgust. 'They'll never believe you.'

'But *you* believe me,' I said, giving her the best searching stare I currently had in stock.

'Of course,' said Stephanie. 'Not even you could dream up anything this crazy. Let me see if I have it. About a zillion years ago, as the ice was melting in God's cocktail glass – '

'It wasn't so long ago,' I explained. 'Much of what happened transpired in my lifetime.'

'As I was saying,' said Stephanie, 'about a zillion years ago, as the ice was melting in God's cocktail glass, Al Capone hops off to prison and before he goes, gives his executive butt-boy, Leaning Jesus, a letter or a document or a map that details where he's stashed all the loot he's plundered in all the years he's been king of the mob. When the feds make things hot for Leaning Jesus, he, for safekeeping, dutifully transfers said document to young Mike McGovern – '

'You *will* make a good lawyer – '

' – who not only can't find said document but can't even remember receiving it. How'm I doing so far?'

'Right on the money, as it were.'

'OK. Now in 'sixty-seven, McGovern moves to New York, where he works as a journalist and lives a lifestyle not calculated to help improve his retrieval system, not to mention twenty-seven fun-filled years passing by. Longer than some of us have been alive.'

'Don't rub it in. So I'm young at heart.'

'You're not young at heart. You're young at dick. All men are.'

'Your sexism appals me.'

'Then sometime during my happy, carefree childhood – '

'Which is still in progress.'

' – some feds or ex-feds or former feds along with Geraldo

Rivera and half the civilized, as well as the uncivilized, world begin to put out their feelers for whatever happened to all of Al Capone's bucks. Nobody finds the mother lode, but maybe some informer squeals, or some old field agent retires with some classified documents and finally manages to connect the dots between Al Capone, Leaning Jesus, and Mike McGovern.'

'I'd like to connect the dots on this credit-card voucher,' I said, putting on my spare pair of reading skepticals. 'The check appears to be written in Aramaic.'

'So this cell, or whatever it is, now proceeds to closely monitor McGovern's every move, throwing in as well a campaign of harassment and threats that is making him crazy so he turns to you, who, as we well know, already are crazy.'

'Nobody called me bad names at the hospital.'

'So now, through the wonders of modern technology, every word that transpires between you and McGovern, whether in person or over the phone, is being picked up by these people and so some of the surveillance spills over on to you. They get you to put one of their people in personal contact with McGovern. They devise ways to get you out of town and comb your loft. They find nothing, so they decide: What the hell, let's let Friedman lead us to Leaning Jesus. Which in time you do.'

'How stupid of me.'

'Careless is a better word.'

'Thank you, Miss Marple.'

'So now you and Rambam are running around after the fact with satellite dishes on your heads trying to jam their signals or something and meanwhile they have McGovern.'

'Which is about like having a Ouija board. But I'm hoping he knows more than he knows he knows. Memories are funny little things. You haven't really had time to have a lot of them yet. At twenty-two, you probably know more now than you ever will again.'

Stephanie almost sulked, but I could see she was thinking

about it. Then she looked at me with the sudden eyes of a child. It was like watching a brooding buttermilk sky just as it clears to be breathtaking, flag-waving, lovemaking, Texas summer blue.

'Don't worry,' she said consolingly. 'They won't hurt McGovern. He'll come back and then you can talk to him. Find out what it is that he doesn't know or what he has that he doesn't know he has. Your mind may be gone, but you have a brilliant imagination. Use it. You can still be my hero, you know.'

'What do I have to do? Fit my scrotum through the eye of a needle?'

Stephanie laughed a loud, primitive, somehow sensuous laugh. I poured us both the last of the Taj Mahal.

'No, Long Dong Sliver,' she said. 'Just find Al Capone's secret treasure.'

FORTY-FIVE

The weekend passed slowly, like rush-hour traffic of the mind. My mind was jammed with thoughts and concerns about McGovern. Both Rambam and Stephanie had predicted he'd be back before I knew it, but I wasn't buying anything retail. Where was McGovern? What were they doing to him? Why hadn't he at least called? For some reason, I felt more like a mother than a friend. Since McGovern's own mother had stepped on a rainbow some years ago, possibly the role had devolved to me.

Late Sunday night, throwing all caution to the winds, I decided to call McGovern's live-out girlfriend, Beverly. If it had been a case of boy meets girl, or if it'd started differently and ended up that way, the last thing I wanted to do was alert the war department. On the other hand, McGovern had been missing for almost a week now. If I hadn't heard anything and Beverly hadn't heard anything, it was not a good sign. Our boy had gone from seeing an MIB to being an MIT to becoming an MIA.

Beverly, among other endeavours, had co-founded an acting troupe called Theater for the Forgotten. The purpose of the group was to perform in prisons, mental hospitals, halfway houses for homosexual hatchet murderers and other places where normal Americans fear to tread. There was always something about the name of her organization that had bothered me, but I never could remember what it was.

'Theater for the Forgotten,' I said to the cat. 'It's a damn near perfect description of what I've been through lately.'

The cat did not seem to care a great deal. For one thing, she'd been ignorant of my trials and tribulations in Washington and Chicago. For another, she had never been enamoured of theatrical presentations. She particularly abhorred *Cat on a Hot Tin Roof*.

'You see,' I explained, 'the entire search for Polly Price's missing husband, as well as much of what McGovern thought was happening to him, could be categorized as pure theatre. The only thing that's really important is what McGovern has forgotten. Which, of course, raises the question: "Is the theatre really dead?"'

I walked over to the desk, picked up the blower on the left, and dialled Beverly's number in the country, as they say. When you live in New York City, of course, the country is just about everywhere else.

'Kinky,' Beverly said, as she pole-vaulted past hello, 'have you seen Mike?'

'Never could see Mike. How about yourself?'

'I haven't seen or heard from him in over a week. I'm very worried about Mike, Kinky.'

As long as I'd known Beverly, she'd been very worried about Mike. This time, however, I was afraid she might really have something. I didn't want to panic her, but I wasn't exactly filled with the even-mindedness of the old Mahatma myself at the moment.

'You know, Kinky, he's been behaving in a very bizarre and paranoid fashion for several months now.'

'Maybe he's practising to be a New Yorker.'

'He hasn't been himself at all lately,' Beverly continued, becoming increasingly agitated. 'And now he's disappeared! And his apartment's been all cleaned up!'

'That's *really* strange.'

'You have no idea where he is?' she said, taking on a mildly interrogative tone.

'That's correct.'

'And you have no idea *who* he's with?'

'That's correct,' I said, a little too quickly.

The conversation seemed to have run into something of a wall. I removed the little deerstalker cap from Sherlock's head and extracted a fresh cigar, upon which I began performing fairly Freudian acts with my lips and teeth and tongue. Then I set fire to the cigar with a kitchen match, always keeping the tip of the cigar ever so slightly above the level of the flame.

'Should we go to the police, Kinky?' Beverly was saying, as I blew a plume of smoke up towards the lesbian dance class.

'I'll be calling them first thing tomorrow morning,' I said. 'And I'll let you know what they say.' I could already imagine what they were going to say and it wasn't going to be anything Beverly was going to want to hear. So I gave her a little something to settle her nerves.

'Look,' I said, paraphrasing Rambam, 'I'm sure he'll come home soon, wagging his tail behind him.'

If that were to occur, unfortunately, I didn't think it was going to be the kind of tail that Beverly was going to like to see.

FORTY-SIX

The first thing Monday morning turned out to be about twelve forty-five in the afternoon. That was the time I'd taken care of my morning ablutions, had enough cups of espresso to clear Charlotte's Web out of my brain, cleaned up some rather distasteful cat vomit from my desk, and sat down to call Sergeant Cooperman. For a change, the desk sergeant put me right through.

'Make it fast,' said Cooperman. 'I'm just leaving for a big, important assignment. It's called lunch.'

I told Cooperman that I wanted to file a missing person report on McGovern. It was not easy explaining to him why I was worried about McGovern. First, I had to try to put everything that had happened on a bumper sticker for him. Second, as I related some of the more unusual aspects of the case, I had to attempt not to sound like I needed a check-up from the neck up. By the time I'd finished my Torah portion, it didn't even sound very convincing from my side of the blower.

'You gotta be kiddin',' said Cooperman, halfway between a laugh and a choke. 'Your friend McGovern don't sound like he needs a missing person report. You ought to be sending him a bottle of champagne. Any fool can see he's shacking up with that broad.'

'I still have a problem with that,' I said.

'Yeah,' said Cooperman, sounding restless. 'What's your problem.'

'Where do I send the champagne?'

'By the way,' said Cooperman, dismissing the question entirely, 'that plate number you gave Fox the other day for the vehicle supposedly belonging to the guy who was supposedly your client's husband who you were supposedly trying to locate?'

'Yeah?'

'Checks out to be a bread truck in Brooklyn. Now, based on these two parallel investigations you say you've been conducting, I've been able to arrive at a few conclusions of my own.'

'Which are?' I said warily.

'McGovern's either bull-fucking your client – '

'Or?'

'He's driving that bread truck.'

The last sound I heard before I cradled the blower was Cooperman either choking to death or chuckling to beat the band. At the moment, I didn't much care which.

The espresso machine seemed to be humming to itself, so I went over and got a cupful and then walked over to the refrigerator and spoke briefly with the puppet head.

' "Education never ends, Watson," ' I said. ' "It's a series of lessons with the greatest for the last." '

The puppet head smiled understandingly.

'But this is not the Red-Headed League. This is not something out of *Treasure Island*. This is New York in the nineties where, all too often, nothing is delivered. Fiction is the ability to imagine and to believe what you have imagined. We like a good mystery because it affords us resolution, something that life itself so rarely does. Now if McGovern ever returns to the city, we can go out and pour a few drinks down our necks and forget it all ever happened.'

The puppet head smiled understandingly.

I smiled understandingly.

It wasn't all that hard to understand. Sometimes you win and sometimes you lose and sometimes you live in a lonely loft in February, freezing your ass off, listening to lesbians, gazing at garbage trucks, smoking cigars, drinking espresso, attempting to relate to an antisocial cat, feeling sorry for yourself and, occasionally, carrying on a rather wooden conversation with a little black puppet head who resides on top of the refrigerator and is the only one with the brains and the guts and the imagination to call this place home.

I walked over to the couch and lay down for a little power nap, pulling Ryan Kalmin's old blue sleeping bag over me for a comforter. I dreamed of Polly Price. Or was it Irene Adler, the woman who bested Sherlock Holmes and revealed that he had a heart by stealing it? It was no coincidence that the bar where Polly had met Ratso was in Washington. She'd got what she'd wanted from me. That was McGovern. Now it was just a question of whether or not she could get what she wanted from him.

It must've been a hell of a power nap, because when I opened my eyes the loft was dark and the phones were ringing like church bells after a war. I felt like I'd just been through one myself as I shivered and stumbled my way across the gloomy room to the desk and with an icy dead man's grip, collared the blower on the left.

The voice that came over the wire was upbeat and very familiar, with a decidedly British accent, which, in time, I recognized belonged to Pete Myers.

'Kinkster!' Myers boomed enthusiastically. 'McGovern's back! I've got him right here at the shop and he's asking to see you.'

'Can you hold him till I get there?'

'It doesn't look like he's planning to go anywhere soon, Kinkster. He's leaning peacefully against the Dikstuffer, smoking a joint, and drinking directly from a bottle of very expensive, very hard to get imported twenty-five-year-old Macallan high-grade straight malt Scotch that I was saving for a dinner party later this week.'

'I'll pop right over, mate.'

I slipped into my blue Oliver Twist coat, put on my cowboy hat, and grabbed three cigars for the road.

I left the cat in charge.

As I hurried down the four flights of stairs I realized, somewhat belatedly, that it really didn't matter who was in charge. There was very damn little left for anyone to be in charge of. McGovern was back. The game was over. The case was closed. I felt a sudden certitude that Polly and her crew had failed to get what they wanted from McGovern. No one ever would. If indeed Leaning Jesus had ever given Capone's papers to the Kid, they'd been strewn somewhere along the pathway from childhood. The Kid no longer existed. He was now, for better or worse a man. No truth serum, no hypnosis, no casting the mind back would ever recover what had been lost, misplaced, forgotten or, quite simply, never there.

No hacks were in sight, so I legged it through the cold, darkened streets of the Village. The bad news was that there'd be no winners this time. No happy endings. I thought wistfully of Stephanie DuPont's statuesque form, caustic wit, stunning smile and heart of gold. No heroes this time, either. No hacks and no heroes. Just God in His penthouse, Satan in the basement, the cat in the loft, me on the street, and the little black puppet head smiling down from on top of the refrigerator. A million years from now, when archaeologists dig doggedly through the tragic and tedious layers of human existence that had once comprised the ancient city of New York, they will no doubt find that little puppet head. Then, as now, men will probably scratch their own heads in amazement and ask the question that no civilization on earth has yet been able to answer: 'Why is he smiling?'

FORTY-SEVEN

It was almost ten bells by the time I sailed up the frozen asphalt river of Hudson Street and pitched anchor at Myers of Keswick. The shop was closed but its proprietor soon responded to my muted tapping on his chamber door.

'How is he?' I said, as Pete took my coat and hung it by the door.

'A sadder but a wiser man,' he said. 'So am I. That Macallan's Scotch runs a hundred and sixty-one dollars a bottle.'

'Has he said anything about where he's been or what he's been doing all this time?'

'I think he's been waiting for you.'

I followed Pete Myers to the back of the shop and into the little kitchen where McGovern was still reclining against the Dikstuffer pretty much as Myers had described him earlier, except that now the joint was just a roach and the hundred and sixty-one dollars had devalued itself to about eighty dollars and fifty cents. McGovern looked high enough to hook up with the Mir Space Station, but otherwise he appeared to be fine. A sort of sad, wistful smile seemed frozen on his face, vaguely similar, I now realized, to that on the puppet head. Of course, you'd be smiling too if you'd just spent a week with Polly Price.

'How's it going, old bean?' he said.

I threw him an old, unfinished song lyric of mine to sort of lighten the mood and to see what he'd do with it.

'Can't complain,
Can't complain,
Ass got bit by a big Great Dane.
Penis run over by a subway train.
Can't complain
Can't complain.'

'Same here,' said McGovern.

'Do you care to share some of your experiences?' I said. 'At least the ones that are family oriented.'

'How would I know? I don't have a family.'

'You're wrong there, mate,' said Myers. 'You do have a family. It's just not the family you were born with. Let's face it, McGovern. You're stuck with us.'

'So come on, Magoo,' I said. 'Spit it. Where'd she take you?'

'We decided to take a drive to a lodge she knew somewhere upstate. It was near a little dairy farm community outside the small town of Manlius, New York. We stayed in a very romantic old bungalow and the first couple of days there I thought I'd died and gone to heaven.'

'When you die,' said Myers, 'you won't be going to heaven.'

'At first, Polly and I seemed to be a great comfort to each other. She needed an understanding man in her life and I needed a gorgeous social worker who was built like a brick shithouse.'

'How poignant,' I said. 'So you helped each other work through your grief.'

'Is that what they're calling it now?' said Myers.

'Polly seemed to be fascinated with my background. She especially loved hearing me tell stories about Leaning Jesus and all the gang in Chicago. She thought of me as some kind of great eyewitness to the lost and colourful past. She felt she was born too late and the only way she could come to life again was through my eyes. Also, her father died when she was very young and I think she saw Leaning Jesus not only as a father figure to me, but to her as well. My relationship with him became almost an obsession with her.'

'Who's Polly?' said Myers.

'Just a girl we used to know,' I said.

'She asked me if I had any letters or papers from Leaning Jesus or gifts from him or pictures. She wanted to see him better, to touch him.'

McGovern paused to take about a twenty-dollar swig from the bottle of Macallan's high-grade straight malt Scotch. He passed it over to me, and I proceeded to devalue further the liquid assets of Myers of Keswick. Pete himself then took a hearty slug from the bottle.

'Sod the bleeding dinner party,' he said.

'Then yesterday morning,' McGovern continued, as if in a

reverie, 'I woke up and she was gone. All I found was this note.'

He took a crumpled piece of paper from his pocket and handed it to me. I put on my reading skepticals, held the page under a heating lamp, and read the few lines of fine familiar feminine hand:

You're a nice man, Mike McGovern. In another time and another place, who knows? I'll never forget you.

Love,

Polly

P.S. If you see Leaning Jesus before I do just drill a little hole and pull me through.

There was a silence in the little kitchen as Myers read the note and McGovern took another rather expensive pull on the Scotch. Then Pete handed him back the note which this time he folded neatly and slipped into his wallet.

'I guess Beverly must've straightened up my apartment,' said McGovern. 'I can't find a damn thing I'm looking for any more.'

'Same here,' I said.

'By the way,' said McGovern, 'I'd appreciate it if you guys wouldn't mention any of this to Beverly. She tends to take a rather dim view of this sort of thing.'

'I'll file it away with all your other secrets I've kept,' said Myers. 'Then one day I'll blackmail your ass for a bottle of twenty-five-year-old high-grade straight malt Macallan's Scotch.'

'And as for me,' I said, 'I've already consigned the entire episode to the precise location where it's always belonged.'

'The Dikstuffer?' said Myers.

'No,' I said. 'The Theater for the Forgotten.'

FORTY-EIGHT

Several months passed and Polly Price was not heard from again. Possibly she'd vanished in the same mysterious way as her husband, whoever and wherever he was. With Polly's disappearance, there were other *desaparecidos* as well, though I don't believe McGovern consciously connected the two events. The Men in Black disappeared, along with the old Indian in the receding turban, the Gene Kelly impersonator on the fire escape, the little green man, and all the other phone calls, threats, and disturbances, real or imagined, that had plagued McGovern's world.

Even the winter seemed to have almost disappeared. Spring cannot always be considered spring in New York, but at least the streets and sidewalks and parks were no longer twelve inches deep in toxic, coffee-coloured sludge. I was no longer freezing my balls off every time I got out of bed, and the cat, I noticed, was no longer hunkering down cowboy-style beside the percolator.

It was a clear, crisp, beautiful Friday night in the city some-time around the middle of April and McGovern was having an intimate dinner party at his place which, I am not terribly shocked to report, was back to its usual state of comfortable disarray. McGovern's guest list that evening was limited to three: Beverly, Stephanie DuPont and myself. The dish he was serving, which he'd laboured all afternoon to prepare, was his famous, incomparable Chicken McGovern.

'That was the best chicken I've ever had in my life,' said Stephanie, across the candlelight and chicken bones. 'You've got to tell me how to make it.'

'It's an Old World recipe,' said McGovern. 'It's rather com-plicated. For about thirty years I've kept it right up here.' McGovern pointed to his very large and handsome head, but Stephanie, being young and impetuous, still wasn't satisfied.

'If it's not a secret,' she said like a petulant child, 'why can't I borrow it? Surely you've got the recipe written down somewhere?'

'Stephanie,' I said, 'if McGovern doesn't want to give away his recipe he doesn't want to give away his recipe. You wouldn't dream of walking up to Colonel Sanders and asking him to give you his eleven different secret herbs and spices.'

'First of all,' said Stephanie, 'I wouldn't be walking up to Colonel Sanders. He'd probably be crawling up to me and asking for my telephone number. Secondly, Mike McGovern can cook absolute circles around Colonel Sanders.'

She favoured McGovern with a stunning, admiring smile of such intensity that it could've launched a thousand cookbooks and floated them all the way to Troy. Basking in the afterglow, McGovern got up from the table and wandered into the kitchen, where he could be seen picking up a steak knife and prying loose a board under his sink. His three dinner guests looked on in mild amazement.

'There's a hidden compartment here,' said McGovern, 'where I keep my old recipes and stuff. I haven't opened it in years and I can't promise, but if I was a hard copy of Chicken McGovern, this is where I'd be.'

'He's such an accommodating host,' I clucked approvingly.

'I never knew that hidden compartment was there,' said Beverly.

'That's what makes it a hidden compartment', said McGovern, as he extracted a sheaf of yellowed papers and proceeded to shake the dust and cobwebs off into the trash.

'He always ceases to amaze me,' I said, as I lit an after-dinner cigar to the disapproving eye of Stephanie. But the main focus of the dinner guests was now clearly upon McGovern.

'Holy shit,' he said, looking over the recipes.

'What?' I said.

'Now I remember where I got the recipe,' said McGovern.

'I memorized it so long ago that I'd forgotten. Leaning Jesus gave it to me.'

'WHAT!' Stephanie and I shouted simultaneously.

Before Beverly could say 'Who's Leaning Jesus?' the two of us were on our feet waiting as McGovern trundled the ancient document over to the table.

'Let me have a look,' said Stephanie. 'A girl knows about these things.'

She gave McGovern another stunner of a smile and he put the recipe in her rapacious hands. I got up and put on my reading skepticals and walked around behind her as she sat back down to read the recipe. The ingredients and instructions were as follows:

The Marinade
three or four pound chicken
cut up with backbone and wingtips used for stock
fresh ginger
three scallions diced finely
drumsticks, thighs, and white meat scored,
skinned, and cleaned of hidden fat pockets
two tsp roasted browned peppercorns
two TB soy sauce
sugar sprinkled to taste

The Sauce
four garlic cloves diced finely and mashed
four scallions diced finely
one stalk celery
a few stems fresh coriander or parsley
fresh grated ginger to taste
two TB light soy sauce
two tsp distilled white vinegar
four TB chicken stock
one TB tomato ketchup
sugar to taste
two TB sesame oil

You Also Require

cornstarch for dredging
non-fat oil for deep frying
toasted peanuts to taste

Putting It Together

Peel and grate the ginger finely.
Dice scallions into very fine rounds.
Divide chicken and put into bowl.
Score or prick with a sharp knife.
Sprinkle with ground peppercorns, ginger, scallions, soy sauce, and sugar.
Rub in well with hands.
Cover and refrigerate for four hours or overnight.

For the sauce, use two separate bowls.
In one bowl place the mashed garlic, diced scallions, and celery cut into very fine rounds.
Mash ginger and cut into minute dice.
Combine and set aside.

In the other bowl, stir well soy sauce, vinegar, stock, ketchup, sugar, and sesame oil.
Set aside.

After chicken is marinaded, set in a row and dust all over with cornstarch.
Pat chicken until mixture is well absorbed.
Set aside for twenty minutes.
Fry in hot vegetable oil until crusty.
Bake in oven at 350 degrees for thirty to forty minutes, dependent upon size of chicken pieces.
Drain on paper towel and place on serving dish.
Mix together the two bowls of sauce ingredients and bathe the chicken.
Sprinkle with toasted peanuts.
Open mouth.
Serve at once.

'Wait a minute,' said Stephanie. 'There's one more page to this.'

'It's already the longest recipe in the world,' I said.

It was also just about the most disappointing recipe in the world, I thought, as I poured myself a very generous portion of brandy and drifted over to the wall above the empty fireplace to share my sorrows with Carole Lombard. Sometimes, I reflected rather grimly, no matter who wrote it, who cooks it, who serves it, or who eats it, a recipe is just a recipe. Behind me, I supposed, Stephanie was still poring over the damn thing. I could hear McGovern describing to Beverly a rather humorous incident from the recent behaviour of one rather notorious Mick Brennan. I downed an extremely large sip of brandy, gazed deeply into Lombard's eyes, and realized they bore an almost familial resemblance to Stephanie's.

Suddenly, either Lombard or Stephanie seemed to be speaking to me. Maybe it was both of them.

'Listen to this,' the voice was saying. ' "If you want to live dangerously (like I used to do), you might want to try".'

'Try what?' said McGovern.

'Just some optional ingredients he lists here,' said Stephanie.

'There *are* no optional ingredients to Chicken McGovern,' said McGovern with some heat. 'It's a very concise, very old family recipe.'

'Hearts of palm,' said Stephanie sweetly.

'No way,' said McGovern.

'Between one and two large stone crabs sprinkled with sea salt?'

'Ridiculous.'

'Just under one large tree-ripened tomato?'

'Insane!'

'Five deep-fried oysters?'

'Bullshit!'

'Simmer for ninety-five minutes?'

By this time McGovern was fairly well simmering himself.

Beverly looked mildly amused. Stephanie appeared to be silently rereading the optional ingredients.

'Hearts of palm,' I said. 'That's Palm Island, Florida, where Al Capone died. He was known as the "Master of 93 Palm Island", his sprawling estate down there. Ninety-five minutes would be right next door. Drop a word or two out of each optional ingredient and I think we've got something.'

'Got what?' asked Beverly.

'The secret to where Capone buried his treasure. A recipe's a perfect vehicle for a treasure map. It's the kind of thing you'd never think of in any other light than what it is. That's why McGovern didn't remember Leaning Jesus giving him anything.'

'There's lots of other things I don't remember,' said McGovern.

'That's why you're happy,' I said.

But by now there were four happy people in the room. Five if you wanted to count Lombard. And I guess you might as well, because when I looked up at her eyes again I'd swear they were smiling.

FORTY-NINE

'You see,' I said to Stephanie as we walked home that night from McGovern's, 'even the spiritual surveillance of all our lives doesn't infallibly turn up every mundane detail. Some little things always tend to slip between the cracks of our sidewalks and our souls.'

A light rain was falling and, in the ancient glow of the streetlights, there seemed to form a canopy of hope and excitement over the city and the world. There were five and a half billion people and four hundred mountain gorillas left, I thought, and though I wasn't exactly sure which group I'd rather hang out with, I was finally beginning to have some fun at the party.

'What is old will be new,' Stephanie was saying with a beatific expression on her beatific features. 'What is lost will be found!'

'And what is tedious,' I said, 'is that Beverly won't let McGovern leave the city because of his recent disappearance. If we find the treasure we'll just give him his half.'

'You mean his *third*,' said Stephanie.

'You *are* going to make a good lawyer.'

As we strolled through the crowded streets of the Village, Stephanie suddenly broke away, running ahead, then spinning round in sheer joy and exhilaration. And it must be reported that many a jaded Manhattanite looked on in a state of mass hypnosis as that remarkable girl jumped up and down, imbuing the stoic sidewalks of New York with a young and hopeful presence. Indeed, I, too, watched with a proud if somewhat prejudiced eye as she stood there shimmering in the grime, a cheerleader in the game of life.

'We're going to Disney World!' she shouted.